CW00410286

was born in Co. Kildar   .... serious Hunting and Fishing Church-going family" who gave her little education at the hands of governesses. Her father originally came from a Somerset family and her mother, a poetess, was the author of "The Songs of the Glens of Antrim". Molly Keane's interests when young were "hunting and horses and having a good time"; she began writing only as a means of supplementing her dress allowance, and chose the pseudonym M. J. Farrell "to hide my literary side from my sporting friends". She wrote her first novel, *The Knight of the Cheerful Countenance*, at the age of seventeen.

As M. J. Farrell, Molly Keane published ten novels between 1928 and 1952: *Young Entry* (1928), *Taking Chances* (1929), *Mad Puppetstown* (1931), *Conversation Piece* (1932), *Devoted Ladies* (1934), *Full House* (1935), *The Rising Tide* (1937), *Two Days in Aragon* (1941), *Loving Without Tears* (1951) and *Treasure Hunt* (1952). She was also a successful playwright, of whom James Agate said "I would back this impish writer to hold her own against Noel Coward himself." Her plays with John Perry, always directed by John Gielgud include *Spring Meeting* (1938), *Ducks and Drakes* (1942), *Treasure Hunt* (1949) and *Dazzling Prospect* (1961).

The tragic death of her husband at the age of thirty-six stopped her writing for many years. It was not until 1981 that another novel – *Good Behaviour* – was published, this time under her real name. Molly Keane has two daughters and lives in Co. Waterford. *Time after Time* appeared in 1983; *Loving and Giving* was published in 1988. Her cookery book, *Nursery Cooking*, was published in 1985.

Virago publishes *Devoted Ladies*, *The Rising Tide*, *Two Days in Aragon*, *Mad Puppetstown*, *Full House*, *Taking Chances*, *Loving Without Tears*, *Treasure Hunt* and *Young Entry*. *Conversation Piece* is forthcoming.

VIRAGO
MODERN
CLASSIC

NUMBER

324

****Young Entry****

MOLLY KEANE
(M. J. FARRELL)

WITH A NEW INTRODUCTION BY
DIANA PETRE

"No pup is a good pup unless it's a wicked pup,"
Inn Saying

Published by VIRAGO PRESS Limited 1989
20–23 Mandela Street, Camden Town, London NW1 0HQ

Reprinted 1990

First published in Great Britain by Elkin Mathews & Marrot Ltd 1928
Copyright M. J. Farrell 1928
Introduction Copyright © Diana Petre 1989

A CIP catalogue record for this book is available from the British Library

Printed in Great Britain
by Cox and Wyman Ltd, Reading, Berks

To

D.

.

INTRODUCTION

The future author of *Young Entry* was seven when the cook turned on her one day, wagging a finger: "Now you listen to me, you *wild little red rip* . . ."

Molly Keane was seventy-nine when I first met her in 1983; small, deceptively frail-looking, no longer a red-head, but still something of a rip, there was little change in the original cocktail of her engaging qualities. Her small alert eyes missed nothing; her face is not photogenic, the infinite charm of it lying in its subtle mobility, but when it is still, perhaps when she is listening to someone, which she does with almost inspired concentration, her eyes are among the saddest I have ever seen. Her flick-knife wit, especially against herself, has never shadowed; she loves the incongruous, the unexpected lapse, the kaleidoscopic disarrangement of values. There is an element of steel in Molly Keane, as there is in most survivors, and this is more than equalled by a desperate vulnerability and a kind heart.

It has been said of Arnold Bennett that he conducted his literary education in public. The same may be said of Molly Keane. She was twenty-one when *Young Entry* was first published. She has said of her own work that its subjects have always stayed within a small canvas

v

INTRODUCTION

because she never writes about anything unless she knows about it *really* well. So what did she know about really well aged twenty? She knew about hunting and flirting and the lives of the Anglo-Irish landed gentry and its adamantine class structure. *Young Entry* has a minimal story line: Prudence, nineteen, who hunts and flirts, is being brought up by three guardians.

Prudence flamed and sulked, growing wilder than ever in her conduct, and hating her three guardians, severally and collectively. She hated Oliver, because he ignored her; Kat, because she was untidy, grubby—almost, and fussing—always. And Gus, Cousin Gus—she hated because she feared her. *The influence of a strong personality which has ruled you absolutely, for almost as long as you can remember, is marked and abiding.*

The italics are mine. It seems that Molly Keane's mother, a linguist, musician and published poet, loved Molly the least of all her four children; she was the "odd one out". In the character of Gus she gives a first and relatively slender example of the matriarch who preys on youth for her own narcissistic purposes. In each following novel this ensnaring, feline character is expanded and refined with irony and intense inner knowledge until in *Good Behaviour* it reaches its apotheosis in the character of Mummie, whose daughter Aroon, the large worm, in the end steps into Mummie's shoes, immaculately trained. A Keane novel without one of these appalling creatures is unthinkable.

Prudence's best girl friend who also hunts and flirts is, inexplicably, called Peter. They talk to each other and, indeed, to their suitors and their dogs, in caricature style.

"Peter, little *little* you!" Prudence picked up one of Peter's hands and crushed it ecstatically in both of her own. "Where

INTRODUCTION

would I be without you? Let's see who has the dirtiest nails."

This absorbing occupation kept them enrapt for quite three minutes.

"You win, Puppy." Prudence sat back in her seat, and pushed some of the damp, yellow mist of hair beneath her small, felt hat.

But the real subject of *Young Entry* is hunting. Will the new Master of Harriers be allowed to hunt its pack over the same country as the resident Master of Fox Hounds hunts his?

For twenty-five minutes, without a semblance of a check, hounds ran over the best of Toby's borrowed country; twenty-five minutes while fire ran in the veins of their three followers, and drunk with the headiest of all wines, the glory of fox-hunting, they flung the fences behind them; nor ever encountered one strand of wire; for the great God of fox-hunters looked down, and smiled, and blessing them, decreed that it should be so.

Young Entry is a juvenile work, extravagantly over-parodic throughout, but the talent of its author is unmistakable. For Molly Keane's worldwide admirers its charm and interest lie in this very factor; it was written before the exuberance and wit and innocence had come under a more conscious control, soon to be evident in every succeeding book she wrote. She has always insisted that after her first novel, published in 1926, when she saw herself as "a second Shakespeare", she wrote the subsequent novels with difficulty and solely for money. But this can only be a fraction of the truth. The difficulties of the craft of writing came as something of a surprise to her after the easy fluency of the first successful attempt, but the exercising of a natural gift and the tapping of hitherto bottled up self-expression must have brought its own reward. To this day she becomes uncomfortable when charged with being a "born writer". In *Two Days in Aragon*, she says of a character:

But life was Nan's province, every aspect of life on which she could lay a finger; some octopus-like quality in her seemed able to reach out its sensitive strength and grasp the essential of what she heard and saw, and hold it tenaciously within herself until the moment for its use should come.

Molly herself had been doing this all her life.

As is now widely known, her first eleven novels were published under the name M.J. Farrell, a name she adopted for fear of ridicule and cold shouldering from the Anglo-Irish hunting set, the only friends she had at that time. Then, still as Farrell, between 1938 and 1946 she stopped writing novels and wrote four plays in collaboration with John Perry, all of which were put on in London by Binkie Beaumont and directed by John Gielgud.

But in 1946 something devastating happened. Mrs Keane's adored husband Bobby suddenly died. Without question this was the most shattering blow in her life. For thirteen years theirs had been a marriage of the most fulfilling harmony and enjoyment. A perfect companion, a sharer, loving and full of life and fun, Bobby was equally at home with the Anglo-Irish hunting crowd, into which he had been born, as with the sophisticated London theatre world. Now this was over, as though by the guillotine. All her friends and her only remaining brother Godfrey know that on the dreadful day of Bobby's death something irrevocably broke in Molly. She was left with not much money and two small daughters aged five and a half and one and a half.

INTRODUCTION

Molly's emotional life had never been straightforward. First there had been her alien status as a child in her own family, unloved by her mother. Following this she claims that at school she was hated and tormented by all the other girls. And she hated them. When she told me this I was surprised. In someone who had formed and held so many long friendships and was herself so gregarious by nature and so open with strangers, it made little sense. At least it turned on its head La Rochefoucauld's axiom: "Les défauts de caractère s'augmentent en vieillissement comme les défauts du visage." The hated schools had exacerbated the feeling of separateness, and when she started writing novels she felt obliged to follow the same pattern of isolation and use a fictitious name. Later, with the newer London friends, theatre people, writers, publishers, who stimulated and nourished her intellect and humour in a way that the hunting crowd could not, the need to compartmentalise became even greater. Only with Bobby had the whole of her diverse nature been able to flourish. Equally at home among artists and sportsmen he had understood her duality and never mocked her. He appreciated her gift as a writer and was proud of her success, and at the same time he loved hunting with her and going to parties and giving them. He was also a helpful and devoted father. He had fitted the needs of Molly's complicated nature like a sheath.

Another blow, though not on the same scale, had hit Molly Keane very hard slightly earlier. Her latest play had flopped. The one she was working on when Bobby died was never finished, but the one before had been put on in London and taken off a few days later. A radical change which would soon proclaim itself with the trumpet blast of *Look Back in Anger*, was taking place in the theatre and the Farrell/Keane style of drawing-room comedy was no longer acceptable. In 1946, disillusioned about her talent and alive only to the constriction of pain in her heart, she stopped writing altogether for the next thirty years.

The texture of Molly Keane's prose is like a Matthew Smith painting, voluptuous, sumptuously rich and curvy; her empathy with nature, her feeling for the changing of the seasons, of dawn through to midnight, has been, from the beginning, one of her great strengths as a writer. You can *touch* a Farrell/Keane countryside, and you can *smell* it:

On they jogged, by blackberry-filled hedges and twisting by-roads. The sky lightened slowly to disclose the witching sadness of the Irish countryside. They rode by little tumbled houses—lonely on the edges of dull, purple bogs; here, was a burnt fox covert—Anthony's face darkened at the sight; there, a haunting, wet, little wood, where the old twisting birch stems were like crooked, silver spells; and the tang of the purple loosestrife rose on the smoke of the morning.

She was writing like this aged twenty; in *Two days in Aragon*, published in 1941:

The scent of azaleas caught in the back of her nose like a fog of honey and pepper. The harsh almost animal breath that is behind its scent was not here yet, only the wild pungent sweet of its earliest flowers.

Every one of her books is dotted with descriptive passages which cause the reader to stop and go back to re-read slowly with joy.

Like the young Molly herself, Prudence is a wilful,

INTRODUCTION

vulnerable, larky girl, brimming with life, attractive to men, very popular and devious. With almost no money she hunts, tears about in cars, flirts, visits friends' houses, goes to the races, hunt balls and parties. Someone or other always pays her hunt subscriptions, lends her horses, gives her clothes. As Molly Keane told me, "You simply didn't need money in those days. Everything was somehow always there."

Always there for the Anglo-Irish in the Big Houses. Molly Skrine, as she then was, grew up in just such a way, but unlike her friends and contemporaries, her unsleeping eye never failed to catch the nuances of speech and behaviour between the privileged and the working classes. In the twenties this was even more marked and unbridgeable in Ireland than it was in England. M.J. Farrell recorded it all. "Peter dropped a half-smoked cigarette behind her back, setting her foot upon it; she did not smoke before 'the people'."

Good Behaviour, published in 1981 is, without queston, Molly Keane's masterpiece, but *Young Entry* (which title might fittingly apply to its author) will give delight to the hunting fraternity with its many descriptions of the chase, and also much pleasure to those readers turned detective in sighting planted seeds in the author's literary greenhouse—seeds which in time grew to such masterly and fruitful luxuriance.

Diana Petre, London, 1988

CONTENTS

YOUNG ENTRY

✣✣

CHAPTER I

PRUDENCE

" So like Prudence ! " the tennis party said. They also said : " God help her when the old ladies hear about it ! "

Prudence, playing efficiently up at the net, concentrated her attention entirely on the game. She seemed to have utterly ignored the fact that a pair of jodhpurs—be they ever so well cut— are hardly the correct kit for a tennis party ; even when supplemented by the best of fair-isle jumpers and undeniable socks.

After all, when one's cousins (who are also one's guardians) refuse to lend the car, what *is* one to do about it ? Bicycle, perhaps ? Not if you are Prudence ; especially when the distance to be covered exceeds one mile. She rode, of course. And if she could successfully overcome the difficulties of playing tennis in so cramping a kit, no one else need object to it. Peter, in the opposite court, obviously approved ; and if Peter approved, no other opinion mattered very much to Prudence,

7

The two girls, Prudence and Peter, exchanged
the unconcerned glances of good friends as, their
set finished, they walked off the court, and made
their way towards the benches and rugs where
the other members of the tennis party were
seated.

They did not speak to each other at once. This
afternoon's show was in the nature of what Peter
—whose ways of expressing herself were concise
and rather picturesque—called, a "distinctly low
party." This only meant that their hostess, and
most of her guests, did not belong to quite the
same strata of Irish county society in which Peter
Trudgeon and Prudence Lingfield-Turrett had
been born and brought up; which fact accounted
for the cousin's refusal of the car that afternoon,
as well as for the almost morbidly polite interest
Prudence was showing in the few remarks volunteered by her late partner.

He was an overwhelmingly shy curate; Prudence
was being kind to him partly because she hated
people to be shy of her; and chiefly because
she wanted so badly to talk to Peter—whom
she had not seen since yesterday—and yet earnestly
desired that Mr. Bennet should not guess that
she felt anything but rapt interest in his conversation.

"Do you fish, Miss Turrett?" Mr. Bennet
asked, quite easily, once the ice had been broken
—or rather, melted—in the lighting of a cigarette.

Miss Turrett shook her head regretfully:

"No, Mr. Bennet, not even trout. You tie
rather a good fly, don't you? Miss Trudgeon

got a four-pound white trout on one you gave her."

Mr. Bennet's glassy eyes popped. He was so pleased.

"Ah, Miss Trudgeon's a grand fisherman. She's a great sport all-round—don't you think so?" Thinking perhaps that he had been too profuse in his admiration of my lady's friend, Mr. Bennet caught himself up, adding as a diplomatic afterthought, "I believe you're a very keen follower of the hounds, Miss Turrett."

Prudence was delighted. The remark was so delicious as to quite repay her for trouble previously taken.

"Indeed, I am, Mr. Bennet," she schooled her speech easily to the subtleties of his, "only I'm awfully frightened of the jumps, you know."

"T'ch, t'ch, they're surely a fright!" Mr. Bennet agreed in a heartfelt murmur. "But I hear you're always the first lady in at the death."

"Oh, not *always*, Mr. Bennet." Prudence was enjoying herself more and more. "And if I am," she continued, "all the credit belongs to the Puckhorn. When hounds are running Pookie takes charge of matters, and all I have to do is to stay with him. He's priceless."

"Oh, yes! He's a lovely animal." Mr. Bennet felt about in his mind for some safe remark about horse-flesh. Finally, he brought it out:

"Lovely gloss on his coat!"

Prudence nodded—wordlessly. Twisting sideways, she battled for a moment with helpless mirth, and the massed attacks of midges on her

9

slight ankles. Then, once again she faced her companion, with lovely, grave eyes.

"Major Countless is cubbing in Knockbeale Wood on Tuesday morning," she told him, casually. "You should put an alarm clock in a tin basin, and get up at 5.30 to hunt on your feet. Didn't you board two and a half couples when the committee gave up? You'd like to see how they'll do for this new fella? I think he's only had them out for road-work, so far."

Mr. Bennet sucked his teeth retrospectively:

"I'll not forget in a hurry the three months I put in with the lot you and Miss Trudgeon landed down on me. Only I was sorry for the poor brutes, I'd have had the whole lot in the river twice over, before your cousin had the new master enticed to take them. Oh, such a crew! What's this, now, their names were? Dimity, and Draughtsman, Ruby, and Ranger and Rally. I could never get their names, at all. It was mostly Spot, and Dot, and Dash, I had on them."

"Well, Mr. Bennet," Prudence rose to her lean, conspicuous height—she was much too thin— "*promise* me you'll be out on Tuesday morning. And—I tell you what—beat up all the people you can who boarded hounds, I know they'd be interested ; and we'd like to have a good field out to, er, to—as it were—welcome Major Countless. I think it would be a nice idea, don't you? "

"T'ch, lovely ! " agreed Mr. Bennet, who was quite aware that, should the alarm clock and the tin basin fail in their functions, Miss Lingfield-Turrett was perfectly capable of rousing him from slumber herself. There was that story about the sleeping curate—but, of course, it was quite among the indiscretions of her extreme youth.

Prudence *was* indiscreet. And yet she had, as she often told one, been beautifully brought up. So, leaving all her sins heaped at the doors of Heredity, she went her careless way—the despair of her guardians, and the joy of all fellow irresponsibles.

These guardians—the Misses Lingfield—were old ladies (or rather, middle-aged ladies) of some character. Character which did not, however, make them the best possible guardians for their young cousin. Still, since Miss Augusta, Miss Kathleen and their brother, Oliver, were the only near relatives that Prudence's father possessed, it was both natural and obvious that he should leave his little daughter in their charge, when he went out to the Great War—from which he never came back. Under their guardianship she was to remain until she should come of age, and inherit both the property of Lingarry and the Turrett money.

This blessed day was still two years distant on the afternoon upon which Prudence wore her Cousin Oliver's jodhpurs at a tennis party—a party given by people whom she knew her cousins listed among the " impossibles " of the neighbourhood ; and imposed her wiles on the long-suffering and indulgent Mr. Bennet.

Now, after a faint smile, and a murmured, " I know I can rely on *you*," she left him, moving across the grass to Peter, with quite unconscious stateliness.

Peter, who had done her duty equally by her late partner, now felt no compunction in isolating

herself and Prudence—for a short space—from the
rest of the party. They drifted vaguely towards
the house ; finally installing themselves unobtrusively in somebody's new Dodge car. Prudence
seated herself before the wheel, and stretching
forth a surprising length of leg, absently took out
the clutch and fingered the various gadgets on
the switch-board while Peter spoke.

"My dear bird," Peter said caressingly, "I'm
so glad to see your face again. But what are you
doing in Cousin Oliver's breeching ? You know,
I don't call it nice. And I'm sure the girls wouldn't
like it, either."

"Oliver is away for the day—with Major
Countless," Prudence explained. "And the girls
don't know one pair of breeches from another.
They'd get equally fierce whether they saw me
walking about the passages in my cami-knickers,
or this perfectly excellent yoke." She passed
approving hands down her lean thighs ; then
turned serious eyes to Peter : "Do you know,
they have an old coat hung on a nail inside the
stable-arch, and I'm supposed to drape my naked-
ness in it, before Tom Hinch or John Strap see
me, when I come in from riding ? 'Exposing
your legs '—that's what they say."

"My God ! " Peter was momentarily deprived
of speech. "My Ma is bad enough, but these
two old——" she flicked past another word, and
finished——" old cats, they take the barbed wire
spittoon. They do, really."

"Peter, little *little* you ! " Prudence picked up
one of Peter's hands, and crushed it ecstatically

in both her own. " Where would I be without
you ? Let's see which of us has dirtiest nails."

This absorbing occupation kept them enrapt for
quite three minutes.

" You win, Puppy." Prudence sat back in her
seat, and pushed some of the damp, yellow mist of
her hair beneath her small, felt hat. " And now
let's think of some serious diversion. It's ages
since we've had a real good crack."

Peter nodded slowly. Screwing her blue eyes
into slits, she trod absent-mindedly on the self-
starter. With the consequent jar, came inspiration.

" Pet—I've thought of it ! "

Prudence remained nearly impassive.

" Sweet one," she said, " tell me. At least—
you needn't. It's what I've thought of too. I
know. We—we'll rag the guts out of that horrid
little fella, Major Anthony Countless, M.F.H. I
hate him, and so must you. You do, don't you ? "

Peter threw up her round chin and laughed.
She laughed with her throat, and chin, and her
whole body, in the most infectious way—but not
noisily. Suddenly grave again, she turned to
Prudence.

" Poor brute ! I pity him from my soul, if you
and I really have taken a dislike to him. I suppose we have. After all "—she ticked off the
points on her fingers—" Oliver Lingfield produced
him, when Toby Sage'd have taken the hounds,
if we'd put up another two hundred. Then, the
girls approve of him. Also, he's a dam' Saxon ;
and, he's been disgustingly rude to you, in your
own house——"

"No," Prudence broke in, swiftly. "He hasn't even taken the trouble to *be* rude. He hasn't asked me anything about the hounds—though he *must* know I took more trouble about them than anyone, when the committee gave up. He hasn't even asked me to go and see the new kennels. He refused to take Jack Stevens back—even as second whip ; Jack, who knows every inch of the country, and I promised him I'd do my best to get him taken on again. *And* he's put down three-and-a-half couples. One of them was Dainty, too."

"*No*, Prudence, he *hasn't !* "

Prudence nodded.

"He has—this morning." An even note of indignation was in her voice. "Oh, I don't find him very difficult to dislike. A nasty little fellow ! A stiff-necked, fox-catching, little Saxon ! "

Peter said : "Dammit, Prudence, fox-hunting is his job ; he is badly wanted in this country. He has the money ; he has the hounds ; he has the horses ; he doesn't even mind if we *do* dislike him. What are we going to do ? "

"Dash ! I believe they are looking for us to play," Prudence jerked abstractedly at the catch of the door nearest to her. "Look here, Puppy. To-day's Saturday. Between now and Tuesday we've got to collect every soul that walked a pup or boarded hounds during the last six months. They've *all* got to come out cubbing at Knock-beale. Be persuasive, but don't over-do it. I'll explain it all, later. Yes, Mrs. Roche—are we to play again ? Come on, Peter." The pair descended and walked across the gravel ; Peter,

ponderously, yet with something of the grace of
a very well-fed cat; Prudence, with a free, impa-
tient stride.

It was not until they were thoroughly engrossed
in their game that a car slid noiselessly down the
slight gradient to the hall door, and there came
to a well-ordered stop. It was a high-powered
car, with very limited seating room. As Mrs.
Roche hurried hospitably forward, two men—preceded by a tall, and excellently tailored, lady—
got out. The lady was Miss Augusta Lingfield,
Prudence's guardian; and the taller of the two
men her cousin, Oliver Lingfield. The little fellow,
with the brick-red, hard-bitten face, and slightly
bowed legs—cased in wonderfully fitting canvas
leggings—was Major Anthony Countless, previously
referred to as a "fox-catching little Saxon." He
looked as though his voice must be a rasping bark;
so that his quiet, almost gentle manner of speaking
came as a slight shock to those who did not know
him well. The shock was not of so staggering a
nature as that which delinquents in the hunting-
field sustained at his truly paralysing flood of
invective—which the gentle voice rendered even
more surprisingly effective.

The trio advanced across the gravel, Miss Lingfield in the van.

"How do you do, Mrs. Roche?" The politeness of her greeting was tinged with annoyance at
having forgotten the tennis party, of which Prudence
had told her. "I wonder if you have met our
new Master? Mrs. Roche—Major Countless. We
have been driving round the country looking at

horses for him, this afternoon. My brother thought you had something here which might possibly suit."

" Don't let us take you away from the tennis, Mrs. Roche," Oliver Lingfield put in, " if we could see your husband for a minute. Had no idea you had a show on this afternoon ;—Ah, here he is, now ! "

As the three men set off for the stables, Mrs. Roche—something of a diplomatist—endeavoured to suggest that Miss Lingfield should accompany them. The elder of the two " girls " put the idea brightly on one side.

" Oh, no, I think not, Mrs. Roche. It always seems to me so much better to leave men *alone* on these occasions. One never quite knows . . . some little question they might not care to ask before a lady—one has to be a little careful. And I should very much like to see the players."

Ignoring Mrs. Roche's murmur about tea, Miss Augusta Lingfield set out purposefully towards the tennis court. Now that she had landed herself in the midst of this undesirable party, she was going to do the thing graciously, or not at all.

" I am so sorry," she said, " that I could not allow little Prudence to come to you, to-day. She has already been to three tennis parties this week, and I really felt that a line should be drawn somewhere."

Mrs. Roche swallowed apologetically :

" I always feel, Miss Lingfield, that really the girls now have so few of the chances we had, that really it's very hard to deny them what little pleasure they can get—especially as this is such a quiet little spot ; no dances ; no officers ; in

fact, there's nothing left at all in Ireland now—
only the hunting and a little tennis."

Miss Augusta permitted herself a faint smile—
more pitying than derisive.

"Oh, I'm all for amusement for the young,"
she admitted it as one does an amiable weakness,
"at the same time, I insist on a few, light, domestic
jobs being done. Now, I left little Prudence
to-day, quite happily stoning cherries for jam."

Mrs. Roche drew in her breath sharply, as if
to speak ; but before she could do so, Miss Augusta
broke in with a slight yelp of horror :

"Mrs. Roche ! Don't tell me that is a *girl*, playing tennis in the far court ! Is she not ashamed
of the disgusting exhibition she is making of herself ?
Ugh ! "—as Prudence ran the length of the court
with amazing speed—" sickening ! "

"Indeed, Miss Lingfield "—Mrs. Roche cast
about unhappily in her mind for something to
say—" it's not everyone could wear them ; but
we all thought they looked very nice. Yes, really
—imagine ! " She tailed off into a stricken silence,
aware of an almost perceptible stiffening in her
guest's attitude. It was really too absurd that
this old aristocrat should make her feel as though
there was something morally wrong, low and
dirty, in the sight of that clean-limbed girl, as she
streaked across the court, with a controlled swift-
ness which was grace itself.

"Mrs. Roche, if that is really my little cousin,
will you have the goodness to send her to me, at
once. *At once.* You will forgive me, but under
the circumstances, I do not feel equal to meeting

your other guests. Please send her to me in the house." As Miss Lingfield turned to walk back to the car, it was obvious that she and Prudence owed the queer stateliness of their gait to some common ancestor.

The hostess paused, indecisively; then, shrugging her shoulders in hopeless amazement, she advanced towards the players. Prudence came to meet her —her chin at a more than usually defiant angle.

"Thanks so much, Mrs. Roche," she said. "I've enjoyed it awfully. Didn't I see Cousin Gus talking to you? I expect I'd better go and explain —I mean, I think she'll probably want me to go home. Good-bye." She shook hands carelessly, and moved off.

Cousin Gus watched her ward's leisurely advance, with pain, grief and anger boiling in her system.

"Puce with suppressed maidenly virtue," Prudence decided, as her guardian's wrathful eye raked her from head to heel. "Damn it!" she longed to say, "I've got *some* clothes on, you needn't look as though I'd forgotten everything;" but ancient custom prevailed; she felt as she had done, when—at the age of eight—she had been discovered (quite unclad) racing the pantry-boy down the bathroom passage. She said nothing; but stormed in her heart, and looked sulky. Cousin Gus continued to look her over searchingly for quite a minute, without speaking. At last:

"If you think we have all been sufficiently edified by the sight of your legs, perhaps you will put on your coat. I will then ask Major Countless to be kind enough to drive you home."

"I have my horse here, Cousin Gus." It was dullish work addressing a covert-coated back, but Prudence persevered. "I've got my horse here, Cousin Gus."

"I repeat—put on your coat."

"But I'm riding."

"For the third time—I will not have you standing about in this disgusting state. Put on your coat."

"I tell you, I'm riding. I've got the Puckhorn here."

Cousin Gus swung round upon her ward, horror deepening in her gaze.

"Don't tell me that you went along the public road as—as you are now? Impossible!"

Prudence remained silent while Miss Gus rummaged in the car, and finally produced somebody's jaeger lining.

"Put this on."

"I can't ride in that," Prudence's grey eyes began to be full of tragedy, "I'm riding the Puckhorn, and he'd go clean mad, with that thing flapping round him."

"In that case, I must ask Cousin Oliver to be kind enough to ride your horse home. You will come in the car with myself and Major Countless."

"I *won't!*" Prudence was in a flame of rebellion. Yet, as her cousin and his friend came round the path from the stables, she was shuffling hastily into the coat which Miss Lingfield held out. The custom of years is not lightly broken.

"Oliver," Miss Lingfield addressed her brother in icy tones, "I am taking Prudence home in the car. She has a slight headache. I am *very* sorry to trouble you, dear, but would you mind—would you be so very kind—as to ride her horse home?"

Oliver surveyed an extreme length of grey-flannelled leg, in silence, for a moment, then he said:

"Yes, of course I will, Gus. Which is it, Prudence?"

"It's awfully good of you, Cousin Oliver, thanks very much. Really, there's no earthly reason why I shouldn't ride home. Anyway, it's the Puckhorn. I should hate to ride him in flannels—especially as John has been polishing my saddle."

"Oh, has he? Well, get some oil on it to-morrow." Mr. Lingfield paused for a thoughtful moment, then he turned to his elder sister: "Look here, Gus—I don't feel brave enough for horse-back exercise on the Puckhorn this evening. You see, I'm wearing trousers. Why can't Prudence ride home?"

Miss Augusta choked. It was really too much—first breeches, and now trousers. However, her horrified resentment of her ward's appearance in the former, overcame her anxieties for her brother's safety—in a slippery saddle, and on a light hearted five-year-old—in the latter.

"Oliver, I have a particular reason for asking this."

"Why not swap? Can't you see that the lady has a perfectly good pair of jodhpurs—much your size too, Oliver." This was Anthony Countless's artless suggestion. He could not understand why the girl should get so scarlet in the face over it—perfectly reasonable idea.

"Er, yes, so they are b'Jove! So we could, I mean What about it, Gus?"

But Cousin Gus had had enough. In other words she was not taking any more.

"This," she said, "is revolting. Oliver, you forget yourself. Prudence, get into the car. Perhaps, Major Countless——"

"Stop that horse!"

The clatter of hoofs, galloping on very hard ground, was plainly audible. A moment later, a bay horse, with reins swirling, came head-long round the hair-pin bend from the stable yard; after a horrified stare about him, and one wild and childish whinny, he advanced perilously on the crowd of cars. Behind him, a wire fence and a spiked iron gate, barred the way home.

Anthony caught him—quite easily, as it happened. As he led the horse back: "I'll ride home, Oliver," he remarked in his gentlest voice, "you drive the car, will you? And don't take it out of the gears more than you can help; I may need her again."

The faint flavour of bitterness in his voice was as gall in Prudence's already overful cup. After that, the crashing and grinding of the Bently's gears made music in her ears. That Cousin Gus should—at the conclusion of their drive—say, "Thank you, Oliver, you drove beautifully," added worm-wood to her gall. She had long since resolved not to grit her teeth against Cousin Gus's idiocies, but the resolution was always broken. Had she had anyone with whom to laugh at them! But she heard them so often, and so much alone. That made all the difference.

·　　·　　·　　·　　·

It was late that same evening, when Prudence sat up very straight in the scarlet bed of her white, and black, and scarlet room—such being the un-restful colour scheme which she had herself thought out and insisted upon—and hurled defiance at the fates, and her guardian cousins.

"Daddy, why must you have got killed? Why *did* Mummie die? Why must I go through two more years of this absurd hell? Why are they such old devils? They're low, they're evil——"

She bit her fingers futilely, as brilliant rejoinders to some of the grosser remarks flung at her earlier in the evening—on the delicate subject of her personal modesty—crowded each other in her brain. "Oh, they've got minds like dam' sewers——" Gradually her own mind worked away from the subject of her cousins. Her hands ceased to fold and twitch restlessly on the sheets. Prudence had lifted dreams from her tears—fair dreams that trembled into ecstasy. One thin, beautifully shaped arm, lay outside the bed-clothes. Her pyjamas—brilliant rags, but flimsy—had torn all across one shoulder; her hair was the colour of ashes round the mask-like gauntness of her face; in the red droop of her mouth lived a promise of passion.

Prudence looked rather dreadful in bed, Cousin Kat thought. So—well, 'abandoned' was not quite a nice word. But, really—that torn night-dress!

"Prudence, are you awake?"

"Yes." Prudence wasn't. She was half-asleep, and very sulky at being disturbed. She pulled

some bed-clothes consciously round her shoulders
and peered up at her cousin.

" I'm not surprised to see you hustle the blankets
round your shoulders, Prudence. Are you not
ashamed ? After the beautiful talk Cousin Gus
had with you this evening on the subject of modesty,
here I find you lying half-naked in bed. It is
disgusting. It quite sickens me."

Prudence sat up straight in bed, dropping the
clothes from her shoulders. Colour flooded her
face—flooded down to the violet hollows of her
neck ; the light spun golden in the misty ashes of
her hair ; her eyes were wide—wide with tears
of rage.

" If you don't like my pyjamas, Cousin Kat, and
if the sight of a little of the human form is such a
shock to your system, why don't you knock at my
door, before you come in ? I'd rather you did,
really. Then I'd have time to get into a good old
jaeger winceyette, or something equally refined."

" That will do, Prudence. I came to bring you
some aspirin—as I believe you have a headache ;
also, to let the dog into your room—since you
forgot her ; *and* to let you know that I finished
the cherries *myself*, this afternoon."

Cousin Gus killed by the deadly weight of her
own personality ; Cousin Kat—by kindness only.
When she had taken herself out of the room,
Prudence sank once more among her pillows ; a
flame of anger consuming her very soul, and pricking in little beads of moisture through the even
pallor of her skin.

23

CHAPTER II

KNOCKBEALE WOOD

It was 5.30, by the clock on a dewy, dusky September morning, when Major Anthony Countless, Master of the Drumferris fox-hounds, mounted his horse in the kennel yard ; while as uneven a lot of hounds as were to be found in Ireland snuffed languorously round the new kennel doors, and the heels of the whip's horse—entirely unappreciative of their new huntsman's presence.

The knowledge—fruit of more than one little experience during hours of hound exercise—that the whip's cat had only to go away in view, for half the pack to break and riot after her, led Major Countless to ride rather hastily out of the yard. That hounds did not require so much turning to him as usual, did something to relieve the sombreness of his early morning feelings.

It was, of course, absurd to think that he could hope to do much with them, as yet. But, in all the years during which he had dreamed splendidly of hunting a pack of hounds, he had never—even dimly—foreseen the quite hideous lack of sympathy which could exist between a body of soulless rioters, such as the Drumferris fox-hounds, and their new huntsman.

24

Anthony had carried the horn for his regimental pack in India. He knew something of hounds, and more of horses ; but so far, in many mornings of road work and in three mornings' cubbing, he had been able to do very little with the undisciplined lot of outlaws which his good friend, Oliver Lingfield, had— with Irish impudence—beguiled him to come over from England and hunt two days a-week, in as bad and trappy an Irish country as could well be imagined.

Of course, he reminded himself, as his unfavouring eye lingered on Nosegay, falling out to scratch lavishly (that was her gratitude for the pungent dressings which he had ordained for all) they had been out of kennels for quite five months, it was not unnatural that their discipline should be bad. Of all the Irish madness he had ever heard of, this boarding out of hounds by couples was the most singular. They were a pretty unutterable lot ; he could almost have sworn to a trace of kennel-terrier in the two-and-a-half couples which he had recently speeded to their ultimate hunting grounds.

On they jogged, by blackberry-filled hedges and twisting bye-roads. The sky lightened slowly to disclose the witching sadness of the Irish country-side. They rode by little tumbled houses—lonely on the edges of dull, purple bogs ; here, was a burnt fox covert—Anthony's face darkened at the sight ; there, a haunting, wet, little wood, where the old twisting birch stems were like crooked, silver spells ; and the tang of purple loosestrife rose on the smoke of the morning.

Anthony saw no magic in any of these things ; his mind was fully occupied with the improvements

which he had made, and was still making, at the
kennels. Cement and inside walls, benches, boiler-
houses and feeding-houses soared and rocked in his
brain. For Anthony loved his hounds and thought
much about their health and comfort—far more,
indeed, than he did of his own. Was not the
plumber (that rare and exotic bird) called daily
from his ostensible work of installing Hot and Cold
at Drumferris (the little house which Anthony had
taken for the hunting) to arbitrate over taps and
hose-pipes in the kennels?

A determined effort on the part of his mount
to turn down an inconsiderable bye-road, brought
Anthony's mind back to the affairs of the moment.
He chastised the Puckhorn—a pleasant little horse
of the cobby stamp, which he had bought from
Oliver after his hack home of the previous Saturday
—and proceeded to his usual riding-to-covert game,
of putting a name to each hound in the pack. He
had just decided that a certain elderly bitch was
Ruby, when Ruby—if, indeed, it was she—flung up
her head with a melodious howl, and together with
Dimity, Draughtsman, Ranger and Rally, departed
in full cry down the foot-path—for they were now
on the high-road leading to Knockbeale Wood.

Galloping furiously, Anthony and the whips came
up with them, in time to see the pack storming
about a small man, who, having abandoned his
push-bike as a means of locomotion, and propped
its front wheel securely between a telegraph post
and a demesne wall, was now endeavouring to
take sanctuary, by standing with one foot on the
saddle and the other precariously balanced on the

cross-bar ; from which momentary coign of vantage
he adjured the pack.

"Here, Spot ! Poor Spot ! Ah, poor girl, you
know me, surely ? Eh, Dash ! Go down, now !
Go down ! "

Dash, Spot and Co. were delighted. They leaped
frenziedly on the wheels of the bicycle, in a creditable endeavour to lick the face of their quarry ;
though they did not succeed in perpetrating this
lovable trait in their dispositions, they were at
least successful in dislodging their late "walk"
from his perch. It was, perhaps, as well, that the
bicycle crashed after, and on top of the prostrate
Mr. Bennet.

"I'm fearfully sorry, Sir——" Anthony Countless schooled his tongue once more to everyday
speech, as he addressed Mr. Bennet. "I really——"

"Oh, don't mention it," interrupted the victim.
"Sure the reason is only that I have in my pocket
a couple of the cheese savouries my landlady makes
me, and I always used to give them to the hounds
I was boarding. I suppose they smelt them this
morning, and that now's the why. I declare, I'm
sorry you whipped them ! They meant no harm
—the poor brutes. Did you, old fellows ? " Taking
a greasy package from his pocket, he flung it, as
accurately as possible, in the direction of the three
most notable sinners.

Ruby had it down, even to the string, before
the red-hot lash could speak.

"My God ! " Anthony turned to the smiling
Mr. Bennet in his muddy grey clothes. "You,
you shouldn't do that, you know."

27

"Ah, I brought it out for them, anyway." Mr. Bennet looked ruefully at his grazed hands. "It's better than having them tracing me round all morning for it." Picking up his bicycle he leant it against the wall. Then, lighting a cigarette, he waited till the now speechless Master and fifteen couples of hounds should have faded round the corner.

"My God!" Anthony repeated foolishly, "the Plaster of Paris Poll-Parrot merchant, b'Gad!"

"Yessir?" said his icily aloof and indignant English whipper-in. But Anthony was again past speech, though this time it was from laughter.

Tom Willis, the whip, could see nothing to laugh at in the affair. From first to last it was a disgrace; just as the kennels and feeding arrangements and, above all, the pack itself, were—to his soul, which loved to see things done decently and in order—a disgrace. He often woke in the night positively sweating as the thought of what the first whip of his last pack would have said to the make-shifts and disgraceful laxity in his present kennels.

Before they reached the lane-way that led to Knockbeale Wood, several hounds broke from the pack and endeavoured to follow persons mysteri-ously abroad at this early hour. It could hardly be possible that even puppy-walkers had been ardent enough to rise from their beds. Anthony sincerely hoped that, if such were the case, they had at least refrained from filling their pockets with strong-smelling dainties for their late charges' consumption. As he rode through the gate-way of the walled lane that stretched darkly between the woods, a girl's voice greeted him coolly. He turned to see Prudence Lingfield-Turrett—Oliver's little, heiress cousin—seated on the wall, her long legs dangling. She held a crooked, little terrier beneath her arm, while another screamed defiance and hatred at the hounds. A girl sat beside her. She was too fat, he decided ; then noticed her quite wonderful complexion and sleepy eyes. She said " Good-morning," too—a trifle less crisply than her companion.

" Good-morning." Anthony touched his cap, " very glad to see some terriers out," and he rode on ; Puckhorn whickering and turning his head excitedly. " Come up, horse ! " Anthony caught up his reins and hit him behind the saddle, whereupon his mount let out with both heels, catching a hound in the ribs with one ; followed confusion, while the Puckhorn was beaten, and the hound yelped and cowered.

Prudence turned to Peter, her lovely mouth, which always gave the lie to the crossness of her eyes, and the haunting unrest of her face, working like a child's with unhappiness.

" You saw that, Puppy ? Riding my horse while I'm on foot and beating him and pulling him about in front of me. Pookie never kicked hounds when I had him."

" You bet he gave him a dig with the spurs to make him show off," Peter suggested. " Nasty little cad ! "

Prudence slid down off the wall and coupled the terriers.

" Come on," she said briskly, " I'm afraid Mr. Bennet won't turn up now, and it's too late to pour his jug over him."

"He's probably got neuralgia again," Peter observed sadly, "he suffers from that—and tooth-ache. Oh, the toot'-ache's a fright—it'd set you mad altogether," she sucked her teeth much after the manner of Mr. Bennet; but was not at all discon-certed when that gentleman dismounted heavily from his push-bike, about two yards behind her.

"Good-morning, Mr. Bennet," she continued easily. "You're very late, and you're awfully muddy. Have you had a fall?"

"T'ch, 'deed I have!" Mr. Bennet removed his hat as Prudence smiled at him—blankly but sympathetically. "I declare you'd have died laughing at me awhile ago, Miss Trudgeon, if you'd seen the way I was. Here I was, standing up on the saddle of the bicycle, with my arms round a telegraph pole."

"But why, Mr. Bennet?" Peter inquired dazedly.

"Why? Wouldn't anyone else have been swarming their best up the pole? But I knew they only meant it in fun. Sure many a time they kept me stuck in my bedroom till I had enough old boots gathered to fire at them."

"What!" There was rapt delight in Prudence's voice. "You don't mean to say the *hounds* had you treed up a telegraph pole?"

"Isn't that what I said?" Mr. Bennet felt that a more tender interest might conceivably have been displayed in the perils of his situation. "The new master seemed rather annoyed. He beat the poor brutes most cruelly, I thought. I told him it was all caused by a cheese savoury I had in my

pocket, intending to give it to poor old Ruby—
she was always my pet ! "

Prudence gasped and flung the terriers' strap to
Mr. Bennet.

" Hold them," she called—" I must get on !
Lend me the bike, will you ? "

" I very much doubt, Miss Turrett——" Mr.
Bennet began, but Prudence had already mounted.
Running, with one foot on the step, she leapt into
the saddle like a boy, found the pedals unhesitatingly and pushed off ; her knees were up in her
ears—the bicycle being a size too small for her—
and her short skirt was anyhow.

" Come on, Puppy ! " she called.

Miss Trudgeon could move. She placed one
foot on the step, flung her right leg across the
mud-guard, and maintained her balance by leaning
heavily on Prudence's shoulders. The pair, coasting swiftly down a hill, turned an impossibly sharp
corner and were lost to sight.

" T'ch, t'ch ! There's two real sports ! " reflected Mr. Bennet. Here, one of the terriers,
suddenly slackening the strain on their strap, which
—up to this moment—had been maintained even
to breaking point, bit him abruptly in the calf.
With nerves badly shaken by the morning's previous incident, Mr. Bennet released his hold of
the strap and watched with starting eyes—the
still coupled pair scramble over the wall, to dis-
appear into the lavish undergrowth within the
woods.

Meanwhile, Prudence—a marvellous colour,
lighted by exertion, in the pallor of her face—pushed

gallantly up a slight gradient. The way was rutty and Peter weighed quite ten stone.

" Let me, pet ! " Peter breathed throatily down her neck ; but Prudence, shaking an obstinate head, gave one more shove (which, she felt, *must* burst her heart) and they were on the summit of the hill—were coasting once more down its farther side.

As the slope grew steeper, and consequently their progress faster, Prudence made the interesting discovery that Mr. Bennet's bicycle entirely lacked brakes. Stretching forth a sinuous length of leg— the shapeliness of which even a checked stocking of futuristic design could not quite disguise—she braked for a moment with one well-brogued foot against the mud-guard. Then, releasing the wheel, she observed casually to her passenger :

" Jump, if you can ; if not, fall off. I'm dashed if this jaunt is worth a pair of Watkin's shoes. And hurry up—the hounds are round the next corner, we don't want to lay any of them out."

" Oh, blast it, pet ! Steady her a moment if you can." Peter shifted her balance, causing the front wheel to swerve perilously.

" Jump ! " ordered Prudence ; then, more severely : " *Jump*, can't you ! "

" Right ! " Peter jumped ; retained her balance by a miracle, and catching Prudence round the waist, swung her clean off the saddle. The bicycle crashed heavily.

When she had recovered herself :

" Thank you, Peter," Prudence observed politely, " tell you the truth, I didn't know how I *was* going to get off this rotten yoke."

Raising the yoke in question cautiously from the ground, she essayed to push it for a few yards.

" No good, buckled and jammed." She laid it gently to rest on a bed of nettles, and catching Peter by the hand, said :

" Run ! "

Arrived at the place where they expected to see hounds go into covert, they paused ; nothing was to be seen of the hounds, but within the wood their huntsman's voice rose and fell in well modulated encouragement.

" Good morning, Miss." Prudence turned to see the deplorable figure of the covert-keeper approaching her. This was Micky Grogan—the worst poacher and best fisherman on the river; a wonderful snipe-shot too ; and he could tie a most killing fly for salmon or trout. He knew all the ways of Fin and Feather ; and had the eyes of a poet and the temperament of a fish. A mournful man—except when in his cups—he could whistle like birds singing and imitate the cry of every bird.

" Morning, Micky," he was a great crony of Prudence's but preferred Peter's company.

" She wouldn't care what hardship she'd get," he would say of her, after a long day's fishing in the cruel blasts of March. He was the apostle of Peter's greatest faith and love in life—salmon fishing.

" Mick "—Peter dropped a half-smoked cigarette behind her back, setting her foot upon it ; she did not smoke before ' the people '—" are there cubs in it, Mick ? "

" There is, of course, Miss Peter. Weren't there two litters raised in it ? I lay near the den myself,

33

one night in June, and seen the whole kit o' them
playing around like puppies—the way ye'd laugh
to see them so cute ; and the eyes of them like
otters' eyes in the dark, and long, little noses on
them. Oh, there's surely foxes in it ! "

" Yes, but are they in it now, Micky ? Wouldn't
they have gone to Cree Hill ? "

" Ah, what'd shift them ? " replied Micky easily.
" Wasn't a chap telling me, e'en yesterday, himself
and another fella was in it a-Sunday, with a couple
o' lumps o' terrier-dogs and a hound, and they
raised a fox just taking his course down one of
the cut-ways."

" H'm," said Peter, " well, that ought to have
scattered them a bit. I wish there was something
for the hounds to push about, this morning."

" Is it them ! Sure any old cat'd come handy
to the like o' those fellas." Micky winked expressionlessly at Prudence, he was ever ready to dis-
parage the hounds, which could prove a stronger
attraction than the river in the days of March.

" I'd wish to see cubs in it, whatever," he continued, " isn't it what they say this new Major
gentleman'll pay a sovereign to the covert keeper
for every fox he'll kill out of it. That's a hell of
an improvement on ten shillings." He winked
again and spat—at an angle from the two girls.

" Whisht ! ye can hear them hunting now—
that's no rabbit out before them."

The trio ran down the wood and established
themselves unostentatiously with a good view down
four intersecting rides, and out on to the open
hillside beyond the trees.

"They *are* hunting, Peter," Prudence said, "something stronger than cheese has moved them this time."

A minute later a large, pale cub slid out of the end of the wood, remained still for a moment, half-hidden by yellowing bramble leaves, then slid shiftily down the hillside.

The excellent screech which hastened his departure was all to Prudence's credit. Its perfection was due to months of solitary practising—practising necessarily far removed from the haunts of men, or, at any rate, from the haunts of Cousins Kat and Gus. Its resonance brought the whip, galloping—a vivid flash of colour—down one of the rides.

"Where'd 'e cross, Miss? Ow, pity to stop 'em, when they're hunting something besides cats, for once."

A crash of music, and the pack swept—a broken sheet of colour—from the cloaking undergrowth on one side of the ride to the green density on the other. Hunting they certainly were.

Their huntsman burst from the wood a moment later, three couples of enthusiastic but uninitiated puppies gallumphing ecstatically down the ride behind him.

"We don't know quite what's expected of us," they seemed to say, "but here we are—anxious to do the right thing!"

"You'll have to ride round and stop 'em, Willis," the master called; and to the covert-keeper: "He's got a start?"

"He have, begor! He's snug in Cree Hill by this," Micky answered.

35

"There's a brace on foot in covert still. Why didn't you stop him breaking if he crossed straight in front of you? God dammit! A man can't be everywhere in this blithering wilderness." The Master proceeded down the steep hillside, quite unmindful of the rabbit holes strewn in his path, his shoulders and seat set easily to the discrepancies of the descent.

Prudence looked at Peter and Peter looked round for Micky. He had vanished as completely as though he had been caught up in the morning mist, which was even now smoking off briar-wreaths and bracken. It was to them, then, that the reproof had been spoken.

"He was quite right," said Peter, "we should have tried to."

Prudence's stormy eyes held no whit of sorrow or repentance.

"The best hunt ever I had," she said, "was on the sixteenth of September, but I suppose he's too correct in his ideas to cross country while there's a briar green in the fences."

"Well, there are three un-cut corn-fields between this and Cree Hill . . . there they are coming back—shall us?"

"Yes, let's," Prudence assented hurriedly. By the time the hounds were up the hill-side the pair had vanished as untraceably and completely as Micky Grogan himself.

It was nine o'clock before hounds were drawn out of Knockbeale Wood. Nine o'clock, with the sun high in a polished heaven, and no faintest vestige of scent in the bracken-filled woods. The

36

Master and whips conned over the pack—twelve couple where fifteen and a half had left kennels that morning.

But the three and a half couples of which they were short,—Rarity, Cobweb, Dauntless and their fellows—were, at the moment, too delightfully occupied to feel more than the faintest shiver of cold anticipation as the summoning notes of the horn reached them in the secluded sand-pit upon the hill-side where they were feasting, richly and furiously, upon the long defunct, and lightly buried, carcase of a sheep.

In a near-by rabbit hole one kicking hind leg announced the presence of the two terriers—Dilly and Blazes—that is, if the couples still held. Their suppressed yelps of excitement, and the showers of sand which flew upon the morning air denoted a near approach to their white-scutted quarry.

It was upon this scene that Willis—the thong of his crop unfurled for instant execution and his tongue tuned to harsh admonishment—bore down, only to find that the sand-pit was firmly fenced all round and its gate locked. Before he could climb the wire, a long scream—penetrating in its intensity—rent the air, as a large rabbit was drawn (loudly protesting) from the mouth of her burrow. The scream was followed by hysterical yelps from the two terriers, as Mrs. Bun, with the energy of despair, tore herself from their jaws, and set off at a creditable pace down the hill-side.

The terriers followed in kangaroo-like bounds, the puppies struggled through the wire and followed the terriers—giving tongue with a fervour which

37

had been noticeably lacking on their lawful occasions earlier in the morning.

Their voices carried clearly to the place on the hill-side where Anthony and the second whip held the remainder of the pack. A shiver of intention swept tensely through the twelve couples and before their huntsman had time even to prick his ears to the sound, they had broken and were away through the wood, getting to cry like a shot from a gun.

Anthony picked himself up—he had been standing by his horse when the rush took place—to find himself gazing into the limpid, grey eyes of Prudence Turrett.

"I think you'd better let me catch the Puckhorn," she said, handing him his whip.

And with the air of a mother who mounts her six-year-old son after he has taken a toss, she held the Puckhorn till he was safely in the saddle; then opened a gate to let him into the wood.

. . . . .

"*Darling* Blazes, Mummy's own funny!" she cooed, when she and her terrier were once more re-united. "*Such* a clever little girl! Did she show those stupid puppies how to hunt rabbits? *Did* find dead sheep, precious?"

Blazes—a woundingly undemonstrative little dog —wriggled from her mother's embrace and, jumping stiffly down to the ground, embarked on a diligent and thorough survey of her person.

CHAPTER III

JAMES had been butler at Lingarry for upwards of twelve years. Even the arbitrary ways of the Misses Lingfield, who treated all servants as either liars or thieves, (often as both) had failed to dislodge him. The two ladies always believed the worst of James, but had never quite succeeded in establishing against him anything nearer thieving than his habit of keeping the dregs of the cream jugs in an old jam pot—which was hidden in a drawer with the knife-powder—until such a time as it could safely be carried down to Mrs. James at the gate-lodge.

Mrs. James had been one of the most iniquitous of the Misses Lingfield's long line of cooks. Her marriage to James having, in fact, been considerably accelerated by—— but neither of the girls could think of that dreadful time without a hot blush of anger and discomfort.

That James had not been sent (characterless) about his business, after such a rending of the decencies, was entirely due to Oliver—whose hunting kit James kept with a stability of fervour and a perfection of zeal which, his master realized, could never be equalled.

39

When remonstrated with on the subject of the
cook, James had replied :

" Ah, the poor girl was always a little careless.
Sure, what matter ? You know, a little accident
the like o' that could happen anyone. You might
say, indeed, 'twas partly my fault. See, Mr. Oliver,
you should get us the back gate-lodge."

Oliver had bowdlerized the reply into a mere
expression of willingness on James' side to marry
the careless Kate O'Mara ; thus he continued—
during the period of Prudence's extreme youth—to
discharge the duties of butler and valet at Lingarry ;
adding to these the wholly honorary offices of scourge
to a long line of suffering pantry boys, and guide,
philosopher and valued friend to Prudence.

Knowing well on which side his bread was but-
tered, he was the cheerful scape-goat (whenever
possible) of the many crimes and lapses of her
childhood, and as she grew older, continued to lie
for her with the same perfection and fervour that
he showed in the cleaning of Oliver's hunting kit.

Prudence, who had loved him with passion in her
childhood, still discussed all her affairs with him.

On a still, windless, perfect morning, early in
September, James was perfunctorily flicking round
the dining-room with his duster, in preparation
for family prayers.

Prayers were read aloud before breakfast by one
of the girls—generally Miss Gus—for the benefit of
her own soul, her sister's, and Prudence's—who
was late, on an average, four times a week. The
pantry boy was also supposed to be present, but
as the hour was that at which another operation,

known as " tending the separator ", kept him occupied in the dairy, his presence was not insisted
upon.

This morning, James laid the faded manual of
devotion open at the page marked by a yellow
ribbon, enveloped the parrot's cage in a heavy
swathe of curtain (which did little to dim the
occupant's protests), and was polishing the apples,
from a dish on the sideboard, on the lining of his
coat, when Miss Gus came briskly into the room.

As usual, she was admirably clothed. She wore
an excellent tweed skirt with a *tabac* alpaca woolly ;
and walked as though brightly conscious of the
exceptional cut and mellow colour of her laced
shoes. Her nose (which, by the way, was just as
well cut as her shoes) was slightly blue in the early
morning.

" Good morning."

" Good morning, Miss." James straightened the
dish of apples, and was making a prim departure
in the direction of the gong—Miss Augusta's appearance being the signal at which he boomed forth
a summons to prayer—when the lady inquired
coldly :

" James, where is the ham ? "

" I d'know, Miss." James, poised for flight, at
the door, hoped that the question would not be
pressed. He hoped in vain.

" My orders were that the cold ham was to
come in for breakfast," Miss Augusta continued,
with pardonable annoyance, " this is the second
morning that they have been disobeyed. I let it
pass yesterday, as Mr. Oliver was not at home,

but I will not have such disobedience in future. Tell the cook to give it to you."

" 'Twould be hard for her," reflected James, as he slid out of the room and went across the hall to the gong. "Wouldn't Miss Gus, now, put stitches across a bag o' weasels ! " Having thus summarized his employer's foible for economy, he was about to strike the gong, when a door opened on a landing above him and Prudence—with tumbled hair hanging about the strained, white urgency of her face—breathed hastily :

"James, for God's sake, don't ring the gong yet ! I'm not half dressed. Go and tell Maggie to bring me up some clean stockings, I haven't a *rag*."

The desperation in her voice might have conveyed, to anyone who knew her less well than James, that she was about to miss a train ; or that her dog had died ; or almost any conceivable disaster ; but that was just Prudence. A ladder in a favourite silk stocking could reduce her to tears, just as a phrase of wild poetry made her drunk with ecstasy, or a witty story moved her to agonies of mirth. She did things to distraction —always.

James, realising her peculiarities, merely ejaculated : •"Holy snipes ! God help us ! " and, moving over to the dining-room door, coughed demurely to attract Miss Gus's attention. When he had done so, he said :

"Excuse me, Miss ! Maggie have taken the gong-stick to bate the wild-cat was roving the landings last night. Will I tell the two ladies prayers is waiting ? "

Miss Augusta nodded ; she was re-filling the sugar basin from a locked store in the sideboard cupboard.

James departed on a protracted tour. He scoured the house for Maggie—the under-housemaid, and sent her up to Miss Prudence, while he himself, " took a race round to the clothes line to see would he get the stockings—what colour are they, Maggie ?"

" Like a kind of a beejy-nude," replied Maggie —a young woman of some sophistication.

" Oh, God be our help ! " murmured James, in bemused consternation, as he set off at a sloping canter for the clothes line.

All things considered, it was hardly surprising that—the belated morning prayers over and break-fast advanced past the porridge stage—Oliver should rake the sideboard fruitlessly with his eye, before observing : " Gus, I think some of that ham we had the other day would be rather——"

" My dear boy ! I spoke to James only this morning about it—he forgot, I suppose. Prudence, ring the bell, please. Really, Oliver, that old man is past bearing. His *carelessness !* Prudence, did you ring the bell ? "

" Yes, Cousin Gus."

" Ring it again, please."

" I heard it sound," replied Prudence, who was engaged in the ticklish performance of helping herself to honey. " Oh, all right, Cousin Oliver, let me ! " But Oliver's thumb was already on the bell-push.

" Perhaps, another time, you might spare *one* minute from your food to do as you are asked," thus Cousin Kat, in gentle reproof. "You see Cousin Oliver had to leave his breakfast and walk across the room."

"A little exercise is quite good for my figure."

Oliver, who, though nearing the fifties was lean and athletic as any boy, could afford jokes on this most sensitive of subjects. "Fat! I'm gettin' as fat as a poisoned pup," he smiled one of his rare and charming smiles at Prudence, and carved her off a piece of bread, after the manner of one who confers a royal favour.

The bell was answered by Michael, the pantry boy. In response to inquiries he stated firmly that it was what Miss Kierney, in the kitchen, said, the ladies had the last of the ham flavouring the pea-soup, e'er yesterday.

"Hang it all, Gus! I'm not really clamouring for ham, but we only embarked on the thing two days ago," Oliver said this more in a spirit of curiosity than for any other reason ; also it rather tickled his humour that Gus—who prided herself, loudly and all day long, on the efficiency of her house-keeping—should have permitted a Fortnum and Mason ham to be consumed by her staff in something under forty-eight hours. His inquiries, however, were as flint to the steel of his sister's ready wrath. A duet of indictments against the cook arose between the two girls.

"To think we should have such a shameless thief in the house!"

"She never puts all the vegetables I give her into the stews——"

"But she will have to account to me for this ham."

44

"And, now I think of it, we didn't *have* pea-soup for dinner on Tuesday night. Oh, my memory! What soup did we have, Prudence?"

"Oh, God!" murmured Prudence beneath her breath; surreptitiously giving a piece of toast to Blazes who, tucking in her stump of a tail, slid quietly across the room, before depositing the morsel beside Cousin Kat's chair, where she nosed it disdainfully.

"I don't remember, Cousin Kat." Prudence glared balefully at Blazes, who could nearly always be trusted to do the wrong thing.

"*I have it!*" the younger girl exclaimed triumphantly. "It was *white* soup. I can remember perfectly picking a bay-leaf for flavouring. Prudence, I particularly dislike dogs being fed at meal-times —you know it. Yes," she rose from her place and began to collect the multifarious belongings which she carried and strewed about her wherever she went, "that *proves* it!"

"How much?" Oliver put in. Unlike Prudence, he rather enjoyed these alarms and excursions, from which Kat had this time emerged quite literally crowned with bays. "What do you deduce from the white soup, Kat? It's too deep for me. Did you have a pain?"

Kat stuffed a decrepit old pair of gardening gloves, a torn silk stocking, three decaying letters and a prayer book into a shattered basket; securing the package with a swathe of ribbon, she moved towards the door.

"It is perfectly clear to me," she said just before she opened it, "that abominable woman has

stolen the ham ; and—what's more—I believe every
servant in the house is in *league* with her. Such
a pack ! " And with a guttural sniff of disapproval
and horror, Cousin Kat left the room.

" Well, Prudence, what do you think ? " Oliver
was lighting a cigarette and stooped to make much
of his very dear little dog, Cobby. Cobby had
come to speak to his master, despite the fact
that Blazes was bolting and choking down her
breakfast, with a furtive eye on his dish—the half-
finished contents of which she knew she might
have for the asking, since Cobby was in all things
an utter gentleman. " You go and finish your
breakfast, old man. I would, if I was you. Yes,
I know—these women !—Well, as I was saying,
what do you think about it, Prudence ? "

" Oh, I dunno," Prudence was collecting food for
the hound puppies, " she keeps chicken bones out of
the dogs' dinners, anyway, and she makes "—she
checked herself on the uttermost edge of an adjective
—" good meringues," she finished, glancing helplessly
at Cousin Gus, who observed with cold decision :

" *This* is hardly a time to allow our personal
likes and dislikes to interfere in a matter where
Duty is clear. Either that ham is produced in
one hour from the time I go down to the kitchen,
or the cook leaves the house to-day. I have suspected her for some time of dishonesty over small
things, but this is a little too much." She rose
from her chair with some majesty of demeanour,
and proceeded to lock the marmalade and sugar
in the sideboard cupboard.

In the doorway, with the hound-puppies' food

balanced precariously, Prudence paused to say haltingly :

" Well, don't think I'm interfering, will you, Cousin Gus, but when you ask her about the ham, do remember that she's frightfully, er, highly-strung ? I mean, she really isn't quite like other people, I don't think."

" Her savouries certainly aren't—like other people's, I mean," Oliver murmured with a faint sigh of regret. " What d'you mean, though, Prudence ? Highly-strung ? "

" Well, you know she was nearly distraught when John Dooly died, having kittens "—here Prudence caught a swift shade of disapproval steeling the expression of Cousin Gus's face, so amended hastily—" when my cat died, you know. And she put the sheep's eyes, that she got out of a head that was for soup, on Maggie's pillow, and frightened her into hysterics. . . . And she's madly in love with John Strap—though she's old enough to be his mother——" perceiving from the deepening disgust on Cousin Gus's face that this piece of news revolted her even more than the reference to John Dooly's fatal confinement Prudence tailed off weakly : " What I wanted to make you see is that she really *is* frightfully highly-strung, so to abuse her would only——"

" Thank you, my dear. Since when, may I ask, have I been in the habit of *abusing* my servants ? I should also be interested to learn how it is that you are so familiar with the disgusting details of their—their private lives ? Yes, tell me that, Miss ! ' Highly-strung,' indeed ! Faugh !

47

disgusting ! Let me tell you, I am perfectly capable of dealing with her without your advice. The impertinence—I never ! " Miss Augusta fumed her way out of the room.

Prudence, slightly shrugging her thin shoulders, followed at a discreet distance, and made her way out by a circuitous route towards the stable yard.

A peculiarly stilled atmosphere pervaded the house and held the very air of the back premises in a strange thrall of quietness.

" All of them upstairs in their bedrooms, discussing it," Prudence surmised, as she prowled about the deserted larder and scullery, in search of scraps for the puppies' meal. Generally, Mary Kierney had a heaped basinful in readiness for the satiation of their morning greed. It was one of the chief points in her character which made Prudence like her. " But how she can feel moved to passion by John Strap——" Prudence frowned and sat on the edge of the scullery sink, with hands pressed to her forehead, trying to realise this thing.

Always—no matter what she was doing—if a thought struck her intensely, Prudence threw all to the winds until she had threshed the subject through and back again across the lost lands of her mind. Any little thing would swing her brain off on one of these voyages of analysation ; Oliver's seat on a horse : Had she passable ankles ? Why did old Kat and Gus reduce all things of beauty which they touched with words to a disgust of dross ? Should she have brilliant knickers and a wrap-over skirt ? Where to buy unscented face-powder ?

This morning, as she walked across the yard,

crying and calling the names of her hound pups she was still pondering the strange charms of John Strap, which had so smitten the heart of Cousin Gus's middle-aged cook.

Gorgon and Gossip were strangely slow to answer their summons to breakfast. Truth to tell, they were, at the moment, very pleasantly engaged in tearing and devouring the body of a newly-slain fowl— one of Miss Kat's prized Barnevelders, to be exact. Their retreat from the outer world was a thicket of rhododendrons, which grew on a steep slope opposite Lingarry House, and in the spring-time dropped their petals, as well as their reflections, into a large-sized pond—the inadequate water supply of which rather spoilt its efforts to be ornamental. However, at certain times and seasons, of which to-day (consequent upon Autumn floods) was one, " the Lake," or " Rosy Waters " —Cousin Kat's touching and poetical names for the pond, which Oliver (who was, by the way, agent for the Lingarry property) summarised as a d—d nuisance—was quite full. Five feet was the greatest depth to which its slightly turgid waters ever attained, and this they measured in one spot only—a spot situated immediately below the dense thicket which the puppies had selected as particularly appropriate for the horrid completion of their crime.

" Gorgon ! *Gossip !* Gossip ! Co-oop-then-little-bitches ; Co-op away ; Gorgon ! "

Prudence's voice was clearly audible to the culprits as they wrangled red-mouthed in their stronghold.

" Blast them ! " Prudence used some more, quite unprintable, words, her gift for inventive being well-developed, before she went back to the yard, to put the culprits' breakfasts safe out of the way of cats.

In the yard she found Cobby, sniffing delicately and restrainedly at a full basin; and observing with disfavour the hurried and conscience-stricken retreat of Blazes, she concluded (and rightly) that at least one puppy's breakfast had found a most unsuitable destination. Kissing Cobby, almost with ardour, she picked up the two dishes and bent her steps once more towards the scullery door.

Before she was half across the yard the door burst open and Mary Kierney—Miss Gus's highly-strung cook—rushed wildly forth. There was something of distraction in the woman's aspect; one hand at her throat, she seemed to choke—was choking, in fact, with sobs of distraught rage. The wind was in her skirts, and in her hair; she ran across the yard in angles, as though blindly; and as she ran, called down maledictions on the head of Miss Gus.

Miss Gus stood at the dairy door. She appeared very angular and very stern; not at all pitiful, Prudence thought, of the poor bellowing fool who ran from her.

"Prudence," she called, "come in here. I've had a most unpleasant scene——"

"I think I'd better go after Mary," Prudence was turned half round, following with her eyes the direction in which the cook had fled.

"Nonsense! Just a wild tantrum—after this she must certainly go."

But Prudence was already half across the yard, calling as she ran:

"John! John Strap! Which way did Mary go?"

"I couldn't rightly say," replied John Strap; then, with sudden enlightenment of his own stupidity: "Sure, how could I know? I didn't see her since last night."

"Well, you're a useless fool," Prudence remarked distinctly, before taking another tack across the yard, and out to the gravel sweep in front of the house.

"Mary!" she called. And again, distressfully: "Mary!"

She felt uneasy, as though Mary Kierney's strong, unstable forces of emotion had roused an answering emotion within herself.

As she still hesitated, uncertain what next to do, the pantry window slid up and James put out his head.

"Mary Kierney went vaulting down through the rosy-bushes not one minute ago," he volunteered, "likely she have Miss Gus's ham hid some place, the way herself and John Strap can be picnicking in it at their ease. Cripes, how cosy they'd be!"

He laughed sardonically and was about to shut the window when his action was arrested by a piercing scream, which came seemingly, from the pond itself.

"Holy Hour!" he ejaculated, "She's in it!" and pushing up the window sash, he climbed out on the sill and dropped to the ground.

"Run, Miss Prudence! Get the old boat. God alone knows what depth of water's in it."

James, while Prudence fled—as though on wings —to fulfil his behest, picked up a rake, which had been left on the gravel, and with it in his hand,

clove a way through the fastnesses of the rhododendrons. As he fought, blindly and painfully,
through their tangle, the screams re-doubled in
vigour—punctuated faithfully by the wild and
youthful voices of Prudence's hound puppies.

Stumbling over some loose object in his path,
James fell headlong. When he picked himself up
it was to discover, with a faint stirring of horror,
that his hands were stained with blood ; dazedly,
he realized that the object which had tripped him
was one of Prudence's silver-backed hair brushes—
it lay glinting among the wet leaves. Feeling as
though he was caught in the toils of some evil
dream, James broke through the last of the twisting
branches which separated him from the water,
and shouted hoarse encouragement to Mary.

Mary Kierney, now nearly exhausted, though
more from the wild energy of her terror than from
the length of her immersion, was alternately beating the water, screaming, and tearing at the bosom
of her dress—that she might at least die with her
hand on her rosary. Yet she was not more than
twelve feet away from the bank, nor did the water
reach above her shoulders.

" In God's name, can ye not walk in, the same
way ye walked out ? " James vociferated angrily
from the bank, where—together with the puppies,
who thought it a new and entrancing game—he
leapt agitatedly from foot to foot.

" Me feet "—she wailed, in answer—" Oh, God
be merciful ! There's snakes around me feet ! "

" The Lord save us ! " was James' somewhat
awed comment. Abandoning his early, heroic plan

of wading out to her rescue, he held fast by an
overhanging bough, and reaching out the rake at
the full length of his arm, adjured her to "ketch
it till the boat'd come."

Mary mastered herself sufficiently to do as she
was told. And a moment later, a flat-bottomed
punt, propelled at some speed by the strong arm
of Anthony Countless, came round one of the
artistically designed bends of the "rosy water,"
and was soon beside the now nearly collapsing
cook.

"We can't lift her on board," Anthony objected,
"I mean—we'll get so wet. We'll have to tow
her. Catch her by the back of the apron, it's sheer
funk that's petrifying her, I expect."

It was characteristic of Anthony that, when
Prudence had fled before him, wild-eyed and quite
regardless of his morning salute, he should have
put his horse's reins behind his stirrup-leathers and
followed her without hesitation. Now he said :

"God! You've missed her."

Prudence tried again ; and this time the effort
was more successful. But if it was, Mary's shriek
fairly pierced the heavens.

Gorgon and Gossip gave tongue *fortissimo*.

"Me feet's cot !" Mary wailed. As the punt
had brought up almost with a round turn, something of the sort seemed obvious. "Holy Jesu !
they're tearing the legs off me—yow ! "

"What *are* we to do ? " Prudence asked despairingly.

"*I* think the woman's mad, I'll pole off again.
Hold on to her."

53

"No—no. Don't! You'll *hurt* her." This time
Prudence loosed her grip upon the apron strings,
and Mary went under in earnest and with a
resounding splash.

"Oh, Joseph!" breathed James, from his perch
on the overhanging bough, "she's gone now."

Anthony Countless' comment was scarcely of so
sacred a nature. When the lady came to the surface,
her cries, for the moment, choked, he climbed
over the punt's gunwale and putting his arms about
her, wrenched her free from the clasp of the sub-
aqueous monster, and staggering gallantly ashore
beneath his burden, sat her down upon the bank.

"Were you, were you just paddling?" he
inquired with some curiosity.

But Mary Kierney had fainted—as well, perhaps,
since her alternative expression of the stress of
the situation would have found vent only in
renewed hysterics.

Prudence, one leg black mud up to the knee,
the other pale and shapely as she knelt beside the
prostrate cook, bade him run to the house for
restoratives and help. Plainly, she thought that
both were too late. Her distraught eyes forbade
utterance to the idea that he should return, as
they had come, by water. Under the circumstances, he felt that the least he could do was to
burst—as James had done before him—a path
through the thicket.

.   .   .   .   .

"And to say 'twas the wire your poor Da had
in it agin the pikes." Thus James, discussing the

situation the same evening, in the pantry with Prudence. " And she to say 'twas snakes had her by the legs. God knows, 'twould be the quare big snake would fix his jaw round *that* leg."

" Well, I've heard some dam' queer stories about pike that have grown into monsters, in old ponds," said Prudence combatively. " And, anyway, I didn't notice yourself was so anxious to go in after her—poor Mary ! "

" Ah, well, poor Mary, indeed ! " James responded easily, ignoring Prudence's innuendo. " I declare, you'd have to be sorry for the creshur, when ye'd see the way she was lying, threwn out on the bank. And for the hairpins to go drop out of her hair in the water ! And to say now the Captain had to take the hair and *smooth* it back with his hand——" James illustrated this touching reminiscence with a gesture which thoroughly deranged his own three grey hairs. In the privacy of his pantry he was wont to discard a remarkably neat wig (that had once belonged to an uncle of Prudence's) and without which few were ever privileged to behold him.

He dwelt on the word ' smooth,' rolling it on his tongue, until Anthony's well-meant action assumed in retrospect a grave flavour of impropriety—almost of abandonment.

" Well, but, James "—Prudence had found some crystallized cherries of uncertain age, in a dark (and probably, noisome) cupboard, and was now eating them greedily—" You know, James, as I was saying, to try and drown yourself in five feet of muddy water, just because you've stolen a ham ! It's not good enough, is it ? "

55

James craned his long neck and thrust his face close to Prudence's ; at the same time shaking a portentous, bony fore-finger.

" Miss Prudence,"—he spoke low and hoarsely —" where did the *blood* come from ? "

" What *do* you mean, James ? What ? Blood ? What blood ? " Prudence's voice was pitched high and she spoke crossly, as always when badly shaken.

James shook his head. " That now's all the why," he declared gravely, if a little abstrusely. " D'ye mind me now, Miss Prudence, there's trouble to come of it when ye'll meet blood in the woods of Lingarry." Then, with a sudden change of tone—" Oh, Christmas ! Look at now, what'll I say to Miss Gus ? Ye have every cherry gone, and they to come in for the dessert to-night. Well, well, aren't you the boy ! "

" Tell her any lie you like, James," Prudence looked quite sick—though it could scarcely have been the cherries that had upset her. " No, don't tell lies, James. I don't think it's lucky—is it ? Say I ate them. And give me a candlestick, for Heaven's sake ! And, and, you might bring these logs along to the study now, please. Hurry up with your wig, you old ass, I'm waiting for you."

" Wait now, one minute "—James begged her, as he hustled round the pantry, opening doors and peering into dark cupboards—" in God's name, where did Michael leave down the candle-sticks out of his hand ? " he demanded pathetically. " Me heart's broke striving to insense that one. I declare, an ass with a blind eye'd have as much cleverality as this fella ! Where now, are the

candlesticks? Aha! I has them now." He re-
appeared after a prolonged dive into a corner
cupboard, with four flat silver candlesticks in his
hand. Lighting one for Prudence, he followed her
along the many dark and winding passages that
led from the pantry to the front of the house.

About ten minutes later the pantry door opened,
to admit James once more. Whistling thoughtfully through his teeth, he deposited the empty
log-basket, and proceeded to arrange, in a small
silver stand, some feathers that he plucked from
a torn and mangled wing, which—judging from
its colour—might once have been part of one of
Miss Kat's Barnevelders. His task completed, he
handed the vase to his satellite, Michael. "Take
a race round to Mr. Lingfield's study with this,
now," he commanded, "he was tearing the house
down for pipe-cleaners, e'er yesterday."

When Michael had departed, as bidden, James
grinned—a rather rat-like grin—at his own reflection in a piece of broken mirror which hung on
the wall.

"Sure the world knows, and Miss Gus knows,"
he reflected, "that every gerrl in the house'd be
off out o' this like the crows on the hills, if there
was ony talk o' the doings was in Lingarry when
they seen blood in the woods before. Ah-ha!
them pups is great jokers." And he fell to polishing a silver-backed hair brush of Prudence's with
zeal and vigour.

CHAPTER IV

WICKED PUPS

OLIVER LINGFIELD was a most endearingly unpleasant person. He took, as though conferring a favour of the highest order; he gave, seldom. When he did, it was always remembered. Men valued his friendship; women generally wanted his love; or, at any rate, his approbation—his liking. All over Ireland, he could put up, at an hour's notice, at the houses where everyone would like to stay—if they could.

His friends delighted to welcome him, and to mount him (on their most intractable horses, if they were his women friends), and to provide him with the best of their shooting and salmon fishing, if they were of his own sex. When he was leaving, they said, " Come again—soon," and meant it.

So Oliver came and went. He shot their bogs —he was a perfect snipe-genius—and shot their pheasants, fished their waters, and rode straight to hounds, on any incorrigible on which they chose to put him up. Above all, he was very discreet with their wives and tactful with their daughters. Thus he retained, for more years than he cared to look back upon, the position of one of the most popular men in the country

58

The secret of his attractive personality—above and beyond his usefulness as a gun, rod, or rough-rider, lay in his subtle talent for interesting himself, particularly and individually, in all his friends. To all, he successfully conveyed the impression that their affairs were to him of paramount interest and importance ; also, that half-an-hour, after dinner, was not too long a space of time in which to listen to the outpourings of their troubled bosoms ; and finally, to agree heartily with whatever course they themselves suggested following.

At his particular job, he was a land-agent, Oliver excelled. In other words, he was very lucky. Besides the element of luck that crowned his work for the estates in his charge, he had a special genius for the management of property—a rare quality, and one not over-frequently found in land-agents. Certainly, he had steered Lingarry well through the troubled years of strife and disorder in Ireland. Prudence would learn to thank him for that, one day. Among the ruined great houses in the country, Lingarry still reared its ugly stateliness of outline ; untouched by fire ; uninvaded by the lawless soldiery of either party.

Oliver had been a good steward of his young cousin's extensive possessions. And in her long minority, his two old step-sisters—Kat and Gus— had ordered her household with irreproachable exactness and a devotion to detail which left not a boxroom uninvaded, not a corner unkept, or undusted.

That the girl, whose guardians they had been since her tenth year, should still appear to the three of them—Gus, Kat and Oliver—as a mere cipher, was not unnatural. Prudence would not come of age for two years more. So why, when she was still under their control, they should put themselves out for her pleasure or amusement, simply because she had left school, neither Kat nor Gus could see. Oliver could have seen—and did too, perhaps—but argued that he was too old to charge himself with his little cousin's amusement. It was often an awkward thing—taking a girl about, who had never been about before. And, in any case, a kid like Prudence (who, mind you, was a very good kid, too) would find it a most infernal bore, trotting round to race-meetings with an old stiff, like himself. And what else was there to do in Ireland—except hunt, fish and shoot? Prudence had all the hunting she wanted; he saw to that most efficiently. And as she was not keen about either fishing or shooting—well, it was a pity, but he could not help it. That was as far as Oliver's conscience went on the subject of Prudence—his young ward and cousin.

Cousins Gus and Kat, realizing that now—schooldays being over—their dynasty was on the decline, sought to improve the shining hours which still remained of Prudence's minority, and their guardianship of her careless spirit, by tireless admonishment, varied by stiff and formal pleasure-seeking. During this—Prudence's first summer of emancipation—they gave an occasional tennis-party for her benefit, at Lingarry. At least, they gave them till the fatal day when Cousin Gus's horrified eyes beheld Prudence aiming gooseberries at the open mouth of Toby Sage. After this, the edict went forth that no more tennis-parties were to be held at Lingarry, since Prudence had not yet learned to behave herself as a lady should.

Prudence flamed and sulked, growing wilder than ever in her conduct, and hating her three guardians, severally and collectively. She hated Oliver, because he ignored her ; Kat, because she was untidy, grubby—almost, and fussing— always. And Gus, Cousin Gus—she hated because she feared her. The influence of a strong personality which has ruled you absolutely, for almost as long as you can remember, is marked and abiding. So Prudence still—as she had done in her tenth year—lied and schemed, with varying success, to hide her misdeeds from the scorching criticism and sure vengeance of Cousin Gus.

To-day, the first of October and Prudence's nineteenth birthday, Cousin Gus was in a mood almost to be described as sunny—at least as compared with her usual bleak, almost malevolent outlook on life and her fellow-creatures generally. She had kissed Prudence quite lingeringly, murmuring, "The *birthday* girl ! " when that happy being put in an appearance in time for the morning prayers.

In the devotions had followed strange and misplaced intercessions (punctuated by long gaps for silent prayer) in which the Deity was implored to grant that some person (name unspecified) might, from this day forward, lead a better, fuller, happier life, and prove a blessing, not a curse, to those who loved her.

Prudence, seated now on the sun-warmed, granite steps of the hall door, recalled how she had held her breath at the time, that every word of Cousin Gus's extempory supplications might be stored in her mind for Peter's delectation. She frowned, as she remembered the subsequent bestowal of a clean and crackling five-pound note. Old Gus was a beast, but she was occasionally appallingly —almost breath-takingly—generous. In common gratitude should one, perhaps, repress (even from Peter) the story of the prayers?

As she chalked and stripped her terrier's stub of a tail, Prudence reflected bitterly that the amount of fun to be obtained from broad-casting the girls' absurdities would never equal the sum total of the annoyance, not to say personal inconvenience, these absurdities caused her. Anyhow, there could be no harm in repeating Cousin Kat's gem of speech, when she had presented her birthday gift—an old paste brooch, lacking most of its stones. Kat, unlike Gus, did not give way to sudden spasms of generosity, in the shape of five-pound notes. What was it she had said?

Wrapped in a haze of retrospection, Prudence plucked carelessly at Blazes'—now much reduced —apology for a tail. Once too often she reft a thumbful from a tender clump ; with a snarl of anger and a yelp of pain, Blazes tore herself from between her mistress's knees and fled, headlong, down the grass slope towards the avenue.

Up the avenue swayed and rocked a very old and much racketed Ford Sedan. It was driven by a small boy at whose side sat Peter. In the body of the car Dilly, her terrier, pressed an anxious face against the glass, until the driver's perilous turning of the up-hill curves dislodged her from the seat and she fell—with a resigned gulp of protest—among the many parcels which had long since bumped to the floor.

Peter was quite unperturbed by their eminently risky progression. She sat silent by her small brother's side, pre-occupied over the lighting of a fresh cigarette from the stub of her old one. It was wonderful how Peter's complexion survived, in all its perfection of child-like bloom, for she smoked continuously—lighting one cigarette on top of another, as she was doing at the moment— ate far too many sweets ; drank as many cocktails as came her way, and never went early to bed. Yet the life she led suited her superbly. From November to March, she hunted three days a week. She rode a line of her own, and was voted, by those who knew, as good as any man and better than most. Born with more wit than intelligence, she never read a book if she could help it ; nor did her thoughts dwell on any subjects more remote than her dogs ; the horses ; her book-maker's account, and how it was to be paid ; and—of course—" The Boy-os."

The Boy-os was the name given collectively to her six brothers—descriptive, perhaps, of their hardened and unapproachable sinfulness. Their ages ranged from twenty years (this was Mervyn —just recovering his balance after Eton and Sandhurst) to three years—Victor, reputed by old Nan, who had suffered from them all in turn and

63

thus should know what she was talking about, to be, " the biggest blackguard and the worst heart-scald of the lot of them."

It was Sammy—he came near the middle of the big family, which leaves him still at his preparatory school—who drove the Ford up the Lingarry avenue this moist September morning. The drive-way was long, and branched over by the dull, grey lace of beech boughs. Blown leaves shone, round and golden, where the night's rain had pasted them flat to the ground.

Quite oblivious of the misty loveliness that surrounded her, Peter pulled hard at her cigarette, and hung an arm across the back of her seat, that Dilly might not feel too isolated ; also by way of a reminder that parental retribution was at hand, should she so far forget herself as to tamper with parcels from the butcher.

Dilly, however, had discovered a far more absorbing occupation than that suspected by her mistress ; one which would not so easily be traced home to her as would the blatant crunching of cutlet bones. She lay with half-closed eyes, rapt and quiet ; the end of a warm tongue just touching a large piece of butter, the brown and white paper wrappings of which she had in one spot, slowly and patiently, melted away. Shivers of exquisite appreciation ran deliciously through her. The butter, which had at first proved hard and resisting, now yielded warmly, so that she could push her tongue into a delicious depression, which ever receded before the advance of her greed. How marvellous it was ! Dilly wondered why

Blazes (who knew all the things one should not do) had never told her about butter parcels. Blazes was five months older than herself, and knew all the Facts of Life—from personal experience, too—so why had she kept this most entrancing form of amusement to herself? A close dog! Dilly resolved at once that with her own body should die the secret of butter-chewing.

At this point the Ford lurched convulsively and came to so sudden a stand-still that Dilly was flung with some violence against the door. Although weighing—in her best condition—not much more than eight pounds, so great was the force of the impact between the small white dog and the faulty door-catch, that the latter burst open, and Dilly was precipitated backwards, with much discomfort and loss of dignity, on to the avenue.

"Sorry, Peter," Sammy apologised, a faint flush of contrition staining his fair skin. "I thought I was over Blazes. Where's the fool of a dog now? She looked like the last lap at a coursing meeting, didn't she? Never saw a dog travel faster, did you?"

"No," Peter agreed, when she had restored Dilly and some scattered parcels to the back seat and installed Blazes on her knee. "Poor brute! I expect Prudence has been plucking her again. H'm, yes, I thought so!" as Blazes, who had inadvertently sat down on her own tail, gave utterance to a shrill yelp of pain.

Prudence came leisurely down the grass slope to meet them. Standing in the centre of the drive, she held up a hand to stay their advance. . . .

65

"Sorry, Prudence!" Sammy gasped his apologies for the second time within five minutes. "My mistake! I thought I was slowing off the juice —did it the wrong way, if you know what I mean."

Prudence, whose side-step before the car, suddenly accelerated from fifteen to twenty-five m.p.h., had been masterly, nodded with comprehension. Then, placing a hand on Peter's either shoulder, she gazed soulfully into her eyes, murmuring the while :

"Dear child—this year is it to be a 'Love in the mist', or a 'Devil in the bush'? *My* little Prudence—or a wild, wilful girl?"

Peter, after she had drawn one long breath of delight, sank down upon the step of the car and buried her face in her hands.

"Prudence, how wonderful!" she breathed when she could speak ; "Kat, of course. Kat, to the life. But did she really—is it possible?"

"I'll swear she did—every word of it." Prudence pulled Blazes out of the car and kissed her face. "Smells foul," she observed, dropping the little dog so that she fell on her back. "My darling— only one! Mother's *child*, did I drop you?" she cried aloud, in an agony of abasement ; distractedly kissing the top of a tan head. But Blazes, though she was not really much hurt, preferred to stay with Peter—who had picked her up. Peter's knee was always such a safe place for little dogs.

Prudence sat down beside Peter on the step of the car. She lit a cigarette before handing her case up to Sammy—as thoughtlessly as though he had been ten years older.

66

"What have you been doing to Blazes?"
Peter asked. "Firing her hocks? I admit they're
curby enough to justify it."

"What are they *saying* about you, my beautiful?
Bite them, darling! Sink your teeth, Blazes!"

But Blazes only blinked and coughed at the cloud
of cigarette smoke which had been blown in her
face. She never *could* do the right or dashing thing.

"Well, girls, if you wouldn't mind finding some
other place to talk scandal, I'd go round to the
yard and have a look at the horses," thus Sammy,
who would not for worlds have admitted that
Prudence's cigarette was already making him feel
sick.

"Right!" They rose to their feet, threw away
their cigarettes and walked off together; their
heads bent; hands in pockets; oblivious of all
the world; utterly content in each other's society.
Their friendship was very complete. To be
together spelt, for them, joy—which meant fun
and amusement.

This friendship did not date from nursery,
scarcely even from schoolroom, days. All through
their childhood, as often as they had met, equally
often had they joined battle—to be separated by
panting, slapping nursery-maids, and later by
coolly efficient governesses. It was not until Peter
was in her fourteenth, and Prudence in her thir-
teenth year, that they discovered a sudden affinity.
No warm, unstable, flapper friendship, but a deep
interest. Peter said to Prudence:

"You've got the most curious mind I know.
I love the things you think out for yourself."

Prudence said : " What I like about you are the devilish amusing things you *do*."

Peter answered : " Oh, rot ! I don't, really."

But that was the day on which the idea came to her of going one morning to arouse Mr. Roberts (the curate) from the prolonged slumbers which, lasting—so report said—till a late hour in the morning, were a disgrace to his cloth. And equally, of course, a disgrace to the parish. While if they were a disgrace to the parish, they reflected badly on the parishioners. It was, as has been already stated, Peter's original idea, but it was Prudence who worked out these excellently logical reasons for the early morning raid which was subsequently undertaken.

The events took place as follows :

Armed with the garden syringe and a hunting whip (the latter, as much for the sorely needed sensation of swagger that it lent the wielder, as for the chastisement of Mr. Roberts' dog), the two reformers stealthily squeezed through a narrow, downstairs window of the curate's lodging, at some seven-thirty by the clock, on a bright morning in May.

" Thank God we chose a holy day, when Mrs. Keogh would be at Mass " ; Peter referred, in a windy whisper, to their victim's landlady.

Prudence assented ; and, as celerity of action was not for the moment their chief object, she proceeded to coast round the damp, stuffy little sitting-room into which they had climbed.

" Hellish dark and smells o' cheese," she opined, or rather, quoted, as she closed the glass-fronted doors of a cabinet and proceeded to examine the photographs of Mrs. Keogh's deceased relatives which hung on the walls. She indicated a peculiarly nauseating example of photographic art.

" Doesn't it remind you of those little memorial verses they put in the *Irish Times* ? "

> " She has gone before us,
>   Nothing's left of her at all,
>   Only her photograph,
>   Hanging on the wall."

Peter nodded absent-minded assent. She had been revising the plan of campaign.

" I think," she said now, " it would be better if only one of us went in with the syringe. The other can look out at the top of the stairs, in case Mrs. Keogh comes back, and explain."

" What good will that do ? " Prudence interrupted. " She'd only tell the girls on us. As it is "—she adjusted a fearsome, black mask, and glanced rapturously down at the suit of boy's clothes which she wore for the occasion—" Divil a one would ever know us ! We'll dash in ; fill the syringe in the jug ; let him have it, full blast ; and dash out again. If Mrs. Keogh does come back—storm past her, and once in the open, we've easily got the legs of the lot of them."

" 'Sides, we've got the key of the back avenue door," Peter suddenly recollected. " Oh, come on ! "

Warm, damp hand in damp, cold hand, they stole up the rickety staircase, and paused outside the door which they had previously marked down as that of Mr. Roberts' bedroom. Here, a fit of caution once more overcame Peter.

" One of us had *better* wait out here—just in case," she whispered agitatedly.

" All right, *wait !* " impatiently Prudence's hand turned on the door handle. It was snatched away by Peter.

" I'm the eldest," she said hoarsely, " and I thought of it."

Tragedy in her eyes, Prudence said :

" I *must* go. I've *never* seen a curate in bed."

" No more've I ! "

" All right ! We'll bof' go." So together and breathing heavily, they tip-toed into the chamber of this Prince Charming.

Prudence took one look at the curate—deep-wrapt in unlovely slumber, one hairy arm thrown across an unclean counterpane—another look at the disarray of his cast-off clothing ; then shuddered violently.

" It's *beastly*," she whispered. " Let's come away, *don't* let's——"

" Damn ! " At the washstand Peter had just made the unfortunate discovery that the gardener's syringe was not in working order.

Really great moments, however, have their inspirations. Carefully lifting the basin in which, over-night, Mr. Roberts had performed his ablutions, Peter strode, as silently as possible, across the room to the bedside. Then, with swift and cat-like dexterity, she turned the basin upside down over the sleeping curate's face.

The effect was instantaneous. So, for the matter of that, was the retreat of the infant reformers. With a yell—resonant in reverberations, since it came from beneath a large, tin-enamelled basin—sounding in their ears, they hurled themselves downstairs.

As she banged the door of the sitting-room, Prudence had a momentary and never-to-be-forgotten vision, of a pale, pink-clad figure leaping downstairs in their pursuit.

A moment, and they had wriggled through the window ; another, and they were flying down the road ; once round a sharp bend and they knew themselves safe. Remained only to open the back avenue door ; get inside unseen ; and all danger was over.

Seated on the sun-warmed tar-felt of a henhouse roof, they gloried in the memory of their evil-doing. Wallowing in a rapturous sense of their security from suspicion, they reviewed—step by delightful step—the morning's happenings. Thus did it happen, and thus, and thus.

Peter looked up suddenly. She had been toying, wordless for the moment, with the derelict syringe. Now, her jaw dropped. Her whole body stiffened.

" Prudence, the whip ! We've left it in the sitting-room. And it has my name on it ; and, ' From Templedarton to Ballyskipeen '—it's the one Daddy gave me after I rode Flyman in that hunt."

.   .   .   .   .

The whole story came out, of course. It delighted Peter's parents so hugely, that her father was with difficulty prevented from adding that date to the inscription on the incriminating whip.

The tale of their ward's iniquity did not reach the girls' ears till some weeks had elapsed. When it did, they were told, as a huge joke—by someone who entirely failed to appreciate their point of view—how Prudence, when questioned as to the curate's night attire, had replied (quite unabashed by the presence of several members of the sterner sex), "Tight pink all-in-ones."

The whole affair was just a little too sickening and revolting, the girls decided. So Prudence was sent to school, where she was very unhappy, a year sooner than had been intended ; and in her holidays all intimacy with the Trudgeon family was strongly discouraged.

Yet it was not entirely because the girls made this fatal error in separating them that Peter and Prudence remained such truly intimate spirits. It would be difficult to tell what the one found in the other, but their very differences formed ties between them. A wild, delightfully irrespon-sible, amusing, and—strangest of all—a most capa-ble pair—thus they were described by the indulgent. Selfish, greedy, totally unimaginative, and lacking in even the most rudimentary sense of decency or fair play—so their devil-may-care partnership appeared to others. Certainly the two had many regrettable episodes to their discredit. Of these, the cold-pigging of the curate might be taken as a sample of youthful indiscretion ; their present campaign against Anthony Countless being the conception of maturer devilment.

"Darling old bird, I haven't seen you for three days," Prudence was saying, as she strode, and Peter lagged—a little ponderous and quite unhurried—down a wide, gravelled way that led from the house to the kitchen gardens. "We'll get a bunch of grapes to eat, and talk somewhere."

"*Two* bunches," Peter amended, "because we've got masses to crack about. Where'll we go? Hay-loft?"

"No. Too fuggy. Pig-sty roof."

On the pig-sty roof then, Prudence—voraciously stripping and eating grapes :

"Heard anything about *me*, Precious?"

Peter did not answer at once. Prudence ate so abominably fast, it obliged her to concentrate too, if she was to obtain even half her share of grapes. However, when the three last (and quite uneatable) green dwarfs on the end of the second bunch had been cast to the pigs below, she propped her back against the two foot of garden wall that projected above the pig-sty roof, lit another cigarette, and referring back to Prudence's last question, replied in her slow, unhurried voice :

"Yes, *heaps*. Anthony Countless came to dinner on Sunday night——"

"Yes?" Prudence inquired insistently, as the narrator paused to re-light her cigarette and inhale deeply, before she continued :

"Oh, well—as I was saying, Mervyn and I mixed him a couple of quite extraordinary cocktails, and told Hodge "—Hodge was Lady Mavis Trudgeon's most irreproachable English butler—"to keep plenty of drink to him during dinner.

73

Well," she paused again, this time to cremate the corpse of a flea, which she had deftly removed from Dilly's back, on the end of her cigarette. "Oh, yes, he got quite amusing after dinner— telling us about your cook trying to drown herself in the pond. I didn't like to ask him why, but I rather gathered James had something to say to it."

"Oh, no. It'd have been John Strap, if anyone. But it wasn't that at all. She stole a ham, or something—that was all."

"I expect it was the way the girls went for James afterwards, that made him suspect the worst. He had Mervyn and Toby and myself sick with laughter—imitating Kat and Gus."

"Yes, they were wild because we broke some shrub or other—carrying poor Mary up to the house. I thought she was dead." Prudence's eyes grew wide at the tragic memory. "And those two old hags gave her an hour's notice, just as soon as she stopped having hysterics—wasn't it damnable? I gave her two-pound-ten; it was all I had."

"Poor brute! But it must have been funny, all the same. I'd have given anything to have been there when you ducked her under. And James praying his best up in the rhododendron— priceless!"

"It wasn't, really—at the time, I mean. It was beastly. Did you say Toby Sage was dining with you, too?"

"Yes. D'you know his latest? He's got a valet. Mervyn and I asked him the most awful

questions about what the valet did for him. We
made Anthony quite shy. Toby didn't give a
curse, though—he's awfully hardened—Tobioh is.
Isn't he? Don't you think so?"

"What else did you talk about? You said you
talked about me."

"Oh, yes. Anthony was asking if many
dangerous women came out—dangerous to his
hounds, he meant. So I said, no; we all went
like distraction, but we were a very knowing lot.
Then he asked me if you were any good; and
I said, 'Yes. Full of ginger.' And then Toby
said, 'rather scientific too,' in that shutting-up
voice he has. Condescending brute! I *can't* rave
about him, like everyone does, I can't even see
that he is so good-looking. Of course, he can
ride a bit——"

"Oh, brilliant——" Prudence was brutally
extending a ladder in her stocking. She spoke
shortly, yet as though she wished to discuss the
point further. Then, apparently changing her
mind, she began calling and whistling for Blazes.

A minute later, a man's figure came into view,
round the corner of a hay rick.

"She saw him coming all right—that's why
she called Blazes," reflected Peter instantly, and
quite without any rancour whatever. Aloud she
said:

"Hullo, Tobioh! Hope that valet didn't ill-
treat you in your bath this morning."

"I always take my bath at night, thanks,"
replied Toby Sage, readily enough. He spoke
with an absurd and most successful brogue—

75

painstakingly cultivated, one perceived at once, for in matters of moment the affectation was instantly dropped.

"Come on down, now, girls, and talk to me nicely," he entreated.

Prudence hung a tentative leg over the pig-sty wall ; then, changing her mind, continued the conversation from her present quarters.

"We *are* talking to you," she observed incontestably, " about baths—wasn't it ? *I* always have mine at night, too. Funny, isn't it ? "

" Funny, yes. But *so* convenient."

" How—convenient ? " Prudence was ready, now, as ever, to give herself away.

"Well," Toby murmured, thoughtfully, " I *simply* hate wasting things—water especially. So I should always make a point of letting you have second go at my bath water. You'd love that, wouldn't you, Prudence ? "

Prudence lowered her other leg, inch by inch, over the wall.

" You're a harmless sort of thing, Toby," she observed compassionately, " an' I *simply* hate hurting you. Still, they tell me chastisement is good for the young——"

Prudence was at her best in a rag. The true spirit of the thing imbued her. Unlike many girls, she neither screamed, when her skirts rose above the border line of modesty ; nor did she hack her opponent on the shins when the farce reached the stage of physical violence.

Peter, who realized that while two make a rag, three make a muddle, remained upon the

76

roof, smoking reflectively, as she looked down on the battle which raged below her.

" Prudence rags just a little *too* well," she criticized inwardly. " She's so madly *chaste*, she never realizes how absurdly beautiful she is. Mostly bone, of course. But it's such superb bone. . . . Is she attractive to men, I wonder ? Toby's different. He's not stung by girls in that way. He likes them to dance with, and for horse-shows and race-meetings—not for love. I can see that by the way he's fooling with her, just like another boy. He *hurt* her then, too——" Round chin propped on square hands, Peter continued, fascinated, to watch the beautiful, writhing, wrestling pair below her.

For Toby was almost inanely beautiful, too. ' Handsome ', does not in the least describe him. He was the son of a triumphantly lovely woman and of a man as ugly as few men are made.

Toby's inheritance of all his mother's good looks was so startling as to appear almost absurd in a boy. His grey eyes were cloaked deeply in dark lashes ; the lines of his chin and jaw were things to leave you gasping in wonder. And then, he was all knit and set together with such elaborate perfection. He had her rather olive and perfectly smooth skin too ; with an identical mole, placed high on the right cheek bone. His black hair, growing low on his forehead, was like a girl's hair —cropped exceptionally short.

It was hardly surprising that Toby's father, who adored him only in a lesser degree than he had adored his dead wife, could, nevertheless, hardly support the sight of this son—so agonisingly perfect a reminder of all that he had lost. So Sir Dominick Sage, with a touchingly beautiful faith in the boy's character, made him a large—even an affluent—allowance, and surrendered to him, more as an occupation than a duty, the stewardship of Merlinstower—its farming and blood-stock, its fishing and shooting—while he, pathetically enough, spent his years in attending to his many foreign interests, ever accumulating new ones and even adding to his already consider-able wealth.

As for Toby—the real Toby—he was not yet quite spoilt by all the favours which Fortune and a misguided parent had delighted to heap upon him. His valet, his beautiful clothes, and his excellently bad manners did not really typify his attitude towards life. The things he had, he held altogether different from the things he did. In this belief lay his way of salvation. What came to him easily and through Fortune's favour, he held in no repute ; he lived to fulfil his strivings. And the ideals he strove after ? These were :

To ride a hunt, or a race, as it should be ridden ; to tie a very taking fly ; fish seriously ; shoot straight ; and some day, hunt a pack of hounds.

As ideals, quite useful, and more difficult of attainment than may be imagined.

Naturally, he had for years been accustomed to amuse himself with each girl who took her turn at the short-lived game of being the prettiest—and, momentarily, the most popular—member of the younger strata of county society. With none

of them, however, did he finally commit himself
to matrimony. His genius in annexing attention
was only equalled by his genius for escape, as
soon as the aforesaid attentions threatened to entail
responsibilities. His flirtation with Prudence was
still in its infancy—a stage in which it had, throughout the summer, been curiously prolonged—chiefly
owing to Cousins Gus and Kat's lynx-like chaper-
onage of their ward.

This morning his interest was more than usually
piqued by a girl who could rag with him as
strenuously as any boy, yet when really hurt (more
by her own fault than his) flung away from him,
and casting herself down upon a hay rick, sobbed
unaffectedly for quite three minutes. He thought
at first that she was laughing; then, dazedly,
that she was hysterical.

Peter, however, said calmly, and as though
reproving an elder brother for harsh treatment
of a junior :

" *Now* you've made her cry. You must have
hurt her. Things hurt her far more than they
do other people. Shut up, Prudence ! Here's
Kat coming to collect the Barnevelders' eggs."

Peter's words had a wonderfully calming effect
on Prudence. The blue-white shoulder, off which
her jumper had slipped untidily, ceased to quiver
to her sobs. It lay still as a dead thing among
the spiky hay. Toby, as he slid down out of sight
beside her, noticed it curiously—only remotely
aware of its loveliness.

Down below, they heard Kat's uncertain voice,
then Peter's, slow and calm, answering her—

measured words, coming clear in the bright stillness.

"Good morning, Peter."

"Morning, Miss Kat. How are the Barnevelders laying?"

"Oh, very well. Wonderfully, in fact. That
reminds me—I'm trap-nesting. It keeps me so
busy—letting them in and out, you know. Do I
know where Prudence is? No, indeed I do *not*!
Picking up the fallen apples in the garden, perhaps.
But now I come to think of it, to-day is her birthday, so she has probably made *that* an excuse for
not doing any of her usual things. And that
reminds me—I must go and get the vegetables
for lunch. Tell Prudence, if you see her, won't
you?" And Miss Kat departed towards the
Barnevelders' trap-nests.

"*Is* it your birthday?" Toby asked; he stood
below the rick and held out both hands to help
her down.

Prudence, in one boneless contortion, slid unconcernedly into, and out of, his arms. All traces
·of tears had disappeared from her face as rapidly
and completely as tears do from the face of a very
young child. They left behind a sort of veiled
radiance, infinitely moving. She pulled down her
close-fitting felt hat over the hair which covered
her ears, and with beautiful confidence refrained
entirely from the use of her powder puff. Then,
slipping an arm through Peter's and a hand into
Toby's coat pocket, she set her face towards the
fields known as the "Plantation Grass."

"Because," she said, "I know now, you came

over to look at the Preceptor filly—not to see me
on my birthday, at all."

" How old are you, to-day ? " he asked. " Just
nine o'clock ? I thought so. God bless us ! Isn't
she very tall for her age ? "

" Puppy, darling, what were we talking about
before this brute came and thrust himself on us ? "

" I think it was about him," Peter answered
leisurely. They had rather left her out of it, so
far—not that she cared. But she was not going
to make it easier for Prudence. That would have
spoilt fun, besides being unnecessary.

" Oh, so we were. Let's go on ! Was it fifty
pairs of silk socks you told me Mervyn found in
his room, or only forty-five ? "

" That's rather a give-away, isn't it ? Sure,
it's a well-known fact poor Mervyn can't count
beyond ten."

An expression of puzzled affront came into
Toby's beautiful eyes. Everyone knew that raillery
on the subject of his clothes he could not endure,
yet here was this amazing girl continuing—in
the face of his evident displeasure—to tell him off
competently and quite unabashed, on that very subject. He was unaffectedly surprised at Prudence.
She had, indeed, surprised him intensely three
times in the course of thirty-five minutes ; first,
by her endurance and quite incredible muscularity ;
then, by her equally amazing collapse into tears,
and immediate recovery of self-control and confidence ; and now, by her perfect disregard of
his feelings. Something, he felt, must be done to
show her that she had her limitations.

81

On their return journey from the inspection of
the Preceptor filly, he observed—noting Prudence's
swift glance in the direction of the hen-houses :

" Which are you most frightened of—Kat or
Gus ? "

" Neither," replied Prudence swiftly, " why
they're as harmless and innocent of guile as you
are yourself—almost."

" All the same, I bet you'd be too frightened
of the pair of them to come off with me now and
go to the Curragh races this afternoon. I've got
a horse running at three-thirty. And—b'Jove !—
I told them I wanted early lunch, too. I'll have
to make myself pretty scarce. Well, will you
come ? "

Prudence, a faint, red spot of excitement on
either cheek-bone, accepted the invitaiton with
hauteur. To no one did she admit her inherent
dread of rows with Gus. " You mean Peter too,
of course," she added affirmatively.

" Yes, of course he does," Peter answered for
him tranquilly. " You know you'd never get
out of this scrape alive, if the girls thought you'd
first lunched and then gone racing—alone with
a young man. Hurry up and change your clothes,
anyway. I'll be at Merlinstower just as soon as
you are. Good-bye, sweetheart. Have a cocktail for me, Tobioh." She departed to find her
Ford and its youthful St. Christopher.

.   .   .   .   .

Later, as she took her place beside Toby in his
quite unnecessarily showy, sports-bodied Vauxhall,

Prudence drew a prolonged sigh of mingled relief and apprehension.

In her mind's eye she could see the havoc wrought in her room during the frenzied fifteen minutes which she had spent dressing herself. None of her stockings had matched ; nor had she been able to discover the flame-coloured knickers which she felt that the occasion demanded. However, now she came to think of it, the sealing-wax red pair she was wearing rather matched her deeply-dented, small felt hat.

This hat (and of course, the knickers) together gave her confidence to carry on the escapade. The hat was so becoming as to be almost too alluring—so Cousin Gus had thought when she forbade it to be worn, at the same time providing her ward with a substitute, equally becoming, and more suitable for a " young girl." Prudence had immediately put both feet into the crown of the substitute and, in an agony of rage, had jumped in it round and round her bedroom floor. After this she wore it sulkily, when she could not help herself, and the red hat only when it was possible to do so without incurring Gus's displeasure.

To-day, she wore the too-alluring hat quite beautifully, so that it cast the clearest of shadows across her deep eyes. She had even put a brazen streak of red on her mouth, so that it matched, in colour, the hat and the flash of knickers as she crossed her long, thin legs, trying to both look and feel jaunty.

The achievement of jauntiness was, fortunately enough, quite outside Prudence's attainments.

Nothing she could ever do would make her appear
jaunty, or even the least bit ordinary. There was
something nearly saint-like about her that forbade
it utterly. She looked, at the moment, rather as
if she had stepped down from a stained-glass
window, strangely well appointed for a race-
meeting. The most rigid and correct of pale
grey tailor-mades hung on Prudence's wonderful
bones like drapery ; her pale, silk stockings were
like fine smoke ; the gold of her hair, an irrepres-
sible aureole, beneath the blatant little hat. Her
field-glasses, in their leather case, suggested absurdly
a pilgrim's scrip or wallet ; her staff—a shooting-
stick.

Toby, who was driving very fast, took it all in
and approved, remotely. When she stepped out
of his car and, after taking the great flight of steps
to the door two at a time, in a manner which
caused her tight skirt to recede impossibly up the
backs of her knees ; and stood, a little lost, like
a sudden shaft of light in his dark hall, he drew
a quicker breath than usual and approved a trifle
less remotely.

" But, but Peter said she'd be here. Didn't
she say she'd be here ? You know, she *said* she'd
be here. Is she here ? " Prudence was dreadfully
bothered. This was really awful. What *would*
Gus say if, and when, she found out. Besides,
truth to tell, she was really desperately shy of
Toby, and the prospect of a *tête-à-tête* meal with
him positively appalled her. She had said all
the things she could possibly think of to say to
him during their six mile drive here ; nor did she

suppose that they could very well fill in the time by ragging madly. It would not really be much fun without the presence of a third party. Where *was* Peter?

"No, Sir," said the man-servant who answered Toby's summons, "neither Miss Trudgeon *nor* Mr. Trudgeon have arrived, Sir." He paused, and added helpfully, "Luncheon is ready, Sir."

"Well, how about it?" Toby asked, when the man had gone. "They're beastly late. I think we'd better start without them. Come on—I'll teach you something Kat and Gus would just hate you to know—the *only* way to mix a 'Manhattan Bobbery.'"

Toby was a wonderful host. Prudence laid down her gloves and her gleaming little bag on a gigantic and sombre oak chest, and followed him towards the dining-room, feeling a little brighter. By the time the cocktail had been concocted and absorbed (Prudence was quite perilously innocent of cocktails) she felt so bright that she hardly knew this sparkling creature which was herself.

Lunch, laid on a small, round table, in one of the wide windows of the dining-room, was an entrancing meal. Prudence, as it progressed, became more and more convinced that Toby and herself were two of the most amusing people God had ever created and brought together.

And Toby became momentarily more positive that never, in all his experience, had he seen a girl more completely, gracefully, and successfully bowled over by two cocktails.

" D'you know the game of ' rabbits-in-a-hole ' ? "
Toby asked her, interestedly watching her consumption of a second helping of iced pudding. He
would have thought, to look at her, that Prudence
simply didn't know how to eat. Observing the
wreck of a cold duck and the litter of plates which
he had removed to a side table, he now knew
better. " Do you know the game of ' rabbits-in-
a-hole ' ? " he repeated, stooping down as he
spoke to pick up Gummy—a minute and suppli-
cating Cairn terrier.

Prudence shook her head.

" Is it a nice game ? " she queried, " I mean,
is it a game I could play with Kat and Gus in the
long winter evenings ? "

" Oh, rather ! I expect they'd love to have
you eating out of their hands. No, on the whole,
I think you could play it better with Blazes. I
suppose you do sometimes give her something to
eat ? "

" She does her feeding more credit than Gummy
does his, anyhow." Prudence regarded the delicate sweep of the Cairn's pale little body, safe
held in Toby's arms. " Is it biting the hand that
feeds it ? " she asked.

" I told you—we're playing ' rabbits-in-a-hole.'
Most people'll only do it once, but "—he kissed
Gummy behind one dark, prick ear—" I'm so awful,
dam' stupid dog I do it again, and again, and
again. An' each time I get my nose caught, I
do, terrible bad. But brains aren't my strong
suit. No. I'm just darlingest dog ever was.
Oh, *I'm* a pup—I tell you—I'm a hell of a

pup !" He opened his fist, in which Gummy
had been vainly nuzzling, yielding up at last the
scrap of dry chicken with which the trap had
been baited.

"An' that's how we play 'rabbits-in-a-hole,'"
he explained. "I'm sure you and Cousin Gus
would have great fun over it. You might tell her
I taught it to you, and see what she says."

"She'd say you were a forward young man,
very forward, and that she was surprised at my
vulgar taste in friends, or else, that I was a 'True
Turrett.'"

Prudence spoke through a bright, light haze,
which seemed to surround her impalpably, and
caused the floor, when she rose from her chair,
to assume strangely uneven proportions and to
recede an immeasurable distance from her feet.

Toby left her in the library, with the largest
cup of black coffee he could secure, also the *Tatler* ;
he had hastily secreted a copy of *La Vie*, for he was
a young man who believed in virgins retaining a
virginal purity of mind, and went away to change
his clothes.

Prudence, in his absence, powdered her nose,
added a new smear of lip-stick to her angel's mouth,
upset her coffee cup, and—having re-arranged
a rug to cover up the stain on the floor—fell to
wondering how it was possible that three-quarters
of a glassful of some rather wonderful cup, preceded by two cocktails, could have combined to
make her feel so jolly and, at the same time, so
uncertain of her true reflection in the mirror of
her powder box.

"I *wish* Peter'd come," she murmured hope-lessly. "What *can* have stopped her? I can't, I simply can't go to the Curragh alone. Why, I've never *been* there, even. I'll have to ask Toby the way to the ladies' cloak-room when I want a lick of powder on my nose. He'll think me such a fool, he'll wish he hadn't brought me. Do I pay at the gate, or will he? I *wish-to-the-devil* Peter'd come. Oh, why did I start? Why did I have those cocktails? Why did I spill my coffee? I know he'll notice the rug has been moved. Damn!" She flung herself into the corner of a wide couch and covered her face with her hands.

Five minutes later, the sound of a car changing gear up the last steep slope of the avenue, struck like music on her ears. Peter—darling Peter! One could always rely on her. "She shouldn't have cut lunch, though. I've got to rate her for that." Prudence, who had rushed joyfully out to the hall, returned whence she had come, to sit in a semblance of aloof displeasure, the *Tatler* held before her face, and her legs crossed over the arm of a ponderous chair.

When the door opened, she spoke coolly from behind her paper.

"You might have been in time for lunch," she grumbled, "I've got beastly drunk and been most indiscreet—all because you weren't here to look after me. Toby's gone to change. I told him his nude shirt made me sick on the spot. Have you had lunch? Why are you so late?"

"*Prudence*——" the voice from the door was almost inhuman in its mingled expression of wrath

and horror. But Prudence, still ensconced behind
her *Tatler*, and half-way through " Pictures in the
Fire ", remained entirely unmoved.

" Rotten poor imitation of Gus, if you mean it
for her," she observed, and re-crossing her legs
contorted herself afresh in the depths of her chair.

" Prudence—*pull down your clothes.* Put down
that paper. Get up. I cannot trust myself to
speak to you. Have you *no* shame ? Does nothing
touch you ? "

A delighted smile upon her face, Prudence
lowered the *Tatler* and turned approvingly to the
able imitator in the doorway. With a little, choking
cry of quite genuine terror, she was on her feet.
She looked wildly about her for a moment, as
though seeking any possible way of escape ; then,
coming forward uncertainly, she faced Gus in the
doorway ; a set, leaden expression freezing up the
beauty of her face. Almost—she looked furtive.

Caught, frightened, more than a little muddled
by the drink, which had not yet died out of her,
Prudence climbed into the Lingarry car and was
driven homewards. The old inhibition of her fear
of Gus, like a fast-rooted fungus, spread its clammy
hands through her brain, to paralyse her will and
fill her with a sickening anticipation of the evil
yet to befall.

CHAPTER V

A VERY NICE MARE

" Well, well, well," sympathized James whole-heartedly, " isn't Miss Gus now the devil's own dart ? Holy Jesu ! I thought the breath'd leave me when I seen herself and Miss Kat walkin' east the garden, a half-an-hour ago. And to put the red hat and the—the other little red yokes on the bonfire was what they done. And not a word out of them, good or bad. Ah, what matter now, Miss Prudence, it's not always beneath their sway ye'll be."

James paused suggestively, and Prudence, who was drooping dejectedly in one of the basket chairs of that dreary and dim old room that had once been her schoolroom, and to which she was still banished in the days of her evil-doing, fell into a yet more languorous attitude, remarking bitterly :

" Two more years' purgatory is a long time, James."

" Oh, it is, surely it is," agreed James, as he gathered up the fragments of the breakfast that Prudence had eaten in disgraced isolation. Before leaving the room, he placed four loose cigarettes on the table near her.

"Whisper, now, Miss Prudence, I whipped them few from the silver smoke-box in the study," he informed her cheerfully.

Prudence lit one gratefully

"Oh, Lord, James!" she exclaimed after the first puff, "you've got hold of Mr. Oliver's Sobranis —I'll be killed if the ladies smell them off me. You'd better put these back."

"Ah, devil a matter! I couldn't get them back now, whatever, I seen Mr. Oliver lock the box up on me." James had picked up his tray and started for the door, when Prudence called him back.

"I'll want you to arrange for two notes to go for me, James—John Strap could take them. One to Merlinstower and one to Kilronan, for Miss Trudgeon, he's to get an answer to it. He needn't wait for an answer at Merlinstower," she said. Seating herself at the dented, ink-stained, old school-room table, she dragged a blotter and notepaper towards her, and proceeded to write.

To compose a letter of any sort was something of an effort to Prudence, and this particular letter would seem to be the outcome of peculiar travail. She wrote the day of the month, and began: "Dear"—After biting heavily into the handle of her pen, she wrote "My", before the "Dear". Plainly, the capital letter beginning the second word did not please her, for—after an abortive attempt to convert it into smaller type—she tore the sheet from her block and began again. Finally, this is the letter that she re-read, before sticking

the missive into an envelope which she addressed
to : " Dominick Sage, Esq., Merlinstower."

" DEAR TOBY,
        " I was passionately sorry I didn't go
racing with you yesterday, as intending to.
Cousin Gus came with Oliver when he came to
see you about the Preceptor filly you came to
look at in the morning. She said my dog Blazes
was sick. I thought she might have picked up
poison, so I came back with her. I hope you
didn't think it was too funny of me to go away
so suddenly. I am sorry for infernal scrawl, but
this is written at speed.
                              " Yours ever,
                                    " PRUDENCE."

The composition of a letter to Peter was a much
less weighty matter. Inspiration, in fact, flowed
so freely that the missive was, upon the whole,
illegible, and entirely ungrammatical.

" SWEETEST LOVED ONE FAR AWAY," (it began
rhythmically),
        " Darling—*such* rows. Declares to God
I thought I'd never get out of this mess alive.
Did Toby tell you I was drunk ? Anyhow,
we had the devil of a good lunch. Why
weren't you in time for it ? And if not why
didn't you warn me about cocktails ? I hate
wine, really. I only got half-a-glass, but it
makes you feel so jolly.
        " Well, darling, there I was sitting in the
library place, aching to see *your* sweet face, when

who should walk in but Gus, herself. Puppy,
I thought it was *you*, and there I was all in pieces,
with my skirt gone in a string round my waist
and the red hat she hates. She hardly said a
word. I can't tell you how awful it was. She
made me get into the car and told John to drive
home. On the way home I was sick, so they
had to stop the car to let me out to be sick behind
the hedge. Gus said : ' over-eaten yourself, I
presume,' just like that. But it wasn't, it was
terrified fright made me be. It couldn't have
been the cocktails, could it ?

" Then, darling, we got home and had a
dreadful tea. Kat sniffed and sniffed, and Gus
said *nothing*. When it was over Gus said I was
to go to the study and wait for her. I felt so
cold after being sick, it was filthy. I saw myself
in the glass. I did look plain. My mouth was
all crooked, and my nose and eyes as pink as
could be, and my hair all greasy. I wished I
could have killed myself on the spot. Then Gus
came in and shut the door. She came over to
the fireplace and stood looking at me ; I could
think of nothing but how indelible my lip-stick
was, I tried to lick it off. I expect she noticed
because suddenly she looked disgusted as well,
and said, ' Suppose you explain yourself. That
is, if you have any possible explanation to justify
your conduct of to-day, which, even you will
admit, *surpasses !* '

" I couldn't think of one word to say, only
I did hate Gus. She said : ' Well ? ' I gulped
out strings of lies, I can't remember what they

were, now, it was all so complicated. But it
wasn't the *least* use. All she said was : ' As far
as I can see, beneath the mass of excuses, if not
downright falsehoods you have told me, one
thing stands out clearly ; that is, you went alone
and unchaperoned to the house of a young man ;
lunched with him alone and intended to drive
twenty miles to a race-meeting with him, *and*
back—still alone. Quite candidly I consider
your conduct is——' I can't tell you, Peter,
all the things she said about my conduct. They
weren't, truly weren't, *quite* nice. Finally, I got
wild and told her that like all pure women she
had a mind which revelled in filth. She didn't
like that, so I am to have my meals by myself
in the schoolroom till I apologise. When shall
I see you again, sweetheart ? Do make some
plan.

" Thine till death,
" PRUDENCE."

" P.S.—In the night they came privily while
I slept and took away my red bockers and my
darling hat. James says they've burned them
in the weed-pile. Surely, *Evil* has befallen
Prudence !
" Don't tell Toby. Please, please don't."

The letter finished, Prudence buried her face in
her hot hands, pressing her palms close against
her burning, hurting eyes. She felt so sick, so
hopelessly unclean in mind and unattractive of
body. Lightly as she had written to Peter of

Gus's tirade, her cousin's words were, nevertheless, blazoned searingly upon her brain.

They had been pitiless words—a stripping aside of all veils from the reservations that exist between young and old. Nothing appeared to Gus in the pleasant guise of youthful folly. Glamour, for her, was not. If your conduct was a trifle unrestrained, so, probably, were your morals. Prudence's morals were, she suspected, non-existent. In this supposition she was quite correct—in so far as that Prudence had no sense at all of the value of the accepted proprieties. What she did not suspect was the fact which Peter, loving Prudence as she did, had discovered in the morning of all these disastrous happenings.

"Prudence is so absolutely *chaste*," Peter had thought. And again, of Toby : "He doesn't want girls for love, only for dances and race-meetings." It was so true, though to Gus it would have been incomprehensible. Indeed, had anyone been bold enough to embark in argument on the subject, she would have shut her ears and freezingly indicated that discussion of the indecencies was not one of her favourite themes for conversation.

This may have been so ; but it certainly had not prevented some rather brutal remarks made the previous evening, the memory of which still scalded in hot, pricking waves over Prudence's body, while their half-truth forced itself sickeningly and unrelentingly upon her consciousness.

"For it's *true*," she reflected unhappily, "I *did* wear red knickers because I thought them attractive, and why should I want them to be attractive,

95

unless I cared about ' showing off my person ' . . .
old *swine* . . . And I got drunk. *God!* If she
guessed that! Why *is* it I can't do anything
ordinarily? Other people go racing, and lunching,
and driving round the country with young men,
without something repulsive being made of the
whole show. Why can't I? I know enough to
look after myself; though, if I'd relied on Gus to
tell me things, I should have been in a home for
unmarried mothers, years ago."

Prudence smiled at the recollection of Gus's only
effort at putting the Facts of Life before her ward.
It *had* been funny. Even at the age of fifteen she
had perceived that.

To-day, she considered that Gus, with her
indubitable talent for deftly ignoring and sliding
away from unpalatable subjects, might have
delivered yesterday's homily on pure and impure
virginity with a trifle more artistry. It should have
been on the lines of that previous elucidation of
the mysteries of sex and child-birth.

Prudence smiled again, remembering that bright
morning on which—her stumbling repetition of a
duty towards her neighbour finished—Gus had
alarmingly taken both her hands into the grasp
of her own strong, cold fingers, and leaning forward
on the wide sofa which they shared, began porten-
tously :

" My dear, you are no longer a child. Soon—
very soon, now—you are to be confirmed. It is
right that you should be equipped at all points.
That is the only way in which you can be a good
soldier, faithful to your Lord, always striving—

well, let me see—yes. Well, my child, I have
something to put before you."

A lengthy pause, fraught with immense reticence
on Prudence's side, and intense discomfort on the
part of her mentor, ensued.

"Do you," said Gus, at last, " in short—what
do you know of Life?"

Prudence, who knew a great deal, gleaned, since
the age of ten, in many unhealthy ways, grew
slowly more and more scarlet in the face. Her
child's mouth gaped a little. She was taken aback.

"What?" was the best she could manage.

Gus sighed. Obviously, the answer to her question was, "nothing." She still held Prudence
firmly by the hands, and continued gallantly on
the difficult subject, her elucidation of which was
really masterly.

"Well, dear," she said gropingly, " it's something very wonderful and beautiful, dear—something you wouldn't *quite* understand." She paused,
adding as an impressive afterthought ; " not unlike
a *flower* unfolding."

At this interesting moment Oliver had come
hurriedly into the room ; whereupon Prudence
had been dismissed, nor had Gus ever again referred
to the subject. Obviously, she considered that her
duty in the matter had been well and neatly done.
Certain it is that the idea of blaming herself for
any of Prudence's misdemeanours never once
crossed her well-ordered mind. For how—she
might reasonably enough have asked—could she
be expected to foresee the nature of the tangents
off which Prudence might, at any moment, fly?

No, just retribution following on sins committed was as much of a check on her ward's wayward spirit as she could compass.

Prudence was leaning perilously far out of the window when James re-entered the room to collect her notes. Perceiving her attitude he started violently forward, exclaiming in horrified accents, " By the Holy Fly ! Come in out o'' that, Miss Prudence, me darling girl, ye have a right to be killed. God above ! " he added, as Prudence slewed her body slowly inside the window-sash, " isn't one death enough from the house, without you striving to make a corpse of yourself this way ? "

" What *do* you mean, James ? What death ? Who's dead ? Do tell me, I'm so bored."

" Sure the world knows, and yourself should know, poor Mary Kierney strung herself on an ash sapling, three days after her leaving this place. Isn't it what they say she must have been two hours there, strangulating like——"

. James dwelt upon the luscious details, all unremarking Prudence's strained silence, the starting horror in her eyes, and the waves of colour which passed, dying to a greenish pallor, over her face. " Well, well," he finished with deep relish, " and to say 'twas the rope-ladder herself and John Strap had, the way he could be climbing up to her room so handy and so neat, she done it with. Yes, indeed—that's what they had made up for their allegations. And look—at ! Tom Hinch—the poor, quiet man—he was persecuted, the way he couldn't leave a bit of rope for lunging the horses down out of his hand a minute, but me brave John'd have it whipped, and to go make steps in the ladder is what he'd do with it."

"But how?"—a dreadful curiosity overcame Prudence.

"Oh, she unpicked it, of course," said James, easily divining the question in Prudence's brain. Didn't Tom Hinch reckernise his own ropes after? He did, faith! Ah, well, you'd have to pity the poor girl for all the trouble come to her. But for her to go make the second attempt, after the first going bandy with her—doesn't that bate out?"

He picked up the two notes from the table and when he had unconcernedly perused their addresses, again bent his glistening gaze upon Prudence, remarking softly and with horrid unction:

"What did I say to yourself, the day we pulled her out of the pond? When you'll meet blood in Lingarry, surely ye may keep an eye out for trouble, afther. Yes, indeed, it's not a nice sign, at all . . . *It's very ugly.*" He sunk his old croak of a voice ominously, over the last words, and sidled gently out of the room.

Left alone, Prudence, with a prolonged gasp of horror, flung herself wildly down on the hard, old schoolroom sofa; so she lay for a few minutes, long shudders vibrating over her back and shoulders. Her grey face hidden against a musty and unyielding sofa-cushion, she strove to shut out the horror that James' gruesome story had loosed about the faded room.

Sunlight poured upon her quietly, through the wide window; within the house, all was silent;

outside, the air was so still that the leaves, which yet stayed on the trees, detached themselves, as it were of their own volition, and spun straight and slowly to the ground. In the colourless, old room, Prudence, now crouching like a terrified child in the corner of her sofa, called hideous images to her vision. Some horrid avidity within her insisted that each detail, unsupplied by James, should be like an evil curiosity in her mind ; while what she already knew filled her with a sickened pity.

Mary—poor Mary ! Mary, who was always so nice about the dogs' food ; whose flirtations with John Strap had been the basis for so much jesting and badinage ; Mary whose *meringues* had been such a delight to greedy Prudence—dead. Was it possible ? And to have died such a slow, cruel death ; Prudence, visualising it horribly, was shaken by an agony of anger against Gus. " She was inhuman—the old beast ! She was cruel—devilish cruel. Why did she send her away—why did she ? I hate her. I hate this house, I hate them all. Oh, what *am* I to do ? What *shall* I do ? "

Hands clasped frenziedly about her knees, she sat up at last, facing the tense atmosphere of the old room. She felt that she could not bear the quietness and solitude any longer. Oh, for something to do ! Anything, to blot out this horror from her mind.

" I'll wash my hair," she decided ; and leaping from the sofa, fled, headlong, down the passage to the bathroom. There, the discovery of cold

water in the cylinder went far to efface, by a process of counter-irritation, the chaotic horror of her
thoughts. Swinging upon her heel, she tore off
in the direction of her bedroom. A fresh idea
had taken possession of her mind. She would
ride—would ride, moreover, the new chestnut mare
with which Oliver had replaced her adored Puckhorn.

Fifteen minutes later she was walking across
the stable-yard. Erect and beautiful, a tattered
Burberry caught about her, she might well have
posed for a statue of Our Lady of Poverty. One
hound puppy, leaping, dragged at her coat—as
it were a child clinging about her skirts. While
she spoke to Hinch, the groom, it mouthed at
her hand, loving a little, after the foolish fashion
of fox-hound pups.

" The chestnut mare, Miss," Hinch was saying,
" ah, she's very unaisy. You'll want to sit tight
on her. I had her out meself e'er yesterday, and
I declare to God ! every old ass-cart that'll rattle
past her, she'll soar into the air, with buck, lep
and kick. Keep yourself quiet, now "—he adjured,
as the mare flung up her head to evade the bit.

Prudence, leaning against the stable wall,
surveyed her prospective mount with interest,
tempered by just a little of the " unaisyness "
with which it would seem that the mare was also
imbued. A nice looking mare enough, she appeared
too; lots of strength and plenty of quality ; a great
jumping quarter, and a nice, sloping shoulder ;
well ribbed-up and well let down ; her lean,
fiddle-head was the plainest thing about her.

Oliver was a notable judge of a horse, and had a happy knack of securing just the right thing for his purpose. Prudence, still surveying in silence his latest purchase, felt bound to concede—albeit grudgingly—that he had not done badly in the way of a successor to Puckhorn.

"Looks like a right one," she said thoughtfully to Hinch, "can she gallop?"

Tom Hinch looked up from his task of oiling the mare's feet.

"That's a race-horse," he announced impressively, "and ye might swear she's a flapping jumper. We met a tractor-engine below Tim Connor's, and she sailed out o' the road, over four foot of a stone wall, like a bloody skylark."

When she had hung her Burberry on a nail in the stable arch, and quietly mounted the sidling, head-snatching mare, Prudence decided that their mutual acquaintance might, perhaps, progress more successfully in the fields than on the highways. After she had sat down with some difficulty to three most disconcerting plunges, she was not quite sure if she had been correct in her procedure ; however, this was not the moment to change her plans, so, with hands always low and head high, she rode the mare out of her difficult mood, and in fifteen minutes' time had her cantering sweetly and quietly round the big field.

Prudence was quite a good girl to ride. Had she consented to ride side-saddle, she might almost have ranked as a finished horse-woman. Although she possessed hands—that rare thing in a girl who rides astride—she was not really strong enough to be at her best with a leg on either side of her horse. A girl may have a tight seat, hands, judgment, and impeccable nerve, but, unless she has in addition, a very large measure of physical strength, she will never ride out the finish of a long hunt so competently and happily as will her sister in a side-saddle.

Prudence had a beautiful-looking seat on a horse. Her flat shoulders moved and set so easily ; unlike most girls, she used her thighs, instead of riding in that hideous, balanced fashion—knees in ears ; proof positive of incompetence. It was a joy to see her swing the big mare about and send her gallantly into a not inconsiderable furze hurdle, correct her swerve towards a broken-down wing, and lean back, far and freely, as they cleared the bushes with quite a foot of unnecessary emphasis.

Toby, who was patiently watching the progress of events from a gap in the hedge, had eyes more for the mare than for her rider.

" That's a toppin' nice, quality mare," he reflected, glancing up from the shielded flame of a match in his cupped hands. " She's a lovely mover too, though you wouldn't think her fast either—to look at her." He allowed his cigarette to hang, unheeded, in his fingers, lost in critical meditation.

Prudence obviously hadn't seen him ; well, it would do him no great harm to wait till she came down the field again. The three several made fences over which she was riding led towards him in a straight line. The first two were a furze hurdle and a loose-built stone wall ; the third, a built up double—plump and new. The mare came for it steadily and kindly, took off fault-lessly—it was no blame to her when newly-laid sods gave under her, and she came back badly on the near side. . . .

For one dreadful minute Prudence felt as though all her lifetime had been a gigantic struggle ; a struggle to escape from something which pinned, and held, and crushed her to the ground ; something ungovernable and violently strong. Then she was caught beneath the arms and swung up and away. . . . It was Toby, she recognised him as soon as she got her wind back.

"My God ! You, you damned little fool, are you hurt ? "

"No," answered Prudence with dawning astonishment, "I don't believe I am. The mare, though——"

Toby was already pulling the mare up on her legs, and now led her gently about, now paused to look her over carefully. "No damage done—as far as one can see at present, anyway. How did you manage to do such a stupid thing ? Didn't you know it was a new-built fence ? "

"I, I forgot, as it happens," Prudence answered as loftily as possible. "Awfully silly of me," she conceded lightly ; adding, with a very different tone of earnest thankfulness in her voice : "Any-how, thank goodness, the mare's none the worse. And Gus—I mean, Oliver—need never know if we put the sods back carefully. Need they, Toby ? "

"Not so far as I'm concerned," he told her, "especially if you're clever enough to think of

some way of removing the mud from your saddle
—*and* your coat."

" *I* know," Prudence replaced the last of the
sods as artistically as she knew how, " you can
produce a hanky, wisp me down first, and then
the mare." She presented her muddied back for
his ministrations as unconcernedly as though he
had been her maid. During the wisping down
she screwed her head over her shoulder to discuss,
with a choice of detail that certainly did credit
to her imagination, the horrors which might have
been attendant on her mishap.

" Stop *talking* about it," Toby said crossly, at
the end of five minutes. " It *was* a nasty fall, and
a very silly bit of work on your part, if I may say
so ; but as the mare is none the worse, and you
haven't broken your thigh (as you should have
done in that mix-up against the wing) the best
thing you can do is to forget it. Hang it all,
girl ! I'm sure no sane person interferes with
wet mud."

" All right, clean the saddle, now," Prudence
returned equably.

" By the way, why are you here ? " she inquired
ten minutes later, as he walked by her stirrup,
up the avenue to the house. " I mean, after yesterday "—she stopped, looking down at him con-
fusedly, colour in her cheeks and a frown at her
own awkwardness ridging her forehead.

" Oh, yes," Toby lit a cigarette ; " well, I came
to have a little chat with Gus. You see, I didn't
like her spoiling my party yesterday."

" Very nicely put, too," commented Prudence.

" Oh, thanks. Aren't you too kind ? Well, as I was saying, I told Gus how revolting she'd been to take you away——"

" *Toby !* What did she say ? "

" Say ? She said there was no one she would rather you went racing with than meself. Only, you were too young to go unchaperoned. . . ."

" Rats ! "

" I told her why Peter Trudgeon didn't turn up for lunch, and she got so excited, explaining to me how badly the Trudgeon family had been brought up, that she forgot all about you."

" Why ? " Prudence asked. " I mean, why didn't Peter come ? "

" Sammy got a heart attack, in the Ford, going 'home—he was driving, too. Sure they smashed the car to blazes. I believe Sammy got fearfully sick, all through smoking a nasty cigarette you gave him, and that's what brought it on."

" Oh, Lord ! I never thought—but even if I had, I'd never have imagined a little thing like a cigarette could make such a hatful of mischief." But whether Prudence was thinking of Sammy's heart attack, the smashed Ford, or the unfortunate ending to yesterday's luncheon party, is uncertain.

" Are you staying to lunch ? " she asked, when the mare (together with a very garbled version of the morning's mishap) had been handed over to John Strap.

" Yes, I am. Gus asked me to. And I must see Oliver."

" Oh, well—good-bye, then."

" Why say good-bye ? " Toby asked, taking her hand and shaking it absent-mindedly up and down. " Don't you eat lunch ? But I know you do."

" Yes, but I eat it with the dogs in the school-room till I promise to be good again," she told him, almost with embarrassment.

" Oh, that's easy ! Just go and tell Gus you're sorry—like a good girl."

" Shall I ? I hate doing it. Shall I really though ? "

" Yes, go on. I've got a mass of important things to buck to you about. And I don't sup-pose, no matter how rude I was, Gus would send me to the schoolroom to have lunch with you."

" All right, then—I *will !* " Feeling a little uplifted that Toby should really have important things to discuss with her, and also that he should feel her absence from luncheon to leave a regret-table blank, Prudence moved off at once in the direction of the garden.

" By the way," she observed suddenly, swinging round to Toby, again, " such a ghastly thing has happened—our last cook committed suicide."

" Good God ! How beastly." Toby was visibly taken aback.

" Yes, wasn't it frantic ? It was the sight of John Strap reminded me. Fancy *doing* such a thing—poor brute ! " Prudence laughed care-lessly and strode off ; so much for the morning's tragedy. The mishap with the mare had touched her more nearly ; the excitement, more intense and more recent, had, for the moment at any rate, quite swamped the earlier trouble in her mind.

In the garden, then, as Gus removed her earthy gloves, and with them dusted the baggy knees of an old gardening skirt:

"Oh, there you are, Cousin Gus," began Prudence uncertainly, "I just wanted to tell you lunch is ready—what I mean is, I'm awfully sorry I was rude yesterday."

"My darling child," answered Gus, with quick warmth and generosity, "I *know* you mean what you say, and I'm so glad you came and told me. I knew it was never *my* Prudence who would speak like that. Was I right?"

"Yes, Cousin Gus."

"And you came and told me of your own free-will—that's what I like. You didn't see Cousin Oliver?"

"Given me away to Oliver, too, has she?" reflected Prudence, with a hint of sourness unbecoming in a repentant sinner. A moment later she was struck by a really bright idea.

"As a matter of fact, Cousin Gus, I saw Toby Sage, and he told me what a beast I'd been," she announced hesitatingly.

"Well, *how nice!*" Cousin Gus fairly beamed. Picking up her gardening tools, she handed them to Prudence. "In the potting shed, my dear." Then, turning to Kat, who at that moment came fussing round the corner of an old clipped hedge, she announced:

"Prudence has come to tell me how sorry she is for her bad behaviour, so now all is forgiven and forgotten."

Kat sniffed doubtfully.

"Well, I suppose I must forgive you, too," she said. "*But* "—with acid emphasis—" I shall never forget the dreadful things you said to dear Cousin Gus. No, I *cannot*. Besides," whirling round to Gus and speaking almost in tones of triumph, "how can she be sorry? Look at her, standing there in that immodest little coat that we have both forbidden her, time and again, to wear. That *proves* it ! "

"Oh Lord ! I forgot—I'm most awfully sorry," gasped Prudence.

"You forgot ! You're sorry ! You're a very naughty girl—Miss. *And I don't believe she's one bit sorry*," this last, in a penetrating whisper, was addressed to Gus ; after which Kat took herself off towards her cucumber frames.

"Go into the house, at once, and put a skirt about you, Prudence," Gus spoke with most of her usual accent of cold reserve. In reality, she was more annoyed by her sister, than by Prudence's last slight misdemeanour. Had Kat brought Prudence to her present right frame of mind, well did Gus know that her reception of contrition and apology would have been very different. But Kat was an adept at lessening any little triumph, or any meed of praise, due to her sister reformer.

CHAPTER VI

PETER

" Oh, how d'ye do ? I say, look here—do chase me away, I'm an infernal nuisance, I know."

Anthony Countless stood in the doorway of Mervyn Trudgeon's study at Kilronan, embarrassedly surveying the only occupant of the room. This was Peter. She reclined upon a wide sofa, a white bandage tied round her head ; a cigarette depended between her fingers. Dilly, seated upon her person, growled morosely at the intruder.

" Dilly-pooks—*not* done ! " Peter cautioned her. Then, to Anthony—swinging her legs off the sofa, and vigorously brushing cigarette ash from her skirt :

" Oh, don't say that. I'm delighted to see someone. It's painfully boring, being shut up like this. I hope you've come to play cards with me ? "

" Oh, I'll play cards with you, of course. But I really came to see that brother of yours."

" Mervyn ? " Peter was not at all perturbed by this direct statement of her caller's business. " He'll be back in about an hour," she said, " if you can bear to wait as long. You don't mind my sewing, do you ? I promised to mend this silk vest of Boodie's. He's got so crazy about his undies since the great affair with Mrs. Wentworth-Stuart started."

Anthony sat down in a chair near her sofa. But for some five minutes he did not attempt to break the silence which reigned between them. Then he said, with an obvious jerk, which showed his thoughts had been far away :

" How are you to-day ? Better ? "

Peter looked up from the garment which she had been laboriously cobbling ; her three-cornered, dark blue eyes gleaming below the white bandage on her forehead.

" Toppin', thanks. Shoulder still a bit crippled, otherwise I'm grand."

" Sammy all right, too ? "

" Oh, Sammy's in great form. Thinks himself so jolly clever now for upsetting us—he's got off another three weeks' school."

" Um. School doesn't seem to worry any of your brothers much."

Anthony's tone was so disapproving that Peter laughed.

" Well, y'see "—she ticked them off on her fingers —" Mervyn is just waiting to join his regiment. Boodie can't *bear* his crammer, and Sammy has this weak heart to produce whenever convenient. But Hodge and Jasper are always at school and even poor Victor has to do his lessons with Nan. Of course," she conceded, " Boodie *is* a disgrace, I'll allow that. *No* boy of his age ought to be leaving his crammer's and having an affair with a divorced widow."

" *What ?* Mrs. Stuart ? "

" Yes, he's crazy about her. And really, you know, she's got a face like a granite horse. I *can't* see——"

At this moment the door opened to admit Boodie. He appeared to be perfectly seething with suppressed excitement ; however, on seeing Anthony, he produced a manner as calm and restrained as he could compass. Hitching up his pale, grey flannel trousers, he seated himself in a chair and fired off a string of aimless, disjointed questions respecting hounds, cubs and coverts—plainly inattentive to the monosyllabic replies vouchsafed to his babblings by the M.F.H.

" Talk *sense*, if you must talk, Boodie," Peter implored him finally, as she bit off the end of her thread and handed over his pink vest.

" Sorry. Did I drivel ? My God ! You have done this badly, Peter."

" Oh, go to hell ! " returned his sister, irascibly. " Di isn't going to *see* it, is she ? "

" No—at least, I don't suppose so. But, look here—talking of Di reminds me—what I mean is, I wanted to ask you how much it would cost me to give a, a fellow I know dinner at the Shelbourne ? "

" Boodie ! Has she promised to dine with you ? How *wonderful !* "

" Yes," replied the rapt and artless Boodie, " and what I want to know now is—what's the least I can do it for ? "

Peter calculated for a moment :

" Dinner will cost you seven-and-six each. And if she has a drink, that's a bit more."

" Well, she just can't *have* a drink," Boodie asserted, almost peevishly.

" Then there's a tip for the waiter, and coffee

and liqueurs," Peter continued, " and if you bring
her on to a show of any sort afterwards——"

" I'm dashed if I'm bringing her on to a show of
any sort afterwards." Boodie sighed, running his
fingers despondently through his hair. " Damn it,
Peter, what am I to do? I thought twelve-and-six
would see me through, easy. It's all I've got, too."

" Why *did* you ask her ? " Peter inquired curiously.

" Oh, she was looking so toppin', or something
. . . I d'know what. But look here, will you be
a *dear* and lend me ten shillings ? Thanks most
awfully, Peter. It'll see me through grand, I'm
deeply grateful. Should I telephone to them to
keep a table, or will there be plenty ? "

" Oh, masses. It's not horse-show week."

" All right. So long, then." He left the room,
but burst in a moment later to add : " By the way,
Master—I'd nearly forgotten—Mervyn asked me
to tell you he'd got that brown horse of Murphy's
in the stables for you to see." He closed the door,
and went whistling down the corridor.

Peter rose to her feet and smiled down seriously
on Anthony, who still remained sunk in his arm-
chair. He thought the wide bandage over her
eyes gave her an austere look—it was not unlike a
coif. A pity that her general outlook on life should
not savour equally of the cloister ; her language
had more than once positively disgusted him.
Now, having made a complete circuit of the room,
she offered him a cigarette ; on his discovery that
he was without matches, she nonchalantly plucked
a coal from the fire, holding it in the tongs at
the right angle for him to light his cigarette.

" Don't you smoke ? " he asked, surprisedly.

" Yes, that and drink are my only vices. Let's
go out to the stables and have a look at that brute
Mervyn has collected for you. God knows when
he'll be back."

Anthony demurred. " Should you ? I don't
think you ought to. Fact, I'm sure you oughtn't."

For answer, Peter pulled a short Burberry coat
from behind the sofa, donned it, and making a face
at Pookie, strode heavily from the room ; her hands
deep in her pockets, her bandaged head bent.

Anthony perforce followed.

The hall, through which they passed, was in its
permanently conflicting state of confusion. Mounted
foxes' masks hung on the walls, jostling terrific
cases of stuffed sea-birds. A badger snarled eternally at the stuffed form of a fourteen-pound brown
trout, which returned the snarl by a glassy and
pre-occupied stare. There were foxes' brushes
hung everywhere upon the walls, too—with the
children's names and a date engraved on many
of them. Wedged between the trophies hung old
sporting prints, their series not always complete.
At one end of the hall was a great, open fire-place ;
a heavy, angled, dark settle taking up one side ;
on the other, a fanner was set to blow up the fire.

The great house-door stood open ; on the thres-
hold—greatly daring—two setter pups endeavoured
to steel their nerves sufficiently for an encounter
with a monstrous tortoiseshell cat. The cat lay
and glared at them from her couch on the broad
head of a magnificent tiger-skin, that stretched its
sleek length across a wide space of polished floor.

Everywhere there were brass Indian pots and bronze jars, filled lavishly with the blue agapanthus lily ; dark oak chairs stood to rigid attention round the walls ; and light came kindly down upon the confusion below from a domed sky-light. A smell of new leather rose, thinly predominant above the honeyed thickness of the lilies' breath, and the mixed air of sandal wood and old camphor which hung on the atmosphere. The half-unpacked saddle-case, from the depths of which gleamed the raw yellow of a new side-saddle, accounted for the leather tang. As she passed the case, Peter peered in.

" Oh, Lord ! There's Zookie havin' her kittens in my new saddle. How annoying ! Well, I suppose I can't disturb her—must be trying enough, anyway. Poor Zookie—mother's sweetheart ;" she bent over the box, while Anthony hastily went out to the steps. He had no mind to be called upon to fill the office of *accoucheur ;* Peter, he felt sure, was not incapable of making the suggestion.

Peter joined him after a moment, a stick in her hand which she had selected from a litter of rods, landing nets, tennis racquets and shooting-sticks that occupied one corner of the hall.

They passed together down the many-windowed length of the big house, under an ivy-grown arch into the stable yard. Here, their companionship progressed to something like guarded intimacy.

Peter was so very sure of herself with regard to horses that she said but little, and what she did say was devastatingly to the point, and notably lacking in quotation marks. At the end of twenty minutes Anthony was inclined to think her opinion was almost worthy of attention. She had told him, without an instant's hesitation, that his prospective purchase was lame, though the unsoundness was so slight that many—himself included—would have passed it over entirely. Hearn, the groom, corroborated her opinion unflinchingly. The horse, he said, was not very sound.

" A horse is either lame *or* sound ; can't have 'em *very* sound," Anthony muttered irascibly ; but his judgment was shaken, he temporised.

" Care to ride a little school ? " Peter asked him. She was sitting on the stone mounting-block, picking an occasional flea out of Dilly's back.

" There's a rather tempting bank, down there," she jerked her head sideways, indicating the direction and left it tilted comfortably as she waited for his reply.

Anthony, who had been morosely studying his excellent boots, looked up to catch for a moment the charm of her pose ; the grave blue eyes, full, for once, of impish suggestion ; the deep flush of perfect health which glowed in the creamy curves of her neck, as well as in the even tan of her face, lifted so serenely to him ; her arms stretched behind her back, with hands flattened on the rough stone of the upper block, gave him the full lines of her firm young breasts, under her long, close-fitting jumper ; this sudden realization of her as a marvellous specimen of the female of the species gave him something of a jar. But—Good Heavens !— he had been staring at the girl like a fool, instead of answering her question. *What* had she suggested ?

A bank? A school—that was it. He assented to
the notion and promptly left Peter's side to go
over to the loose-box and watch the saddling of
the brown horse.

Nevertheless, when, a little later, the brown
horse—in a manner utterly piggish and self-willed
—entirely declined to consider the meanest of
Peter's temptations in the way of banks, it was
with an unaccustomed touch of self-consciousness
that he tried severe and successful conclusions
with his mount. The brown, after his one refusal,
acquitted himself with grudging adequacy round
the remainder of the school.

As they walked back towards the house, Anthony,
warmed and soothed in spirit after his ride, became
(for him) almost communicative. That is, he
spoke to Peter of those subjects, so near to his heart
as to be almost sacred, the hounds and the sanita-
tion of the new kennels.

Peter, listening to the true, inward history of
the subtle differences existing between Anthony's
ideas and those of the master-plumber ; and to
the tale of their amalgamated plans of drainage
versus the objections foreseen daily by his kennel-
huntsman, felt moved to deep sympathy. How, she
asked herself could this little Saxon be a match
for Denny Connor—that arch-fiend of plumbers ?
She found the maintenance of that attitude of
unfriendliness enjoined by Prudence increasingly
difficult.

"And then, y'know," Anthony was saying
despondently, "I get a letter only yesterday, from
my second horseman's wife. Wanted to know why

he didn't have her over. Said, would *I* speak to him. So on. Well, why write to me about it?"

"What did you answer?" Peter asked, with some curiosity.

"Answer? I just wrote back that this was such a desperate, heathen sort of country, and the house so bad—drains up and all—she shouldn't think of coming. Damn foolishness."

"He's not such a helpless innocent," Peter thought, slouching along beside him, with an occasional sideways glance in his direction, from beneath the bandage, "he might best Denny Connor yet. I don't know about him; Prudence may be wrong, I think she is. I almost like him."

Following on a somewhat prolonged silence, Anthony observed, *apropos* of nothing, unless, indeed, it might have been the rabbit which Dilly was optimistically hunting through the laurels:

"I should have thought all the hares in the country were poached to blazes—judging by the numbers of long-dogs and half-hounds you see in every cottage."

"So they are," replied Peter, "there isn't a wild hare in the country."

Anthony stopped and bent his cane on his boot, while a frown of incomprehension drew deep lines in the red tan of his forehead.

"Well, that's a funny thing." He unbent his cane and walked on. "Young Toby Sage wrote to me last week, asking leave to hunt harriers one day a week in the Knockderry country. I told him to fire away, as far as I was concerned. But it's a queer idea, if the country is so short of hares. Take him some time to get them up."

"Yes," said Peter tranquilly, "but you know, they aren't short of foxes up there."

"What?" For a moment Anthony failed to take in the full import of her remark. As it dawned upon him:

"Good God!" he muttered faintly. "But, but the fellow said *harriers*."

"In Ireland, and indeed, I believe in some English countries too, harriers hunt foxes, *not* hares," Peter pointed out gently.

Anthony, whose head up to this moment had been sunk in his hands, sheer stupefaction almost stunning him, lifted it suddenly. A fierce light, kindled at his very soul, burnt in his eyes.

"He doesn't imagine he's going to hunt the coverts, does he?" Anthony's voice snapped off. It was the cry of a soul in travail.

Peter understood it perfectly. They were back in the yard now; she seated herself once more on the mounting-block.

"Look here," she began slowly, "I'm not taking sides; but you'd better listen to me. Look here——"

"Yes. He doesn't think he's going to hunt the coverts, does he?" Anthony demanded obstinately.

Peter shook her head reassuringly. "This is your country," she began again, "you have the say-so. You're hunting hounds, aren't you?"

"If he thinks——" interrupted Anthony monotonously.

"Yes, but he won't," Peter spoke almost swiftly in her earnestness.

The country, she said, was a big country; a four day a week country; the Knockderry end

was the best part of twenty miles from the kennels
—two days in the season was the most he could
possibly do in it ; it was a filthy country to ride,
and a terrible place to cut a horse. The coverts ?
Gorse, covering miles of rocky mountains. Neglect
it and he would see what would happen ; trapping
of foxes and poison laid at once. Whereas, let
it be hunted and the people would keep quiet.

" Toby, you see "—she wrinkled her eyebrows
till they disappeared from sight beneath the bandage—" Toby is the right sort. Say ' no ' to him
over the harriers, and he'll give up the notion at
once. What do you suppose'll happen then ?
Some buckeen starts a proper, pirate pack, and
does more harm ruxing out the country one day
a fortnight, than Toby and his twelve couples
would do in six. Tobioh knows what he's doing,
he won't *poach*."

" Well, I'll think about it," Anthony promised,
" it's been a deuce of a shock, you know."

Peter got up from the block. " Let's go into the
house," she proposed, " the sun is beastly hot."

" I say—I'm most awfully sorry. I'm *dashed*
sorry ! Like an ass, I never thought——" Anthony
apologized feverishly.

But Peter only shook her cropped and bandaged
head, and maintained a strong silence—recuperating,
perhaps, after her lengthy dissertation.

The sight of Toby Sage's car, its pale yellow
length drawn up near the hall-door steps, moved
her to speech.

" Talk of an angel "—she grimaced comically—
" if that's not Toby, himself. How funny ! "

Anthony stopped, confused.

"I—don't think me rude," he hesitated, "fact is, I don't want to meet the fella till I've thought about this harrier game a bit more. Awkward, you see, deuced *awkward*. Well, look here, I must say ' good-bye ' now. And thanks so much——"

"What on earth for ? " Peter eyed him calmly, but without disfavour.

Anthony didn't know, quite. But he got out of the difficulty by an entangled and urgent invitation to her to come over and inspect the building of the new kennels.

"I *want* you to see that feeding-house," he declared with a fervour almost more surprising to himself than it was to Peter.

She gave him her brown, serious-looking hand, and shook his with gravity.

"I'll tell Mervyn you're satisfied about the brown horse—provided he passes the vet," she said. "He'd make quite a useful one for a hunt-servant," she suggested, "a sticky ride, I should say, but awfully respectable." A very slow smile displayed a dimple in the corner of her mouth, as unexpected as it was delightful. "Mervyn and I'll come over on Sunday, probably. Good-bye." She left him and sauntered slowly and heavily back to the house.

A minute later, as Anthony was starting his car, Dilly—covered in red earth—shot from the laurels, and nose to the ground, raced like a thing demented along her mistress's tracks, to be swallowed from sight in the gulf of the hall-door. Plainly, a long separation from Peter did not bear thinking about. Anthony, as he let in his clutch, smiled, for the first time that afternoon ; dogs, he could understand ; about girls, he was not so sure. In any case, they did not interest him in the least. His mind, as was usual in those days, passed at once to the tortuous consideration of kennel drainage.

Within the hall, Peter encountered a white-faced Toby.

" Prudence has just fainted," he announced without preamble.

" Where is she, Toby ? " It was characteristic of Peter that she did not ask why Prudence had fainted, or when, or how.

Toby nodded towards the door of Mervyn's study, where Peter had been sitting earlier in the day. " In there," he said. " I was just off to get a spot of brandy," he disappeared into the dining-room.

In the study, out-flung upon the sofa, Prudence was coming to herself with long shuddering breaths. She raised her haggard face, that had been bent on her arms, when Peter opened the door.

" I'm going to be awfully sick ; I shall cat my soul up," she announced with faint distinctness.

Peter moved over to her and laid her flat on her back.

" Rot," she said, " you won't be. I know. Shut your eyes."

" All right, Puppy." Prudence's heavy, blue lids closed down obediently.

Before many minutes had passed, she reflected, almost comfortably, that wherever Peter had found

the eau-de-cologne and salts, they made a marvellous difference. Almost—she didn't feel sick ; the
next moment, she was sure she didn't.

"Now, for heaven's sake, girl, will you be quiet
and drink this ; and don't, if you can help it,
give me any more shocks to-day."

It was Toby's voice that she heard behind her,
as she tried to struggle up into a sitting position.
She drank obediently, what they gave her ; then
lay, lapped in drowsy peace, thinking of nothing,
save how comic was the pattern of the chintz on
Peter's sofa. Soon, she didn't even think of that ;
for she sighed, and tucking a hand beneath her
cheek, fell into sudden, child-like sleep.

In the hall, Peter permitted herself a question.
And Toby, when he had lighted a cigarette—a
trifle unsteadily—set himself to answer her.

It was all those beastly kittens—ran the lucid
explanation—and the cat, of course. Cat-bite was,
so he had always understood, second only to fox-bite.
After all, what should he have done ? It *had* to be
done at once, and Prudence was perfectly game
over it. And then, when the thing was finished,
went off like that. Wasn't it extraordinary ?

"Perfectly incredible," Peter agreed. "But do
let's get it clear. Did the cat bite her ? "

"It was like this," Toby was calming down
considerably under the influence of a cigarette,
"I drove her over, you see, to ask after you—
how are you, by the way ? "

"Me ? Oh, topping. But get on——"

"Yes. Where were we ? Oh, yes. Well, we'd
just got into the hall, and I was lighting a cigarette ;

Prudence started mooning round—reading off the
dates on the masks and so on. Then she saw
your saddle, sticking out of the case over there,
and started to pull it out. Next thing, I heard
her call out and she pulled her hand out of the
packing-case with a perfectly good cat hanging on
to it like grim death. I tell you, I had a moment
of my own before I got the brute's jaws opened;
she'd sunk her teeth all right."

" How perfectly awful ! What did you do then ? "
Peter was almost shaken.

" I slit up the tooth-marks with my knife and
poured in half a bottle of iodine." Toby lit another
cigarette on top of this statement, and shook out
the flame of his match. " Then she fainted,"
he added quaintly. " I'm glad you came when
you did, I was getting so worried."

" I wouldn't have had the guts to slice her up,
but she'll be all right now," was Peter's only comment. She climbed down from the oak chest
where she had been sitting and went over to the
saddle case.

" Six kittens," she observed cheerfully. " Poor
Zookie—I *didn't* mean to. No, I wouldn't ever."
On her knees, she bent over the cat, stirring the
damp new kittens with an unshrinking forefinger.

" There's a white one, and a black, and, I think,
a tortoiseshell ; the rest are only commoners."
She raised her face, flushed and pleased, to Toby,
who stood behind her.

" Why, what's up, Tobioh ? "

Toby, shuddering, looked as though something
had violently disagreed with him.

"The sight of those damn cats makes me feel perfectly sick," he told her, "how *can* you play about with the little brutes, Peter?" He turned from her suddenly, strode jerkily down the steps, and began to do things inside the bonnet of his car.

Peter, her eyes full of light, continued to look down at the cat, sumptuous and expansive in her so recently achieved maternity. She scratched her sympathetically at the base of her ears.

"It's all right, old lady," she murmured, "I'd have done exactly the same myself, I expect. An' *now* we've got to see about a slop-pail for these little commoners. You weren't *very* clever to have them, darling." She moved her saddle gently away, in case of further accidents, and re-settled the packing round the young family.

About an hour later, Prudence—her hand now in a more adequate bandage than Toby's silk handkerchief—was sitting up on the sofa, drinking tea. She was also able to venture pensively on a substantial chunk of iced chocolate cake. She did not speak much. Peter had straightened out her green silk jumper, but her hair was still just anyhow. As a matter of fact, the pale loops and looseness of her tumbled hair became Prudence marvellously better than a sleek coiffure would have done. There was a quality in her that rose, not so much above, as beyond smartness, and that made every *outré* thing she did, or wore, become the only correct procedure, or apparel.

Peter and Toby were talking about those harriers; he had told Prudence all about them during

125

their drive from Lingarry, so she listened now, only half attentive ; regarding them mournfully over her second slice of cake. She thought that it might be fun ; only, Toby's meets would be so far from her always ; she knew it would be difficult to manage a day with him.

Mervyn came in, very fair and brown in the face ; only less assured in manner than Toby. He drank tea, solemnly considering the sit of his jodhpurs. He had been schooling a young horse and there was mud on the shoulder of his tweed coat. Boodie appeared too, before the end of the meal. He talked feverishly, wiping his hands on the slack of his trousers ; he was getting this dinner properly on his nerves. And when tea was almost over, Bims—baptismal name, Victor—the youngest of the Trudgeons, rolled in, dressed in his afternoon suit of pink linen. He was an agreeable, puppy-like infant ; fat, but not unduly greedy. His elder brothers abandoned themselves immediately to his entertainment.

Peter continued to talk to Toby solemnly about the harriers. Above the not inconsiderable noise created by Bims and his elder brothers, Prudence made out that Toby was bothered and on the edge of annoyance, from which state Peter soothed him with skill.

Presently, Lady Mavis Trudgeon added her vague bulk to the already crowded room.

A solidly beautiful woman, she was one of God's own muddlers. Her carelessness ! The six children that she had unintelligently and unwillingly produced testified to that, simply by their existence.

She moved creakingly across the room, and shook hands with Toby and Prudence in a vaguely pleased manner; but more as though they were welcome strangers than constant *habitués* of her house. She was about to greet one of her sons with equal politeness when, realizing her error, she sank into half the wide sofa, explaining to every one how it was all on account of that appalling check coat of Mervyn's—she simply *could* not get used to it.

"Or else he's had his hair cut," her eyes dwelt on Mervyn's head, attentive for a moment, then perfectly unseeing. She had played bridge all the afternoon, and recalled with fervour what wonderful hearts she had held—a pity that she had not put her partner up again; still, there was that King, guarded, somewhere. . . .

"Good bridge, Mummy?" Peter asked.

"Yes, darling. *Excellent.* Toby, how is your ear-ache?"

"I haven't got any, thanks awfully, Lady Mavis."

"No? How stupid of me! Of course, I was thinking of old Jimmy Brennan. He's a martyr to it, poor man! Prudence, are you going to the Jamison-Hoare's little dinner-dance?"

Prudence looked up from the nastiness which she was busily creating with cigarette ash in the dregs of her tea-cup.

"It was last Friday-week, you know," she reminded her hostess gently, "I did go; it was a dreadful show."

"Oh, *yes*," a reminiscent light glowed in Lady Mavis's fine eyes, "of course! I remember now.

I was so anxious for Peter to go, you know. I thought it would be nice ; but she simply wouldn't. I tried to persuade her. Yes, she was so wicked and naughty, driving home, I *cried*. I did, indeed ! "

" Oh, Mummy, you didn't ! *What* a whopper ! "

" Indeed I did. Yes, I cried in the night." This with evident inspiration. " Well, the language you used was too awful. ' I'll be damned in Hell,' you said——"

" Badly behaved girl, she is. Had drink taken too, probably." Toby rose from the hassock, round which he had been writhing his long legs for the past three-quarters of an hour. Obviously, he wished Prudence to make a move.

In the hall, Prudence pulled Peter aside.

" My stockings are coming down," she murmured brokenly. " Did *you* interfere with my suspenders ? "

At Peter's emphatic denial, she grew exceedingly pink.

" Some one must have," Prudence was cross and bothered. She repaired the damage, powdered her nose, and pulled down her ancient, pale felt hat over her ears without once looking into a mirror.

Then, answering the imperious summons of Toby's melodious horn, she ran across the hall, nearly slipping up on a loose rug, tore down the steps and was at once confronted by the difficulty of climbing into the door-less body of Toby's car.

" I think you'd better let me lift you in," Toby suggested, slipping from behind the wheel, " one hand's so awfully crippling."

" I've got both my legs, thank you, Toby."

Balanced, with one foot on the tool-box, her other leg over the door, knee bent up and straight-hanging foot seeking foot-hold, she might have been a life-size radiator nymph—fully clothed. The next moment she slid down beside him ; lost, in the lengthy depth of the car, to all eyes but his own.

Half-way home Toby said, " You *are* an event-ful person. We can't do the most ordinary things together, that something disturbing doesn't occur. Aren't you ashamed of yourself ? "

A silence followed. Then : " I, I *am* awfully sorry, Toby." It was a very small voice, and the shake in it was ominous.

Looking down, sideways, Toby saw a piteously drooping mouth, and slim hands driving futilely into side-pockets in search, he felt sure, of a hand-kerchief.

" *Prudence !* You absurd kid. I, I *like* events. Didn't you know, silly ? "

At a loss for words, they both felt uncomfortable ; each found the other a trifle inadequate. Prudence pulled down her eternally ascending skirt. Laugh-ing, Toby raised his eyebrows. It was so much easier to return to banalities.

" Such a pity," he murmured, " I love the cut of those green yokes. Do you get them specially tailored ? "

" That will do, thanks." Prudence was really trying to be repressive ; it was unfortunate that a sudden bubble of laughter should, at that moment, break from her irrepressibly.

" What are you laughing at ? Tell me. Go on, tell me, Prudence. You might ! "

Prudence gazed through the wind-screen. "Suspenders," she said; then, flinging herself back in her seat, moaned in an agony of mirth.

Toby's grin was entirely adequate.

" 'Lay the patient,' " he quoted, " 'flat on his back. Loosen any garment of a, er, constricting nature. Administer restoratives.' Dammit, how *was* I to know where the brutes began or ended."

" *What* began, or ended ? " Prudence inquired with *hauteur*, just touched by anxiety.

" Your—oh, well, *all right !* I know now you don't wear any." Toby slowed the car down at the Lingarry gates. "We'll go on, shall we ? " he proposed.

" No. Home, Toby." She thrust out an arm to indicate to a car behind that they were turning.

Toby obeyed her regretfully.

" When are those harriers arriving ? " she asked him.

" Next week," he told her, " I'm going down to see about it on Wednesday. By Jove ! If you and Peter could come—there's an idea." He slowed up and looked down at her anxiously.

" Oh, I don't know," Prudence answered, with unassumed carelessness, " I'd never be let go. It might be quite fun. Would it be worth the effort ? "

Toby accelerated again before the ascending slope.

" It is most essential," he announced importantly, " that your acquaintance with the harriers should begin without delay. I shall need you badly to turn hounds to me, you know," he finished on an utterly serious note.

As seriously, Prudence thanked him, but declaimed with fervour her fittedness for such a post of honour.

" I know best," Toby answered her supremely.

Stopping before the door, he climbed out and was round at Prudence's side before she had moved.

" All right, Tobioh. It's worse, getting out."

He lifted her up bodily, and set her on the ground without an instant's unnecessary delay.

" Thanks, Toby. I'm going in now." She was in one of her dreaming moods—for herself, full of colour ; for others, less exciting.

Still, Toby wished to keep her a little longer ; that was the worst of Prudence, no one ever wanted to say " Good-bye " to her—*just* yet.

" Have you christened the chestnut mare ? " he asked.

" Yes."

" When ? "

" Just now."

" Oh, what d'you call her ? "

Dreaming still, she looked in his eyes. In hers was an absence of all coquetry. " Suspenders," she almost whispered. Her face, seen by the evening light, against an evening sky, was like a pale, pointed piece of jade.

Toby choked. " You're a nasty, brazen girl, aren't you ? What'll Gus say to such a lewd name ? "

Prudence hardly raised her heavy eye-lids.

" ' Suspenders '," she murmured again, " by ' Suspension ', out of a mare called ' Look-again '. Don't be silly—Toby, *darlin*' ! "

CHAPTER VII

PEARLS AND PERILS

"I DON'T like the idea, at all. I may say I dislike it exceedingly. It is—well, 'fast' is a word I hardly care to use, but I consider that in this case it is almost justifiable." Miss Gus lifted another fold of the linen sheet, into which she was firmly stitching her disapproval of the proposed visit to the present kennels of Toby's harriers.

Kat, who was seated in a low chair, warming her shins at an ample fire, sniffed superbly.

"If you ask *me*," she said, "I think the idea is nasty. These young people, indeed! Setting off by themselves for an entire day. And *do you know*," she spoke with sudden energy, "young Miss Peter had the impertinence to inform me that it was 'quite usual'? I never! If that doesn't *prove* it!"

"'Prove!' Prove, what?" inquired Miss Gus, snipping off her thread and glancing at her sister distastefully over her spectacles.

"Prove that they are a horrible, fast crowd. *Moderns*—that's what they are; tearing round the country in motor-cars all day, and half the night. It's not *nice*."

That her sister should be so entirely in agreement with her was quite sufficient to make Miss Gus trample on her own feelings on the subject.

"One must try," she said, "to be fair. After all, things have altered since our young days; I don't say for the better; perhaps I don't even think so. But they have altered. I hope I am not a reactionary, I try to keep an open mind. No, on the whole, Kat, I am inclined to think this day's trip may be quite a harmless little outing. After all, Peter goes with her brother, Mervyn; Prudence goes with Peter, who is—I must admit— a *rock* of sense; *so* unlike Prudence. And as for Toby Sage—Dominick, I should say; there is nothing I loathe like the present day fashion of nicknames—if Prudence *must* have a young man to trail about after her, there is no one I would rather she went about with. He is, at least, a gentleman." Cousin Gus snipped off her cotton, and threaded a needle with deft precision.

Kat snuffled in a disgruntled manner. In argument, she knew herself to be no match for Gus. Still, she hated giving in.

"What I do dislike," she observed, almost pacifically, "is the fact that there are four of them in the party, and not one, solitary one of them is Prudence's brother—there! You can't deny *that!*" she ended with something like triumph.

Gus glanced up from her work; she was unaffectedly puzzled.

"My dear Kat, what do you mean? Of course they are not her brothers. She never had a brother."

Kat fidgetted and grew uncomfortable. Her extreme delicacy of mind made it nearly impossible

for her to say what she meant. However, since
Gus insisted on being so stupid, she was now
bound to explain herself to a coarser extent than
she had intended.

"Well," she said, "it's not a nice way of putting
it, but since you insist on having things so very
broadly—who is Prudence going to sit with, alone,
(there are just four people in the car, remember)
for this long drive? And, this is the question,
will she sit in the front seat or the back?"

"She will sit with Peter," Gus prophesied firmly,
"in the back seat. Naturally, the two young
men will want to sit together in the driving seat;
and, in any case, Peter will not care about sitting
with her brother——"

"Yes, but neither——" Miss Kat was beginning
triumphantly, for the second time, when her sister
interrupted her by announcing with finality:

"In any case, I shall settle nothing until I have
seen Oliver. Oliver always knows the right thing
to do."

"Yes indeed, dear Oliver," mused his other
affectionate sister, "of course we'll ask Oliver;
how stupid we were not to think of it before!"

"I," said Augusta coldly, "had intended to do
so from the first."

Kat sniffed again. It was her one, rather
monotonous, form of repartee. However, since she
knew that Gus knew that she knew the idea of
asking Oliver's advice had been an inspiration
born of the throes of argument, she felt that her
elder sister had not scored too complete a victory.
And the knowledge helped her to preserve a modi-

cum of dignity, as she got up from her chair, collected her multifarious belongings into several untidy heaps, and went out to attend to the Barnevelders' trap-nests.

In the soft dusk of the big hall, where all the light there was seemed to strike upwards from the old, carefully polished surfaces of the furniture, she met Prudence and Peter. She peered at her niece distressfully, in the half-light.

"What have you got on your legs *now?*" she asked fretfully.

"I've got waders on my legs *now*, Cousin Kat," returned Prudence with defiant virtue, born of the consciousness of a long-skirted mackintosh.

"Have you taken Cousin Oliver's waders without leave? Put them back in the rod-room immediately; this moment, please."

"Only, as it happens," Prudence's voice was bright with frosty politeness, "these waders don't belong to Cousin Oliver. They are James' waders."

"Do you mean to tell me that a cousin of *mine* could be guilty of such a low, horrible trick—to borrow a pair of trousers from a servant? Prudence, have you forgotten yourself utterly? Faugh! Why, a low woman of the streets—ugh!—of all disgusting . . ." Cousin Kat broke off, words literally failing her; while shudders of unaffected disgust chased one another down the outstanding ridges of her long, and slightly curved, spine.

"Well, Cousin Kat, as the waders were only given to James on his last birthday, he hasn't worn them yet—and won't, till the fishing begins next spring. Not that I'd care a d-ash, if he had," she concluded untruthfully and with more than a hint of defiance.

Kat had never succeeded in inspiring awe in any creature. Unless, indeed, awe describes the state of the Barnevelders' feelings when the trap-nests fell upon them during their consummation of the laws of nature. At any rate, beneath her reproofs, Prudence was never visited by that pa-ralysis of the powers of repartee, and indeed, of consecutive thought, which overcame her so devas-tatingly whenever Cousin Gus vented her wrath upon her. To-day, she swung upon her heel and left the hall without deigning to explain further.

Kat, still rooted in horror to the floor, saw her join Peter on the steps and watched the pair—preceded by two joyous terriers, and followed by the hound puppies, for once demure,—take their careless way down towards the river.

Peter was laughing at Prudence's rage.

" Why *do* you get angry, darling? It's such a wicked waste of energy. They're frightfully harm-less, really ; and you know you can generally get what you want out of them. *I* was taught from my youth up never to rux a hornet's nest."

" I don't stir them up. It's they who stir me up, till I feel like a good old hornet's nest, myself. All very well for you to talk, Peter. You only see them in snatches, when they're stupid, like Kat was just now. I have them *all* the time—day and night, breakfast, lunch and tea. They come and poke me out of the bathroom if they think I've been in it too long. They send me to bed at ten, every night ; and come in at half-past ten to take away my candles—at least, they do when they remember to ; I can never be sure they'll forget. I tell you, Peter, it's an awful life. If I could only read and write I'd go and do secretary to someone for the next two years. Only, I can't, and there's the hunting and "—she caught Peter's hand and squeezed it fervently—" little, darling you. Sweetheart, I can't bear to be parted from you for one single minute."

Peter returned the pressure of her hand without embarrassment ; then, dropping it and thrusting an arm through Prudence's, she muttered with deep feeling :

" My God, old girl, we have the *hell* of a good season in front of us. We'll ride some good hunts together yet."

Prudence nodded. Peter always saw life through such a good medium—their hunting. It was everything for each of them ; yet each enjoyed it in a different way.

For Prudence, a hunt was, from find to finish, one delirium of excitement. It was lucky that Oliver saw to it that she was adequately mounted ; for, when the fever of the chase raced in her blood, Prudence would have ridden (or endeavoured to ride) anything on four legs over almost any obstacle which God or man had seen fit to place in the line of country across which hounds were running ; not that she was altogether lacking in judgment ; but it was of a different order from a good many other people's. Also, she possessed the priceless gift—outcome only of an iron nerve—of riding a horse really well into its fences.

Peter was different. More of a purist than Prudence; the hounds and their work was her joy, her interest and delight. It supplied for her the poetry of existence. She rode a fast hunt well enough; but in a slow one, with hounds working out each yard of a stale and twisting line, almost walking after their fox, she was nearly as happy. While Prudence fretted and chafed, longing to get on, Peter—her eyes alight, alert for every whimper, watching, always watching—was content to see hound-work at its prettiest and most difficult. Her soul blasphemed in chorus with that of the huntsman, when his hounds were pressed upon; and was with him also in ecstasy when the line was hit off afresh after a successful cast.

The unmistakable tang of Autumn was in the air this afternoon. Peter sniffed it appreciatively as she sat on the river bank, searching her person for cigarettes. The smell of burning weeds hung on the faintly chill air. Across the river she saw the blue smoke rising from a pile of scutch-roots burning in a dusty, ploughed field; beyond the fire, she could see the low, quiet outline of a dim white house—the keeper's cottage, it was—and above, shelving gloriously to the pale sky, Lingarry woods blotted from sight the purple distance of the mountains.

She found her cigarette case; and her eyes travelled from its contents to Prudence, who had discarded her Burberry, and clad now in the waders and a rough woollen jumper, was sliding rapidly into the river.

" Look at, Miss Turrett," Peter called, " I'll join you when I have the cigarette smoked. Devil a mussel you'll get in that stream—let alone a pearl."

Prudence did not reply. They had come out pearl-fishing ; and she, personally, was going to wade for mussels. It was chilly work, even with James' waders. She wondered how Peter, who had said she would wade in her knickers and tennis shoes, would enjoy herself.

Staring absorbed through her glass-bottomed bucket into the golden, dark water, Prudence would plunge down an arm and pick up stone after stone, in mistake for the dark, elusive mussel shells. It was a maddening game, only fascinating for the first five minutes. From time to time she would call to Peter, who had now waded across to the opposite bank, and was slowly working her way up-stream, prosaic blue bockers pulled over her tweed skirt :

" How many have you got ? "

Peter at first shook her head, but later she held up two fingers and then a third and a fourth. Soon she called out :

" I've got twelve, now. Shall we open them ? "

" Oh, Peter—*no !* I haven't got *one*, yet. We will when I have." Prudence dived her arm in again, cursing when the sleeve of her jumper unrolled itself in the water ; but this time she did pull out an ancient and hoary shell-fish. " Right, now ! " she screamed across to Peter ; and splashing out of the water, she scrambled up the bank, and sat down to prise the shell open—rather impeded by her still bandaged hand. Peter had the knife in her pocket ; but to wait was perfect torture to Prudence. She broke a stick and cut her other hand before she prised the shells apart and with an eager forefinger explored the mucous consistency of the unhappy fish within.

An instant later she sprang to her feet, almost sick with excitement, and shrilled across to Peter :

" Puppy ! Puppy — I — gotta — whoppin'—*pearl !* Quick—come over. I believe it's *pink.*"

Peter, when she got across, found her fellow fisher of pearls sitting on her haunches, breathing hard with excitement over something that she held on the wet, pink palm of her right hand, the wrist supported by her left. She tilted up an eager face to Peter, bending down over her shoulder.

" Is it, Peter ? Is it ? "

Peter picked up the pearl between careful finger and thumb.

" Yes, it's a topper," she declared. " A pink one, too. How marvellous ! I am glad." She fingered it curiously ; then gave it back. " It's lovely. Let's slice mine open ; we may have hit on a bed that hasn't been disturbed for years." She produced a knife and slitting each shell, probed them, one by one, fruitlessly.

" What a shame, Peter ! However, we'll go shares with this one. We ought to get a bit for it, you know."

Peter shook her head vehemently.

" Rot ! my dear girl, it's easily the best you've got, so far. You mustn't dream of selling it. That makes four pink ones you've got, now."

"Six," corrected Prudence, "with the one Toby gave me."

"Did Toby give you a pearl? You never told me about that."

"Didn't I? I meant to;" Prudence became a trifle confused; "yes, it's quite a nice one. I'll show it to you." She sought for and opened her green enamel cigarette case, which held everything in the world, except cigarettes. From it she produced a small screw of soft paper that yielded to Peter's eager gaze a pink pearl, almost as good as the one which Prudence had just found. She compared the two minutely. Meanwhile, Prudence smoothed out the piece of tissue paper, and removed a photograph from the cigarette case to a pocket of her jumper.

When both pearls had been replaced in the green case, Peter rose to her feet. Kicking her empty shells back into the river, she lit a cigarette.

"Well," she said philosophically, "it's a little bit of life, it is. I find twelve mussels, you get one ewe-lamb, and there's the pearl, if you get *me*."

Prudence, still caressing her cigarette case, nodded—wordless.

"Darling, don't let's go on fishing. James' waders are leaking in the seat, or else it's that sharp rock I sat on. Let's find a really decent spot and crack."

Peter, putting on her stockings, agreed. At the same time, a relentless voice within her argued aggressively that had she, and not Prudence, been the one to find the pearl, Prudence would have obliged her to wade and amass shells until the petrifaction of her nether limbs was an accomplished fact. However, as a prickling glow of warmth ascended her legs as she donned her stockings, a like glow, of joy in Prudence's company, ran like gladness through her heart. She pulled her skirt out of the bloomers, smoothing down its wrinkles over her ample thighs.

Prudence's eyes, watching her, grew troubled :
"Oh Lord, Puppy ! I wish I was a bit fatter."

"Why on earth ? I ride over ten stone, you ride nine nothing. What more do you want ? "

Prudence surveyed the firm, full curves of Peter's body with an appraising eye. But what she said was :

"Great bone, haven't you ? That's what really weighs."

Peter considered her legs ruefully. "Um, yes. I carry it low down, too. But don't talk as if I had hips like a stallion ; it distresses me too terribly."

Prudence laughed. "Darling, you know you're absurd."

There was silence for a time. They left the river bank and mounted the rising ground towards their destination—a scrubby thicket of hazel, which caught and held all there was of the slanting afternoon sunlight. Within its sheltered warmth, Prudence—her back propped against one of the more stable of the hazel growths—continued the conversation between spasms of nut-cracking.

"Personally, Peter, I think it's eight times more attractive to be fat. I read a book by Anatole

France, the other day, and all the women in it
were positively bursting."

Peter, whose reading did not include the works
of Anatole France, nevertheless criticised the same
with some adequacy.

" Filth ! " she pronounced.

" No, wonderful." Prudence corrected her.
" Both, perhaps ; but his words are too marvellous,
like bridges built across—you know ? "

Peter, who was not interested in the subject,
cracked and ate nuts, while Prudence dreamed.
A rude shock awoke her.

" Puppy, you greedy brute ! You've eaten all
the nuts. How could you ? "

" Have a cigarette instead," suggested Miss
Trudgeon composedly, " nuts are awfully thin-
ning—didn't you know ? "

Prudence lit her cigarette, expelling a cloud of
smoke to extinguish the match.

" Peter, darling—I notice you're distinctly progressing with little Antonio, master of chasse," she
observed ; there was ever so slight an edge on her
voice, and anxiety to observe the effect of her
speech written plainly on her face for Peter to
read.

Peter looked up steadily. " If you mean by
' progressing ' that I'm getting off as hard as you
are with Toby Sage, you're quite wrong." She
flicked the ash expertly off her cigarette. " You
are, you know. Aren't you, Prudence ? "

Prudence grew pink up to the eyes.

" What rot, Peter ! " she defended herself hastily,
" I *like* Toby, all right ; he's quite fun and jolly

useful ; besides, he's the only man Kat and Gus allow near the place. But, honestly, I don't *care* for him—sure wouldn't I tell you if I did ? " She pulled hard on her cigarette. " Do you think," she added ingenuously, " that he likes *me* ? "

Peter laughed—a rich chuckle. The counter-charge had been so extraordinarily successful. " Oh, Prudence, my pet, he likes messing round with you, I suppose, or he wouldn't *do* it."

" He doesn't ' mess,' Peter. He never touches me."

" No ? I shouldn't have thought he was one of the mauling sort," Peter became a little thoughtful. " Are you in love with him ? " she asked directly.

" Oh, *I* dunno," Prudence was busily pulling off her waders. " What's it like—love ? "

" How can I tell you ? Well, I suppose if you were in love with him you wouldn't mind him messing you up to—to any extent."

Prudence, the waders half off, clasped her face in her hands and swayed her body from the waist upwards ; then made evil faces, as though there was a bad taste in her mouth.

" I should just hate it," she announced fervently, " in fact, I wouldn't let him, you know. I'd scream, or lock my door, or something. I hate Toby now. Why did you say that, Peter ? "

" My dear ass, I don't imagine he thinks of you in that way at all. Toby ! Toby only plays about with girls, he doesn't fall in love with them. Doesn't know how."

Prudence renewed her struggles with the waders. When she was at last clear of their encumbrance :

" I thought you said he liked me ? " she observed aggrievedly.

Peter didn't even smile ; she knew and loved Prudence so well, and understood her as completely as it was possible for anyone to understand the shifts and charms of such a nature.

" Do you think the girls will let you come and look at the harriers ? " she asked. " You must, Prudence. We'd have *rather* fun."

" Good God, yes ! I'd die twenty deaths to go," Prudence laced her hands about her knees and gazed raptly at Peter. " Just think what fun we'd have. Do you think these harriers are a scheme, Peter ? "

" I think they're a very good scheme, and badly needed in the country too. But they jolly nearly didn't happen."

" What d'you mean ? " Prudence was consumed by curiosity.

" Oh, didn't I tell you yet ? It was the best bit of crack I had, I s'pose that's why I nearly forgot it. Anthony came over to Kilronan—the same day you distinguished yourself with poor Zookie—he came to look at a horse. Mervyn was out, somewhere," she drew on her cigarette with little jerky puffs, " so I went with him to see the horse. And in the course of conversation——" she slid her eyes round to see if Prudence had noticed this.

" Oh, so he did talk, did he ? How surprising ! " observed Prudence sourly.

" Yes, he talked away. Well, in the course of conversation, he asked me if there were many hares in the country. I couldn't think why he was so interested in the subject till he told that Toby had written to him about hunting harriers one day a-week in Knockderry. Even then, it took me a minute to tumble to it," Peter chuckled. " It took him longer still to digest the fact that *harriers* hunt foxes only in this heathen land. When he did, his state of mind was simply pitiable."

" What was it like ? "

" Like stomach-ache, I should think. I tried to make him see light, and he went away to sleep on it."

" D'you mean he was going to stop Toby hunting hounds ? "

" No, he won't do that."

" How d'you know ? Has he said so ? You never can tell with these little prigs of Saxons."

" They may be prigs, but they mean what they say, and stick to it all right." Peter ached to add : " And as a matter of fact, he's not half such a prig as your little pal, Tobioh," but judged it more politic to withhold the opinion ; especially when the dogs, bursting frenziedly through briars, at that moment joined the party, with effusive explanations of their delay.

" Dilly, I don't believe you for a moment. Why lie to Mother ? You smell all dead sheep ! How *could* you say it was a water-hen ? Yah ! nasty. *Dead !* Oh, no, Mother didn't love—no, *never* did——"

Dilly, scraping her tummy abjectly on the ground, craved remission of the smacking she so richly deserved.

"God! Don't they stink? No, go away, Blazes! You're simply foul." Prudence rose to her feet—a dryad of the hazel-grove. Blazes (the pet fawn) she repulsed with evil words. "Wherever the carcass is, we'll have to find it," she announced, "or the puppies will roll till midnight. What a bore! What are you going to the spring for? Thirsty? I'm sure that water's bad."

Peter squatted above the low-sunk well:

"I'm just washing out Dilly's mouth—Mother's little dog is quite unkissable at present." She accomplished the task with diligence and the use of many dock leaves; then, producing her own vivid little shingle comb, ran it carefully through Dilly's side-whiskers. Dilly took it all as a matter of course, if not of necessity; only shuddering slightly when the water got up her nose the wrong way. She was a very human little dog, of almost over-developed character—after all, Peter had loved her for close on three years.

Prudence caught Blazes.

"I think we'll get our face washed too—darling," she announced. But Blazes, freeing herself with a sudden and skilful wriggle, got clear away, and slunk off into the fastnesses of the brambles, tail well down.

"Oh, bad luck to her! Let her *stay* dirty then, if she won't be pleasant about it. Come on, Puppy, these pups have got to be found." She led the way out of the pleasant place of hazels and waited in the field for Peter.

"Gorgon! Gossip! *Gossip!* Come-away-the-little-bitches! Pups! Pups! Pups! Curse the

little brutes ! Half my life is spent looking for
them, and the rest of it goes getting into rows
for the mischief they do." Prudence was distinctly
put out. She called again, and descended the hill
still calling.

"They've gone home by themselves, probably,"
Peter suggested. "Let's do the same and have tea."

"Peter, *darling*, that's just what I want, an' I
didn't know. *Tea*—and of course they've gone
home—Come on ! I'm simply weak with hunger.
I couldn't think why I felt so cross." She strode
out across the fields towards the house at a swift,
driving pace which hopelessly out-classed Peter's
slouching gait. But Peter did not fuss herself to
keep up ; she lagged, so soon Prudence slowed
down. They went arm-in-arm over the short
grass ; climbing a fence and two fishing stiles in
single file ; and talking all the time ; slow unforced
remarks ; questions and answers ; almost wholly
without point—disjointed and familiar.

"I think your hair wants a trim, Puppy."

"Mm. Boodie took the small hand clippers to
it the other day—hasn't done it a lot of good."

"Oh, do tell me—how did Boodie's party at
the Shelbourne go off ? "

"Yes, that was *too* nice. He came into my
room yesterday morning, radiant. I said, ' Hullo !
did she let you kiss her in the car coming home ? '
' She let me hold her hand,' he said, ' and here's
your ten shillings by the way.' I was awfully
surprised. I said, ' Didn't the dinner come off ?
What a *shame !* ' ' Oh *yes !* ' said Boodie, quite
delighted with himself, ' it was grand—*Toppin*'.

You see there was a waiters' strike on, so I could only get her tea and bread and butter. Wasn't it luck ? ' "

" How perfect," Prudence breathed, " too good to laugh at, almost. . . . Shall we have lunch in Dublin if we go with Toby ? "

" Expect so. If we go. They're *bound* to let you go, Prudence."

" Yes, sure to. Let's be awfully nice and polite at tea. Wipe your feet on the mat, for a start, Peter. I see Gus looking out of the window to see if we do." They had reached the porch now, and scraped their shoes with vigour.

In the dining-room an excellent tea was ready. Tea was a meal which Gus thoroughly under-stood. Therefore, on the white cloth-covered table (the fashion of bare mahogany did not prevail at Lingarry) were many good and pleasant things to eat. There were honey and blackberry jam ; the butter—made daily—tasted like Devonshire cream. There was griddle bread, and little flat hot cakes that you might butter for yourself, as thickly as you pleased. A great fruit-cake gaped richly beneath its pent-house of almond paste ; and brandy snaps curled, thin as paper and a little greasy, on an old blue and white patterned plate. In the centre of the table a huge silver cup, engraved with a good horse's name, held late-flowering roses—quantities of them.

Peter sat down beside Miss Gus, who was pouring out tea.

" The big tea-cup belongs to Prudence, doesn't it ? " she said, handing things. " Didn't you get

it for her to have for after-hunting teas? She told
me. Do you know, Miss Lingfield, when I envy
Prudence awfully? After a long day's hunting,
when I know she's coming back to one of your
teas—and I'm not. I am greedy, aren't I?"

But Gus smiled on her indulgently, begging her
to eat; pleased that Peter should appreciate her
teas, which were something of an effort—especially
with the new cook, who was not nearly so good
as their late unfortunate. . . . Peter had heard
about that? *Too awful*, wasn't it?

At the other end of the table Kat was squeaking
with excitement over Prudence's pearl. She was
nearly as thrilled and excited as if she had found
it herself. She looked at it in every light, and
then dropped it into her tea-cup—the contents of
which were, fortunately, cold. However, its rescue
and restoration to its owner provided some thrilling
moments.

"So lucky," Kat said, "that it was tea—not
vinegar, like the lady in the poem."

"What happened to her, Cousin Kat?"

"Well, really, I haven't read it since I was a
girl and it is quite confused in my mind. But
at any rate, that proves it."

"Yes, Cousin Kat," said Prudence, instead of
saying, "Proves what?" and she had her reward.

"Proves that pearls do melt, you know," explained Miss Kat, triumph in her tone. Nobody
contradicted her.

Half-an-hour later, replete and smoking a Balkan
Sobranie which Miss Gus had herself abstracted
from the silver box in Oliver's study, Peter joined

Prudence in front of the house ; together they went round to the yard to get Peter's cob.

"Well, did she say anything ? I left you alone on purpose to give her a chance," Prudence asked eagerly.

Peter nodded, expelling a rich cloud of expensive smoke.

"She said, ' I am quite ready to let Prudence go, so long as *you* (that's me) are in the party. I know you have some sense '——"

"So have I," put in Prudence.

" ' And I can trust you to see that Prudence behaves properly,' " finished Peter, without heeding the interruption.

"Well, I'm blowed ! Does she expect me to produce a kitten, nine months from the day I drive fifty miles alone with a young man ? Evil-minded old tripe ! "

"Now, Prudence, you're being absurd. You've practically got leave to go—by the way, she said, ' I must ask my brother first, of course ' . . . for goodness sake don't put them off it in any way."

"I don't know that I want to go," said Prudence, defiant and sulky. " ' Behave properly,' I like that ! Why can't she trust *me ?* Suspicious old fool. I jolly well won't go."

"Darling, don't be wicked and naughty. Your eyes are getting perfectly black with rage. I know you'll rush in and have a frightful burst with them over something, and then get forbidden to go. And you did say you'd come, for my sake, precious. I'd hate each moment without you. In fact, I don't think Ma would let me go. You'll *try* to come, won't you ? "

" All right, Peter. If you really want me——" Prudence assented loftily. But she stood silent and abstracted, hands linked behind her back, while Peter climbed gingerly on to an over-fed pony of Mervyn's—mad to get home, after her afternoon's incarceration in a strange stable. Prudence grinned as the pony dived out of the yard gates, and simulating panic at some harmless object in the laurel hedge, plunged crabbedly, and did her valiant best to take the avenue at a useful gallop. Ponies and cobs had such amusing ways with them, she thought. And that was a nice shaped little thing of Mervyn's. Peter had her walking now ; but her back was still up, like an egg. Prudence, when she had watched them out of sight, sauntered slowly towards the kitchen regions ; it was time to see about the puppies' suppers.

Still ruminating with growing bitterness on the suspicious and untrusting natures of her guardians, she wandered aimlessly into the scullery and proceeded to amass scraps for the puppies' supper. It was a job she loathed. But the new cook was not to be bribed or coerced into preparing meals for either dogs or cats ; both species of animals being, so she stoutly averred, the scrapings of Hell. She was an intractable creature of a stolid disposition ; it was, therefore, with some surprise that Prudence, as she rummaged in the scullery, heard long wails, interspersed with snuffling sobs, coming from the direction of the kitchen. Outbreaks of the kind—so usual in the days of Mary—

were an unfamiliar occurrence of late. Perhaps it
was one of the other servants—probably bewailing
the falsity of man's nature. But no. That was
certainly the cook's nasal voice, rendered still more
muffled in timbre by the sobs which impeded her
utterance.

" I'll not stop in it," Prudence heard ; nor was
she surprised. Gus had a way of changing her
cooks with alarming frequency.

" No, nor I wouldn't stop another night in it—
not with the like o' *that* about——" Sobs.

" No, but look-at, what you should do, Mrs.
Kelly, is to knock the bed down, and put it up in
Bridgie's room. That'd be like company for you,"
suggested the voice of Maggie, the housemaid, in
low tones of conspiracy.

" O-my-God-is-it-sleep-in-that-bed ? " came Mrs.
Kelly's voice, in a hyphened crescendo of horror.
" I wouldn't lie to ye," she continued in more
hushed tones, " but there's a dizzy sickness on me
all day after. Me stomach's bad," she averred
imperiously, her tears forgotten in the recitation
of her bodily ills, " I feels like I had a combulsion
o' the brain, after the womp I knocked out o'
the floor ; there's a confusion of blood in me left
arm ; me heart shifted——"

" Oh, great God above ! " chorused the recipients
of this alarming account in awful unison, and their
voices sank forthwith to whispers.

Prudence, suddenly realizing that she was doing
something very like eaves-dropping, clattered the
puppies' dishes before tearing off down the many
dark passages to James' pantry.

James was cleaning silver, an employment that his soul abhorred ; therefore Prudence sought to humour him by picking up a spoon and a leather. Seating herself on the corner of the table, she said :

"Oh, James, thanks most awfully for the loan of the waders ; they were topping. Wait till I show you the grand pearl I got," she dropped her spoon, produced her cigarette case, and passing over the screw of paper to James, awaited his comment.

"Faith, that's as nice a pearl as any ever I seen," he pronounced judicially. "Bedom, luck'll folly you, Miss Prudence, whatever ye do. But this other little fella "—he held Toby's pearl up to the light to look at it better—"That's a pearl Micky Grogan got a month past, and young Mr. Sage give him two pound for it. Sure if he'd been ruled by me, he'd have got five pounds for it—no less. Yes, in Dublin. He would, faith !" as Prudence looked sceptical.

"The waders were *excellent*, James," she announced as she put away her pearls, and resumed work on the spoon.

"Ah, thim's a right snug invention," James admitted, "sure in the wettest water ye'd be as cosy with them yokes on ye as if ye were in the bed itself. Wait till I has a twenty-pound salmon, now, taking me down-stream—then I'll know their value. Wasn't Mr. Oliver, now," he continued affably, "very nice. To say he'd give me these for me birt'-day. Nor I didn't forget the nice flannel vests and pants yerself gave me, agin the

bronchitis. But Miss Gus "—he lowered his voice
and spoke behind the soup-ladle he was cleaning—
" it's six years last October since she tore the face
off me—an' all I done was to ask her for a little
breeches. Now ! " James nodded his head vigorously, as much as to say, " What do you think of
that for a just and innocent request ? "

" I say, James," Prudence dropped all pretence
of helping him to clean the silver, " there was
the most awful row going on in the kitchen, when
I was getting the pups' food just now. The cook
was roaring crying, and she had some long story
made up about her bed. What the dickens is
the matter ? All the maids are in there, drinking
tea and whispering away like mad."

" And how would I know what'd ail a nest o'
women, the like o' that ? " demanded James.
" Ye'd want to be a fairy before ye could say what
has them the way they are."

" Then they *are* upset about something ? "
Prudence demanded swiftly.

" Well now," James' tones grew confidential,
" I'll not conceal it from you, Miss Prudence,
they're a little unaisy."

" ' Uneasy ' ? But why, James ? What's the
matter with them ? "

" Ah, sure where's the sense o' talkin' ? " James
demanded pathetically of the spoons he was collecting and laying, in serried ranks, upon a tray.
" There's things will happen, and—believe you
me, Miss Prudence—the less said about them, the
better for all. Ah, they generally always passes
over," he added lightly ; then, with an ominous

shake of his head : "Though there's troubles in some places ye'll *never better*. No, nor ever lay, and them that meddles with them has long sorrow, after."

James had picked up his tray of silver and started for the door, when Prudence, white and shaken, caught at his arm.

"You're a horrible old man, James," she said, speaking with a ghastly attempt at lightness, "*I* don't know what you're talking about—always making a mystery out of something, aren't you ? You're six times worse than the maids, yourself."

"I am, may be——" James cast one lightning look at Prudence. Then, changing the subject said casually :

"D'ye know, Miss Prudence, them pups o' yours is below in the ash plantation this two hours. Sure the sheep wire around it has them baffled altogether."

"Well, James, as you're so clever as to know where they are, I do wish you'd go down and let them out—yes, and give them their supper too. I, I have a little job to do for Miss Gus."

"And what about James ? " demanded that gentleman, with a hint of asperity. "Haven't he one-hundred-and-one little jobs to do for Miss Gus ? God is my witness, Miss Prudence, the feet is bet up under me this living minyute, and how I'll stand out the length o' dinner in the boots is unknown to me. Send Michael after the dogs. I have work enough to do tending Christians, let alone the like o' them outlaws."

Still muttering, James hobbled off down the passage, Prudence close in his wake. At the dining-room door she parted from him, with strict injunctions that Michael was to be sent immediately, and with all possible secrecy, on his mission of rescue. Then she went off in search of Kat, or Gus. She did not care which she found, so long as she did not have to endure her own company till dinner time.

"Michael, go bring the two dishes o' food out to Miss Prudence's puppies. They're shut in the far loose-box," directed James, ten minutes later. To himself he added, "Aha, I knew well the devil himself wouldn't get her to the plantation ash by dusk light. Well, isn't she very frightful? I declare, ye'd have to laugh."

·   ·   ·   ·   ·

Purple dusk fell into night. Stars bloomed in in a frostless sky. Prudence gazed out of a drawing-room window, hypnotised by the dark tree-shapes, strangely blotted against the sky. An absurd, childish dread of the darkness without seizing her, she dropped the curtain back quickly, looking with relief towards the lamp-lit table where Kat and Gus sat, wrangling over the matching of embroidery silks.

After an hour, spent with her back to the turf fire, she had forgotten her unformed fears. She took up her bedroom candle with not more than her usual reluctance.

"Good night, Cousin Gus."

"Good night, Cousin Kat."

"Don't delay in the bathroom, Prudence."

"Hold your candle straight, dear. You're spilling the grease on the carpet."

As she went slowly upstairs, Prudence remembered, with a faint stirring of anger, her indignation of the early evening against her guardians. How *had* she forgotten it? Ah, she knew now. With a rush, memory swooped on her.

The darkness of the scullery; the servants' hushed voices and hysterical sobbing; James' half-veiled hints; what had they all meant? What had James said to her the other day? "When you meet blood in the woods of Lingarry . . . not a nice sign . . . trouble, trouble after."

One hand at her throat, and the candle tilted, guttering, in the other, Prudence stood suddenly still and rigid on the staircase. Little, separate, running shudders passed trickling over her body; leaving her, not cold, but sweating, shaking, terrified. "Mary. It was Mary, of course. *Walking*. . . ."

Prudence threw one long, agonising look over her shoulder; then, sobs shaking her, choking in her throat, she ran, stumbling and crying, down the corridor to her room.

CHAPTER VIII

TOBY'S HARRIERS

" TIM HEARN did a right job on those benches,"
asserted Toby contentedly. He stood at the door
of one of the well-built houses in which his father
had once kennelled the Drumferris Fox-hounds,
regarding with pleasure the completion of his
preparations for the harriers' reception.

" Did you get that cow from Jackie Ryan ? " he
asked the henchman who attended him.

" She got better, Master Dominick," was the
illuminating reply. " And the old donkey I had
marked down in me own mind for soup, they
whipped it to the other hounds on me. But sure
I'll have to see and get some flesh before them
fellas'll come ; though there's a great scarcity
of things dying in the country now, whatever way
it is."

" Well, you'd better have something ready for
them, Jim, for they mightn't be above making a
chop at yourself—as old and tough as you are,"
with which pleasantry Toby sauntered back to
the house. Donning an overcoat of a rather wonderful brown colour, he found the hat that blended
with it most surprisingly, and took his way round
to the garage.

He drove fast all the way to Lingarry ;
purposely going there first, that he might have
the three miles on to Kilronan in Prudence's
unadulterated society. As he drove, he studied
his bare, brown hands on the wheel, with
absorbed attention ; his mind interestedly concerned with what the day might bring forth.
He knew he would want to kiss Prudence (and
would probably do it, too) before they got home
that night.

Prudence's entire lack of response made this
faintly progressing affair with her more amusing
for Toby than any of his previous experiences,
when things had been so easy for him as to render
attainment puerile. And never before had a flirtation of his prolonged itself in the subtle stage of
doubtfulness for so long—for four months, nearly,
he had jested, played and flirted, just a little, with
Prudence. Not once had she shown the faintest
shade of the emotion he aroused so fatally in most
girls ; it was amazing and intriguing. But if her
marvellous coolness intrigued him so deeply, what,
he wondered, would she be like if he could touch
and hold her, school that daring, red mouth to
helpless submission ?

He simply didn't know. And for Toby, that
was the whole fascination of the thing. In all
their friendship he had never found her twice the
same ; maddening, one day—the next, adorable.
Dreaming, sulky, despondent or madly jesting,
the only stable thing about her was her strange
beauty ; and that had the quality of flowing
water—the same changing changelessness.

As he sent his car along Toby's thoughts were something like this :

" I'll have to mount one whip, I suppose. I'll enlist Prudence to turn hounds to me too. She didn't seem too keen when I told her, she'd *do* it all right though . . . now, if I'd asked Betty Kane or Judy they'd've been all over me at once. She's a funny kid—those old aunts are rum birds. How they'd hate it. *I* don't want to kiss her. . . yes, I do, though. I'd like to hold her . . . Jove, that's not a nice sound I hear. Nut loose, perhaps. No, it's in the engine. H'm, must take her round to the garage during lunch. That van ought to take twelve and a half couples all right. Gad, I should have some fun with these harriers. . . . Shall I manage to get Prudence to sit with me, there and back? Peter's all right. Does she let that little stick, Anthony Countless, make love to her? Girls are all alike, of course— except one. And a pity she doesn't take after the rest. Just the sort to go to the bad when she comes into all that money, the *deuce* of a lot of it. She'll make it fly, though . . . wild as a hawk. . . . *Someone* ought to look after her a bit. . . ." And by the time he had turned the car in front of Lingarry steps, the thought that he must manage to have Prudence beside him, alone, had obliterated all the other shifting swarm of ideas from his mind.

He had forgotten Blazes. Prudence stood on the steps holding the end of a long, red strap that branched out into innumerable other straps, which were wreathed round Blazes's skimpy little body.

Prudence's mouth was down at the corners, her face was drawn and haggard with misery.

" I don't want to come," she announced, almost before the car had stopped.

" Oh, well—don't come, then," Toby would not for worlds have shown that he was surprised and hurt. A trifle of annoyance he did permit himself. " If I'd known you weren't coming I'd have saved myself five miles and gone straight to Kilronan."

" I *am* coming, I *must* come—I promised Peter."

" You promised *me*, too, you know," Toby reminded her, " but I suppose that's a matter of very little consequence. Well, as you *are* coming, suppose you hop in now."

" Jump in, Prudence—jump in ! " commanded Cousin Gus. Alert and swathed in veils, she too came down the steps.

" Good God ! " Toby was horror-struck. Surely the old lady was not coming too. Anyway, there was no room. What could he say ? He advanced uncertainly, and shook Miss Gus's admirably gloved hand. " Er——" he began.

" Jump in, Prudence," repeated Miss Gus, with a faint flavour of asperity. " Good morning, Dominick. A lovely day for your drive. I wonder if you would be so very kind as to take me with you as far as Kilronan village ? I have shopping to do there, and Oliver will drive me home later on."

" *Rather !* Of course—yes——" Prudence, he noticed, had climbed sulkily into the back seat, towing the unwilling Blazes after her—" Yes, that will be toppin'," he finished futilely. " Oh, good morning, Miss Kat. I say, you know there *are* rugs in the car. Let me take some of these."

" Can't have enough. Get your deaths of cold," gasped Miss Kat who, staggering beneath her burden of heavy rugs, was cautiously descending the steps. She refused to relinquish any of them ; approaching the car, she climbed into the front seat, and bending over, endeavoured to envelop Prudence in a heavy green plaid.

" I don't *want* it, Cousin Kat."

" Don't be a silly girl—always thinking of your appearance ; if that doesn't *prove* it, what does ? " Leaning over to tuck the rug more closely about her ward, Kat lost her balance, lurched forward, saving a header by a grasp at the back of the seat, and crimson in the face from her exertions, stepped backwards. As she did so, she inadvertently placed the large, flat heel of her house shoe upon the knob of the self-starter.

" Get off it ! " screamed Prudence.

" Take your foot off," suggested Toby more mildly.

" Grr-errr-errrr," went the self-starter.

" What is it ? Where ? What ? " shrilled Miss Kat, quite unable to understand anything, save that the noise, created somehow by her agency, was a dangerous one, and " the thing " might " go off " at any moment. Paralysed by fright, and determined not to leave Prudence's side in the moment of danger, she continued to stand on the self-starter.

It was Miss Gus who rushed at her sister and pulled her bodily out of the car. She then turned furiously upon Toby :

" The *idea* of leaving a motor so that it might
go off at any moment. I never ! I should have
thought, Dominick, you might have exercised a
little more care. But you young people are all
alike—no consideration. When I *think* that Kat
and Prudence might be drowning in the pond at
this moment ! "

Toby looked at the angry lady in mild amazement. Plainly, apology, not explanation, was
indicated to stem the flowing tide of her wrath.

" Awfully sorry. Swear I won't do it again,
Miss Gus. Frightfully careless of me. Er, shall
we start ? "

Gus, as she settled herself beside him, swathing
her body in some of Miss Kat's supernumerary
rugs, felt that she had, perhaps, been a trifle harsh
in her admonishment of one who, after all, was
not a relation. Therefore, as they swung smoothly
out of the gate :

" And is *this* what you call a Ford ? " she asked
brightly and with becoming intelligence.

Toby's surprise rendered him dumb for a moment.
He accelerated so that their rate of progression
mounted with some rapidity from twenty-five to
forty m.p.h.

" No," he said at last, " not, not quite."

" Ah," observed Miss Gus, cheerfully consoling,
" I daresay it's a very nice car all the same. And
what a lot of little taps and wheels you have in
front. How do you remember what they are all
for ? "

" You get quite used to them," answered Toby,
with divine patience. Then, looking over the back

164

of the seat : " Are you all right, Prudence ? Have another rug, won't you ? "

Prudence's reply was muffled ; but decidedly she did not want another rug.

In the village they dropped Miss Gus. She thanked Toby for her drive and took a cautionarily affectionate farewell of her ward. As her tall figure disappeared into a grocer's shop, Toby leaned across to Prudence.

" Nip over the back," he said, " won't you, Prudence ? "

Prudence shook her head. " It's hardly worth while is it ? " she asked, with an attempt at *hauteur* which was unsuccessfully sulky, " we've just got to drive up the avenue."

Toby said nothing. But as he turned the car, the crashing and grinding of his gears spoke for him.

Prudence sat bolt upright in the back seat ; miserably aware that she was spoiling all her own fun and making Toby bad-tempered too. Well, it was entirely the girls' fault. Their consent to the expedition obtained, with it had also been received a lecture on *nice* and *nasty* behaviour with young men that had left Prudence in a very flame of wrath and vague discomfort. It spoilt things so—all this endless and exasperating stress which they laid so painstakingly on her virginity. For, really, it amounted to that and nothing else. And Prudence hated to be reminded that young men could ever be more than good friends in their relations with her. Well, they wanted to kiss you, occasionally, but never in a way that counted—

or at any rate it had never counted with Prudence, any more than Cousin Kat's matutinal salute did. Love, passion and the world well lost, they were all empty words to her. Gus's half hints and vague warnings only served to make Prudence feel cross and conscious in Toby's company. In her wisdom, Gus had indeed succeeded in awakening a measure of sex-consciousness which, like a barbed entanglement of mushroom growth, for the moment effectually separated Prudence and Toby.

At Kilronan, Toby, ignoring his passenger, climbed sulkily out of the car and pushed the bell.

Mervyn, struggling into a coat, called greetings from inside the hall ; and Peter, ably tailor-made to-day, in a ling-coloured tweed, shapely cromwellian brogues on her large feet, came down the steps to talk to Prudence.

Toby came behind her and spun her slowly round by the shoulders.

"Admirable suitings," he commended, interrupting something that Prudence was saying, "devilish good, they are."

"What ? I hate that cloth, Puppy. All flecks ; looks as if the hens had been peckin' it," thus Prudence from the car. "It'd be all right if you took it out to the yard and got them to run the clippers over it. As it is——" she broke off and began to collect rugs, throwing them on to the gravel. "Take these in, Toby, we shan't have an inch of room."

"Thanks." Toby would have liked to shake her till she cried. "But d'you mind, if you must throw the rugs about, throwing your own, not mine.

I *hate* the idea of gravel-rash," he added pathetically as he stooped to collect the scattered rugs,
and to shake (with what he felt to be mis-applied
energy) the loose sand and pebbles from their
folds. He would so much rather have given
Prudence the shaking for which she was spoiling.

"Peter," he said, turning to deposit Kat's
contributions to the expedition in the hall, "sit
with me up to Dublin, will you? I've got some
things to discuss with you—rather important."

Peter agreed; having done so she knew better
than to remain in Prudence's stormy company.
So with a despairing cry: " *Cigarettes*—my God!"
she dashed back into the house. "*I* don't want
any of her d—d nappiness," she decided. "What
can have upset the child like this? It's not altogether Gus. There's always something else at the
back of these moods—the thing she won't tell
you about generally. . . ."

On the way up to Dublin she wondered what
it could be. Also, what was the matter of vast
importance that Toby wished to discuss with her?
For he sat almost silent by her side, intensely pre-
occupied with his driving. Peter did not feel the
silence to be any sort of strain; she leant back
in her seat, tranquil and unbothered. Having
long ago come to the conclusion that young men
did not sparkle in her company, she very wisely
restrained all impulse in herself to sparkle in theirs;
and left matters at a satisfactorily comfortable
companionship.

These companionships were many. Brilliant
young men liked Peter, because she gave them

time to make their cleverest remarks. Lazy men liked her because she never attempted to stir them to energy. Non-dancing men sought her out fearlessly, for she never tried to drag them to hunt-balls ; and dancing men always danced with her because, though a trifle on the sticky side as a partner, she was such a rest to sit out with.

Two men had loved her, not passionately, but comfortably and securely ; and though Peter had shaken her head sadly at their proposals (she had no mind to become the wife either of a struggling younger son colonist, or a penniless foot-soldier) she still wrote to each of them, regularly once a month ; one letter to Canada and one to India ; and heard from both by nearly every mail.

Peter's secret and unconfessed fear was this : That no man would ever love her with the passion of which she read in books. For, beneath the outward phlegm of her nature, Peter loved herself, a few people, some animals and her idea of perfect marriage with a flaming ardour, the height and depth and strength of which she was not herself quite aware.

To-day, she smoked a vast number of cigarettes as she sat, unheedful of the silent and preoccupied young man beside her, and half attentive to the snatches of badinage occasionally audible from the back seat. Obviously, Prudence was recovering her poise ; of this she was more than glad. It would be too awful if that deplorable fit of sulks had continued further into the day. Prudence in a bad temper could, and sometimes did, success-fully spoil any party ; when in the right mood

she could make the dullest affair go from start
to finish.

As they drove through the suburbs and into
Dublin the almost uninterrupted flow of eager and
serious talk in the back of the car argued well
for Prudence's return to a state of grace. Peter
screwed her head round, for the first time during
the drive.

" What's the matter, children ? " she asked.

Prudence leaned forward eagerly ; her eyes
grave beneath the brim of her small hat.

" I've made up my mind," she said, " Mervyn's
going to hold my hand."

The car swerved a little in passing a tram-car.
" Sorry ! " said Toby.

" How nice "—Peter answered Prudence—" for
how long ? "

" For all the time he's doing it, of course."

" Yes, I suppose so. But when, and where ? "

" I don't know the address. But Mervyn says
it's a quiet little place—you'd never guess."

" It's the place you go to, Peter," Mervyn put in.

" I *don't*," Peter said indignantly. " I don't
know what you mean. Do explain," she finished
on a more tranquil note.

" Oh, here we are at Stephen's Green," Prudence
raised a violent commotion among the rugs.

" Stop, Toby ! Stop at the top of Grafton
Street. I've *got* to dash down and get some mauve
crêpe-de-chine, before lunch."

" Hadn't Mervyn better go with you. He could
be holding your hand," suggested Peter, as the
car slowed down beside the pavement.

169

"No, no thank you, Mervyn. I won't have time to get it done now," Prudence was climbing into the front seat and out over the side of the car as she spoke. "Give me Blazes, will you? Thanks"—as Blazes was disentangled from the rugs and handed out, red straps trailing—"I'll meet you at the Shelbourne at one o'clock. That's right, isn't it?"

As the car moved on, Mervyn and Peter both looked back. There was Prudence, pale and grey-clad, standing on the edge of the grey pavement like a hopelessly lost wood-nymph; while the streams of grosser mortals passed and re-passed unheeding. At the end of the thin red strap Blazes sat firmly on her tail, entirely declining to move. Prudence pulled. Blazes slid a short distance along the pavement; then, sticking in her toes and bending her neck, pulled too. The tall figure stooped; Blazes was picked up and stowed beneath an arm, and Prudence disappeared round the corner of Grafton Street.

At the door of the Shelbourne hotel Peter consulted the little gold wrist-watch with its half-hunter face, that four of her brothers had given her.

"It's not one yet," she said to Toby. "If you're really going to the garage, I'll go off and get my hair trimmed. I promise you not to be late for lunch, Tobioh." She disappeared among the crowd—a distinctive, well turned-out figure. Obviously of the country, her good tweeds seemed still the only possible wear among the short, tightly clasped coats of the hordes of pretty, painted little

Dubliners who thronged the pavements. She walked among them, large and sweet and pleasant, a creature from another sphere.

Back at the Shelbourne, not later than five minutes past one, Peter stood a moment in the hall.

" No," the porter told her, " Mr. Sage had not come, nor Miss Lingfield-Turrett, nor yet Mr. Trudgeon." He knew them all, as the staff of Dublin's best hotel does know individually the sadly depleted members of Irish country gentry who, coming up by car for a day's shopping, go there to feed, to be sure of meeting their friends, and to pass out through the doorway storing in their minds the latest scandal which somebody's husband has heard at the Kildare Street Club.

Peter repaired to the lounge, there to await the arrival of the rest of the party ; and there Prudence found her when she came in, ten minutes later. She smiled from the doorway and threaded her way unhurriedly through the crowded room. Prudence knew how to move—in restaurants and other places. She paused on the way to greet a friend, sitting alone ; coolly recognised a male acquaintance, who was enmeshed in another party ; then continued on her stately, rather aloof passage towards Peter. Her demeanour in public places was totally perfect. Had she been a boy one would have looked at her and at once said— Eton. As it was, those who knew her, if they saw the back of her head and shoulders across a crowded room, said : "Prudence Turrett—couldn't be anyone else." And those who did not know her asked immediately who she was.

"Hullo, darling! There are the boys, at last,"
Prudence said; she led the way back to the hall.

"What have you done with Blazes?" Mervyn
asked suddenly, when lunch had progressed as far as
cold snipe. Prudence laid down her knife and fork.

"All the devils in Hell," she announced solemnly,
"wouldn't equal what I went through with Blazes
in Grafton Street. Wait—I'll tell you." She proceeded with her snipe at a tremendous rate, so
that they waited quite three minutes to hear the
end of her story.

"Well, *what* happened?" Mervyn inquired,
when he could bear it no longer. "We saw her
whipping round on the start, with you. After
that?"

"I carried her for miles. And when I put her
down she ties her lead round the legs of the nastiest
looking young man she could see. At least, I
don't want to be unfair, he *looked* nasty. But when
he got himself undone, he most nobly offered to
carry Blazes for me, anywhere I liked."

"Oh. Yes, he *was* nasty. Waiter! What are
you going to have next, Prudence?" Toby asked.

"I d'know. Anything—pêche-melba, that'll do.
Yes, and then, when we got to Switzers, she wound
herself round and round a stand with fifteen
guineas worth of a dress on it, brought it smashing
down. I had a fearful job disentangling it before
the woman came back with what I wanted. I felt
absolutely flustered."

"Pity Mervyn wasn't there to hold your hand,"
Toby remarked acridly. "Have another pêche-
melba?"

"Yes, please. Yes, wasn't it? We shan't have time to go to that little place to-day, shall we, Mervyn? Did you get the address from Peter?"

"This *is* rather much," Peter said. "I know of *no* haunts of this nature. They sound low to me."

"Besides, I should have thought the back of the car was good enough for most people," Toby remarked. "Have another pêche-melba, Prudence."

"Yes, please. No, I think I won't. Could I have one of those cream-horn things? I can't understand what you're getting at, Peter," she observed plaintively, "what Mervyn couldn't remember was the address of the man who does your shingle. All the way up this morning he was encouraging me to get my hair off. Weren't you, Mervyn?"

"Yes, I think it'd look very well indeed hogged," Mervyn announced decisively.

Peter turned and rent him.

"Well, I think it's deuced smart," he replied to everything she said; varying the monotony of his rejoinder with: "Yes, it's neat."

As they wrangled, Prudence caught Toby's eyes across the table. Her own were kind, perhaps because she was full-fed.

"Shall I do it, Tobioh?" she asked softly. "You say."

"It's your own show," Toby answered, with as much carelessness as he could manage, "but if you want to know, I should simply hate it."

"Oh. I did want to know. I won't."

"Have another——" Toby broke off. How could he tease this creature, with her angel's mouth, and pure, pale gold hair flowering softly against the wistful angularity of a heart-shaped face. Her very presence was exasperating, uplifting and adorable, all at the same moment and not one of the three for long at a time.

Toby paid the bill a few minutes later. Peter feeling the faintest constraint, as girls just occasionally do on these occasions, gathered up her hand-bag and rose to go. But Prudence, as the waiter departed, folded her hands together on the edge of the table and looked across into her host's eyes :

"Thank Toby for my good lunch," she murmured gently, before she followed Peter out of the room and along the dim passage towards the lounge. In courtesy she was perfectly at her ease.

As they were getting into the car, Prudence touched Toby on the arm. Coffee, liqueur and a good cigarette had lent their inevitable, faint flush to her cheeks and brightness to her eyes.

"Tobioh," she said gently, "could I please, do you think, sit with you driving back—so's then we can talk about the hounds. I can't do both ways. Peter might——" she left it at that ; but got her own way with enviable ease. For, when the car left Dublin, she and Peter were sitting together in the back seat ; hands clasped beneath the rug in perfect concord ; talking easily—without brilliancy, without boredom. Blazes, who for once had ceased from troubling, was asleep at their feet.

174

About two hours out of Dublin they began to lose their way. Although their destination, according to the manifold directions they received, was never farther away than about a mile and a half, it took them quite thirty-five minutes to cover that distance.

" Rum thing," said Toby, as the party, leaving the car in a gateway, proceeded to walk up a lane to the residence of Mr. John Kelly—Master of Harriers, " first time I came down to have a look at these hounds I found the road without a stagger. To-day, when I *am* in a hurry, can't do a thing."

" That's the worst of having an eye for a country," said Peter, with quite unintentional sarcasm. " The thing *I'm* afraid of is that the van has gone by now."

" No fear. It's only three-thirty. Here's old Kelly himself."

A tall, lantern-jawed individual, wearing riding-breeches, advanced upon them. He shook hands all round, without varying the brilliance of his smile, rendered beautifully monotonous by a very new set of false teeth.

" I was very sorry," he addressed himself to Toby, " for not telegraphing you to put off coming. But indeed, I only heard two hours since that the van I had engaged to take the hounds over to your place was broke up since yesterday in Tailor's gerridge."

" Well I'm——" Toby refrained from saying what he thought. " Can't you get another van anywhere ? "

" Ah, these things are *not* so easy come by, are they ? " Mr. Kelly included the rest of the party in the conversation with pleasant ease. " And I assure you, ladies, I'm sick, sore and sorry taking ' no ' for an answer, everywhere I go making inquiries for a van. I've been to two fellows below in the village, let alone going to a friend of my own who has a nice motor-hearse ; and would you believe me, not a-one o' them would hire out their old concern for the trip."

" Well, I should say the motor-hearse would be a most suitable conveyance if twelve-and-a-half couples of hounds are to travel fifty miles in it. Wouldn't there be a few corpses at the end of the journey ? " Peter struck in.

Mr. Kelly surveyed her tolerantly. " Ah, it's roomy enough," he said easily, " roomy enough." He turned again to Toby :

" I don't at all know would you be interested in the matter, but I have two couples o' nice puppies in at the present time. They were out at walk with a cousin o' mine when you were here before. Sure there's no reason for you to take them if you don't want to, but I'd like your opinion of them. Indeed, I was saying to myself, 'twas a pity you didn't see them last time you came."

" I'd like to have a look at the hounds, Toby," Prudence said. " I hear they're a very useful lot," she turned and smiled on Mr. John Kelly, thereby making him her friend for life, or, at any rate, for the duration of this afternoon.

" They're as good a lot of hunting hounds as there is in Ireland this minute," he told her, as

he led the way through a tumble-down gateway
into an enormous yard, part farm, part kennels
and part stabling. " Bred to nose, they are, and
not to tongue, nor yet to fashion——"

" Don't run mute, I hope," put in Peter.

Ignoring her remark freezingly, Mr. Kelly swept
on : " B'Gad ye'd sooner see them at their work
than be snug in the bed. Here ! " he called to
a thin-faced boy who was cleaning out a stable,
" I'll have Rally and Mary out, Philly."

Prudence and Peter, exchanging glances, realised
a shade ruefully, that the right remark would
now have to be sought for, as the hounds were
had out, couple by couple. They need not have
harboured any fears on that score. For Toby,
rapt, enamoured, bringing thoughtful attention to
bear on each hound as it came out on the flags
(or rather, cobbles) engaged Mr. Kelly's entire
attention. The pride-ful sense of ownership was
on him ; and in a very mixed lot of under-sized
fox-hounds, he saw the nucleus of a pack such
as he hoped to see grow and flourish at Merlinstower.

" That hound now——" Toby surveyed an
elderly and unattractive specimen with less favour
than he had accorded to its predecessors—" that's
a rough-looking hound."

" Ah, old Samson. Hey, Samson, *boy* ! Well,
Mr. Sage, that's a fourth season hound that never
made a mistake yet since he learnt his business.
That's a hound that never deceived me." He
went up to the kennel door ; as he spoke to his
hounds they greeted him melodiously. " Ringlet,

Philly," he said, "We'll have Rarity and Siren out together."

Philly's harsh snarl could be heard, admonishing the rest of the kennel, before two smart bitches enough, well turned, smooth and neat, and with a good show of bone, were had out on the flags, to fill Toby's eye and gladden his heart.

"That's a smart bitch. *Siren!*" Mr. Kelly got her up on her toes with crumbs of biscuit from the pocket of his coat.

"There's strength for you," passing his hand over back and loins, "I give her a very high character too," he continued; then waited an unhurried minute that her points might be well taken in, before he passed on: "This is a second-season bitch by Ranger from Mary—a neat mould of a hound for you."

"A very pretty neck and shoulder," Prudence commended Rarity in a low voice to Toby, "got lots of strength too. She'll make a great matron, Toby."

Toby turned to her, a grave light shining in his eyes.

"Yes, she should," he said, "she should."

And so they went on through the twelve-and-a-half couples, till the kennel doors closed on the last of them—Ruby and Tanner, a wise bitch, from the famous Black and Tans. And Mr. Kelly spoke his concluding word in their praise.

"Four-and-a-half brace of foxes in thirty-five days, they killed last season; and in this badly stopped country too. Ah, they're fox-catchers all over. And I wouldn't let them go to any man but yourself, Mr. Sage. It'd break me up—it would, indeed."

" Four-and-a-half brace in thirty-five days is good enough, for harriers," Peter observed, " it says a bit for their huntsman too."

Mr. Kelly took her in with a favouring eye. " Those little hounds would hunt by themselves and kill their fox too ; yes, and come back to kennels like Christians in the evening."

" I've no doubt they would," reflected Peter.

" I'll tell you what "—Mr. Kelly smote Toby excitedly between the shoulders—" we'll have a little hunt this afternoon till ye see the sort o' them. Here, Philly ! " he called to the thin-faced boy who had disappeared into a boiling-house, from the open door of which issued a truly awful smell, " Put the saddles on old Gallagher and Roguey. We'll go see can we find a fox up in Kiln hill. That's the right place to view a hunt from," he informed his guests. " Excuse me now one minyute, ladies, till I run to the house for me whip and the poor little horn."

" The poor little horn," echoed Prudence as he departed, " he must hate the hounds going awfully, doesn't he ? "

" If I hadn't got them the bank would have sold them up on him," Toby told her. " Anyway they say he won't ride the country now, he's stiff."

" H'm. Mervyn, ask the boy if we can get the car up Kiln hill."

Mr. Kelly, returning at that moment, bustled into a dark loose-box from which he pulled out an old bay horse with a big knee and a wise eye.

179

"By the Holy Fooks!" he swore to Prudence gallantly, "if I'd known Mr. Sage was bringing *you* down to my little place, I'd have had a horse for you you might *call* a horse; yes, and made sure you saw a hunt on him too."

"Oh, you're too generous, Mr. Kelly. Mind I don't come down one of these days and take you at your word. I might, y'know."

Mr. Kelly winked at her delightedly:

"I *love* the look in your eye," he informed her in a hoarse whisper from behind the hand that held 'the poor little horn,' "but *don't* tell the father!" after which pleasantry he bade Philly, "let them all come—all but old Melody and Warrior." Sitting big and square on his big bay horse, he answered with words of cheer the greeting of his hounds as they poured out of kennels, and round his horse. He had donned a battered, old red coat, for the hounds knew the old coat, he said. Philly too, when he pulled out the redoubtable Roguey, they saw had done the same.

"Mind now, Philly," the master told him as they rode out of the yard, "we have to show sport to-day. In the name o' God try your best to keep the hounds together."

"Well, may the Man Above see to it there's none o' them nasty hares about," was Philly's reply.

"Amen," echoed the M.H. adding with feeling, "nor yet rabbits."

"They hunt well in all weathers. Warm days and cold days, in dry, in rain, in heat, in storm,"

Prudence, in a low voice, reproduced the very intonation of Mr. Kelly. " But I don't know what hounds could hunt to-day, Toby. It's absolutely sultry and the ground's *parched*."

The four of them stood at the corner of Kiln hill, a rocky eminence, on the sheltered side of which a remarkably snug little gorse gave the impression of a very holding bit of covert ; Mr. Kelly's harriers stormed into it in a way that was pleasant to see.

Philly sat his horse immovable, at the upper corner ; and the huntsman on his old bay horse rode slowly up one side, cheering his hounds on through the thick covert.

The party on the hill-top waited for some minutes, warm in the incongruous sunshine. Then Prudence touched Toby on the arm :

" There's their fox, Toby," she murmured. She pointed down the hill to where, slipping across a corner of the boggy bottom, was a dark red, grey-hound of a fox.

" By jove ! what *eyes* you've got, Prudence."

Toby ran down the hill and they saw him speak to Philly ; saw Philly catch up his reins ; heard, at the same instant, a hound speak, and another. Till, with music good enough to stir any heart, the pack burst out of covert and down the hillside. On this seemingly impossible scenting day they romped away on the line of their pilot in a manner which rendered valid Mr. Kelly's loudest boast on the subject of their hunting capabilities.

The huntsman, though still cheering his hounds to the line, rode away from them as hard as he could go in the direction of a cattle gap which had befriended him often of old. Philly, they saw drive his rangy brute of a chestnut undependable into a stone-faced bank of no mean proportions, and watched him, over with a bad peck and a great recovery, taking the shortest possible way to be with the hounds.

"Philly's the lad," Peter murmured to her brother, " if Toby could get hold of him, now . . ."

And Toby was saying to Prudence : " Jove ! if I had *that* fella to turn hounds to me——"

Prudence, her eyes on the chase, nodded but said nothing. Below the hill where they stood the country stretched out like a map ; they could still see the hounds, running on well, and once had a view of the hunted fox.

"You wouldn't see a hunt like this twice in a lifetime," Peter said, and she was right.

Prudence suddenly clutched Toby's arm. " Toby ! dashed if that isn't a fresh fox jumped up right in front of them. Look ! They've divided now. Hang it ! Aren't these toppers the way they stuck to the line of their hunted fox."

" Philly's staying with the main body."

" Where the deuce is the Master ? "

" That fresh fox is coming right back for the hill."

" Not often you see two distinct hunts without moving three yards from where you stand."

" By Jove ! How they are sticking to it ! " This last from Toby who could still see Philly and his seven couples, now almost out of sight and still running on.

"There's a bit of scent in spite of conditions," he said when he could see them no longer. His sigh was all pure rapture. Soon, so very soon, he would be hunting these hounds in his own country.

"Prudence! My arm is black and blue this minute. Stop squeezing it, like a good girl."

Prudence pinched harder in her excitement.

"They're back in the hill, Toby," she said, "and the Master got a grand nick in, below in the bog. He's with them now. They're storming into it, aren't they? But I bet he's to ground."

And ten minutes later the distressful, "Wind-'im! Wind-'im-in!" was audible from far down the rocky hill-side. They descended to find the hounds marking their fox in a fissured wall of rock. Their huntsman was gazing with one eye into a crack that one would have thought incapable of admitting a rock-rabbit; his old horse, ears and head alert, standing at a little distance, the reins on his neck.

"Well, well, well," Mr. Kelly withdrew his eye from the draughty fissure, "these things is the will o' God, I suppose. Did Philly go on with the hounds? Ah, he did, of course; he's a right boy—better than meself in me old age!" he included them all in the wink which spoke of parallel lines and open gates, pulled gaps and rare nicks in of all sorts. "I declare the old horse tells me I make a holy show of him altogether," he said to Prudence. "But these little hounds minds me yet."

"Well, what matter about riding the country if you're there when your hounds are at fault,

Mr. Kelly," Prudence replied diplomatically. " All the same, I bet that old lad with the knee has carried you in some rapid hunts."

" Well, he has, he has," Mr. Kelly admitted. Hoisting himself once more into the saddle, he collected the hounds with a couple of wheezy twangs on his old horn, and set off down the hill, determined to jog by short-cut and by-way till he hit off the hounds and Philly once more.

" You may say good-bye to your harriers for to-day, Toby," Peter told him as gently as possible. " You mayn't believe me, chaps, but it's a quarter past five now, and, I don't personally think we'll get home to-night."

" Never ! Come on, girls, we'll get to Dublin in time for some dinner, anyway. It's no mortal use waiting to discuss matters with old Kelly now. I suppose he'll send them along as soon as they're sound after to-day's show." And Toby, his beautiful head held high and his eyes shining like a girl's, newly kissed, strode freely, rapt in his own high and lofty thoughts, down the rocky hill-side.

CHAPTER IX

SHOCK

" I WISH we knew what they'd done with their fox."

Putting her bare arms behind her head, Peter looked across at Prudence and Toby who, that same evening, at the hour of eight-thirty, were sitting opposite to her in the lounge of the Shelbourne.

Toby did not answer her question at once, because he was thinking how odd it was that Prudence's arms could be so transparent, and yet miss being knobbily bony.

Prudence did not answer because she was only slowly recovering from the effects of two cocktails and a glass of champagne ; both strongly recommended by Peter as antidotes for the nervous strain involved in the composition and despatch of a wire to her guardians. The wire announced, or would announce the next morning, that, owing to the break-down (fictional) of Toby's car, she was obliged to spend the night in Dublin.

" Why don't we stay the night, and go to one of these awful dances at Clery's ? They're really quite good," Peter had suggested on the way home.

" You boys can stay at the club, and Prudence and I will split a room at the Shelbourne."

Objections had come tumbling from Prudence and Mervyn.

" *Puppy*, you're mad ! *Gus.*"

" Clothes."

" Yes, we can't dance, Peter. I haven't got a rag."

" Mervyn can borrow some clothes from his little friend Giles Cranford. And, as a matter of fact, Prudence, I can get hold of two dresses I brought up to be altered—one of them's that red thing you swapped to me."

" Shoes," said Prudence firmly.

" I brought them up with me," Peter confessed sweetly, " for you and me. Also stockings, also——"

" Peter, don't forget yourself ! Gentlemen present."

" Damn it all, Puppy ! What *am* I to do about Gus ? She'll break me over this."

" She can't kill you—to-night anyhow."

Prudence felt Toby's eyes running over her and thought, quite wrongly, that he was criticizing her mean spirit.

" All right," she said, " I'll wire. What lie shall I tell ? "

" Do not lie," Toby leaned out of the car, listening, " it's not a bit expedient. Just say that— put it in simple language—Toby isn't one bit happy about that curious, clanking sound in his back-axle."

Prudence had laughed, throwing back her head till the beautiful fine lines of her chin and throat were etched beneath the drawn skin ; and looking

at Toby with shy solemnity, had suddenly slipped
an arm into his.

That drive back to Dublin had been, for him,
the most perfect thing. He had felt roused and
warm at heart after the successful doings of the
afternoon. And now, as he leaned back in his
chair and drew hard on his cigarette, he could
remember the live excitement which had run
ridiculously through him when he had put
Prudence into her coat, and later, when she had
climbed in beside him ; her shoulder touching
his ; her eager face turned to him ; her trick of
looking away for a moment, and down at her
knees, listening to his replies to her questions.
Every most ordinary thing about her was maddening and disconcerting, and the cool evening
marvellously sweet.

A hundred times before they had driven so—
alone too. And Prudence, jesting or sulky, rallying
him about his clothes, or seriously talking of dogs
and horses, had never yet made his heart contract
with a perfection of longing, such as he had felt
all through that long drive. The urgency of it
went through him in strange, distorted waves. At
one moment he longed to pull her up against him
and drag her mouth under his. Again, he was
utterly content ; content because of little things ;
that Blazes, who insisted on flea-hunting in the
seat beside them, should push Prudence closer to
him in her gyrations ; content when she slid a
thin hand into his coat pocket, fumbling for his
cigarette case ; and when, being Prudence, she
failed to light her cigarette till (at the third last

match in the box) he must stop the car and do it for her. Glad, yet aching and fearing, unsure of himself, trying desperately to be the everyday, imperturbable Toby.

As he dressed for dinner in his room at the club he told himself the truth :

" I'm mad for her—that's it. I guessed it, now I know." He surveyed his reflection solemnly in the mirror. " Gad ! this suit of clothes has seen five reigns now ; Dot Harding—married. Judy—married ; twins. Bardie Kane and Betty. And now, *Prudence*." He straightened his tie, collected Mervyn, and went out to get into the car and drive round to the Shelbourne for dinner.

And now, dinner over, they sat in the lounge waiting for Mervyn before driving down to Clery's ball-room. He would have to wait twenty minutes at least before he could take her in his arms and dance with her. Absurd, that the excuse of dancing should be necessary before he could take her and hold her, have the feel of her and the funny, sweet scent, only describable as a wild scent, which was the very spirit of Prudence's personality ; it reminded one of the dappled shadows of leaves, of a fog of blue-bells, of sudden rifts of light, of streams and storms—all of which things and places are, it is well known, beloved of dryads.

Not that she reminded Toby of any of these things. He did not think clearly at all, his mind was too full of the desire to put his arms about her and kiss her mouth, kiss it till he must feel its swooning sweetness on his for ever. . . . Suddenly he caught her looking at him, a little

askance, sideways, from the corners of her eyes.
He had given himself away properly, he supposed.
Well, no matter, she'd have to know sometime.
He plunged into conversation with violence.

" Blazes ! " he exclaimed, " where the dickens
is Blazes ? Don't you want to take her ball-
dancing, Prudence ? "

Peter leaned forward and touching his knee,
spoke in a low voice :

" Anatole is taking care of her."

" Anatole ? "

" Ssh. Don't say it so loud. The management
doesn't permit dogs downstairs, but Anatole is
rather a pal of mine. He's looking after her."

" Yes. Mother's poor little girl," Prudence
sighed. " She doesn't understand one word of
French either. But Anatole reminded her just a
little of James, I think that helped her to bear
the wrench of parting."

" That, *and* the cutlets," Peter put in drily.
" Pull up your shoulder-strap, Prudence. Your
dress is struggling off inch by inch."

" My clothes *never* stay on," Prudence jerked at
the descending garment and rose to her feet. " Oh,
there's Mervyn back at last."

They watched her slowly striding across the
hall ; saw her pause to laugh with Mervyn—
immaculate now in his borrowed tails. She turned
from him with some injunction, for he nodded
assent or agreement, and went towards the lift.
They noted her down-stretched, long, white arms,
and the shrug that narrowed her gleaming shoulders ; her head was like a proud, pale flower ;

her chin held arrogantly, so that one saw the lower
line of her jaw—a trick of hers. She passed from
their sight, leaving an impression of total unreality.
One could not think that Prudence ate and slept,
and drank and lived, like other people. She was
—just was—Prudence.

．　　　．　　　．　　　．　　　．

In the lift which took them to the ballroom on
the upper floor at Clery's, Toby touched Prudence's
hand—touched her shyly, this girl with whom he
had so often ragged and wrestled.

" We'll have the first, shall we ? " he suggested.

Prudence answered carelessly :

" Oh, I'm dancing that with Mervyn—the next
if you like," continued what she had been saying
to Peter ; then, as the lift stopped, stepped out,
without so much as a glance in his direction, and
went away to deposit her wraps.

Toby felt chilled and absurdly hurt ; angry
with Prudence ; angry with Mervyn because he
was to dance with her ; angry with Peter because
he and she must dance together ; and to dance
with Peter meant less than nothing to him.

A little later the girls joined them. Prudence
and Mervyn, smiling at each other, went off side
by side in a very pre-arranged manner, and slipped
easily into the tide of other dancers.

All through his dance with Peter Toby observed
them, raging inwardly that Mervyn should dance
so well.

Mervyn, the pretty boy with his crinkly fair
hair, who never had much to say at any time, was

at last having a proper good innings. For they danced together, the pair of them, as though they had done nothing else all the nights of their lives ; and as though life held nothing else worth doing. If Mervyn could dance, his partner was a conspicuous performer. Looking at her at first, in her tight red dress, one thought only how stiffly she moved ; she made things appear so difficult of accomplishment. Next, one perceived that her interpretation of dance music was the very antithesis of sloppy, careless, shuddering round a room. Her erect body, her stiff, lengthy steps were the perfection of poise. Her slightly hunched shoulders never moved, nor did her long white arms. Save from the hips downwards she was immobile. And Mervyn and she strode across the time of the music, and into it suddenly ; then balanced easily against the rhythm ; in their eyes and set faces an utter oblivion of each other, and of everything save the music which held them in entranced movement.

When it was over Prudence sighed ; stood an instant as if a little bewildered at the cessation of the music, then collecting herself, went off to look for Toby and Peter.

Peter was looking adorable this evening. Her very ordinary, jade green frock set off to perfection the creamy thickness of her skin. She was a little tired too, which took the edge off her usually rather purposeful manner, and lent the shadows that gave a sweetness and depth to her three-cornered blue eyes. She did not show Toby that he had bored her badly ; nor did she permit the other two to imagine that she had bored him. When the next dance started, and Prudence and Toby sidled crab-like among the agglomeration of chairs which blocked the way to the ballroom, she said to Mervyn :

" Prudence dances extraordinarily, doesn't she ? "

" Masterly," replied Mervyn with simple fervour. He added, " come on."

But Peter shook her head. She knew her dancing to be much inferior to Prudence's, and did not choose that even a brother should realise the fact too plainly.

" No thanks," she said, " I want to finish my cigarette."

Yet, when a moment later, a friend of hers came past them with a small, fat girl in tow, she greeted him instantly, introduced Mervyn to the girl, whom she knew slightly, and had once heard described as God's worst clinger in a ballroom, and grinding out her cigarette, accepted the youth's invitation to dance without an instant's hesitation.

" Missing one, Mervyn," she said as she moved away.

It was when they were again sitting out, Mervyn slightly exhausted after his efforts with God's worst clinger, that they were joined by an outwardly calm Prudence and a ruffled and sulky Toby. Peter made room at once, accomplishing introductions placidly.

" Oh," the youth had instantly asked Prudence for a dance, " if you *could* give number ten a home ? After that I'm going to sleep in the cloakroom—

if you don't want to leave, Peter. I'm so tired."
Had she said, " I'm so frightened," Peter would
not have been surprised ; for suddenly the cool,
collected expression crumbled from her face ; a
look of pale, scared aversion taking its place ; and
Prudence seemed to shrink from sight, till all one
saw of her was the confusion and terror that looked
out of her eyes.

Glancing from her to Toby, who was sitting in
sullen withdrawn silence, Peter wondered instantly,
" what's up ? " Aloud, she said : " I'll go *now*,
if you like."

But Prudence, shaking her head, plunged into
breathless conversation with the new member of
the party. She laughed with him, and sparkled
for him, the strained look all the time pulling at
her mouth and the corners of her eyes. They got
up instantly when the music began and went in
to dance.

Toby, when he had said to Peter " shall we ? "
and had been told that she was dancing this with
Mervyn, turned to the fat girl (whom he suddenly
hated violently) and after a stiff, " may I have
this dance ? " threaded his way behind her to
the floor.

She goggled at him and clung tenaciously, till
Toby's very soul revolted equally from her proxi-
mity and from her pitiable efforts at bright conversation. He ground her unfortunate foot, it was
also fat, and tightly shod, into the floor. Then said :

" Oh, *damn!* I mean, I beg your pardon.
Shall we sit out ? My dancing is hopeless," and
nothing else during the ten minutes in which they

waited, sitting at opposite ends of a settee, for the rest of the party.

By the time they came the poor, fat girl was almost in tears. She loathed Toby with an unquenchable hatred, and wished she had the spirit to get up and go into the cloak-room. But he would never notice her departure and she would have to explain it to the others.

Prudence and her partner were the first to come in. She stared about her for a moment, then sat down and talked over her shoulder to Mervyn, who had followed with Peter. Peter, with an amused little lift of her eyebrows, immediately occupied the gap which gaped between Toby and his late partner, and leaning back, remarked generally and conversationally:

"How ghastly hot it is, isn't it?"

"Yes, *isn't* it?" the fat girl was glad to have a chance to say something at last, "it was so beastly hot, Mr. Sage and I stopped dancin', we stopped on account of the heat, you know."

"Hot? I thought it was perfectly perishin'," Toby, who had only caught the word 'heat', did not intend to be brutal, merely contradictory. He was feeling savage and it was in a savage voice that he presently remarked:

"I'm going to get the car, you want to go back, don't you?"

Peter raised her eyebrows again. "I don't know if we *still* want to—we *did*."

"I think this is about the most rotten show I've ever been mixed up in," Toby said sourly, "but don't make a move on my account."

Peter did not answer. She leant across to Prudence ; what she said was not clearly audible to Toby, but Prudence's reply he heard distinctly.

" Oh, I just must dance this with Mervyn, Peter. He's squared the band to play something good. Tell him he can bring the car round after this dance."

' *Tell* him to bring the car.' Use him and ignore him, and throw him aside at his own party, that she might dance with the offal of Clery's ball-room. By God ! who did she think she was ? How much more of her dam' nonsense did she think he was going to put up with ? His face white with temper, Toby rose to his feet, muttered something and walked off towards the bar.

When he had had a drink he felt once again the urge of all his senses ; the thrill with which he had taken her into his arms to dance ; the disappointment of her withdrawn and utterly impersonal contact. He had not seen her face, for she held her head inwards and down. But the lack of response of her body should have told him as much as the scared aversion of her eyes.

" You're dancing rottenly to-night, Tobioh," she had said. For answer, he had ceased at once, and with an arm through hers, had propelled her, with firmness and ease, through the door which led out to the darkness and softness of the night, and to the many-angled corners of the flat roof that abutted from the ball-room.

" I don't want to come out here, Toby," she had said crossly.

" No. But I wanted you to, you see."

" Oh, Toby ! Why ? "

He mistook the breathless shake in her voice ; and dropping the arm he still held, pulled her up to him and stooped for her lips.

She had been too quick, though. Below her ear he had kissed her as she slewed her head aside ; he could still feel the back of her cool hand laid across his mouth, as if in jest ; still feel the shock of the sudden, violent wrench with which she had freed herself a second afterwards ; still remember, with a sort of hurt wonder, the disgust so manifestly written on her face, seen later in the glow of the electric light. Disgust—that was the word . . . oh, *damn*. . . .

. . . . .

" Prudence, stop being silly and tell me what happened," thus Peter, brushing her hair violently with two men's brushes.

Prudence hunched, fully dressed, in a chair gazed at her miserably.

" I told you—Toby was *too* foul. I hate him. Swine ! "

" Did he kiss you ? "

" *Yes*."

" Anything else ? "

" How ? ' anything else '—I won't be mouthed and mauled over. It makes me sick."

Peter laid down her brushes and began to smear cold cream slowly over her face.

" Prudence, you are amazing," she said, " you've got the *most* impure mind, and some of the most improper ways of any girl I know. And yet when a desirable youth like Toby comes along and really, *badly*, wants to kiss you, you go right off the deep end and shudder with horror for hours afterwards—after a perfectly ordinary kiss. Haven't you *ever* been kissed, precious? "

Prudence, pulling her dress viciously over her head, lied, in a muffled voice, from its depths.

" Yes. Heaps of times," she stated defiantly.

Peter began to rub her cold cream off with a towel.

" If Gus had been a divorcée with six co-respondents," she said, " you would have grown up a Sunday-school miss in cashmere stockings. I know ; it's all reaction."

" I don't understand you, Puppy ; except that you're being horrible."

" *Do* you like Toby? " Peter asked, leaning forward to the glass and pulling up the waves in her hair with precise touches.

" Yes, awfully," Prudence straggled across the room to the washstand, one stocking in rings about the ankle, the other leg bare, " when he's nice and his ordinary self, I do—I love him," she added.

" But when he's just ' nice ', and rags, and so on—that's not *him*, you know," Peter said. " And what *are* you washing your ear so viciously for? Itch? Right ear your mother, left ear your . . . that's right, isn't it, Prudence? I expect Gus is thinking of you too, though."

Prudence did not answer. She knew both Peter's suppositions to be perfectly correct.

CHAPTER X

SUNDAY AFTERNOON

A SUNDAY-AFTERNOON party from Lingarry and
Kilronan were contemplating, with expansive
interest, and a certain amount of suppressed
criticism, Anthony's now nearly completed kennels
and drainage schemes at Drumferris.

"You must have put in the dickens of a lot
of money, Tony." Oliver contemplated the roomy,
new yards in front of the sound and airy new
kennels ; their ventilators and well thought-out
inside walls. His eye wandered to the kennel
huntsman who stood, a little apart from the Master
and his group of visitors, a pile of clean white coats
over his arm. "B'Gad, the old ones were snug
enough, too. I suppose the hounds don't know
themselves now, you've got 'em so smartened up
since you took over."

"*Sulphur* dressings are about all they've had—
bar a bit of feeding," Anthony announced in his
short, clear voice. "And as for the snug old
lodgin's, Oliver, they were about ready to blow
down, if they hadn't been pulled down." He took
two of the coats and held one for Peter to put on.

Prudence slid her arms into another which
Mervyn gave her.

"You've got to see this draft I've had from Jimmy Smollet," she heard Anthony say to Peter. Peter said something in reply that Prudence could not quite catch ; but it was obviously sympathetic, for Anthony's small, red face looked less preoccupied than usual by the cares of the hounds and drains, as he turned away to give an order to his K.H.

Thereafter followed the inspection, conducted almost in silence as far as the spectators were concerned. Prudence, yawning, felt how boring it all was compared with that delicious Wednesday afternoon among the harriers.

To-day, the three men—Oliver, Mervyn and an elderly cousin of the Trudgeons—stood in a stolid group ; white linen coats over their good suits of clothes ; well-polished, flatly-cut shoes hardly shifting on the flags ; as they watched, in strongly preserved silence, the new draft ; and later, with more interest, the hounds they knew. How contented they were, Prudence thought ; full-fed after Sunday lunch ; smelling of cigars and good hairwash. The incredible neatness of Oliver's bowtie caught and held her attention for a full minute ; then her gaze became fixed and lowering. How Peter was getting off with that little brute, Anthony Countless ! They stood apart from the group of phlegmatic men ; and Peter, quiet but intensely interested, put grave questions to Anthony ; occasionally ventured a criticism or a word of praise.

Plainly, he thought her worth attending to ; more worthy of attention than Prudence ; for she had to repeat a remark twice over before he heard

her ; and when he had finally taken it in, laughed
shortly, repeating :

" Rosebud ? Thought that was Rosebud, did
you ? She was among the first lot I put down.
No. That's not Rosebud. Cobweb ! *Cobweb*—
put her in, Jack."

Prudence flamed with discomfort, a flame which
burnt down to sulky chagrin. Why had she
spoken ? And why had that little brute seen to
it so well that the others should write her down
as one of those fools who imagine that they know
one hound from another—while they don't. She
supposed that, in their silence, each was thinking :
" Little ass—shoving herself into it. Showing off."
Catching Peter's eye, she detected faint pity in its
expression ; and between sulks and anger could
have cried ; tears were, in fact, very near her
eyes. At such a moment Toby's sudden appearance was, to her, not less than a god-send.

Absurdly well-dressed in a marvellous suit of brown
clothes, he shook hands composedly ; murmured :
" They told me I'd find you down here. These
kennels are quite an improvement. I like your
boiling and feeding." He looked into the kennel
where the hounds lay in their benches, and sniffed
in lofty approval : " Warm. Dry." He withdrew his head and shoulders, then, looking round
him once more : " I just want another look at
that boiler," and turning on his heel swung out
into the yard. He was about to pass Prudence
by on his way to the absorbing boiling-house, but
she called out to him from the seat on the mounting-
block to which she had betaken herself :

" I *wish* you'd help me get this thorn out of my finger, Tobioh. It's giving me *Hell*."

He sat down beside her immediately ; a warm, little rush of absurd pleasure coming over him.

" Are you sorry ? " he asked her, ignoring the thorn. It was the first time they had met since a frigid drive home on the morning after the dance at Clery's.

Plainly, Prudence was taken aback. " Are *you* sorry ? " she countered, not unkindly.

" Oh, *no*." Toby stared past her to the white-coated group, still conscientiously making its way through the kennels. His grey eyes with their violent lashes came back to her face again :

" I'm not *sorry*, Prudence, but we won't let it happen again, because you might turn nasty ; and as I'll want your assistance badly this winter, you won't be a lot of use to me if you're producing pretty exhibitions of temper all the time. We've got a lot to do. I'll want you over at Merlinstower any day you can come. Can you square Gus ? "

Prudence glowed. This thrilled her, if you like. To be wanted—badly ; considered helpful ; looked up to ; and asked for advice ; these things went to her head like wine.

" *Of* course, Toby. You're going to show great sport with these harriers."

" Yes, we'll show sport, all right. My God ! Y'know the country's stiff with foxes. We'll get after them stopping a bit, and push 'em around. I tell you, Prudence, we'll have a right winter."

His enthusiasm caught her like a flame. Raptly they spoke of this covert and of that, which farmers

to propitiate ; which to avoid ; the pity of it that
his best gorse should be adjacent to Paddy Doyle's
of Coolvogue—a sour old customer.

" But anyhow," Toby said, " we'll never have
a big field out, riding across the land and doing
damage. Yourself and meself, and Philly, only a
couple or so more."

" You don't tell me you've got Philly away from
old Kelly ? "

" *I* didn't charm him. But you know, the way it
was, he couldn't part with his hounds. And b'Gad!
he's a *topper*—I'd never know the hounds without
him. Dammit, Prudence ! Once I get bucking to
you I can't be stopped. Come on with me now and
take an intelligent interest in this boiling-house."

Prudence came ; she hung about over the soup,
and empty buckets, and sacks of biscuit and meal
for some time ; then with cheeks flushed and hair
damped with steam, leant against the wall outside and lit a cigarette while she waited for Toby
to finish his pokings round and investigations.

" Seen the rest of the family ? " he asked, when
at last he came out to her. He held her wrist
steady, lighting a cigarette from hers. " Thanks.
No matches."

Prudence, whose eyes had not moved from the
contemplation of a closed door in the row of kennels
opposite, answered harshly :

" Peter and the Master have been in there for
the last ten minutes ; the others went to look at
the horses."

Toby raised his eyebrows, expelling a cloud of
smoke from his nose.

"Ah," he observed, looking down at it, "yes. I thought it'd come to that before long."

Prudence continued to watch the closed door with anxious eyes and she said :

"D'you mean Peter's getting off properly ? "

"You should know more about your extra-half than I do. But she's an awfully sympathetic soul —Peter. An' that's what that fellow requires, sympathy."

"The dickens he does ! She *said* she hated him, Toby. And what d'you mean by his requiring sympathy ? I never knew anyone less likeable."

"That's just why," Toby nodded sapiently, "he's in need of sympathy, and Peter's capable of, of passion "—he hurried out the unusual word— "you're only capable of sympathy, and I want, something else," he laughed embarrassedly.

But Prudence had only taken in the first half of his odd little speech. She was frowning over it aggrievedly, and when Peter joined them a moment later she considered her curiously by the light of Toby's indictment.

Peter capable of passion ? Passion—that was not just mere love between a man and a woman ; it was something far more stark—overwhelming. As Prudence saw it, an experience to be achieved— the stage carefully set, brilliant pyjamas and ruffled hair, in a hotel bedroom—and only desirable with that man and lover whom she had yet to find. To make things really perfect, an elopement, with Gus left, badly hipped, on the field of battle, was essential. But the idea of the hotel bedroom, pyjamas, hair and so on, in connection with any of her present admirers (Toby included) made her feel, as she had once told Peter, as though her system was full of ammoniated quinine.

As she walked up to Anthony's little house between her host and Peter, she looked from one to the other with covert curiosity. Peter, gazing ahead of her into space, was smoking one of her eternal cigarettes ; her thoughts seemed far away ; or rather, Prudence thought bitterly, too damned near at hand. She looked reflectively from Peter's strong, serene beauty of face and form to the little, hard-bitten man, with a face like some not altogether lovable fox-terrier, who walked on her other side, talking to Toby about the coverts ; and wondered, as once before she had wondered about Mary and John Strap, how it was possible that Peter should feel herself moved to the sacrifices of passion for him.

A rush of feeling overcame Prudence. Peter married ! Given to this little, short-spoken, dried-up man ; made over to him for good ; herself, her beautiful body, her life—he would order that for her—and the friends she was to have, too. Prudence felt a nasty jag of misery, thinking that she herself would be, perhaps, the first one proscribed. All her love for Peter rushed over her. She longed to cry out : " *Don't !* Don't *do* it, Puppy. Puppy, darling, I'd miss you too terribly. Life wouldn't be bearable for me." The desire to have Peter hers always swept her with longing. Married to Anthony Countless, she knew she could not keep her like that. There would be a house and a garden—

Peter would be sure to take up gardening when she could not hunt on account of the babies coming ; masses of them, probably ; pink, stupid little brutes that would fill up all Peter's time, love and attention—nothing was to be left for Prudence.

Exasperation took the place of her love for Peter and pity for herself when, arrived at Glenferris Lodge, and in Anthony's bedroom, where they had gone to wash their hands, (Peter's activities behind that closed door had, it seemed, included the dressing of a canker in an old spaniel's ear) she noted Peter's eyes straying, with curiosity faintly tinged by sentiment, from Anthony's shaving gear, visible through the open door of his bathroom, to his boots, ranged against the wall, and hunting whips hanging in a neat row above them ; and observed their almost pointed avoidance of his white-quilted single bed, with striped pyjama suit folded on the pillow.

" She does—she *does* love him," thought Prudence, a little wildly ; and recalled how, when Peter and Anthony had crossed the yard towards herself and Toby, she had said, noting their careless demeanour after a lengthy disappearance : " That's not *love*, Toby." And his drawling answer : " Well, it's not *hatred*, anyway."

Certainly there was no hatred in Peter's solemn, almost shy scrutiny of this room. For the usual reason it made her heart ache a little. She wished that it was not quite so orderly and comfortable ; that there was something about it to be put right ; anything, it did not matter how slight it might be, that she could do for him. But, glancing round, she realized—not for the first time—that Anthony

205

could, and did, make himself exceedingly comfortable without requiring female ministrations of any kind.

Peter sighed, a shade ruefully, and went out to join the others in the oak-furnished, white-distempered living-room, with its dormer windows, bright chintz, and excellent hunting prints on the walls. It was no good staying behind to talk to Prudence ; realizing her to be in one of her very worst moods, she waited patiently for the storm to break, as she knew it was bound to do, sooner or later, leaving a clarified atmosphere in its wake.

That the coming storm was immediate and irrevocable was evident as soon as Prudence joined herself, with a lofty air of detachment from her surroundings, to the party hilariously awaiting the arrival of tea in Anthony's dining-room. She frowned upon Peter who, seated on a fender stool, was pensively scraping a dog's front with the end of her cigarette holder.

" You're using the mouth-piece," Anthony informed her, on his return from one of a series of journeys to the kitchen regions, which he told them he undertook to hurry up Bridgie.

Peter, unmoved, continued to do so. " All right," she said, without a smile, " I never use a holder myself. Only carry it because Dilly likes the feel. So do you—don't you, *boy ?* " She bent over the absurd Yorkshire terrier that lay on his back in her lap, waving all four legs fatuously in the air.

" I say," said Mervyn suddenly, " can't *I* go and hurry up Bridgie. Is she a pretty girl ? "

" No, damned awful." Anthony was producing drinks. " But she means well. I'm putting in a ghastly time with her."

" What's happened to that excellent fella of yours, Tony ? George. What's happened to George ? "

" George ? Honeymooning. I swore him to be back before the season started. But I wake up in the night all of a muck-sweat, thinking how perhaps Mrs. George won't like Ireland."

There was a bump of a tray against the door ; and with the remark that the noise *must* be Bridgie, Anthony got up and went over to open it. He certainly had an attractive way of doing things in his own house. Having shoo-ed Bridgie kindly but firmly out again to the kitchen regions to fetch more cups and glasses, he fussed over the pouring out of tea himself, without asking either of the girls to do it for him.

" See to the drink, if you like," he said to Peter, " you told me once it was your only vice."

" Tea's another," Peter said. Prudence noted with annoyance how she seated herself carelessly by her host's side, and heard her say :

" What wonderful short-bread. Bridgie never made it, did she ? "

" Bridgie ? No, never. Bridgie's limit is this burnt toast, which I *don't* recommend." He handed it to Prudence all the same ; she thanked him prettily and ostentatiously gave her slice to the Yorkshire terrier.

" I brought that short-bread back with me, last time I came over," he told them, " and you'd never believe what I endured getting it through

the customs. Bad crossing—awful cold morning.
I thought there'd be the dickens of a fuss over
my saddle cases ; well, they chalked 'em off without
a word. Asked me if I'd anything to declare.
I thought of a box of biscuits—cheese biscuits,
you know. So I said, ' Yes, biscuits ; just biscuits ; perfectly plain—plain biscuits.' They
ripped up everything I had till they found the
box of biscuits. When they did find it, they prised
it open, and the customs chap bit one of the biscuits. Said he wanted to find out if it was sweet
—sugar was dutiable, or something. I said to
him : ' You may have the *whole* of that biscuit.'
He didn't like it at all. Threw it behind him—
like that. Yes, really. After that he went through
everything. Found the short-bread of course. I'd
absolutely forgotten the short-bread. Gave him my
word I had. No good. Biscuit still rankling, I
suppose. He made a hideous scene ; lugged up
officials of all sorts ; brought sheaves of papers
for me to sign. And all over that dam' short-
bread. Well, *anything* else I shouldn't have minded,
but I hate to be classed as the sort of fella who
wallows in short-bread. It, it outrages me."

" Then what did you bring it over for ? "
Prudence asked urbanely.

" Must have had some occasion like the present
in your mind," Peter suggested quietly. " I *am*
the type that wallows in it."

" Oh, please have some more," Anthony begged
her earnestly. " Tea ? Cake ? Bridgie has forgotten the cake—or else she's eaten it. Go an'
ask her, Mervyn."

"Ask her if she's eaten the cake? Tony, I haven't the nerve. Do it yourself; she's probably fairly used to your face by now."

Peter said rudely :

"Yes, I suppose yours *would* be too much of a hell of a jolt for her system."

Prudence glared at her plate ; and Oliver said :

"I'm inclined to think you're jolly lucky to have anyone at all in the kitchen. How many cooks have we had in the last month, Prudence? Three, isn't it? *I* don't know what's got them at all. The wear and tear on the car, taking them back and forwards to the station is something frightful."

"What happened to the one we pulled out of the pond?" Anthony asked Prudence. "I should think she might have stayed out of common gratitude."

Prudence said nothing. Her eyes grew larger and darker in a whitening face. Across the table they met Peter's—blank and incurious. She knew what had happened to Mary. Then Toby's, grave and eager. "Go on—tell them," her own said. Toby, leaning over just an instant before her silence became remarkable, said :

"Don't tell us the beastly details, Prudence. I hate nightmares." Then, solemnly, to Anthony :

"There was rather a tragedy, you know. She, well, she hung herself."

"Yes, ghastly bit of work," Oliver sought to dismiss the matter, without avail. Anthony's curiosity was roused.

"D'you mean she was trying on the same game when we pulled her out of the pond?" he asked Prudence.

"Yes, I suppose so——" Prudence looked over to Toby again. He had understood a moment ago her terror and horror of the subject; he ought not to *let* them go on asking her about it. And, surely enough, he produced the very remark to turn all their thoughts in another direction:

"Talking of corpses," he observed pleasantly to Anthony, "did you by any chance send to Pierce's of Graiga for a dead horse? Because they sent me a notice, but when I sent a man to fetch it over to the kennels they told him that 'the captain of the other dogs had commandeered it off them.'"

"I don't see to my own flesh. Can't give you much information I'm afraid. Jack got a notice about it and sent one of the boys, I suppose. It's not a pet amusement of mine—going through the country looking at dead horses. The strings of live ones that come up to this door daily give me enough to do."

"Perhaps," Toby suggested evenly, "you'd send the worst specimens along to the harriers; they might be useful for soup, if nothing else—that is, if the farmers are going to continue selling their dead ones twice over, first to me and then to you."

Anthony's little, fox-terrier face sharpened itself into a hundred angles. Aloud, he said nothing; but his expression was one of agonizingly acute disfavour towards the harriers and their Master.

Peter, glancing from Anthony to Toby, whose expression was one of precise propriety, said to herself that this was only a faint fore-taste of the rows which would be. And almost as soon as the idea occurred to her, she decided:

"I'll back Anthony—only thing to do. Pity. I thought it'd be fun with Toby this winter."

As she walked down the avenue with Prudence, Peter broke the stormy silence which lay, like a heavy cloud, between them.

"Go on, say it," she urged pleasantly.

Prudence withdrew the arm which, more from force of habit than for friendship's sake, she had thrust into Peter's. She was choking with anger —the hurt anger we cherish against our friends ; but she could find no words in which to convey to Peter any adequate idea of the enormity of her offences. Neither could she trust her voice to speak. She loathed Peter, for the moment, and the loathing returned to her own heart, stabbing and vehement, till she could have cried aloud in her hatred and her pain. And all the time she did not say one word. It was Peter who spoke again.

"Prudence, you're such an intense person, darling. You don't think one little bit. You just *feel* things, till they hurt, and *then* you think of murder. Listen now, Prudence ; I *know* what's biting you to-day. Darling you don't think you could hate me for a whole afternoon, and I not know it, *do* you ? "

Prudence walked on, her head tilted up ; she kept her pale, still profile turned blankly to Peter.

"Well, look here"—Peter spoke resolutely— "to cut the cackle and get to the horses, or rather, the hounds. I wonder if you realize the fact, that unless some of us keep on the right side of our friend in front "—she nodded towards Anthony —"Toby's going to get a damned poor show with his little lot of rioters this winter."

" Oh ! " Prudence was so taken aback by the suddenness of the idea that she was almost surprised into a normal state of mind.

" Yes," Peter continued to make her point with precision and dexterity, " of course you imagined I was well away with him this afternoon. You're too imaginative, Prudence. That's your trouble, darling. You've got an extravagant *mind*. You buy twenty-one-shilling face-powder, and then use it for putting in your hunting-boots. You're the world's most kissable person, and you see red when you're kissed. You're the most marvellous pal any woman ever had, and you'd chuck a friendship like ours away, break it up, on account of an afternoon's bad temper. You would, Prudence, you know you would ; and then go off with your chin up, and your heart nearly broken. That's you."

Prudence's eyes shone at this description of her own entrancing personality. How wonderful Peter was to see just how she felt ; to know and understand ; to explain another's feelings so intimately. What a gross fool she had been not to have trusted her more. Peter was everything to her—the whole world and a bit over ; of course she would hate those whom Prudence hated, and love where Prudence loved. There was only one Peter, and Prudence must matter to her beyond all created things. So, finding no words to express the relief which flung itself through her, Prudence smiled, one of her rare and heavenly smiles, and said :

" I expect I was in a Hellish temper. Darling Puppy, I've been so worried I can hardly think.

We must talk about it, and we haven't time now.
Come over to-morrow, *whatever* happens—come at
dawn, and stay till dark. I love you so, sweet one !
Just little you and me. . . . Hullo, Toby ! You
made me jump. You shouldn't, you know, it's
bad for my heart. What do you want ? "

" I've got an idea," said Toby solemnly.

" You shouldn't, you know. It's bad for your
brain," Peter told him. " Anyway, I don't suppose it concerns me." She stopped to light a
cigarette, then fell behind to walk with Oliver.

Toby was saying :

" You know my old motor-bike . . . the second-
last I had, before I got my first car ? Well,
Prudence, she'd carry you flying, and there you
are . . . a perfect way of getting over to the
kennels."

" But Gus'd half kill me. She wouldn't think
a motor-bike a bit a nice way of getting about."

" Oh, *rot !* How could she object ? "

" I'll tell you what, though ! " Prudence turned
to him excitedly, " I've thought of a *right* plan.
We'll stable it in James's house, at the end of the
far avenue. She need never know. I can get
over to you by the lanes. Oh, Toby, that's a
grand notion ! "

Still entranced by the idea, Prudence climbed
into the Lingarry car ; and leaning out, talked
to Toby over the back, while John Strap (who
combined the offices of chauffeur and strapper)
endeavoured to tuck a rug about her knees.

" When you're quite ready, Prudence——"
Oliver, behind the wheel, was very patient.

Prudence settled herself down in her corner with
a jerk ; her face immediately lost all its radiancy ;
while dismay and evil-temper laid their clutching
hands on her heart again. And with them,
stronger every moment as the day closed in, and
the car brought her nearer to Lingarry, a trailing
haunt of fear overcame her ; suffocating in its
intensity, more gruesome for its total incertitude.
She could not reason against it ; she could only
feel (with all the extravagance of mind of one
who uses twenty-one-shilling face-powder in her
hunting-boots) that fear, of she knew not what,
which James's inexplicable sayings had first
awakened to be her nightly torture, and her daily,
pricking discomfort.

Beneath the rug, Prudence's hands grew clammy
with heat, and beneath her tight, little hat a band
of sweat broke out on her forehead. If only she
could have someone with her—always with her ;
someone who would hold her hand and go down
the long passage to the bathroom with her in the
dark evenings ; who would sleep with her all
night, and when she woke, her body straining
stiffly away from the nameless terrors of the close
dark, would hold her in kind (not passionate)
arms, and speak of small, cheerful things till she
fell asleep again.

But, in the back of the big car, Prudence crouched,
alone with her fears. Shivering, she slid down
beneath the rug.

. . . . .

Peter did all her thinking in her bath. Life's
problems, she usually found, relaxed their stern-

ness in the steam and fume of bath-salts. Many complexities were oiled and soothed from her mind, as the lather of soap creamed on her body. But this evening, matters refused to clear themselves, according to custom, and she lay long, reflecting on the devious ways that were before her. She frowned and used her *loofah* viciously :

" I *had* to lie to Prudence about it, especially about his stopping Toby hunting. He won't do that, but it's a good excuse for mucking about with him. *I* couldn't stop it, if he wanted to. He's got the world's worst mouth and a funny temper, I should think. Of course, Toby has got his consent, *and* the committee's ; still, I know he wouldn't draw a yard of gorse if he thought the Master was against it. He's orthodox, and he's right. It'll be a pity if Anthony creates and makes things impossible. . . . I *am* interested in him, I like him awfully. Wonder what Prudence would think if she knew ? " Reflectively, she sponged the water over the firm, smooth flesh of her shoulders ; the light, striking down on her, broke up the drops into separate, shining reflections on the smooth dullness of her skin. Reposing full-length again, she manipulated the hot tap skilfully with her toe, and then proceeded to think some more.

" It's absurd, and ridiculous and, and divine," she thought. " I'm *not* in love with him, and Heaven knows, all *he* cares about are the hounds. I've got to marry, of course ; I want that——" she considered the matter further, intimately and unashamed. Then, climbing reluctantly out of the bath, enveloped herself in a towel, and lighting a cigarette, sat down to think about Prudence. Calculating and far-seeing, her mind moved in careful progression : " *Prudence*. She's more to me than anyone. But I'd do without Prudence, even . . . to marry." She drew in her smoke and thought again, with decision : " I *must* have that. I want it. Anthony is obviously getting interested, I'd be a fool not to encourage it. Still "—her mind went forward three years—" if I keep in with Prudence she'll be able to do most things for me—some day ; will, too. She's like that. Going about with Prudence isn't *really* much catch though, for another girl. *She's* always the centre of every show. Still, I'd meet masses more people. Anthony's old, well, getting on. How old, I wonder ? Thirty-five, about . . . I loved his room." Her eyes smiled at the memory of his farewell :

" I *wanted* you to see that draft," he had said.

That was it ; the hounds and coverts, the kennels, drains, boiling and feeding houses, his mind was so full of them. She loved him for it. " He's *fond* of his hounds, I like that," was how she put it to herself.

She got into the two clean, folded silk garments which, before her bath, she had laid with precision in the warmest spot of the hot-air press, and donned her primly-frilled, mauve flannel dressing-gown, without having come to any decision. But as she went down the passage to her bedroom, she thought :

" I've got to do both, marry Anthony if I can, and keep up with Prudence, whether I do or not. It'll be complicated. But Anthony comes first."

CHAPTER XI

HOODED in their shawls, two ancient country-
women clustered together in whispering discourse
before the side-door of Lingarry. Upon Miss
Gus's appearance they broke into an impassioned
duet, the one supplementing the other, their pauses
punctuated by a silence of frigid inquiry on the
part of their audience. It went something like
this :

" God save ye, me lady——"

" I come out on me two feet from Bungarvin——"

" So did I, my lady——"

" We come to a weddin'——"

" Was to be above at the Crosses——"

" Sure it wasn't in it, me lady——"

" A little pair o' boots, Miss—look at the cripples
I has on me, I'm kilt walkin' in them."

" God may lave ye yer health, me lady ; if ye
had as much as a little florum idle, I'd be thankful.
For look-at, I haven't as much on me as'd scare
the birds. God knows——"

" That will do," Miss Gus interrupted firmly.
She was, perhaps, more easily frightened than the
birds. At any rate the idea of the exhibition
(which she knew to be imminent) did not appeal

to her. " I have neither boots nor clothes to give away to strangers," she stated, " what I have must go to the poor round this place. However, (she sternly ignored a whispered demand for the price of a night's lodging) you may go round to the dairy door and have a drink of butter-milk, and some bread and meat from the kitchen." She turned from them and went back through the door, a storm of blessings hastening her retreat.

Down the long, sand-stone passages she walked crisply, her taffetas petticoat whispering audibly beneath a tweed skirt. The tinkers had passed from her mind ; she had even ceased to wonder what make or shape of under-garment might be described as a ' florum.' She was planning her afternoon's work in the garden ; whether to divide the double primroses in the south border ; or whether to plant the daffodil bulbs in the new sheet below the larch tree. Both needed to be done so badly. It was a pity that Oliver could not spare them another man in the garden ; however . . . Miss Gus pushed open the swing-door into the hall and came face to face with James.

" Her lady-ship is within in the drawing-room, Miss," James informed her, in tones almost as respectfully triumphant as though he had divined her plans for an uninterrupted afternoon in the garden.

" Lady Mavis Trudgeon, James ? Is Miss Peter with her ? "

" Miss Peter's gone to play herself with the dogs, Miss. She's taking a race-round now, to see could she get Miss Prudence."

Miss Gus inclined her head, and went on to the drawing-room. Here Lady Mavis Trudgeon struggled gamely out of a deep sofa to greet her hostess.

"So *long* since we've met," she intoned dreamily, "I saw you at Lackettstown last week though, didn't I?"

"The day before yesterday," corrected Miss Gus with precision, "my sister and I were both there. How lovely their garden is. Those glorious chrysanthemums! Now what do you suppose they use?"

A gleam of companionship leaped into Lady Mavis's fine eyes as she leaned across to Miss Gus. Here they were on common ground.

"My dear, I *don't know*. Some people *are* so funny about their gardens. They *tell* you nothing, and as for giving away as much as one seedling—they'd rather die. Now Marion Hogan-Grey is so *secretive*, and she rivals her own gardener in meanness."

"Extraordinary!" Miss Gus agreed. "Now, to *me* half the pleasure in a garden lies in getting plants from my neighbours; but some people can't *see* it. Shall we go down and look at the Michaelmas daisies? They really are a sight."

Peter joined them on their way down to the garden; Dilly demure, and Blazes foolishly up-lifted, kept her company. They had been hunting a cat, and for once Blazes had distinguished herself; having put her quarry to ground up a tree, she had, with reckless bravery, climbed along a

219

branch in pursuit, sustaining in consequence a perfectly crashing fall.

"How d'you do, Miss Gus?" Peter shook hands. "No, I can't find Prudence. But it doesn't really matter; I can come to the garden with you. Are Dilly and Blazes allowed in?"

"Only on a lead," Miss Gus wavered; "however, as you know how to manage dogs—I do wish I could say the same for Prudence—perhaps you could keep them off the flower-beds."

Peter laughed. "I doubt it." She bent and coupled the pair with her silk handkerchief, and slipping the thin, leather belt off her jumper, used it as a strap. "This ought to keep them out of mischief."

The garden door was opened, and the sight of a blackbird, hurrying deliriously out of an apple-tree, sent the little dogs up into their collars at once; their small flags straight as pins, ears forward and eyes alight, they strained raptly forward. Were they not in the garden?—that forbidden Eden which *must* hold all delight.

Peter walked sedately in the rear of the two ladies who paused ever and anon to examine, with thrills of excitement, some minute growth, scarcely apparent to the eye of the uninitiated, but to them full of the promise of future glory. Peter yawned and ate an apple, lit a cigarette, and fell to wondering fretfully where the dickens Prudence had got to.

They were in the rose-garden. Late blooms, perfect and seemingly undismayed by Autumn frosts, flowered in reserved purity, a little more

stiffly than had their opulent elder sisters of the
summer.

" Now, *my* roses "—Lady Mavis began—" are
nothing to these—absolutely nothing ! "

" Oh, nonsense, Mother ! Don't make such a
poor mouth," Peter interrupted. " Didn't *you*
think they were very nice in the summer months,
Miss Gus ? Roses and lavender in an old-world
setting—my mother's the old world setting ! "
She flicked an affectionate, and not at all respectful, glance at the fashionably dressed redundancies
of her mother's figure.

Lady Mavis smiled indulgently, murmured :
" Peter, *darling !* " and let it pass ; while Miss
Gus thought, not for the first time, how strange
it was that Prudence should not be as companion-
able with her guardians as Peter was with her
parent. Different temperaments—that explained it
—very different.

" Yes, indeed," she agreed with Peter's remark
about the roses at Kilronan, " they were quite
a sight."

" Mulching ! " ejaculated Lady Mavis fiercely,
" Filth ! Give your roses *plenty* of it."

" That's the spirit." Peter, no longer even
amused, lagged behind again. Those old things
and their gardens ! Where *was* Prudence ?

Miss Kat joined the party presently, which
made the garden tour appear more endless than
ever to Peter, since they must now retrace
their steps to view many neglected treasures.
Even Miss Gus grew weary at last, and firmly
repressing her sister's suggestion of a visit to the

Barnevelders, she led the way towards the house and tea.

Peter fed thankfully.

"*Such* good cake, Miss Gus!"

Miss Kat sniffed wrathfully. "Well, if it is" —she said—"*I* am the person to be thanked for it. Paugh! These horrible women!"

"Now, *do* tell me, is it your cook?" Lady Mavis bent towards Miss Kat. "I am always ready to sympathise with anyone on that subject."

"My dear Mavis, do not, I *beg* of you, allow Kat to open up her soul to you about the cooks. The matter is too—just *too*—awful." Miss Gus's voice held a note very nearly tragic.

"We've had no fewer than three in the last six weeks," declared Miss Kat. "Yes, indeed—the brutes! And after I had had the servants' bedrooms all distempered—if that doesn't *prove* it! Such black ingratitude!"

"But why? Why don't they stay? I never heard anything like it. Three in six weeks, it's rather awful. Don't they give you any reasons?" Lady Mavis was patently horrified.

Peter said:

"Six weeks—isn't that the period since you had the suicidal maniac?"

Miss Gus started violently; then, assuming her most repressive expression, answered coldly:

"Really, Peter, I see no connection whatever between the two things. None *whatever*. And I do beg that you won't spread any ideas on the subject abroad. It might do infinite harm. Never shall I forget the terrible time we endured, eight years ago, when the servants took foolish notions about the place into their heads. The less we talk about this last business, the better for all concerned."

" I see, Miss Gus," Peter answered equably. " Yes, of course you're quite right. They do get up a panic about nothing so easily."

" I think this is *so* deeply interesting," Lady Mavis broke in energetically. " And, now I come to think of it, I have been conscious of a sort of red aura—an angriness—in the atmosphere of the house, ever since I arrived. Quite indescribable, but there, you know, most palpable to the sensitive ; more a sort of dragging nausea than anything else I can think of."

" *Mummie !* Don't start getting psychic. You are awful. Besides, you *know* it's just that you've made a pig of yourself over the potato cakes. You mustn't mind her, Miss Gus ; it's her latest craze, you know—collecting atmospheres." Peter was quite severe.

" Darling, what a really *nasty* girl you are," her mother reproved her gently. " She's quite the most unsympathetic subject I've ever tried to do anything with," she explained to the mystified, but disapproving, Miss Kat, " she just *won't* respond. No vision about her. Prudence, I should imagine, is immensely psychic ; there's an interesting radiancy about *her*——" Lady Mavis half closed her eyes and gazed raptly into space, breathing heavily through her nose the while.

Peter, after one glance across the table, stooped to give a piece of toast to Dilly, before addressing herself in clear accents to Miss Gus; she said:

"Did you know that Mummie has practically promised to give me a Bradley suiting? Isn't it excellent of her? And it is to be a seventeen-guinea one, too——"

"Peter, *darling!*" Lady Mavis's eyes were wide-open now, and her stertorous breathing a thing of the past: "You do tell such dreadful untruths! You know I never did."

"Yes, Mummie, you did. When Mervyn got those frantic checks you said you'd like one member of the family to be decently turned out—and I might go to Bradley next time I'm in London. You can't deny it—you did."

"Well, if I did say one of you was to have new clothes, I kept my word. What about Victor's new pink woollies? He looks a perfect scream in them."

"'Right, Mummie. I'll let you off this time. I admit Victor does look rather class in the pink suitings. Hullo! There's Prudence."

Without, Prudence's voice could be heard calling:

"Blazes! Blazes! *Blazes!* Duck—Duck—Mummie's little girl! *Blazes*—blast you!"

Blazes got under a chair and made no response.

"I suppose she knows it's time for her medicine," Peter observed, pityingly. "Come on, Blazes. You won't know yourself when you've got outside a bottle of Tonic—Elixir." She smiled at Miss Gus, picked up the reluctant Blazes and, preceded by Dilly, wandered out of the room.

On the steps she met Prudence—a rather dishevelled Prudence—deeply engrossed in the book

224

of words which was wrapped round the bottle
she held in her hand.

"All right," she answered Peter's greeting with
a worried nod ; "how many pounds would you
say Blazes weighed ? I can't get the scales, because they're all in at tea in the kitchen."

Peter shook her head.

"Oh, give a guess ! Well, never mind—I'll
risk a dessertspoon. It can't really damage her.
Hold her steady, you, and pouch the corner of
her lip. I'll pour it in."

Blazes wriggled, strove and ducked her head,
but the major part of a dessertspoonful of nauseous-
smelling liquid was finally inserted into the corner
of her mouth. "Hold on, Peter ; she doesn't
swallow it for ages," Prudence massaged Blazes'
long, weedy throat. "Toby gave me this, to-day.
He says it's grand stuff—nothing like it for getting
up condition on a dog. I *thought* I heard her
swallow that time, did you ? "

"Yes, she may have. Let her go, a minute."
Peter held the little dog firmly and gently between
her two hands. "Blazes—d'you see 'im ? *Rabbits*,
Blazes ! " Blazes swallowed hard in her excitement. "D'you see 'im ? He's a *bad* fella—*send
—'im—away* ! "

Blazes, suddenly released, sprang forward, a
little, swift, white flame, she doubled across the
smooth, green spaces of the lawn.

"That went down all right," Peter rubbed
some dust off the knees of her skirt. "Poor Blazes !
This is the third tonic she's had in the last month.
It's nearly as bad as your cousins' cooks." She

225

picked up the bottle and read aloud : " ' Loss of condition ; appetite ; general falling off ; parasites '—h'm, *she's* safe-guarded. Well, look-at, Prudence—what *have* you been up to ? "

" I thought I'd better clear out to-day, Peter. I rather put my feet in the trough last night. I made an unfortunate mistake with Cousin Kat."

" She seems rather pale and anguished-looking, this afternoon. What did you do ? "

" It was altogether a mistake. She came to me quite late and asked for her Aspirin tablets she'd lent me. I went off to look on the dog's medicine-shelf, where I thought I might have left them ; and in the dark I'm blowed if I didn't get hold of the wrong bottle——"

" What *did* you give the unfortunate woman ? "

" For God's sake don't breathe it to anyone, but it was those patent pills I got for Blazes in the Spring. I'd put them into an Aspirin bottle by mistake. Beastly error, wasn't it ? " Prudence shouted with heartless mirth.

" Don't laugh, Prudence. You might have killed her. Does she know ? "

" If she does, nothing in the world will make her confess to the extreme indelicacy of her situation," Prudence went off into another fit of mirth. " It's damn funny. Toby simply rocked when I told him."

" Did you see Toby to-day ? "

" Oh, Lord—yes. I spent all the afternoon there. I started off on the cob, stuck her into James' cow-shed, leapt up on the old mo'-bike, and that was how it was done."

" That Toby's old bike ? He's made it over to you, has he ? How pleasant ! So that you can skip back and forth to Merlinstower. Well, I wouldn't be you when the girls get to know it. And for once I think they'll be in the right of it. You're playing about too much, Prudence. I used to think Toby didn't care two hells about you ; but now I'm sure he does. It's bound to be awkward."

Prudence hitched herself up on to the stone balustrade of the porch ; her face and drooping shoulders were altogether weary ; her voice irritable, as she answered :

" Oh, Peter—don't be so *alarming !* Can't I muck about the kennels with Toby ? What's the *harm* in it ? We crack away about the hounds and the hunting, and not a word more. I'd shut him up, jolly quick, if he started to get stupid. But I *swear* he doesn't. After all, I must have something to take my mind off this foul place, and those two old beasts inside. I *could* express what I think of them—in one word—but I'm far too fond of dogs. Sweetheart, aren't I ? Mother's only—only. Her Tom—Tom—Duck ! "

Blazes struggled down from her mistress's arms, and wound away round an angle of the steps— tail down, and a wary eye cocked at the medicine bottle.

" All right. Cats, darling ! Hi—*Cats !* " But Blazes showed none of the enthusiasm she had evinced a minute or two earlier at Peter's fictional rabbit. She took one hasty and rather scared look about her, before embarking on an intimate revision of her personal cleanliness.

"That's a fool of a dog. Come on into the house, Puppy, and I'll sell you two jumpers."

On their way up to Prudence's room they encountered one of the housemaids.

"Excuse me, Miss"—the maid's face bore traces of recent emotion of some kind—"do you know where is Miss Lingfield? The cook says she'll not stop in it. Sure she's clapping all she have in her boxes, and she says she'll go off now, on the red, raw miny*ute*."

"Lordy, how gaudy! Not *another* cook going." Peter was on the verge of amusement, but sobered hastily as she caught sight of Prudence's face. Even in the darkness of the corridor she could see how it had whitened.

"I don't know where she is," Prudence spoke in a strangely stifled voice, "tell James to look in the drawing-room."

"Isn't that what I'm after doing, Miss? He gave out to me all sorts, below in the pantry; and in the latter end he allowed he'd carry none o' them trash o' tell-tales to the ladies. But sure when the cook's so eager to go, what can be done?"

"Oh, blast the cook! Come on, Peter." Prudence ran down the passage to her room; banged the door; and going to her cupboard, flung two crumpled jumpers on to the bed. "There you are"—she said furiously—"I don't want you to buy them. Isn't this awful?" Turning from Peter, she collapsed into a chair; her hands shaking; and her lower lip caught between her teeth.

"Good Heavens, Prudence ! What is there to get so rattled about ? Tell me, and perhaps you'll feel better."

"What a beast you are, Peter ! I've nothing to tell you—absolutely nothing. It doesn't matter how rotten things are for me, *you* don't care. And I'm dashed if I tell you anything, anyway." Prudence flamed ; then, as suddenly, cowered in her chair and sobbed.

"Prudence, don't ! You mustn't, really. It's awfully bad for you, Precious. I simply can't allow it. Get up and put a lick of powder on your nose ; I'll say you'll feel different then."

As she affected to examine the jumpers up for sale, Peter ran over in her mind any possible reasons for Prudence's sudden collapse. "Badly frightened," she decided at last. "Shaken to the core about something ; I can't force it out of her, and it's obviously quite trifling or she'd tell me at once." Aloud, she said :

"I'll give you four and sixpence for this jumper with the collar. It'll just do me for cubbing. By the way, let's have a look at that tweed coat you got made."

"Right." In the same measure as she effaced the traces of her tears, Prudence recovered her composure. She fished the garment in question from its habitat amidst a collection of fragile dance-frocks, and slipping her arms in, ripped off her skirt and paraded for Peter's inspection with a studied grace that might have made the fortune of any mannequin.

"Not bad, is it? But do you think he's made it just on the long side? I don't know. It's rather good when I'm up on a horse. Still, I think I might be allowed just half-an-inch more breeches."

"Oh, I *don't* know, Prudence. You're awfully on the leg, in any case. I don't think it's a bit long. Hang it, woman! It's as short as any man's now."

Prudence craned her head to glance approvingly down as much of her back as was possible. "That's what I like," she said, "to be properly turned out astride one *ought* to look exactly like a man. The flat-hat and coat-and-breeches-to-match brigade really *are* enough to make one pop a gut. Painful." She got out of the coat and mooned about for a while in knickers and a jumper; did her hair; then announced, almost cheerfully:

"It's the nights that are the dickens and all, Peter. I lie in that pathetic little bed, all of a muck-sweat, sometimes—simply terrified to move. It's frantic."

"Darling, frightened of what?"

"Oh, just—things," Prudence laughed evasively. "My cupboards and curtains, and all sorts. I hate a room with cupboards; but Gus won't let me change now. I think I'll get married, Puppy. A husband will be something to clutch, don't you think?"

"H'm, yes. Bit too much, sometimes, I should imagine," Peter glanced at Prudence's narrow, red bed with thoughtful eyes. "How about Toby?"

"Oh, not Toby! I don't really want to marry, Puppy. All men are offal. Look here, your Ma

230

has been screaming for you for the last ten minutes. Hadn't we better go down ? "

Peter acquiesced unhurriedly.

" I'm taking this jumper," she said. " By the way, the hounds are in Cloonbeg, on Thursday. Eight o'clock is time enough to be there. Are you coming out ? "

" Yes, I'll ride the new mare. She's going to be one of the best—Suspenders is."

" Why on earth—' Suspenders ' ? "

" Because Hinch says where another horse would fall she'll make suspensions of herself. Quite true too. But she's the ' Lily Maid ' to the girls. Also, her breeding fits in. Good-bye, darling Puppy. I'll see you on Thursday, shall I ? That is—if I don't hunt with Toby Wednesday."

" ' I'll see you on Thursday,' " reflected Peter sombrely on her homeward way, " and to-day is only Monday. A month ago it'd have been awfully different. However, it's as well perhaps ; I shan't have to explain why I'm going out for hound-exercise with Tony to-morrow morning."

CHAPTER XII

MIDSTREAM

" PETER, what are you doing to-day ? "

" Nothing painfully particular, Mummie. That is—I may be going with Anthony Countless to look at a horse."

" You were out with him this morning, for hound exercise, or whatever you call it. *I* don't know. Do you ever tell me what you are doing ? " Lady Mavis was becoming ponderously fractious.

" I was *not* out with him," replied Peter with some heat. " Mervyn went by himself."

" How *stupid* of Mervyn. How awfully *tire*some ! I should have thought you might have managed things a little better, Peter."

Peter did not answer. She was painstakingly glueing a piece of toffee on Dilly's front teeth. Her head on one side, she watched with absorption Dilly's efforts to end the protracted delight. " I hate being *compelled* to enjoy toffee," she murmured, extracting the half-assimilated sweet in stringy morsels, and then wiping her fingers on Dilly's back. Dilly, swallowing the residue at a gulp, thanked her mother prettily.

" I cannot bear the modern young man," Lady Mavis announced weightily from her sofa, " no,

I cannot say I like the type. My dear, when I *think* how different things were in my day. They crawled, literally *crawled*. Yes, with boxes of chocolate, like worms——"

" The chocolates were wormy ? How insanitary, Mummie—wasn't it ? "

" Peter, you know perfectly well what I mean. The modern young man simply makes use of you. Puts you up on his *brutes* of horses—for a treat. Yes, he did, I know he did——" as Peter opened her mouth to refute this imputation. " Well "— with a fine stroke of oratory Lady Mavis again retrieved the subject under discussion from the particular to the general—" all I can say *is*, in my day if they gave you a box of chocolates that was how you *knew* they were paying you attention. The present-day youth gives you a blow, I sup- pose, and you're just as pleased."

" Well, I must say I'd rather have a blow—one can hit back, then. Besides, I hate chocolates. Anyway, Mummie, you needn't think I'm having either—from Anthony," Peter ended the conversa- tion on a devastatingly candid note ; leaving her mother feeling unequal to the situation and com- pletely powerless to deal with this unfeminine daughter, she went out of the room.

Lady Mavis would have liked a daughter whose humours she could render pliable by lavish spoiling ; whose tears would flow readily when outraged parental authority became retributive. The daughter of her dreams resembled accurately a Lewis Baumer etching (all big eyes, fluffy hair and fluffy skirts) and should have had every young man in the country side, desirable or otherwise, prostrate and pleading at her slender feet. She would have enmeshed herself in the most astounding and indiscreet flirtations ; her extrication there-from giving ample opportunities for the display of the parental powers of tact and diplomacy. This ideal being would have worn the clothes selected by her mother with ravishing grace, and so doing prove herself the walking example of the superior good taste of an elder generation. Finally, having ploughed her furrow through the hearts of many, she would achieve matrimony with the Right Person (equally, of course, selected by her parent), and having done so, would obligingly set forth on a sea of marital difficulties, that mother's genius might neither rust nor lie fallow. Whether all difficulties should end from the moment when Grandmamma laid the Fluffy Paragon's child in the Right Person's arms, Lady Mavis could never be quite self-sacrificing enough to decide.

Poor Lady Mavis ! Instead of this creature, whose life she would have ordered to their mutual entertainment and profit, Fate had given her Peter for her only daughter. At least her mother wrote all Peter's peculiarities down to Fate ; but, as she was in many ways extraordinarily like her dead father, it is just possible that he may have been in part responsible for her idiosyncrasies.

From her very earliest days Peter had resolutely declined to become the daughter of her mother's dreams. Her hair never fluffed and she herself neither flirted outrageously, nor lied in a compre-hensible and natural manner to cover her irregularities of conduct. Few men crawled ingloriously at Peter's feet—those large feet, her crowning short-coming in her mother's eyes—and those who did crawl were not the rich and the dashing, but more often the impecunious and retiring, to whom Peter always extended her large kindliness.

It was therefore with an anxious hopefulness, which she spasmodically strove to conceal from her daughter, that Lady Mavis had, for the past month, watched the progression of Peter's intimacy with Major Anthony Countless, M.F.H. She had, as she thought, kept a sensitive finger on the pulse of the affair, from its lowly start among the kennel drains, to its present satisfactory condition when, almost daily, Peter was absent for hours at the kennels ; or on one of those lengthy expeditions optimistically undertaken under the fond delusion that the horse of dreams will ultimately be found, if only one travels far enough from home to look for it.

To-day, in spite of her casual method of conveying the information to her mother, Peter was pleasedly aware that the afternoon would almost certainly bring Anthony to Kilronan, and that together they would set forth on one more horse-coping expedition.

Nor was she wrong ; an hour from the time when the last of the dogs had received its mid-day portion—an hour spent by Peter in rather aimless ragging with Sammy in the hall—she heard his car coming up the avenue. Pulling out her strictly utilitarian powder-puff, she powdered her face with unhurried precision ; and quite oblivious of a derisive and knowing titter from Sammy, in the hall behind her, she strode down the steps to meet Anthony.

Anthony got himself jerkily out of the car and looked at her hard as he shook hands.

" I was thinking of going over to Derryhook to look at the horse Mervyn was telling me about. I suppose you wouldn't care to come and see I'm not too infernally stuck ? " he asked her.

" Yes, I'd like to come," Peter said, " not that I'm any safeguard against John Regan's prods. You mustn't think that."

Anthony did not really think that any girl could know one end of a horse from the other, but it speaks eloquently for his condition of mind that he should vehemently assert his complete reliance on Peter's eye for a good thing.

" What did you do this morning ? " he asked her presently as the car turned out of the avenue gates. " I *thought* you were coming out with us."

" I over-slept myself instead," Peter answered.

" Oh." Anthony paused to think about this. It was a tranquil and pleasing vision—that of Peter over-sleeping herself. She would, of course, sleep, as she did everything else, to repletion. " But you didn't sleep all the morning. What did you do when you got up—had breakfast, I mean ? "

" Schooled a horse with Sammy, and cleaned a pair of breeches before lunch."

" Good Lord! Don't you send your hunting clothes out to the yard to be cleaned ? " There was a sort of mild horror in Anthony's voice as he asked the question. He waited with surprising interest for her reply.

" I always wash my own breeches," Peter told him ; " because I like them well done," she added in explanation.

Anthony nodded. When you came to think the matter out it was obvious that she would choose to clean her own breeches for just that reason—because she herself could do them better than other people. Sitting there close to her, strong and fractious as she was strong and calm, Anthony felt that the fulness of content was to be found in her. He desired content materially, and Peter particularly ; and knowing this, knew that he would tell her so quite soon. And it would be easy and satisfying.

It was a long drive to Derryhook ; quite twenty miles from Kilronan. Peter wished the distance had been twice as far. She only wanted to drive on and on, sitting by Anthony's side, peaceful and altogether sure of her love for him and his—well, at any rate—his interest in her. Yet not once during their progress from Kilronan to Derryhook did Anthony use the opportunities of the way for love-making. Peter was not surprised, nor even disappointed. She waited, calm in the assurance that soon, very soon now, he would take because he could not help himself ; and she would give and give, because her love for him was tireless and she was strong and generous.

Years afterwards Peter was asked what she and Anthony had talked about on that drive preceding his proposal, " because," the friend said, " I can *just* imagine Anthony proposing to a girl, but I can't imagine him leading up to it."

" He was telling me the breeding of every horse in England," Peter answered seriously, " I wish I had his head for remembering pedigrees ; Anthony

is a walking blood-stock-sale's catalogue. It's a
unique gift."

The friend said no more.

But the discussion of pedigrees had in this case
led on to other things; Peter did not mention
that. Before Derryhook was reached Anthony and
Peter knew a great deal more about each other
than they had had leisure to learn in many mornings of hound-exercise and cubbing. For instance :
Anthony now knew that Peter considered the
wearing of bed-socks a filthy habit ; that she and
her lady-mother fought, ' like tame cats and tom
cats in spring ' ; that she knew more than a little
about fishing and had (this was told him shyly)
killed a twenty-five pound fish on a fly of her own
tying ; and that she could put a name to every
yard of covert they passed likely to hold a fox ;
could tell whether it had held one within the past
ten years, and if so recount the hunt which had
ensued with painstaking detail.

Peter, on her side, learned that Anthony's married sister had two grand little boys—toppers to
ride ; and—talking of the hounds—that he proposed to send his Woodlark to Belvoir Helmsley—
finest stallion-hound in England ; also that he
shared her dislike of bed-socks, and hated girls who
' put stuff on their mouths hunting ! ' Peter, who
lip-sticked unobtrusively, made a mental note of this.

When at last they arrived at Derryhook, Anthony
had not hurried over those twenty miles, he turned
the big car round in the rather cramped space
in front of Mr. John Regan's tall weather-slated
house ; saying to Peter, as he reversed to a nicety

and locked his wheels round again : "You're going to drive her home, do you know that?"

"All right," said Peter. She was sensible that an almost crushing honour had fallen upon her.

From behind the lace curtains of the dining-room Mrs. John Regan surveyed the pair indulgently, at once scenting a romance. She knew Peter, who often came over with Mervyn and others to look at horses, well ; and Anthony at least by sight. In the three minutes which elapsed before she greeted them hospitably at the door, she had swept a dog, suffering from red mange, from its lair on the sofa, beaten up every cushion in the room and *cached* two dirty teacups beneath the sofa ; on her way to the hall she hissed instructions to an unseen domestic concerning a clean cap and apron, and the slapping of a cake in the oven. She was then ready to greet her guests with entire freedom from embarrassment.

"Well, Miss Trudgeon, how are you? Won't you come in? How do you do?"—This, as Peter accomplished Anthony's introduction to his hostess—"I declare John'll be mad he was out ! I suppose you came to look at horses. T'ch, it's too bad *really*, and you taking such a long drive."

"We came to look at a chestnut horse Mr. Regan was telling my brother about," Peter explained. "Don't you think," she added persuasively, "you could let us have a look at him?"

"Is it me?" Mrs. Regan laughed indulgently, "sure I'd know what horses he has in it. John'd eat me, that's as true now as I'm standing here, if I was to stir a finger in the stables."

"Is he likely to be back soon?" Mr. Regan's peculiar dietary did not strike Anthony as the least amusing. He wanted to see the horse, as that was what he had come to do, and then he wanted to get away with Peter as soon as possible.

"Ah, he mightn't be back till to-morrow," said Mrs. Regan. Her manner was abstracted; she was, as a matter of fact, coming to a decision. "Tommy," she screamed at a boy who was desultorily raking the sparse gravel of the drive-way, "go tell Michael, here's a lady and gentleman to look at the big horse. And tell him he should hurry and trot him out here, and not have us waiting on him."

"I will, Ma'am," replied the boy, removing himself with alacrity.

"Couldn't we go round to the yard"—Anthony was beginning when Peter quelled him with a look of warning. She knew better than he did how much Mrs. Regan was taking on herself in showing a horse to them in Johnny's absence and realized how unwelcome to her would be his suggestion of a visit to the stables.

"What a pretty creeper that is on the house," Peter observed tactfully, after a slight pause. "I don't think I've ever seen one quite like it before."

"Did you not, really? Well now, that'd root on a rock and no bother to it," Mrs. Regan tore handfuls of the creeper off the house as she spoke and dragged furiously at its roots. That it had indeed rooted on a rock seemed probable from its stubborn resistance of all her efforts to dislodge it. And that it should yield suddenly was only to be expected; Mrs. Regan's collapse upon the

gravel was equally sudden ; and the appearance
of a scaly rat, which dropped like some horrid
fruit from the upper branches of the creeper into
her lap, added a touch of drama to the situation.
With a yell Mrs. Regan struggled to her feet ;
with an intrepid spirit, which can never sufficiently
be extolled, she clasped her skirt about her—the
rat still caught in its folds—and reaching in three
steps the rake which the messenger to Michael had
left behind him, she dropped her skirts and meted
out to the rat, as it loped dazedly away, a very
nasty, sticky ending. She tossed the corpse into a
neighbouring laurel hedge and turned to her guests.

" I wouldn't like them jokers at all," she assured
Anthony ; adding, with great seriousness : " Them's
able to cut your throat."

" By Jove, I've seen a few brave things done,
but I've never seen a braver woman." Anthony's
admiration was heartfelt.

" Ginger for pluck," murmured Peter, just indicating Mrs. Regan who, with two hair-pins in her
mouth, was adjusting a third in the coils of flaming
hair, which her fall and the combat with the rat
had loosed from their moorings.

At this moment the chestnut horse, with an
old groom at his head, came smartly round the
corner of the house. And Anthony proceeded to
walk round him and to say things to the groom
which nobody else could hear. The chestnut horse
was walked and jogged, (showing bad action)
examined and (Peter felt sure) thoroughly dis-
approved of, before Anthony sent him back to the
yard to be saddled up. Ensued half-an-hour when

he was galloped, ridden across three uninspiring fences, pronounced to be a grunter, and returned once more to his stable.

"Well, I'll write to your husband," Anthony said to Mrs. Regan ; and to Peter : "We'd better be making a move, hadn't we ? "

But their departure was not to be achieved so simply. Anthony really did not quite know how it happened but he found himself seated on a hard, velvet-covered sofa in a dreadful little room, waiting for the tea—which he had no desire to drink—to come in ; and listening with a wondering respect to Peter's easy flow of conversation with her hostess.

The tea, carried in in relays by a flustered handmaiden, who twice fell over his feet in her precipitate exits from the room, was ready at last. There was a faint crash of china as Anthony in rising disturbed the cups which Mrs. Regan had secreted beneath the sofa. Anthony started, and Peter, growing scarlet in the face, repressed a giggle with difficulty, and gave her entire attention to her hostess's conversation.

"Did ye know Jimmy Coffee ? " Mrs. Regan was asking. "Oh, he's a *lovely* man, but he's a terrible size. Well now,"—she surveyed the bulky expanse of her own reflection in a wavering mirror upon the wall opposite to her ;—"I'm a fly to Jimmy. I'm a *tiny* little thing compared to him."

Anthony, as he stirred his cup of strong tea, reflected almost with awe on the probable bulk of Jimmy Coffee. It was surprising to hear that Peter should know, or even know of, such a person. It was at this point that he felt a tug at his sleeve and looking down saw an indescribably nasty little boy, whose long fair curls descended nearly to the collar of his velveteen blouse, at his side.

"Ha are ya?" Anthony inquired with more irascibility than heartiness in his voice.

"Say 'how do you do?' to the gentleman, love," prompted Mrs. Regan from behind the teapot. "Shake hands nicely, now."

"I will *not*," replied the child; he eyed Anthony's out-stretched hand with manifest disfavour, and sidling round the table to his mother, squirmed his head against her in a frenzied affectation of shyness. Mrs. Regan stroked his curls fondly back from his forehead with a rather buttery hand.

"Will ye take a *tasse-o'-tea*, *petite*?" she inquired tenderly. Then, to Peter, by way of explanation: "I always speak French to the children, Miss Trudgeon."

Peter's murmured reply was rendered perfectly inaudible by a prolonged roar from the child, who proclaimed with unprovoked passion: "It's Johnny McReery that *I* want." The hideous lament continued unappeased for several minutes after his parent had carried him struggling from the room, and slammed the door upon his howls.

"Johnny McReery is the yard man's little boy," she explained on her return, "the child's cracked about him. Only, really you know, I can't have him going around with Johnny McReery; he'd pick up a common way of talking off him too quick."

.   .   .   .   .

Half way home Anthony, who had broken his promise of allowing Peter to drive, stopped the car and kissed her.

Peter eyed him calmly : " There's *no* excuse for that," she said.

" Well, Peter—it's a non-hunting day ; that must be my excuse, darling. Besides, I love you. Didn't you know ? "

" I didn't—know——" Peter yielded, almost readily. Kissing her his need fired suddenly.

" Don't *bully !* " Peter's voice was firm, though still drowsy with the rapture they had caught together. He couldn't have everything—not all at once anyhow.

" I shouldn't bully you, I know, darling. But you're such a wonder. Put your arms up. Kiss me—ah, Peter, properly——"

Ten minutes later they drove on into the setting sun ; the glow in Peter's heart was scarcely less radiant. She loved and was loved again. The glow in the sky faded out ; the grey of evening and the little bitter chill of the coming night was with them, but Peter was all one throb of living warmth. And Anthony discovered a remarkable and (he assured her) heretofore unknown gift for changing a left-hand gear with his right hand.

They called in at the kennels on their way past. Anthony had orders that he wanted to give before he drove her back to Kilronan for dinner. The orders concerned horses for the morrow. Anthony would ride Puckhorn ; Willis and Carter, the two whippers-in, were to have Twinkler and Uncle ; he would bring over Miss Trudgeon's saddle, she was to have Christopher. Seven o'clock would be time enough to leave the kennels ; he did not say where he was going to draw.

On their way back to the car Peter asked him what he was going to do.

"I'm going to Knockree," he told her. "I'll spend the morning there and kill a fox in it if possible. There are about two square miles of gorse there ; it just sickens hounds drawing it. They tell me there were two litters bred there this year ; I'd like to kill a fox in it—they'd leave quick enough then. As it is you *can't* force one away."

"Pity some one wouldn't put a match to three quarters of the covert," Peter commented.

"I don't know. It's a perfect stronghold for foxes,"—Anthony broke off as a boy ran up to the car, in his hand the green envelope of a telegram.

Anthony, when he had torn open the envelope and read its contents, swore softly. "No answer," he told the boy. And to Peter : "Stick your toe on the self-starter, dear." After that he hardly spoke to her for quite two miles. Peter, her cheek against his sleeve, did not care. When he did speak it was to ask :

"Peter, how soon can you marry me ? "

Peter raised her face, one cheek crushed and pink from where it had lain against his coat. Over her left shoulder she saw a thread of the new moon gallantly riding the sky—a good omen. She turned a worn sixpence in the gritty lining of her pocket as she answered : "At once, I suppose. Or else we'll have to put it off till the end of the season. I suppose one *has* to go and honeymoon, for ten days at least—not that I want to."

Anthony looked at her. "*I* do," he said, "I think we might even spare ten days from this country and have some of them round about Melton."

Peter put her cheek back against his coat. "All right," she said, "you say when."

In her large, orderly bedroom—compared to which Prudence's was such a scarlet piggery—Peter sat late that evening, a little tired, her thoughts yet held in a stilled enthralment—wonderfully, completely satisfying. She undressed slowly, folding her clothes up with all her usual care for their well-being. Padding bare-footed across the deep pink carpet to her cupboards, she pulled a clean pair of pyjamas—very sane pyjamas—from the well-filled, scented shelves.

Pushing her head and arms into the silk jumper, Peter reflected that Prudence would certainly have made such an evening an occasion for something really extravagant in the way of night-wear. Thinking of Prudence her mood changed a little. A chilly current joined itself to the warm stream of her thoughts. She loved Prudence, yes. But with a love that wavered pitiably by the side of her love for Anthony. She was sorry if her engagement should put any strain on their friendship, but also she knew with utter certainty that she was ready unhesitatingly to sacrifice her friendship to her love. She realised that the sacrifice had begun that very evening when she had unquestioningly accepted Anthony's suggestion of a bye on the morrow, nor given more than a fleeting thought to the meet of Toby's Harriers to which she and Prudence were to have fared forth together.

Having completed her preparations for the night Peter bent over Dilly's basket, tucked in a corner of blue blanket and received in return two weary

grunts of thankfulness ; she kissed Dilly ' good-
night,' extinguished her candle and slid into her
bed. For perhaps five minutes she lay stiffly on
her back staring wide-eyed into the darkness ; then
suddenly she flung herself round, her face buried
against the pillows, her bright, shingled hair ruffled
out of its ordered waves ; her body and mind in
sudden unreasoning tumult, she lay near to ecstasy.

" Peter," said Sammy's voice at the door.

" Yes. Come in."

" Oh, Peter, I've got such an awful stomach-
ache. Believe I'm dying."

Abandoning her dreams, with hardly a sigh for
their broken glory, Peter rose to minister to him.

" Hop into my bed, Sammy. I'll get you a
hot drink. Found the hot water bottle ? "

Sammy, as he curled himself round the life-
restoring heat of his sister's rubber bottle, reflected
with gratitude that anyone but Peter would certainly have asked what he had been eating before
ministering to his pains. However, as he was not a
very gracious little boy, his only remark when Peter
got beneath the eiderdown as she waited for her
spirit-stove to heat a drink for the sufferer, was :

" Get up. Your *bloody* heels are stickin' into
my *bloody* legs."

When the hot drink had done its work and
Sammy drowsed, blissfully at rest after pain, a
slight, peaceful hiccup coming from the heart of
the blankets the only reply to questions as to his
well-being, Peter wrapped herself in her flannel
dressing-gown and took her way to Sammy's room
where she spent the rest of the night in Sammy's

disordered bed. It seemed such a pity to disturb
him.

.　　　.　　　.　　　.　　　.

At Drumferris Anthony knocked out the end of
his last pipe and laid it carefully down on the
mantel-shelf. He looked round the small, comfortable room and tried to imagine what it would
be like with Peter there. He frowned. At least
she would not allow the Bridgies of her reign to
leave their dusty brooms in corners. On the dark
oval of the oak table lay the green envelope of the
telegram which he had received on his homeward way with Peter. Picking it up, he re-read
the message. His frown deepened. It was from
George. George, his valet for years ; his guardian
angel ; the one perfect man-servant in all the
world ; from George, whose surname was now
Benedict. And this was what it said :

" Wife ill unable return to work at present in
any case cannot come Ireland."

Anthony tore the paper across and put it into
the dying fire. Then he drew back the curtains
and looked out into the soft night. The very
young moon just outlined the roofs of his new
kennels ; the Irish smell of wood-smoke caught
him happily by the throat ; the thought of Peter
was as if kind hands had been laid upon him.
Remembering the morrow's early start Anthony
turned to go up to bed. As he undressed he
thought : " Well, if I can find a silly fox, and they
leave a silly earth open, and we can persuade
him to push his silly face into it, we'll have him
out and eat him. I want blood."

CHAPTER XIII

A GOOD HUNT AND A BAD MISTAKE

" Miss Prudence, let you take a nice fresh egg
for your breakfish. Sure what nonsense ye have—
to go out and gallop the country fasting."

Prudence looked up from the banana skins that
graced her plate. She was pale and tired in the
young, morning light, and snapped at James with
a break in her voice. " Go away, James. You
make me sick."

" Well now, what about the least sign of rum and
hot milk? " James suggested appealingly.

" Don't be stupid, James."

" The devil a-matter! Show me here the coffee-
milk." James manipulated the milk jug over the
flame of the egg-boiler for some moments, finally
concocting for Prudence the one essential of an
early-morning start for a cubbing fixture. He
noted with approval the slow colour that came
to her face after she had gulped the beverage
down. " Ye'll be the better o' that," he promised
her, " and look-at now, what I whipped for
ye."

" Oh, James! That's Miss Gus's plain chocolate, she got from the stores. Don't you know
she has every stick counted? "

"Ah, there's nothing only the sign o' chocolate in that," James re-folded the end of the flat, white package, "and the Man Above alone knows what time o' day it'll be before you get a bit to eat."

"Right you are, James. Thanks awfully, anyhow." Prudence rose from her chair and went out to the hall, feeling distinctly benefited by James' ministrations.

"Have you your gloves?" he asked, scuttling, and peering after her in the dim, early-morning light of the long passages: "Don't leave the whip after ye, whatever."

Prudence turned and smiled at him. The rum and milk had certainly done much to lessen the edginess of her temper. "How fussed you are, James. Did the ghosts in the woods tell you I wouldn't come home, I wonder?"

"Oh, God be between us and harm!" muttered James piously. "I wouldn't wish to hear the like o' that talk at all."

Prudence laughed; stamped stiffly down the stone steps in her field boots; and strode off along the flagged path in the direction of the stables. At the corner of the house she turned, and seeing the grey, old man still looking after her—drawn and bent together he seemed, in the thin autumn air—she raised a hand to her hat in a gesture of salute or farewell, before she turned the corner and passed out of his sight.

In the yard, sounds of activity were audible from the chestnut mare's box. Prudence, as she pushed aside the wet branch of a rose-tree that trailed across her path, untethered by a recent storm, overheard scraps of conversation between Hinch and his satellite.

" . . . Well, I was black asleep," she heard in John Strap's voice, evidently in extenuation of some charge. An almost inaudible reply from Hinch followed. But, obviously, it concerned itself with those who, in his opinion, no person could pick apart for badness, and whose proper sleeping-hours were devoted to far other pursuits.

" Well, it was me stomach was sick," John Strap averred in injured tones, " me mother can tell you that's the truth for me. At ten o'clock last night, I declare I'd be glad to die. I had prods in me digesture rose like flames half way in me t'roath ; me heart bate ex-*tra*. Sure the way I was——"

" Ah, shut-up ! You and yer lies," Hinch interrupted agreeably, " passing low, dirty remarks and tossing with the chaps at the crosses, is what'd suit you better, at ten o'clock in the night or any other time. Such delicacy ye have—yourself and your stomach ! " This last in tones of biting scorn.

Prudence leaned over the door of the hound puppies' house, shamelessly listening for more. But John Strap was obviously too rebuked for further excuses or recriminations. A minute later Hinch looked out of the loose-box, a cloth in his hand.

" Pull the mare out, Hinch," Prudence told him. " I hope she's in good form—we might get a bit of a hunt this morning."

"Well, she is. She's hellish rakish in herself, altogether. Bring her out, Johnny. Look at that, now"—as Suspenders, with a pale and dissipated John clinging to her head, issued skittishly from her box—"you may swear she's stepping as light as a thrush." Hinch moved over to feel a girth, and Prudence, joining him, laid a quiet hand on the mare's shoulder.

"Got her back well up, hasn't she?" Prudence laughed with very natural uneasiness. "Lead her about a minute, John. I don't want a repetition of yesterday's games."

John grinned in respectful sympathy. "Nothing at all she done, only go clean up in th' elements altogether," he volunteered, in answer to Hinch's look of scorn.

"Did she offer to buck with you, Miss Prudence. Oh, go to God! Keep the stick to her—that's the only dart. And look-at—take a wink at the girths when you'll get to the meet; if the saddle slipped back on her, she'd put you, or me either, to hell out o' that—too quick."

Prudence did not answer. She beckoned to John Strap, and sticking a foot in her stirrup, mounted in gravity and silence: "Open the gate, John," and she was out; was riding quietly down the leaf-mould paved back avenue. She opened the two tall gates which divided the back avenue from the farm lane and the lane from the high-road, off the back of a surprisingly compliant Suspenders.

After the first mile of the road had been accomplished, Prudence—satisfied that (always barring

the advent of a motor-lorry) Suspenders had now
settled down and would, with luck, maintain the
perfect lady attitude until the meet was reached
—lapsed into meditation. The grass siding was
sound here, the mare might jog on.

Peter. She hadn't seen as much of Peter lately
—not so much as she had of Toby. Dear old
Peter ! But she was hanged if she could stand
the Anthony Countless craze. Peter must drop
him. Would she ? Not likely. . . . Hold up
mare ! What are you going all over the road
for ? Funny, how little one minded all the beastli-
ness at Lingarry when one was going out hunting
in the early morning. Why should one mind ?
There was really nothing *to* mind. Only, at night
it was so awful. After all, she smiled with half-
shut eyes, there was always Toby. She could
have him—if she wanted him enough. . . . If
she wanted him. But did she want him ? Toby
was a darling ; a miracle to look at ; far the
nicest young man in the country. It was a comfortable thought that she, Prudence, should be
the object of his devotion. Comfortable, and so
useful. Hunting, dancing, racing, meant for her
Toby, and Toby's car ; gave her the pleasing
consciousness that less lucky girls were saying :
" That ? That's Prudence. Prudence Lingfield-
Turrett—Toby's last. He doesn't do *badly* for
himself, does he ? She's a bit of an heiress too.
Gets it all when she's twenty-one. Desperately
attractive, don't you think ? *Wild* as a hawk."
And the knowledge that even those who were,
perhaps, her detractors, nevertheless accepted the

least recognition on her part with some small stir
of excitement. Still—a husband. . . . Prudence
felt the mare's mouth with deft consideration.
. . . A husband—she didn't want that, not
yet.

Oh, Lord ! What a morning. Throwing up
her head to its characteristic angle of intolerance,
Prudence snuffed the air with appreciation. On
one hand a stubble-field gleamed palely—a week
bereft of its corn-stacks. A low mist lay over the
country within a mile's radius of the flowing river.
Looking across the low banks that fenced the road
to her left and right, Prudence decided that the
banks, though still on the hairy side, were more
or less jumpable. Autumn rains and early frosts
had deadened colour ; and the indescribable
feeling of coming winter, with its near promise of
the best fun in the world, caught Prudence with
stinging gladness. She pulled up the mare to
look into a covert which lay near—too near—the
road ; not a holding gorse, at all, and it had grown
up tremendously in the last couple of years. It
was to be hoped that Major Countless would turn
some of his money and attention into the coverts
—that would do the country some good.

She rode on for another four miles, thinking
how she was going to have her first hunt with
Toby's harriers ; and it would be a good hunt
too—she felt that somehow, in the half-cold trickle
of excitement coursing through her. Anticipation
is not always the best part of a hunt (especially
in the smaller hours) and it certainly lacks the
fine glow of retrospection.

At a cross-roads she pulled up, and waited. Toby and his hounds would have to pass this way, and as yet there appeared no trace of hoof or hounds' foot-marks on the wet road. Mindful of Hinch's warning she dismounted and shortened her girths by one hole. Then, lighting a cigarette, waited patiently for the arrival of the hounds. Peter would have hit them off at a cross-roads nearer the kennels, she decided. " She and I and Toby —we'll have the *hell* of a good morning," Prudence reflected happily. Then, the tension of the mare's shoulder and the prick of her ears, warning her of the hounds' approach, before she herself could either see or hear them, she re-mounted. This she did as carelessly as any boy ; her eyes on the turning round which the hounds should come ; a firm word of admonishment to the mare as her foot found the off stirrup. For Suspenders was not a lady on whose nice behaviour much dependence could be placed.

Toby : He looked rather *devilishly* good, Prudence decided, as he came into view, the hounds well on in front of his horse. They were topping, too ; wonderful, what three weeks' close (even passionate) attention from Toby had done for them ; Prudence, the mare's heels carefully embedded in the briar-wreathed bank, and the lash of her whip down, called a greeting to their huntsman and his whipper-in, Philly—who had put up condition in much the same degree as had the hounds.

Toby's good bay horse was fighting his bit and going wildly ; excited by the mare and the hounds ; sure now, that he was to go hunting again ; was to know once more the delirium, catching him with the twin strengths of fire and water, when the cry of hounds came surging back across wide fields ; an ecstasy forgotten during the fat months of summer, when he had fed richly from the generous bosoms of Toby's best fields.

"Hullo, Prudence ! Can that mare keep her heels to herself ? "

"I wouldn't ride a horse that kicked hounds." Prudence, nevertheless, dropped her whip-lash again, warily, as a little pied bitch loitered just too close. "That's a green sort of brute you're riding yourself, to-day."

"Do you think so ? " Toby answered pleasantly. "Well, of course, *I* haven't got Oliver to go round the country, picking out the right thing for a little, only child ; if I had, I might be as nicely mounted as you are yourself."

"Well, I don't know." Prudence considered the big horse, "he may be a bit on the leg, but you've got bone there, all the same. You had him out a couple of times the end of last season, didn't you ? I remember him giving you a crashing fall coming off Carn hill."

"I rode that good hunt we had from Knockbeale on him, and he carried me well," Toby reminded her. "He's bred right ; all steeplechasing blood on the dam's side. He *likes* jumping, and given that in a horse you can teach them anything."

"Out of your good old mare, 'Familiarity,' is he ? She's done you proud, Toby. You'll call him 'Contempt,' won't you ? "

" ' Contempt ' ? "—Toby was puzzled.

" ' Familiarity breeds Contempt,' " Prudence reminded him.

" By Jove, Prudence ! You're a topper to christen a horse," Toby told her, in open admiration. " I'd sit up half the night mucking up pedigrees, and in the end of all things I wouldn't be a bit further on."

" Well, Toby—to change the subject—these little hounds of yours are going on nicely, aren't they ? "

" Gad ! They're toppers, Prudence. We had a little hunt ; the day before yesterday—oh, it was no more than a mistake, we were out for hound-exercise, really—they just stormed through Duff-carry covert, and they were every one out of it together, like a shot from a gun."

" Are you by way of cubbing, to-day, Tobioh ? Or do you mean a hunt ? "

" Well, really, all the crops are carried, and the fences are getting so naked now, it's simply indecent not to cross them." Toby and Prudence smiled at each other, like two naughty children.

" Where's Peter ? " Prudence asked after a lengthy pause ; just a slight rasp of annoyance edging her voice.

" Peter ? At Drumferris, I suppose ; that's the game she's at most of these mornings. They are having the deuce of a gallop, those two. Do you approve, Prudence ? "

Prudence laughed.

" Oh, well—everybody loves *some*body," there was a covert sneer in her voice ; but the next moment her manner changed completely. "No, Toby, I don't. I hate it. I wouldn't care if Peter told me, but she doesn't. At least, only the bits that don't count. *I* always tell her things, and it—it hurts."

"Do you? I thought girls never did tell— everything, I mean. Here we are, now——" Toby's face grew stern with the business of the moment ; his voice sharp and absent as he sur- veyed the steep hillside—a tight, close tangle of hazel-coppice, ash-saplings, bracken, and great, toppling grey stones—which was Garrytom covert ; and gave his orders to Philly and Prudence.

"Prudence, you go and watch the lower corner ; the old vixen's sure to break towards Knockowen. I'll lift them to your holloa, and never mind the cubs. Come on up here with me, Philly."

The hounds poured across the low, stone-faced bank, that Toby's young horse took with more zeal than discretion ; Prudence watched him cantering up the misty, hill-side field as she rode off to her post.

"Toby," she reflected, as she pushed at a broken, wooden gate with the handle of her hunting-whip, "is just a little too fond of a hunt to be a good huntsman. Lift them to my holloa, will he? When they're hunting in covert, perhaps. What a liberty ! Well, God help me if I tally a cub away ; I wish Peter was here—she'd know the difference."

Sitting on her horse at her allotted corner, Prudence waited and watched ; every nerve tense ; her senses of sight and hearing alert, like thrum-

ming wires. The mare, cross at being taken away
from the other horses, now strove furiously with
bracken-fronds, now flung her head in the air as
Toby's voice, cheering his hounds, was borne to
them. Prudence drew the snaffle rein through
her fingers and spoke quiet reproof.

An eternity seemed to her to pass before she
heard a hound speak in covert ; and a different
note leaped into Toby's voice as he cheered the
rest on.

Prudence nudged the mare with her heel, and
moved back a little ; her eyes were intent on the
covert-side ; the blood raced through her veins ;
and the hounds' voices and Toby's voice laid
violent hands on her heart.

Now their music died, and the masterful lust
of the chase left their huntsman's voice. In her
mind's eye she could see them, at fault ; whimpering,
feathering, busy in the undergrowth.

A pause. Again Toby's voice. And now a
hound speaks once more. Their music grows and
swells and then fails, as they turn and hunt away
from her. Prudence's hands tighten on the reins ;
they are right up the hill-side now. The deplorable
fear of being left seizes on her, like a cold, mental
nausea. Be with them, she must ; life holds no
other thing.

Yes, it does though. Her trust in Toby. Certain
it is that he will not slip away with hounds, and
leave her. And even as she knew this with beautiful surety, she could hear hounds turning and
hunting back through the wood.

" A cub, a—my God ! "

Slipping along the edge of the fence, like a stain of yellower rust in the dead bracken, Prudence viewed their fox. No cub this, but an authentic old campaigner—not a doubt about it.

Her breath coming fast, and her heart beating quick-time in her dry throat, Prudence waited, motionless, while their fox loped across two sides of the field, and set his mask determinedly for the open country. Then it came :

"Tally-Ho ! *Garn-aw-aii !* "

And, an instant later, Philly's voice across the hillside :

"Tally-Ho, over, Master ! "

Then the quick notes on the horn ; the sound of Philly's whip-lash ; a heart-breaking delay, which gave Prudence time to damn Toby for the slowest fool that ever tried to lift hounds to a holloa ; and then the bustle and jostle as they came out of covert. Toby, with a white, strained face and crackling voice ; saying : "Where, *exactly*, did you see him go ? " An instant of hesitation, and the hounds owned to scent—their voices an anthem to glorify the morning.

No need for Toby's uplifted hand ; before they were half across the second field from the covert, hounds were running on well ; and Prudence, Toby and Philly—those three who loved to hunt the fox—knew, with blessed certainty, that this was going to be a great hunt indeed.

"My *God !* There's a bit o' scent," Toby said it, as Prudence and Suspenders, taking a second fence abreast of him, landed with a bit of a peck in the plough beyond, righted themselves, and

260

were off down a head-land—Suspenders pulling double.

" Sorry, Tobioh ! " Prudence sailed down first at a furze-filled gap. " She'll come back to my hand after another five minutes."

" Right ! Prudence, you're a champion. Come on, now, me old pal, till we see a bit more o' this hunt together." Toby, his eyes all for the hounds and scarcely at all for his fences, spared attention to note that, one more field put behind them, Prudence and Suspenders were going together in the sweetest accord.

For twenty-five minutes, without a semblance of a check, hounds ran over the best of Toby's borrowed country ; twenty-five minutes while fire ran in the veins of their three followers, and drunk with the headiest of all wines, the glory of fox-hunting, they flung the fences behind them ; nor ever encountered one strand of wire ; for the great God of fox-hunters looked down, and smiled, and blessing them, decreed that it should be so.

Twenty-five minutes before hounds were brought to their noses ; a welcome breather for the horses ; and, as it transpired, an added glory and crown to Toby's morning ; for, as he held them on, the line was hit off once more, and they were running again—scent, perhaps a trifle catchier than in the first burst out of covert. They were up in the hills now and the scent (though not the going) improved.

Prudence was the first to slip out of her saddle and allow Suspenders to tow her up the steep hillside.

"We'll be right into the Drumferris country in another half-mile," Toby announced, as they re-mounted on the crest of the hill-side.

"He's hunting this end to-morrow, too. God send we don't run through a covert!"

But as their horses bucked over a loose, stone wall, at the foot of their perilous descent, any ideas respecting the country, save the potent desire to get across it, faded from their minds.

And still hounds ran, and still Prudence, Toby and Philly stayed with them. They were right in Anthony's country now—the worst end of it too—bogs and stone-faced fences, narrow as knife-blades, their portion.

As the hounds burst into Knockree covert, right on top of a failing fox, Toby took on wire, and came a real smeller into the road.

It was not by any means a nice fall; and when Toby and Prudence, who had waited for him, got going again, and arrived at the covert-side, heated, dishevelled and (as far as Toby was concerned) distinctly sore as to the ribs, the one idea upper-most in their minds being to get the hounds out as speedily as possible, it was to hear—above the jealous growling of hounds that have marked their fox to ground—a violent altercation taking place.

"No man ever called me a liar and lived! Wait till I'll catch a hold o' ye to strip ye, an' t'row ye in a bed o' nettles——" this in Philly's unmis-takable voice.

The challenge was received in complete silence; a silence into which Anthony Countless' voice barked the question:

"When Mr. Sage's *harriers* have quite finished marking their fox in my covert, perhaps he'll have the goodness to remove them to his own country? "

" 'Twould be hard for him, sir, and he lying dead in the ditch above "—this again from Philly, but in more respectful tones. So much they heard as they strove with a locked gate which, finally yielding to their joint efforts, permitted them to add their presences to the scene which was in progress in the covert. It could hardly have been one of greater confusion ; for, round the main earth in the heart of the gorse, shoved and growled not only Mr. Sage's harriers, but sixteen couples of the Drumferris fox-hounds. While Anthony, scarlet in the face as his coat, confronted Toby and his companion in crime, speechless for the moment with righteous wrath.

" I'm most confoundedly sorry, sir," Toby dismounted ; " I'd have stopped them if I could, but we've had an hour and ten minutes——"

"And as you're in the covert, yourself, there's not so much harm done as if you were coming here to-morrow," Prudence struck in soothingly.

" Harm done—*harm ! You* talk about harm, you nasty, poaching harriers ? Harriers—harriers *cub-hunting*——" his voice cracked. " My God, sir ! I tell you while I hunt this country I'll have none of your damned poaching ways, and hunting my coverts will have to cease, sir, or my resignation goes in to-morrow."

" Running through a covert after an hour and ten minutes is unfortunate, but it's not poaching," Prudence pointed out ; for Toby, now oblivious

263

of all matters save that his hounds should mark their fox with all decent ritual, had thrown his horse's reins to Prudence, and was now standing over the earth sounding the sorry "wind 'im in."

"When you're quite ready"—there was a cold and ugly gleam in Anthony's eye, as he rode up to Toby—"perhaps you'll remove your *hounds*. And, by the way, I should be glad to know which of my coverts, within a radius of five miles, you have *not* been through this morning?"

"This is the first covert we've touched since we left Garrytom," Toby's manner equalled the other's in stiffness. "I hope you may enjoy as good sport." He touched his cap to Peter and moved off.

"I think it's hardly probable," said Peter evenly; it was the first time she had spoken. As Prudence rode by her, she spoke again: "A *rotten* thing to do; I can't say I congratulate you, Prudence." She looked her friend up and down, unflinchingly; then turned to Anthony. She had chosen.

Prudence stared at her for one uncomprehending moment; then, with flaming cheeks and smarting eyes, she turned her horse's head round and rode after Toby.

CHAPTER XIV

RESULTS

HOME : Riding home through the bright haze of the Autumn afternoon ; a swelling sense of content in her tired limbs ; a feeling in her heart for her tired horse, akin to no other feeling in the world, so full was it of the consciousness of glory shared ; of the supreme, triumphant knowledge of a hunt well-ridden ; Prudence raised her face to the wind that blew softly from the West, and cried a thanks-giving to a kind God.

In such a maze of full content she rode, that a large car drew near her and passed, unnoticed. Only when it had gone some distance down the road did she recognise the backs of its two occupants. Peter, in her familiar, brown tweed, was driving—driving Anthony's cherished Bentley—and beside her sat the Bentley's owner, obviously content that it should be so.

A tide, akin to panic, came over Prudence. It flooded out of mind and body the glow of satisfaction that had been hers ; brought to naked light the realization that Peter—the Peter she knew— was gone from her ; would never, she knew, be the same to her again. Instead of Peter, her friend, here was a Peter who told her off in icy tones ;

who passed her by in Bentley cars ; who rode to
hounds, when Prudence rode to harriers ; who
would—without the smallest doubt—marry Anthony
Countless. And in the long years before them,
Prudence saw Peter's life. She would hunt all
the season, in a manner bordering on the religious ;
take a fishing in Norway in the summer ; return
for Peterborough hound-show, Clonmel, and the
Dublin Horse-show ; and after that, cubbing to
do all over again. Lost to Prudence—lost for
ever. What should she do without her ?

Marry Toby ?

A little, clammy fear clutched at Prudence's
heart. In memory, she rode again by Toby's
side, all the miles back to the kennels ; while every
minute of that hour and ten minutes was faithfully
dealt with ; later, when they sat down to lunch
together, the tale of the morning had been yet
again retold. And Toby's eyes, one short week
ago all for Prudence, were now filled with a new
light ; a burning ardour was in him, leagues
removed from the love of women. And Prudence,
knowing it, fretted in her heart, wishing contra-
dictorily that things might stay between them as
they had been.

Luncheon over, it was Gummy's turn. Gummy
was picked up and his rough face held against
Toby's smooth head, while inquiries were made
respecting his doings of the morning :

" Oh, what I do, all day ? I was a darlin' dog !
I was an-alligator-cat-'ound ! Oh, *what* I do, all
day ? I saw me master get up, hellish early. I
went to sleep again like sensible dog. Got up for

me breakfast ; then I had terrible morning, chasing dam' black kitten. I did a hundred yards, fast-pace, an' put him up a tree. I tell you, he's a *bad* fella——"

Prudence, a cigarette in her mouth, which Toby had neglected to light for her, felt curiously blank and cold ; while an insistent voice cried in her heart, and would not be denied : " Toby—I *do* care for him ; because he is rude ; because he doesn't care about me ; because when he kisses Gummy I want him to kiss me—I love him." Aloud she said :

" Toby, I've *got* to go home."

" Right you are. . . . Kisses, Gummy. More kisses. . . . The darlingest dog as ever, *ever*. My name Mister Doggy-Wise. I tell—I know where one dam' fat rabbit do lie. I was. . . . Come on then, Prudence."

And in the stable-yard he had put her up on Suspenders ; said :

" My God ! Prudence, *what* a morning," and swinging on his heel, was off in the direction of the kennels, before she was well out of the yard.

Remembering all these things, and with Peter's casual passing stabbing her afresh, it was not surprising that Prudence's high contentment of soul in the morning's achievement should abate, giving place, before she had reached Lingarry, to a most pitiable discontent.

" There'll be a row about this," she reflected gloomily, as she left the stables, even the recounting of the morning's hunt to Hinch having failed to cheer her spirits ; she went up to her room to struggle out of her hunting clothes, an angry throb of excitement alternating with the dull ache of misery in her heart.

Pulling down her short skirt, she fastened one shoe-lace inefficiently, leaving the other to its own devices ; then wondered vaguely what to do with herself in the blank hours that were left of the day. The rain was coming down too, which made matters, if possible, more despondent. Prudence banged the door upon the chaos in her bedroom, and set off towards James' pantry. On the way thither she encountered Oliver ; he called her into his study, and shutting the door firmly, offered her a cigarette. Realizing this to be the invariable prelude of a peculiarly trying interview, Prudence at once assumed an expression of sulks and defensiveness, and thrust her body into ungainly angles in a chair.

" Well, what sort of morning did you have, Prudence ? And what do you think of the mare ? " Oliver's pleasant voice was almost silkily suave.

" Oh, a *right* one," Prudence forgot to look cross for a moment. " She gave me the best ride of my life. Takes her fences on the fast side, but you couldn't put her down. No matter what sort of place it is, she always has a leg to spare."

" You sound as if you'd a bit of a hunt."

" A hunt ? We had seventy minutes, and never touched a covert till the end. Found in Garrytom and ran over the best of the Milltown country into Crana hills, with only one slight check. They hunted slowly across the hill, but scent improved the other side ; they left the railway on their right, and fairly raced into Knockree gorse, where they

marked their fox to ground in the main earth."
Prudence had been early drilled to give an unvar-
nished account of a hunt, and she permitted no
interruption of the narrative. When she paused,
Oliver spoke, almost hesitantly :

" You had a right hunt, Prudence. But, look
—there's going to be quite a lot of bother over
it. In the first place, Anthony Countless has been
here since lunch, trying to hand in his resignation
to me—as Hon. Sec. All on the head of this
morning's work."

" But, Cousin Oliver, it was simply, sheer bad
luck, running through the covert. It's rot to talk
about poaching, and hunting the coverts, and
so on."

" I know all that as well as you do. But what
I have to think of is the good of fox-hunting in
the country. And if Tony Countless says he won't
have a pack of harriers hunting on the outskirts,
and ruxing out his out-lying coverts, (when he's
drawing them himself too, b'Gad !) then they
have to stop hunting—that's all about it."

" But, Cousin Oliver, he might have thought
of that before Toby took these harriers. It was
all done in order ; Toby asked permission, and so
on. You don't mean to say you'll *stop* him hunting, now ? It would be too infernal. He's not
doing harm—he's doing good."

" Well, I've got to have a talk with Toby about
it. He is coming over to-morrow, to shoot Kilconnel with me ; he can dine and stay the night,
after. Don't you see, Prudence, I've got to back
up our own Master. He's in a rotten position

269

too. I understand that he only consented to harriers hunting when he was under the impression that they were going to hunt *hares*. We've got a right good man in Anthony ; he'll spend money in the country, and get up the coverts, and all the rest of it ; that is—if he stays. So far, he hasn't had much of a show, and—my God ! Prudence, you and Toby dam' nearly put the lid on it this morning. If it hadn't been for Peter Trudgeon, I believe he'd have taken the mail-boat back to-night."

" Why, for Peter ? "

" I'd have thought that you'd have known, before most people, that Peter was engaged to him. In fact, he told me he'd sent the announcement to the *Morning Post*, to-day. D'you mean to say you didn't know ? "

" Yes, I, I knew quite well," Prudence answered truthfully ; while a voice within her brain echoed drearily : " Yes, you always knew." Aloud, she said : " But why are you asking *me* about the harriers, Cousin Oliver ? "

" To speak quite candidly, Prudence, I think your influence in that direction is fairly strong ; and I want you to use it——"

" Well, you're quite *wrong*," Prudence broke in suddenly, " I haven't the faintest influence with Toby ; and I may tell you, you'll find it a harder job, to make him give up hunting hounds, than you think. He doesn't care a curse about anything else. And why *should* he give them up, anyhow ? "

" Oh. All right, Prudence—that's about all I wanted to know." Oliver spoke coldly and finally ;

so that Prudence left the room with the galling sense of having been dismissed as useless strong upon her.

In the hall she met Michael, the pantry-boy, who handed her a note. It was from Peter; tearing the envelope open, Prudence moved across to read the contents by the dull light of a stained glass corner window.

" It was a bit of a shock to find you mixed up in this morning's show "—she read—" I'm afraid I said what I felt, rather ; but I hope you'll forgive me, as it was in the heat of the moment."

That, by way of apology, Prudence thought, as the memory of Peter's speech stabbed her afresh. She stood erect, like a pale spear, in the shadowy dusk of the hall, and read on with painful haste :

" You won't approve of my engagement," Peter wrote, " but I want you to know that it is such a big thing to me, that I almost don't care what you think about it, one way or another. I expect you'll feel the same whenever your own comes off. Anyhow, I wanted you to know *first*, and wish me luck—even if you do hate Tony ! Really, he's the funniest, nicest thing. I'm afraid I shan't see you again for a week, as I'm going over to London Friday night, with Mummie. Tony is coming for a day or two. We want to choose a really smashing one !

" Tony and I are just off to Jimmy Cashels to look at a horse, so I must stop.

" Yours ever,

" PETER."

"Tony and I, Tony and I"; as it was in the beginning, is now, and ever shall be. . . . Prudence's thoughts were wandering off on cold, shuddering little expeditions. Out in the chill, she realized how warm and safe it sounded, after all—that, 'Tony and I.' And Prudence was alone; alone in this cold house; alone in this grey, raining world; alone always; with fears and despairs; little hatreds and sorrows at her heart. Her ways were never set for her in pleasant and sure places, like Peter's; the art of living was not hers. With a start, Prudence realized that this was just the trouble; she had no gift for enjoying life. Toby had been hers, and she had let him go. Well, he had found a madder love. And that, it seemed, was to be taken from him too. Was it to be? Not if she could help it. Tears squeezed themselves between her eyelids; they fell on her clenched, cold hands.

An amazing thing had happened. She was consumed with hot pity, crying out in championship, not for herself but for another. For Toby.

"Excuse me, Miss Prudence; but one o' yer hound pups has the yella jaundice on him. He used no food at all, to-day; and ye'd say he was very anguished looking altogether."

The interrupter of her reverie was James; James, whose one quick glance had taken in the tears on her face, not to mention the letter which she still held crumpled in her hand.

"Oh Lord, James! Did you put him in the kitchen? Is it Gorgon or Gossip?"

"Is it to put him in the kitchen? In God's

name, Miss Prudence, do you wish the cook to rise up out of it altogether ? "

" No, but I want the puppy kept warm, you fool ! "

" Well, *want* must be the master," James returned with faint acerbity as he prepared to leave the hall.

" Wait a minute, James. What about a fire in the old gun-room ? "

" Isn't that now the very spot I have him nested," James told her triumphantly. " Come with me now, till you'll see for yourself what way is he."

" By the bye, James "—Prudence asked, on the way to the gun-room—" how did Mr. Oliver know I went out with the harriers to-day ? I didn't tell him."

" Faith, I d'know," James replied cautiously, " how would I ? "

" I believe you let it out, James."

" Oh, fie, Miss Prudence."

" Yes, *you* told on me. I know you did. You're a horrible old man, James. I hate you ! You know you did ! "

" Well, God knows I did *not*. Nor I wouldn't. Nor how could I ? Sure I never even knew ye were in it. And what's more, if I had known, I'd have *concealed* it ! " James finished on an exalted note of complete self-abnegation.

" Who told them, then ? "

" It must have been the fairies, indeed," said James with mistimed facetiousness.

Prudence ignored him sternly. As she ministered sombrely to the needs of the prostrate puppy, she remembered that, of course, Anthony had been the informer.

273

CHAPTER XV

THE day following Toby's good hunt opened inauspiciously enough with heavy, sloping grey rain, which slashed malevolently at the bleak, grey walls of Lingarry, and drove in at the western windows of the house.

Prudence, waking completely and beautifully, as she always did, was immediately aware that the clothes, which she had left over-night on a chair beneath her window, must now be hopelessly wet. A minute after the pleasing idea occurred to her, she had thrust a slim handful of wet silk out on the window-sill, closed the window upon it, and hopped, shuddering with cold, and mournfully conscious of a general sense of injury, back into bed. The re-attained warmth filled her with a sudden sense of luxury ; brief and passing quickly as her mind grasped anew at the troubles and perplexities of yesterday.

Everything was just too awful to be borne. She was out of everything ; Peter had given her up ; Toby cared for her no longer—if indeed, he ever had cared. Shaking, she drew the bed-clothes up round her aching throat, and stared out upon the rainy world with eyes that burnt in her head like hot ashes.

" Prudence ! " A sharp rap at her door caused Prudence to recede still farther beneath her blankets.

" Prudence, the bath is ready for you." That, and no more ; delivered in the sharply admonitory tones of Miss Gus, it was sufficient to bring the tears welling to Prudence's eyes as she slid unwillingly out of bed.

Breakfast finished, she shrouded her scarlet jumper in an aged " burberry," and set off for the stables ; stubbornly resisting the newly-found temptation to hang about the hall, waiting for the coming of Toby's car ; he was due at any moment to pick up Oliver, and go to shoot Kilconnel bogs.

However, on her way round to the stables, she encountered him. He slowed up the car and Prudence slid in.

If there was rain in her hair, and if—beneath the loose coat—the lines of her were sure and sweet, Toby did not seem particularly conscious of the attraction. He said :

" Good morning, Prudence. How's the mare after yesterday ? "

Prudence answered:

" I'm just going round to see." Then, after a second's hesitation, she added : " There's the devil's own work over yesterday, Tobioh."

Toby stared stolidly through the wind-screen, and made no answer. At the end of a minute he spoke, " It's a good day for the duck," was what he said.

Prudence, as she continued her interrupted journey to the yard, reflected bitterly on the hardness of a fate which lost her, within two days, and through no fault of her own, the love and confidence of the two people she cared for most in the world. For Toby was obviously unprepared to be communicative on the subject which must, she knew, be uppermost in his thoughts.

In Suspenders' box, Hinch informed her dourly that the mare had a knee on her as big as his head, and was as dismayed with whatever conflict she put past her yesterday, that she never took her feed, good or bad, since she come in the stable door.

Prudence, as the mare toyed languidly with the apple she had brought her, shoving an inquiring nose into the pocket of her wet coat, felt that indeed every man's hand was contrary to her, and the world properly awry.

The remainder of the morning, spent in nursing the hound pup—to-day yellower than saffron— and in the perusal of a work of fiction, which Oliver should never have left on the study table, reduced her to a state bordering on mental suffocation.

That she should take the great—for her, almost soul-shaking decision of going for a walk, shows her stress of mind. For never, if she could possibly help it, did Prudence set forth a-foot. To-day, Cousin Kat's suggestions for the profitable employment of a wet afternoon may have decided her against a sojourn within doors. At all events, three o'clock found her giving last instructions to Michael on the subject of the puppy's diet, before she sheathed herself once more in a rain-coat, and

set forth into the wet. Blazes came too ; unwillingly, and only as far as the avenue gates ; whence
she returned, by devious ways, and tail tucked
well down, to the house and the warmth of the
gun-room fire ; from the fore-front of which—by
a patient process of wet, shuddering pushes—she
at last succeeded in ousting the sick puppy.

Meanwhile, without even a dog to attend her,
Prudence walked with her sorrows in the mourning
day. She did not think much ; or if she did,
only little, futile thoughts, without connection or
sequence. Toby *used* to care—what's happened
now ? That new coat of mine's a *rotten* fit. I
must ask Peter what she thinks—can't do that
now, I suppose. Peter's clothes always fit her.
. . . Anthony Countless wears good leggings. . . .
I suppose Peter'll pinch some off him. I'd
like to pinch that red silk jumper of Toby's. I
could have—ten days ago. Can't be done now.

As her mind dwelt miserably on her colourless
present, contrasting it sadly with her careless past,
her feet carried her on and up a twisting
laneway ; up to where, on a bare, rock-faced
hillside, three tortured Scotch firs blotted their
flattened shapes against the stooping sky ; and a
lonely, little house clung, limpet-wise, to the face
of the hill ; squalid it was, to the point of ruina-
tion, but defiant still of the winds that had twisted
its fir-trees to abortions and, before now, carried
its weighted thatch away.

Over the half-door leaned a very old woman ;
she tipped out a basin of water ; clumsily, because
her strength was so slight. After an instant's

hesitation, she called a shaking greeting to
Prudence.

Prudence started, and stopped ; then she went
on up to the house. For many weeks she had
purposely avoided the dwelling of Mary Kierney's
old mother ; to-day, she could not have told what
reason had led her there. Within the almost
totally dark kitchen she sat down on the greasy
chair which the old woman brought for her, and
addressed herself to the over-topping heights of
conversation.

"Look-at, me lady, 'tis too trouble I put on
ye, altogether—to say ye should sit down in this
lowly, backward, rakish little place. God knows,
Miss Lingfield, only for the sorrow come to me——"
something, midway between a cough and a faultily
produced sob for the moment choked the old
woman's flow of eloquence, and gave Prudence
time to insert a tactful inquiry, respecting the
health of her companion.

"Well, well," a mournful, yet satisfied cadence
swung into the creaking voice, "isn't it what
Doctor O'Flaherty says to me, I might as well
be dead, out and out, as to be the way I am.
Sure he give me a bottle, but he says it should
take the full o' *three* bottles to cure me. Oh, I
have a bad cough, and—saving yer presence—
a, *arrr*, very dirty spit."

"I'm very sorry to hear it," Prudence interrupted the recitation of further ills with some
brusqueness, "but if the doctor is looking after
you, I suppose you'll be all right. Who have
you living with you now?"

" I has me bad, *bad* daughter, Miss Lingfield. Ah, the creature, she's astray altogether, these days. You couldn't tell now the minute she wouldn't go roaring round the country like a bull in a bog ; or like a falling sickness wouldn't take her ; or like—God help us !—the speech would leave her. And to say I has her little trouble on me too——"

Prudence forebore from questions as to the nature of the little trouble. A feeble wail, penetrating dimly from some remote and airless corner of the cottage, announcing, clearly enough, the presence of a baby. Some infant unfortunate, this ; born to Mrs. Kierney's crazy daughter, and destined to struggle pitifully for life in that dire seclusion from the sight of man (and equally from air and light) which is, in Ireland, the fate of most of the illegitimate offspring of the peasant, for at least the first year of life. After which period, if the child survives, its presence comes to be accepted by the country side simply as the misfortune of the grand-parents—its usually self-contributed guardians.

"Well, well," Mrs. Kierney dragged herself back from a perfect ecstasy of coughing. Fixing an unwinking and malevolent eye, red-rimmed and lashless, like a scalded bird's, upon Prudence, she resumed the conversation : " I got hardship every way and always. I rared me two good lumps o' girrls, and when I should look to get a little assistance from them, in the place o' that to draw down the world's disgrace on me is what they done. Well, we has to take the will o' God."

"Yes. But poor *Mary*"—Prudence interrupted—"she could hardly help it." Pity for the
dead girl, and a feeling akin to nausea towards
her living parent wrestling within her, Prudence
rose to her feet; determined, with an access of
nervous fear, to leave the cottage immediately.

As she turned to make her farewells, a sudden,
leaping flame illuminated for a minute the smoky
darkness of the low room. Before its glare died
Prudence had seen the contorted face and writhing
body of a big woman who crouched between the
angle of the wall and the dark dresser; one arm
was flung behind her, her nails scraping on the
rough, plaster walls; with the other hand she
dragged at her throat, like one choking. A heaving,
cumulative effort, and she broke from her corner,
spun three times round, and clapping her hands
over her mouth, ran, tittering and chattering, out
into the rain and wind.

Prudence brought her ghastly eyes back to the
little coughing, blinking woman, who crouched
against the hearth, her old face evil with anger.
Even when the anger died, and a simulated whine
of fright came from the shawl, Prudence felt that
Mrs. Kierney was perfectly capable of dealing
with any daughter, sane or insane.

"She has me this way, the heart's going hither
and over in me chest. I declare to God she'll
cut some right capers. There's times I'll go
around here in dread o' me life. But, sha! the
creature—she's harmless enough. I declare ye'd
sooner have *her* about, than to have the like o'
the Ugliness in the big house, below."

Prudence gasped. Almost, she was beyond speech. The darkness and closeness of the tiny room held her and penned her in. Her eyes, smarting in the bellying turf smoke, were held fast by the two, reddish gleams in the old woman's white face. The thought came to Prudence that Mrs. Kierney, swaying there, in the half-darkness, was like a malignant, giant ferret. The hooped back and down-thrust head heightened the illusion, till the likeness became almost unbearable. . . .

" Sure they tells me," the grating, feeble voice crept on, " there's not a night she isn't in it. And they sees her by dark-light, and dusk-light, and at all times——"

" See who? Who sees her? " Prudence asked incoherently.

" Oh! Oh! " Mrs. Kierney began to sob and cough : " Don't every cook comes in the place have the same ugly story. There's a woman comes by night-time to pull them from the bed. And the signs of death, and the sweat of death, and the ropes, and all on her. Oh, my child! God pity her! He is good—God is good."

The wailing, ghastly cry of a child, waking alone to fear, came to them ; and Mrs. Kierney, with a muttered exclamation of anger, hobbled purposefully towards a closed door.

As the door slammed upon her exit, a gust of smoke and rattle of soot rushed down the chimney, Prudence, seizing on the moment for possible escape, flung two shillings on the corner of the table, and averting her eyes from the darkness around and behind her, fled out into the storm.

CHAPTER XVI

RISK

"Excuse me, Mr. Sage. But Miss Gus is within, and she'll *not* come out till the gentlemen goes," thus James, in a gusty whisper; interrupting Toby's vigil at the bathroom door.

"Oh, thanks, James. I thought it was Mr. Lingfield. How long till dinner?"

"I'm going down now, this minute, to scuffle Michael in with the soup," James told him. "Only, I took a race upstairs to tell Miss Prudence the hound-pup has like a strong wakeness.'"

"What's up with the pup?" Toby asked.

"It have the yelly jaundice, sir. Sure I knows the signs of it well. Wouldn't a Christian take it, leave alone dogs? They would, faith! I seen my poor mother dying down altogether with it, oncet. 'Faith, Doctor,' she said to the old doctor, was in it then, 'it must be the hell of a complaint I have, for the fleas is left off biting me!' Well, a dog itself—you'd pity the creature."

Parting from James at his bedroom door, Toby, when he had lit a cigarette, paused to consider whether he should cut the bath he had been waiting for, and go down to the gun-room on the chance of seeing Prudence alone, and helping her with the sick puppy.

With a long pull at his cigarette, and a morose shake of his head, he finally decided on the bath. If Peter's advice was to be of any use he must put it into practice thoroughly. "Leave her head alone," Peter had said, "you'll find she'll come back to your hand all right." For the last ten days he had conscientiously done so ; yet no very marked results had occurred. Prudence had come over to the kennels occasionally—true. And they had had that grand morning together, yesterday. Beyond this he was no farther advanced, less far, in fact, than he had been before that night at Clery's. Always, he felt a tension in their comradeship ; as though she slid away from intimacy. He felt that she might, at any moment, take the bit between her beautiful teeth and get clean away from him. A passenger in her life, he knew neither confidence nor control.

Toby sighed, flicking the ash sorrowfully from the end of his cigarette. His thoughts left Prudence, and went back to his day and evening spent with Oliver. He quite saw Oliver's point about the harriers. If his hunting harriers meant the resignation of a rich Master, such as the Drumferris country needed so badly, and had at last found in Anthony Countless, then there was only one thing to do about it. He must give up his dream, which had found so great a reality, and get rid of the harriers.

"It's all up to you, Toby," Oliver had said, "you've got the committee's consent, and you've got the Master's. You're a recognised pack. But if you hunt harriers, Anthony's resignation goes in in February. It'll be a bad job for the country; look what he's doing for the coverts; and what he'll do for the hounds. I know Tony—he's thorough. And now that he's getting married to Peter, he may stay on as a permanency. He'll do the country all the good in the world. And, by the time he comes into his old Aunt's money and goes, you may be in a position to take these hounds yourself, my boy."

Toby had seen; seen everything; how little good argument would do; how much harm resistance; how much good compliance. After all, fox-hunting was the thing to support in the country. What matter about one's individual sport, if the fun of one should prove the confusion of all? The good of fox-hunting came before all else. Yet the wrench of giving up his hounds, of putting down the cup of glorious intoxication he had so lately supped was, to Toby, as if a part of him had been torn away and buried, live and full of feeling. Well, it had to be faced. And now, about this bath. . . .

In the dining-room, Prudence sat opposite to him. Looking across at her, Toby could have believed her a wraith.

The blue shadows, which lay like still water, beneath haunting eyes; the droop of her neck on the smooth shoulders; the shaded lights weaving colour in the ashes of her hair; these things made him helplessly aware of her. Yet Prudence, the essential, the unexpected, the distracting Prudence, seemed to have quit her lovely,

gaunt body to-night, leaving an automaton of
self behind. An empty body was there, with
burning eyes in which was the harshness of fever.

Twice during dinner she lifted her head, and
looking across, spoke in answer to some question
of his. Each time, her words came heavily, as
though with a conscious effort she had dragged
her mind away from vaster places ; and yet there
was an almost eager sweetness in her replies, which
showed she was not sorry to be recalled.

Horses—they talked of chiefly. He remembered
that afterwards. Paddy Doyle—he had a horse
with a leg he'd be glad to give away. Toby had
a four-year-old, struck itself, out at grass ; lame
as a tree. Was there any heat in the joint ? No,
what was worse, it was stone-cold. That was a
bad job. That good old mare Oliver had, went
wrong as a four-year-old. Took up her maternal
duties young. Dam of winners, she was ; the
right sort of chaser, she bred. All this flat-racing
blood was doing a lot of harm in the country.
Yes, and the gamble of it. Old Crumlin, now,
he never did anything but break himself, with
his blood-stock ; and there was the little bit of
a mare, John Regan picked up at his auction—
£400, he sold her last colt for. Wonderful.

In the library after dinner, Toby brought
Prudence her coffee cup. She twisted her shoulders
away from him ; lighting her cigarette awkwardly
at the match he held ; then plunged into breathless conversation with Miss Gus. After a moment's
hesitation, Toby isolated himself and Cobby in a
distant arm-chair ; while Prudence, quiveringly,

sickeningly aware that he had left her, could have
sobbed with the anguish of her dreadful, sweet
need, so lately discovered.

From across the room, she watched him covertly ;
her eyes half-shut ; her hot hands clutching the
sofa-cushions. She saw him, holding Cobby close
and safely ; half-heard the idiocies he murmured
down to the rough head ; and longed, with a
vehemence, the strength of which held her helpless, for his arms.

" Toby, Toby. He doesn't care. . . . Oh,
it *hurts* . . . everything hurts. . . ." Anything
to keep herself from crying out ; to hide the tears
which came, stinging and squeezing, through her
dropped eye-lids. The *Tatler*—Kat was reading
it, with faint sniffs of derision or disgust. Ah !
But there was the hound-puppy. . . .

With one long, slow movement, Prudence had
risen from the depths of the low sofa, and was on
her feet. She steadied her voice carefully, to give
the explanation for which Gus looked up from
her work.

" I'm going to the gun-room to give the puppy
his soup."

" Didn't you feed him before dinner ? "

" Yes, Cousin Gus, but he has to have it fairly
—often——" the catch in her voice was very
nearly apparent.

Toby put down Cobby from off his knees.

" I'll come too," he said, " I'm an expert on
Yellows."

Cousin Gus, folding up her work, caught the
flood of colour which ran mercilessly over Pru-

dence's face, staining even her neck ; saw her
hand going out to steady itself on the sofa-back.

" Yes," she said, rising briskly to her feet, " that
will be very kind of you, Toby. I daresay you
will be able to tell us what to do for the poor
puppy. Prudence is so inexperienced."

In the gun-room, the inexperienced Prudence
dealt, neatly enough, with the hound-puppy ;
manipulating a flannel bandage with care ; pouring
down soup with skill. Gus wandered about the
room, vaguely tidying.

" He's pretty bad," Prudence, looking up from
the sick puppy, caught Toby's eyes. The look in
them sent all thought flying. Just before Gus
turned towards them, he leant forward :

" Prudence, come down here again. You've got
to."

Prudence nodded. " Right. . . . Yes, *quite*
right, Cousin Gus. I think he'll do for to-
night."

Across the dimness of the room, their eyes met
again.

All very well below stairs, when the thrill of
his nearness was on her ; but up in her cold, little
room, a very different matter. Not quite so easy
as she had thought, to slip past Gus's door and
grope her way down through the darkness of the
house, to the dim light of the gun-room. Not
easy ; and the distant clap of a door, banging
and swinging in the wind, while the flame of her
candle went shooting and leaping with her pounding heart, made difficulties seem impossibilities.

Her hands flattened, and gripping on the edge of her dressing-table, Prudence bent forward to her mirror, looking for encouragement from the reflection in its wavering depths.

The purple of her dressing-gown framed her pale hair, and was like a heavy sheath round the brilliant jade of her pyjamas ; old brocade dancing slippers hid her cold feet in their tarnished brilliance ; her mouth had a particular gift for loving ; but fear looked helplessly back at her, from her own eyes in the glass.

Twice Prudence opened her door, and peered down the immeasurable length of the dark passage. And twice the scurrying of wind, and the hushed bellying of a heavy curtain sent her back to fling herself on her bed ; torturing thoughts of the naked Ugliness that walked at liberty in the house, a chaos of fear in her mind. Finally, with a bursting sob of resolution and dismay, she flung herself out into the darkness.

.   .   .   .   .

Toby had very nearly given up hope of Prudence's coming ; he sat quiet and still, gazing meditatively into the slow fire ; and listening, rather anxiously, to the sick puppy's breathing. He was on his knees, administering a last spoonful of soup, when—above the tearing of the wind and slash of the rain—he heard a sound, like the smothered shriek of a woman in fear, or pain. An eerie sound to hear at twelve o'clock of a stormy night, and in the isolation of a distant wing of Lingarry—a house which had its stories.

At the same moment when Toby discovered that the electric torch on the mantel-shelf was out of commission, the hound-pup, raising itself on unsteady fore-legs, put its nose in the air and found strength for a prolonged and soul-shaking howl.

" Shut up ! " said Toby, with a brutality which was the result of a slight attack of nerves. " Shut up, damn you ! *Shut up !* "

The puppy, every hackle on end, rose from its bed, and with various flannel wrappings trailing grotesquely, slunk weakly beneath the sofa, where its howling died to a faint and concentrated growl, if possible, more disquieting.

The futility of the lighted match as a means of illumination was fully born in on Toby, as he vainly endeavoured to light his way down the windy murk of the passage leading from the gun-room to the front regions of the house.

Poor as the light was, it served to show him Prudence, lying either unconscious or collapsed, where she had stumbled and fallen forward over two upward steps, the whereabouts of which must have been as familiar to her as life itself.

The musty reek of old curtains and the damp passage in his nostrils, Toby stooped over her— so warm, and sweet to smell. Back down the dark passage he carried her ; her long arms and legs trailing, puppy-wise ; her face and hair turned against his neck.

In the warmth of the gun-room, she sighed and sat up straight on the sofa, in an absurdly stiff and childish position ; remarking in an almost ordinary, if rather strangled, tone of voice :

" Toby, stay with me. Don't let them get at me. Swear you won't. Stay with me all night—till it's light—will you, Toby ? "

" Prudence, my precious—bed, darling. I'll take you back to your room."

Then the voice of a wild, terrified thing cried in his ears ; desperate hands plucked at his coat ; and Prudence's body, taut and convulsive, was in his arms.

" Toby, *Toby !* I *saw* it, Toby. *Don't* leave me ! She, she might *come* for me——" her sobs shook through him.

" Prudence—steady, baby ! No, of *course* I won't leave you ; *ever*, darling. Only you mustn't cry so awfully. Gus will hear you." He pulled down her hands from his shoulders, so that she could not strain away ; her body sagged forward against him ; and her mouth, for an ageless moment of soaring, rocking, delirium, was a reaching, passionate flame on his.

Ecstasy : Shivering sweet to touch, to be touched. Hands that caressed, Toby's hands : arms to hold her—nearer, *nearer* : His mouth, showing her how to love. For Prudence, time and thought were flung to a stand-still. Fear had never been.

It was Toby who found himself first. With a crash the fire had fallen in ; by the sudden, leaping light he saw Prudence's pale, thrown-back head ; the shut eyes, and beautiful, laxed mouth, abandoned to him ; utterly helpless, his—as she was his—to take and spoil for love.

And then the Toby, whose training was to do all difficult things, dragged his arms from the

warmth and feel of her ; his mouth from the
angle where neck met shoulder ; and putting her
gently down on the sofa, he stooped to make up
the fire. When he turned to her again, his hands
were less steady than his voice :

" Prudence, you aren't frightened any more,
are you, Precious ? "

" Not *now*, Tobioh." Prudence leaned over to
the warmth of the fire. Its leaping light gleamed
on jade flashes of pyjamas ; ruddied the pallor
of her throat and hands ; and, when she had
kicked off a shoe, dimpled across pale feet. She
sighed, and put up her hands to him :

" I *was*, awfully. I saw her, you see ; she
almost knocked me down."

" *What* did you see ? "

Prudence huddled her shoulders away from the
darkness behind her, with the very gesture of a
frightened child.

" Don't ask me, Toby. Not at night. At least,
you may—if you let me hold on to you, or something. I'm, I'm *cold*——"

Knowing at last that she needed to be held and
kissed ; knowing his own love, and desire, and
great fear for her ; realizing something of the
shock which, for the moment, would seem to have
thrown her right off what little balance she had,
Toby—with those marvellous hands held out to
him—was in a sorry way, indeed. Kisses, given
and taken like the last, he knew he dared
not risk again. God !—anything but that ; Prudence—his precious—she was too sweet and wild
for it.

" I'm *cold*," she repeated ; the injury in her voice was so manifest that he could have laughed, if they had not been quite so much on the edge of things.

It was then that he saw—in Oliver's pink hunting coat, spread on a chair-back near the fire, a way of salvation ; and clutched at the way desperately, like a drowning man at floating wreckage.

" Cold, darling ? Well, look here, put this on."

" No."

" Put it on, Prudence."

" I don't want to. I want you to——"

" *I* say you're to do what's good for you."

He dressed her, absurdly, before his arms went about her again. The thick, scarlet stuff was something between them ; something more distracting from her nearness than the gleam of slipping silk. He hid her in it—his darling. Its cuffs fell over her hands, and her long, enthralling hair was cloaked away. The lines of her throat and springing breasts were gone ; she was Prudence —a child, inviolable.

" Prudence ? "

" Yes."

" Are you very nice ? "

" *Yes.*"

" Are you very good ? "

" M'm——"

" Are you *very* sweet ? "

" *Yes*, Toby."

" Then give me an *awfully* sweet kiss. . . . Thank-you, darling. An' go to sleep now, or you won't wake up till James finds us in the morning, which would *never* do."

And Prudence, though she felt safe beyond all things, falling asleep with her cheek against Toby's, knew—even in her dreams—that this was not quite, *quite* what she wanted.

. . . . .

Toby had put Prudence down in the corner of the sofa where she slept now like a good child. Her sad face was tucked away in the collar of Oliver's pink coat. He could only see the pure, round outline of her fair head and, when the fire burned more brightly, the thin, curled soles of her feet ; for she slept with her back to the fire and her knees clutched up ridiculously.

Toby watched her feet, fascinated. He felt that —properly speaking—he should cover them up for fear they might be cold. But when he looked round the room for a possible covering he could only see the puppy's blanket, and this he did not think she would care for ; besides, the puppy needed it far more than Prudence did.

In the drear hour between midnight and to-morrow Toby cautiously heated the puppy's soup and bent solicitously over the invalid. She wasn't very grand, he decided, anxiously watching the first spoonful of soup trickle out of the corner of her mouth. The next went down better, but the third was returned labelled ' unwanted.' Toby warmed the blanket at the fire and wrapped the sick puppy in it. Then he knelt up beside her . . . listening. . . . Yes, there was that sound again ; a sound like running feet. Steps were coming towards the gun-room door and going

back again ; returning, to beat an immediate
retreat—strange, distracted sounds ; even ghastly.

Toby looked over at Prudence, wondering if
she heard. But Prudence still slept. She did not
stir until the puppy rose gauntly from its blanket
(as it had done once before on this night of alarms)
and whimpering weakly, crutched itself on unstable
legs over towards the sofa. Then Prudence sat
up straight. Her eyes still deep from sleep, she
stared about her.

" What is it ? " she asked. " What is it ? Toby
—are you there ? Toby ! " She crouched, hiding
her face in the back of the sofa ; pulling the coat
round her head to shut out she knew not what
fear.

" It's all right, Prudence." Toby's voice was
not particularly reassuring. The continuous sound
of those indeterminate, hurrying feet was the sort
of strain to which his nerves were not accustomed.

" A cat, I expect "—he spoke from the door
to which he had fumbled his way—" if it's not
a cat it's a——"

" Ah, Toby *please* don't open the door ! "
Prudence's voice rang thinly with anguish. " Can't
you *hear* it ? "

" Well, I can't sit listening to it any longer."
Toby pulled the door ajar and leaned out, peering
down into the darkness.

All was absolutely silent. Even the wind had
dropped. Only the cold dank of the passage air
seemed to stand still, thick and palpable, as Toby
stood and waited for the feet to approach again.
He waited minutes before he heard them coming

—distant and uncertain, but always nearer. They were hurrying now ; flying feet ; the feet of a thing in panic-driven haste.

Toby, resisting an over-mastering desire to slam the door and lock it, was aware of Prudence's hand, like a fine, ribbed stone, in his, and her breath hot and gasping against his neck. She too leaned out into the passage—that passage which had assumed the strange unfriendliness of another world—but her eyes were tight shut.

They waited together, a horrible moment ; Toby reached for the hope that the steps would turn back as they had done before, reached and clung to it desperately ; while Prudence shifted her bare feet on the floor, moaning a little, helplessly. The steps came flying on. This time they never faltered or stopped till the two straining into the darkness know only that *Something* fled past them in the doorway—was at last in their own warm world of the gun-room. Turning, they saw It cringing before the fire. Then :

"Shut the door," said James' voice, a dreadful whisper. "In the name o' God's pitiful mercy *keep her out !* " He collapsed on the top of the hound-puppy.

Prudence it was who shut the door firmly. She pulled a heavy box full of papers against it and grated the rusty key in the lock for extra security, while Toby occupied himself in reviving James— in which business the puppy's brandy proved most efficacious. The door fastened, Prudence came over and watched the affair distastefully, her feet tucked away on the sofa.

"Well, James," she said as the old man sighed brokenly and sat upright, "perhaps you'll tell us now what you were playing at in the passage. Toby, don't give him all the brandy, we may want a drop for the pup later on. Go on, James. Tell us."

"Wait now, one min*ute*, Miss Prudence, till I'll re-gain me conscious," James rose slowly from the floor and put a faltering hand up to his bald head. "I didn't lose it very long," he went on weakly, "with all the thraffic I put past me."

Toby sat down beside Prudence on the sofa and the pair regarded James in awed silence for a moment. Curiosity had for the time displaced the sheer horror of the last few minutes. Those awful footsteps had after all proved to be only James', and whatever might have caused his panic, the locked door and warmth of the gun-room gave them a species of false security from the darkness of things without.

"Tell us, James," Prudence repeated, "who were you playing hide-and-seek with?"

James' eyes hunted shiftily round the room before he too took comfort from the sight of the locked and blocked doorway. He stooped to the fire, warming his stiff, shaking fingers; but, as the puppy stirred faintly among her blankets, he jumped about again, and in telling his story never turned his back on the room; his eyes strove into the shadows beyond where Toby and Prudence sat.

"Hide-'n'-seek, is it?" his laugh was a poor thing. "Miss Prudence, *she come for me*. 'Twas herself. Only I seen her with the sight o' me eyes I'd never believe it. But (God between us and harm) 'tis true—'Twas herself."

" *Mary?* " Prudence breathed it out.

"Mary. Listen now till I tell yez the whole of it. It might be I wouldn't see a priest till to-morrow or next day, and I'll not last out with the like o' this buggy on me. Sure 'tis too strong for me. I'll tell all.

"D'ye mind now, Miss Prudence, the nice little wife I has—as useful a little handful of a woman as any?" He asked with sudden irrelevance; and, Prudence nodding, he went on:

"Well, when poor Mary done what she done to herself and the ladies here was in trouble for a cook, she was at me ever and always to get her back in this job. I seen no way at all for it—the ladies being as severe as what they are—but to quieten the woman I said I'd do me best. Look-at! Ye might recall the way the cooks hoisted away out o' this as fast as Miss Gus'd bring them out from the station. Well, the creatures! I declare I done no more than draw down the name o' Mary to the first one that come after her, and she had the story complete in no time at all. And Maggie and Michael and the whole click o' them had it ready to tell the next one come in it. Well, it frickened them out of it, whatever. It frickened them out of it. And the only words ever I spoke was to say signs was horrid, and bad luck'd *always* follow when ye'd meet blood in the woods, (yes, for all 'twas only poor Miss Kat's hen the pups tore asunder in the rosydandrum) but sure cooks is frightful easy frickened——" James paused a moment as though in reminiscence, before he continued : " Little I'd heed them ! I had enough to do minding me work, leave alone the wife deaving and teasing me always to know when would the ladies think to give her the job. As if I wouldn't get torment enough with that imp Michael—and he to go put the hand-candles in the hall at five o'clock o' th' afternoon because he'd not walk the passages by dark. And divil a hand thim girrls'd stir in the evening without they'd get that notorious, imdipent whelp to folly them and they going the rounds of the rooms."

" But what was the story you told them ? " Toby asked while Prudence squeezed his hand convulsively.

" Sure 'twas what they said Mary was walkin' in it always," James evaded authorship with some small skill, " and they said she'd strip the bed-clothes off o' them in the middle o' the night. Didn't they swear by black, blue and candle-light they seen her walkin' out the doors and walkin' before them in the passages ? Ah, the pack o' fools ! Not one o' them seen her—*only meself*." As James croaked the words he seemed to shrink into his clothes—an old, frightened man. There was no malevolence left about him, only a real and genuine fear. Toby felt the same shapeless fear flowing into him through the channel of Prudence's hand in his. Quite suddenly the locked door became the trivial barricade it was ; the warmth of the room faded, sinking away from them. They waited helplessly for James to continue.

"I rose up at twelve," he said, "the way I'd give the puppy a bit to keep it going on till morning. Well, when I passed out the bedroom door and went to go down the back stairs, I seen *her* there on the landing waiting on me. I made the blessed sign then and took a dart back to the bedroom but—God help me!—she was before me always. She folly'd me when I run down the stairs, and when I thought I had her misled in the passages she was at this door again before me. God is my witness, 'twas her very self! Is the door shut fast, sir? Ah, what use is doors? What use is talk? A pairson might give up when the like o' this'd happen them. But God is good——" James fell to his knees, gabbling prayers below his breath; forgetful of Toby and Prudence. At last the repetition of words soothed him so that he sank down and slept; his old ghastly head leaning against the arm of the chair where the puppy now dozed comfortably.

Toby and Prudence kept watch, whispering and smoking cigarettes till, sleep overcoming them too, they fell away from each other, lying in angular attitudes of utter weariness at opposite ends of the sofa.

CHAPTER XVII

AGAINST TIME

"WHAT do you think it all meant?" Prudence asked. She was riding beside Toby on the lovely morning which followed that night of storm. It was early still—not seven o'clock yet—and the hushed beauty of the September morning was like milk and wine. They had gone with the first light to feed the horses, bath and change their clothes; and now, as they rode out of the high gates of Lingarry, the past night was a memory striving for the reality of which, to both of them, it fell so short. Other things were more real to them now than the night's wonder of kisses and coldness of fear.

Looking at Prudence as she rode beside him—a lovely cool thing—Toby felt a helpless frost of awkwardness coming across his love for her. And Prudence, filled with a strange new shyness, avoided agonisingly any word or gesture of love. How ghastly if Toby thought she had thrown herself at him last night—made herself dirt cheap. And perhaps she had, rather. That time he wouldn't kiss her as she meant? It was all rather vague to her now, save for the perilous reality of those kisses that had gone before. . . . But certainly

Toby had drawn back, held away when she would have given again—given utterly.

" What do I think it means ? " Toby repeated her question. " James' story ? I'm not good at these psychic shows, but I, I'm quite sure he *did* see—what he said he did."

" Mary ? Yes, I saw her too," Prudence pointed out importantly. " At least, I'm sure now that was what I saw. Though before James told us he'd seen her, I was beginning to think it was only a curtain flapping in the passage that tripped me up."

" So it was, probably—just a bogey ; you know —a ghost you invent for yourself."

" P'raps James only saw a bogey, then," Prudence suggested in scornful tones. She was fighting to justify the validity of her terror.

" Well, I don't think so." Toby considered for a moment. " You see for weeks he's been calling up the ghost of that cook to frighten the other servants. Of course it was he who started those yarns about her haunting the passages. And you can't play with that sort of fire without getting burnt sooner or later ; at any rate an amateur like James can't. He has too much superstition and ignorance to keep right outside it all. And constantly terrifying other people got this thing at last properly on his own nerves. I don't doubt that he saw her, or his thought-form of her, or anyhow something that jarred him properly— poor old lad ! "

" And all to get the girls so dissatisfied with their cooks that they'd have his wife back. What a devoted husband ! " Prudence laughed.

"Yes, b'Gad! He rattled them out of covert properly too, didn't he?" Toby agreed. "Do you think," he went on, "he'll stay on at Lingarry after last night's doings?"

"James go?" Prudence was horrified at the idea of such a calamity. "Well, if James goes I'll go too," she announced with finality.

Toby looked at her from under his blocky eyelashes:

"Darling Prudence, I should say so. 'Specially after last night's show. How soon?"

"How soon, what?"

"Silly! How soon will you marry me and come to Merlinstower?"

"Oh." Prudence rode on in silence for a moment. "Last night's show," she repeated his words to herself. That was it then—he thought he was bound to marry her. Between them they had stripped the proprieties pretty bare, true. And James' sensational appearance certainly put them in a bit of a hole. But, terribly real as she now knew her love for Toby to be, Prudence, mortified to her wild soul by her swift surmises as to his reasons for urging a speedy marriage, chose to be her most difficult and unreachable self.

"Oh," she repeated, "after last night, you think?" Her voice was icily sweet; her very coolness a glamour. "Well, I don't really know. I'll think about it, Toby. Some time, perhaps. . . . Not at once."

"But *Prudence*," Toby was utterly taken aback. "I thought—after last night——" he repeated unfortunately.

Prudence swung round on him. A fine, faint colour flowed from her neck to her shadowy temples. Tears were in her eyes. Her hands, holding the reins and whip, were strained and tense. She spoke with cold venom, in tones not unlike those employed by Cousin Gus in moments of corrective stress.

" Toby, what *has* last night got to say to whether I marry you or not ? Damn last night ! If you ever dare to mention last night, Toby, I'll never speak to you again. I don't want to remember it. I *hated* it. If you think because I was frightened and wouldn't go back to bed that I've *got* to marry you——"

" I *don't*——" Toby almost shouted.

" Why did you say so then ? "

" I never said so. All I meant was——"

" Whatever you *meant* you've said nothing else since we left Lingarry. You said it was *because* of last night you—you wanted—to——" Tears choked her utterance.

In her sorrow she was more remote than accessible. Toby, who had always believed the opposite to be the case with girls when they cried, despaired at last, sulkily.

" I'll never make you see," he said, after an intolerable silence.

" No, you certainly won't ; that's the first sane remark you've made."

" Oh—*Damnation !* " said Toby violently. He turned his horse's head round and rode back the way they had come. The green four-year-old, who resented this sudden parting from her stable-companion, he treated with a severity to which she was hardly accustomed. Toby, suffering and puzzled, had little sympathy for her mood which was, in truth, so like his own. He was hurt— hurt to his very bones. Sore and angry and hope- lessly in love, he rode away from the girl who could give only to snatch again the wonders she had granted ; who loved with such disjointedness that her evil tempers (times indeed of wrath and coldness) far outnumbered the rare moments of passion and the dim sweet moods of silence he had also found in her.

And Prudence rode on with a high chin and a bursting heart. Tears poured down her cheeks, while a secret voice echoed over and over : " Now you've done it. *Now* you've done it. Clever, weren't you ? "

" Toby," she moaned through shut lips. " I didn't know what I was saying, darling. I do love you. I do—terribly. I don't care *why* you marry me so long as you do marry me. *Precious*——" Her want of him sank helplessly back upon her- self. She turned the mare round to follow the way he had gone, then rode away again. She could not call him back. If he came to her again she would be a fairer, softer Prudence. But would he come ? Probably not, she decided miserably ; and bit her lip to keep back further useless tears.

Half-a-mile farther she rode down the lane, till the sound of a horse's galloping hoofs made her pull the fidgetting Suspenders to a stand and, one hand soothingly on the mare's shoulder, she turned half round in her saddle, wondering amazedly

whether this were Toby returned to make his
peace. And if so, why, in the name of all ignorance, should he gallop Oliver's valuable young
horse along a hard high-way.

It was Toby. He came up the road sitting
forward in his saddle as though he were riding
the finish of a race; steadied the youngster as
he passed Prudence, to call out, above the clamour
of eight hoofs—Suspenders pulling every ounce
she knew to keep her nose in front of the four-
year-old's:

"There's poison down in Cloonbeg covert—
I've just heard. The hounds are there this morning an' we've got thirty minutes to get to it before
they do."

"Are you certain about it?" The dreadful
urgency of the matter swept all else out of count
in Prudence's mind.

"Certain." Toby nodded grimly. "I met
Micky Grogan, the earth-stopper, just after I left
you. It's those cursed Croleys. Can we do it,
Prudence?"

"With luck." Prudence took a pull on the mare.
The plain snaffle in which she rode her for exercise
was of very little use. "We keep on down this
road and take to the country at Hogan's farm."

"A three mile point from there," Toby swung
the mare round a bend so that she nearly slipped
up—Suspenders following suit in almost comic
imitation. "Here's where we've got to put on
the pace. It's a stinking awful country. Oh,
hang these turns! This mare been schooled over,
banks at all, Prudence?"

" She's as green as grass." Prudence spoke through the wind in her teeth as she jammed her little felt hat tighter on to her head. This galloping on a road struck her as a horrible business.

" Can't be helped. The little school'll do her good. Two of us have got to come in case one falls by the wayside. I have the legs of you now, in any case, old girl ! "

The legs of Suspenders the bay four-year-old certainly had. Toby was so well in front that his cry of horror and warning came back to Prudence round a blind corner of the road ; and the almighty, sawing pull which she took on Suspenders' mouth was only just enough to steady the mare before she too saw the reason for Toby's horrified shout.

Clever as a polo pony she stopped up with a clean suddenness that very nearly sent Prudence flying out over her shoulder. Her chest was against a tough strand of wire stretched across the road, from which depended the unsavoury wearing apparel of a family of tinkers, whose encampment was situated a couple of perches farther down the road.

Half in and half out of the ditch Toby lay, rather horribly still ; while the four-year-old—her bridle off and hanging in a whirl of reins from the rings of the martingale, expressed her suitable horror of the tinker's tent.

" Oh, God be good ! He's killed ! Ah, the poor young gentleman. Did he not see the wire, lady ? Joe, ketch the horse ! Take down the wire you, Micky ! " A handsome tinker woman, in hideous *déshabille*, dashed out of her habitat, followed by a swarm of offspring, and launched herself loudly upon the scene of action. She helped Prudence to lay the unconscious Toby flat on a nauseous sheet of sewn sacks, and feeling him over with grimy fingers, announced in tones of triumph that 'twas what the bone of the shoulder was burst for ever, and with the spang he hit the road ye'd *have* to say he was dead. At Prudence's request for water she dashed to the tent and re-appeared with a black bottle of whisky.

"That now's every sup in this world we has," she said. "But if 'twas the last ever we'd hope to see the poor young gentleman should have it— the creature!"

Very deliberately Prudence poured out by the roadside every drop of whisky in the bottle. Ignoring the woman's angry cry, she spoke with her young face white and stern; one foot in her stirrup and her haunted eyes on Toby who lay so awfully quiet.

"Look here," she said, "he's not dead, but if you give him one drop of whisky he jolly soon will be. Give him water if he asks for it when he wakes, and don't let him move. He may wake queer in the head. Send one of your boys flying to Doctor Mahony's house, and send another back to Lingarry with the horse. I've got to go on, and I'll send people up at once from Hogan's farm."

She mounted and pushed the mare into a canter again, riding away from poor Toby whom she left surrounded by the whispering, filthy crowd of tinkers. Prudence swayed a little sickly in her

307

saddle at the thought of him, then sent Suspenders
along, horribly aware of the short minutes left
her in which to reach Cloonbeg covert before
the hounds were put in.

It was just part of the morning—so like one of
those interminably malign dreams, when delay
follows evil delay—that she should hear again the
clatter of hoofs behind her, and the four-year-
old, escaped from her tinker-groom, should join
her once more—her bridle only partially restored
and the reins still trailing. Prudence, how she
never afterwards knew, crooked up the tangle
with the handle of her whip ; (it was unthinkable
that Oliver's good youngster having escaped her
proper bustle with only a cut from the wire across
her chest, should now be left to a fate of bioken
knees, or worse) and, with a led horse in her
right hand she turned sharp to the left down a
narrow, high-banked lane, and was soon shouting
frantically at the locked gate of Hogan's farm-
yard.

An interminable wait before a stupid-looking
boy appeared sent Prudence near the edge of
delirium. Somehow she conveyed the urgency of
the situation to his slow brain, delivered over her
second horse and was gone before he could frame
a question. She followed a circuitous route round
the hay-ricks and manure heaps in the yard,
popped over a wooden pole that stopped a gap
out into the fields ; and then, with a determination
that was good to see, she set off to ride something
more than a steeple-chase over as nasty a bit of
country as could well be imagined. But she knew

the line she meant to ride and rode it as straight
and prettily as if it had been a flagged course.

It was a three mile point from Hogan's farm
to Cloonbeg, where the covert—part woodland,
part gorse—straggled down one side of a hill.
The many fences lying between Prudence and her
goal varied from single stone-facers, high and
uncompromising, to the big, rotten double at the
far side of a strip of treacherous bog that lay in
the valley bottom.

As Suspenders, all the best of her awake, galloped
across the first field and, steadying up almost of
her own accord, was on top of the big bounds-
fence, neat as a dog, and over the blind, briar
wreathed ditch on the other side with the spring
of a travelling kangaroo, Prudence felt the first
quiver of elation awake in her. The glory of
riding a good horse for the moment swamped
from her mind the desperate meaning of her ride,
and the anxiety for Toby that had eaten at her
heart up to now. Sliding her reins short again
between her hands, she leaned forward, praying
for luck and no wire.

Her prayer was answered in so far that she
crossed three more banks, in various stages of
rottenness, but all alike as to utter blindness, before
she saw the dread posts topping another bounds-
fence, which ran to left and right of her as far as
she could see.

"This stops us, old girl!" Prudence pulled the
mare together and strove to consider. "Oh,
curse Jimmy Murphy!" Prudence anathematised
the owner of the farm-land with bitter emphasis.

Then (most heart-breaking of businesses) she rode helplessly along parallel with the wired fence, seeking in vain for a possible place. As she did so an old cart-track leading across the field caught her attention. Why a cart-track going down to a bounds-fence ? Following it in the forlorn hope of a gap that could be pulled down, Prudence, to her amazement, beheld that it led towards a gate. She rode up to it, hope high in her heart, only to turn away in sick dismay. The very solid gate was stoutly locked, and a stark, evil strand of barbed wire was stretched taut above its fifth bar.

Now Irish horses, unless schooled to it, are not, as a rule, over fond of timber ; and some Irish people (of whom Prudence was one) simply hate it. Ordinarily speaking she would have rightly called such an obstacle unjumpable. Moreover, the very unpleasant results of charging wire were still remarkably fresh in her mind. It is therefore greatly and eternally to her credit that, with her heart pounding sick in her side, she should have taken Suspenders back into the field, and swinging her about, have ridden her with at least a fair show of determination—into so unprepossessing an obstacle.

It is still more to Suspenders' credit that knowing (as what good horse would not know ?) how her rider's heart was but half in the business, she should have charged her pannel with so great courage, and sailed over it with a hoist and flick of her strong quarters which—if not pretty to sit —at least put paid to the account of that nasty, terrifying erection.

Kicking her foot back into the stirrup she had lost, Prudence felt the jubilant warmth of relief run through her like a fire. But on—she must get on. Precious minutes had been wasted on the wrong side of that desperate wire. Suspenders was ridden hard into the next two fences ; and, encouraged by her success over timber, flew the awkward, little banks with more zeal than discretion ; luckily, in neither case was there a ditch on the far side.

How she got through the bog in the bottom, Prudence never afterwards knew ; more by good luck than good guidance, and with the assistance of a country fellow who shouted warnings to her before, she was quite into the worst of it.

Suspenders, from as bad a take off as could well be imagined, got bravely on top of the big double that fenced the bog, but pecked on her landing, so that Prudence had one hand on the ground. Her recovery was epic ; as was also the manner in which her rider regained the saddle. " I caught the martingale with my teeth," she told Toby afterwards—not that he believed her.

" Stick to him ! " roared the man who had guided her in the bog. " You're right now ! By the Holy, you're a topper ! " His voice, still shouting applause and encouragement was soon faint on the air.

Uphill now, and the going began to tell on Suspenders. No horse is exactly fit before the end of the cubbing ; and the best, if unfit, will be dropping pretty short off their fences after twenty-five minutes of very varied going at the pace which Prudence had made.

Suspenders was no exception to this rule. Prudence still remembers with horror the blind ditches that yawned so thick and green below her, at each of which she expected to meet her Waterloo. The glow that flowed through her when she put the wired gate behind was as nothing compared to that which sprang up in her heart at the sight of a cattle-gap in one most formidable fence. She pointed Suspenders' nose towards it and sent her along as hard as she could.

That there should follow a chain of three gaps and an open gate was almost more than she could believe. Her luck still held. At this rate she would be at the covert in time—in time to stop the hideous poisoning of the hounds ; that terrible thing which is anathema, the sin of witch-craft ; a cursèd and infrequent horror. She had not up to now had a moment to dwell on the thought ; but at last—with two fences only between herself and the covert—it seized on her mind. The terrible fear that she might be too late—just too late by the edge of a minute—caused her to grip her saddle between her knees, and all judgment in her dead, send the failing Suspenders into a tall, furze-topped single bank ; a nasty enough obstacle for a fresh horse, for a tired one an impossibility.

Suspenders failed to get right on top, and came off that tall fence end over end—as bad a looking smash as one could wish *not* to see when engaged in the nasty dangerous game of fox-hunting.

So thought Anthony and Peter. And so most certainly thought Anthony's first whip, Willis, who was new to an Irish country ; for, as they took the hounds in at the back of Cloonbeg covert (so the wind served) they were in time to witness Prudence's and Suspenders' sensational arrival. At Willis's shout Peter and Anthony looked round to see the mare standing on her head in the field with her tail coming over her back ; and Prudence, at the full stratch of her reins, standing on *her* head with her heels coming over her hat.

They picked her up—rather shaken, but otherwise none the worse. The mare, completely done, lay where she had fallen.

"Oh, Lord ! So there you are—and I needn't have had that brutal place after all," was Prudence's first aggrieved exclamation, as her dazed mind took in the presence of Peter and Anthony. Willis's rate of a straying hound roused her mind afresh to the urgency of the situation.

"There's poison down in the covert," she told them. "This is Croley's land you're on now, and it may be poisoned too. Get the hounds out of it as quick as you can—don't mind me. The mare will be on her legs soon enough." She hardly saw Peter, who waited beside her, or turned her head as the hounds were hurried away.

Peter touched her on the arm:

"Prudence, *what* sort of a ride have you had ? You—you wonderful thing ! "

"Oh, do you think the mare's all right ? " Prudence asked despairingly. "I've ridden her right out, haven't I ? Twenty minutes from Hogan's to here and—I nearly forgot—Toby's badly concussed, at least I think so. I left him with the tinkers above Hogan's farm. Lend me

your horse, Peter. I've *got* to go and see how he
is."

"The mare's all right, Prudence. Come up,
girl! Poor pet! Ah, that's better. She's up
now. We'll lead her on to the road." Peter
slung Suspenders' saddle across her own, while
the mare stood, her nostrils wide, her neck a lather,
and her flanks giving out and in like the sides of
a bellows. "By Jove, Prudence, you've given
her a gruelling! You must have come as straight
as a bird. How did you manage Jimmy Murphy's
bounds-fence? It's all wire."

"Had to have that awful gate—*don't* talk about
it."

"Prudence!—And Toby? We've got the car
down here so we can get to him. Hogan's, you
said? Try and get the mare along."

"Yes, I must get to Toby. Good Heavens!
Peter, there's one of the Croleys."

A man came running into the field. His face
was crimson with exertion or rage and he waved
his arms wildly above his head.

"He's going to turn us off," Peter said quickly.
"Dirty brute! Thank God you were in time to
save the hounds, Prudence."

"Rot!" Prudence led the mare a few steps
on to meet the man. "That's not a Croley. It's
the fellow who directed me through the bog. What
can he want?"

"Well, here's Tony back," Peter spoke with
relief, as Anthony's red coat became visible returning up a narrow lane. "*He'll* have something to
say to Mr. Croley—for it *is* him, Prudence"

314

Mr. Croley, it would appear, had a good deal
to say to Anthony, and was still saying it when
the two girls joined them. Anthony's face was
scarlet with mingled anger and incomprehension.
He turned to Peter despairingly.

"As far as I can make out," he said, "the fella
is warning us about the poison. An' it looks as
if he should know what he's talking about—because
he says he put it down himself. Can you understand him? Is he mad? Look-out! He's going
to kiss, er, Prudence."

How Prudence evaded that salute was as great
a mystery as how she came unscathed through
her previous perilous ride. Both her hands were
seized and shaken till they were nearly wrung
from her wrists, while Mr. Croley poured forth
his passionate flood of appreciation for her prowess.

"Ye're a right one, ye're a topper, b'Gad ye're
a darling!" So ran the encomium. "By the
Powers why wouldn't ye be? It's the way ye're
bred! When I seen ye alone on the hill throw
the lep across the gate, the heart shifted over in
me chest. And when the mare fell with ye down
in the bog—I said ye were the boy! Sure it come
to me all in a minute what had ye so determined
for the fences, and I declare I was as taken out
o' meself to see ye goin' so courageous, I took a
race up the road to get the little bike I have. For
if she never lives to warn the Captain o' the dogs,
says I, I'll be in it before them. More power to
ye, ye have me bet! I may give up now! I'll
lay no more poison, I'll trap no more foxes—for
surely courage is a grand thing! And all is between

315

me and the hunt, sir "—he addressed himself again to Anthony—" is the price of a heifer these hell-dogs chased on me poor father this twenty years past. She died under whatever hardship they gave her, and we was never rightly compensated."

" I'll make a note of that," Anthony promised. "Twenty years ago, you said? H'm. Yes, I'll let you know. And I'll draw your coverts another day, sir. Perhaps you'd let *me* know a day that would suit you? "

" Anthony's learning his Ireland all right," Prudence murmured. " But, Peter—*couldn't* we get on to Toby. We'll leave the mare with Croley. He'll see she doesn't die on me—won't you, Mr. Croley? "

" I will, b'gor—and proud! What'll I give her, a feed an' a sup o' water? "

Prudence, shuddering, looked at Anthony. He nodded reassuringly.

" I'll send one of my men back now," he said. "John's in the car—he'll look after her for you. What's that you say, Peter? Toby Sage concussed? Left him with the tinkers? Good God, what a girl! What a morning! And Toby concussed in the cause too. Peter, after this you and I will have to attend the opening meet of Mr. Sage's harriers—good luck to them! "

" Toby's giving up the harriers "—Prudence spoke a little stiffly—" didn't Cousin Oliver tell you? "

" Giving them up? No, he's not—not after this morning's effort. I wrote to him last night too. It took Peter forty-eight hours to make me see reason on that subject—didn't it, Peter? Get into the car, both of you "—as they talked they had progressed out of the field and down the lane to where the Bentley, with three terriers straining out over its doors, stood—" Peter, be kind to my gears. So long, Prudence! Hope you'll find Toby sitting up and barking. I'll be over at Lingarry to-day—tell Oliver." He lifted his cap and rode off down the road to his hounds.

As the heavy car slid forward, a wondering Prudence turned to Peter :

" Peter, he's changed. I, I *like* him. It's not the same Anthony."

Peter spoke softly : " Well he's *my* Tony now. I'm glad you like him, Prudence darling. I thought I could bear life if you didn't, but p'raps I was wrong. Darling, you and Toby? "

" *Yes*, Puppy ! At least, we *were*, but I think it was broken off just before he took on the tinkers' clothes-line. Still, we might patch matters up yet. But you know, he seriously *is* giving up these harriers."

" No, he's not. Tony is determined about that, now."

" We owe it to you, then."

" And who do we owe the fact that the hounds weren't poisoned to? You've got to tell me this morning's doings properly, Prudence. So far my mind is a hopeless tangle of wired fences and locked gates, tinkers and clothes-lines, and broken engagements and broken heads—I hope to goodness Toby isn't too bad."

" Peter, *don't!* " Prudence put her hands up to her face as if shielding off a blow. " They've brought him to Lingarry by now, I should think."

" This chap might know——" Peter slowed up the car and leaned out to speak to a passing bicyclist. " Did you see Doctor Mahony's car ? " she asked him.

" I did, Miss. He had a dead man in it an' he drivin' in at Lingarry lodge-gates, not a half-an-hour ago. Yez should get him in it, if ye'd hurry."

" Thanks." The car shot forward as Peter trod on the accelerator.

Doctor Mahony's battered Chevrolet was still standing before the door of Lingarry when Prudence, white and breathless, almost fell out of the Bentley and fled, wordless, up the steps, and into the hall.

" How's Toby ? " she gasped as she recovered from a violent collision with the little doctor, who was standing in the hall giving last instructions to Miss Gus.

" Dear me, Miss Turrett——" the Doctor, who had reeled painfully against an umbrella stand, felt himself aggrievedly. Then, for he was a good, kind little man, he smiled cheerfully at the white-faced Prudence and forgave her her forgotten apologies.

" He's conscious now," he said, " and should do nicely. It's only a touch of concussion, and of course the broken collar bone is nothing—nothing at all—he won't feel it in a day or two. Though he mightn't believe that if you told it to

him at the present time ! There's something on
his mind tho'—makes him very restless. If we
could only quieten him, he'd do better. Perhaps,
Miss Turrett "—the little doctor's manner was
impersonal in the extreme—" as you saw him last
before the accident you might know what it is.
If so, just go up——" He never finished, for
Prudence was already half way up-stairs.

James, a shining can of hot water in his hand,
was coming out of Toby's room—a quiet, important presence. He cocked his head, bird-like, at
Prudence, and wagged an admonitory fore-finger.
" Well, well," he said, " yez is a caution—the
pair o' yez. Go in Miss, go in——" he slid the
door open for her, and shut it again gently. Then
he turned to face Miss Gus who—ever-faithful to
her duties as chaperone—was hurrying wrathfully
up the stairs in Prudence's flying wake.

" I beg pardon, Miss—Mr. Oliver is tearing
the house down looking for ye. He's below in
the library this minute and says would ye go to
him." And as Miss Gus, thus ably deflected from
her course, turned obediently to obey the fraternal
summons, James closed one eye expressionlessly,
and fell to polishing a passage table with entirely
unnecessary diligence. His duster—a flaming
sword turning every way—kept trespassers without
that indoor Eden.

.   .   .   .   .

Within Eden, Prudence—a hand clinging in
Toby's—bent over him, so bandaged and quiet,
to say :

319

"The hounds are all right, Toby. I *was* in time. An', an', darling—you're to carry on with the harriers——"

Toby hardly seemed to take in what she said. His eyes wandered restlessly, till, with an obvious effort, he collected himself and spoke:

"Prudence, it was about last night. Listen! I only meant that last night made me think you really *did* care enough about me—that's all. I saw what you thought afterwards. I didn't mean that. I swear it never occurred to me——"

Prudence, bending lower, kissed his mouth. "Darling Toby—just as soon as *ever* you're well enough," she breathed out the words with her kiss. And Toby, still holding her by the hand, pushed his face against the pillows and slept.

THE END

VIRAGO MODERN CLASSICS

The first Virago Modern Classic, *Frost in May* by Antonia White, was published in 1978. It launched a list dedicated to the celebration of women writers and to the rediscovery and reprinting of their works. Its aim was, and is, to demonstrate the existence of a female tradition in fiction which is both enriching and enjoyable. The Leavisite notion of the 'Great Tradition', and the narrow, academic definition of a 'classic', has meant the neglect of a large number of interesting secondary works of fiction. In calling the series 'Modern Classics' we do not necessarily mean 'great' — although this is often the case. Published with new critical and biographical introductions, books are chosen for many reasons: sometimes for their importance in literary history; sometimes because they illuminate particular aspects of womens' lives, both personal and public. They may be classics of comedy or storytelling; their interest can be historical, feminist, political or literary.

Initially the Virago Modern Classics concentrated on English novels and short stories published in the early decades of this century. As the series has grown it has broadened to include works of fiction from different centuries, different countries, cultures and literary traditions. In 1984 the Victorian Classics were launched; there are separate lists of Irish, Scottish, European, American, Australian and other English speaking countries; there are books written by Black women, by Catholic and Jewish women, and a few relevant novels by men. There is, too, a companion series of Non-Fiction Classics constituting biography, autobiography, travel, journalism, essays, poetry, letters and diaries.

By the end of 1990 over 350 titles will have been published in these two series, many of which have been suggested by our readers.

Also by Molly Keane (M. J. Farrell)

LOVING WITHOUT TEARS
New Introduction by Russell Harty

'She was in a torment of mistrustful jealousy, despairing at their escape from her, catching at lives as uselessly as though she caught at straws on a flood of water'

Angel, a woman of extreme charm and warm-hearted selfishness, awaits her son's return to the fold. She is the pivot of her children's lives – for haven't they always succumbed to her smiling manipulations? Now she has plans for each of them: Slaney, her beautiful daughter (who will make the perfect match with Angel's assistance); Julian, her young hero returned from the War (though still her baby after all); and even Tiddley, her niece (who lacks the sophistication of her own children, yet will surely be delighted to hover at Angel's beck and call). But sometimes a mother's plans run less smoothly than anticipated. When Julian arrives accompanied by his new fiancée, a stylish American widow, when Slaney seems adept at romancing without a mother's guidance, and even Tiddley shows signs of rebellion, Angel must sharpen her wits and struggle to maintain her tyranny.

In this delightful comedy of manners, originally published in 1951, Molly Keane reveals once again her irresistible wit and dexterity.

TREASURE HUNT
New Introduction by Dirk Bogarde

'"I'm afraid,' Mr Walsh proceeded, still with satisfaction, 'the time has unfortunately come when the Bank is taking every notice.'

That, too, she took magnificently in her stride: 'Banks have *such* bad taste and display it at such unnecessary moments."'

For Consuelo, Hercules and Roderick, life has been a round of carousing, gambling and champagne in the Irish house, Ballyroden. With Sir Roderick's death, however, all grandeur must cease. Though boots are polished on dusty Chippendale and exquisite vases languish on floors, his legacy to the younger generation is a host of debts. To the outrage of their elders and the servants, Phillip and Veronica decide to do the unspeakable and take in paying guests. A battle of wills commences, with Consuelo and Hercules doing their utmost to thwart the new regime. In the midst of it all is old and dotty Aunt Anna Rose, who *insists* that she has some rubies. If only she could remember where she hid them . . . Originally performed as a play, *Treasure Hunt* (1952) shows the inimitable Molly Keane at her comic best.

THE ANTE-ROOM

Kate O'Brien
New Afterword by Deirdre Madden

'Passionately, as if afraid of finding out its casuistry, she
hurled this faith of hers to heaven – but without pausing in it
was swept on to where, in human terms, her great guilt lay'

The events of this rich and intricate novel take place over
three October days in Ireland of the 1880s. As Teresa
Mulqueen lies dying her family gather round her, and beneath
this drama another, no less poignant, unfolds. In a house of
stillness and shadow her daughter Agnes awaits the return of
her sister Marie-Rose and brother-in-law Vincent,
remembering the old days of radiant inconsequence long past,
of flirtations, *billet-doux* and shared sibling secrets. But she
dreads the arrival of Marie-Rose for, in seeking refuge from
their unhappy marriage, both husband and wife turn to her.
Agnes adores her sister, but secretly, passionately, loves
Vincent; ahead lies a terrible battle between conscience and
desire . . . In this delicately imagined novel, originally
published in 1934, Kate O'Brien lays bare the struggles
between personal need and the Catholic faith with the
sympathy and insight which is the hallmark of her craft.

'A grave and beautiful story, exquisitely composed and cut to
a jewel-like fineness' – *Daily Telegraph*

Kate O'Brien (1897–1974), one of Ireland's best-loved writers,
was born in Limerick. She is the author of nine novels, in
addition to plays, travel books and biography.

HESTER LILLY

Elizabeth Taylor
New Introduction by A. L. Barker

'The strategy was based on implanting in the girl her own –
Muriel's – high standards, so that every success Hester had
would seem one in the image of the older woman . . . Patience,
tolerance, coolness and amusement were part of the plan'

Muriel, the elegant wife of a conscientious headmaster fears
the arrival of his orphaned cousin, Hester Lilly, though when
she meets her, Muriel experiences a sensation of relief. How
can someone so ill put-together pose a threat to her carefully
nurtured marriage? But Muriel is quite misled; almost before
she knows it she's locked into a desperate struggle with the
waif-like Hester Lilly. In this, her first collection of short
stories (1954), Elizabeth Taylor beautifully charts the
territory that so much became hers. Here we also encounter
the poignant, muted agony of long marriages, the frittering
away of lives in the polite English countryside; the oddity and
freshness of children's vision in opposition to the adult world,
and much else besides. These tales are superb examples of
Elizabeth Taylor's art.

Elizabeth Taylor (1912–1975), author of sixteen works of fiction,
spent much of her life in Penn, Buckinghamshire.

THE LAND OF SPICES

Kate O'Brien
New Introduction by Mary Flanagan

'She admitted that human love . . . must always offend the
heavenly lover by its fatuous egotism. To stand still and
eventually understand was, she saw, an elementary duty of
love'

On an early October day in 1912 three postulants receive the
veil at the *Compagnie de la Sainte Famille*, a lakeside Irish
convent. When Eileen O'Doherty, beautiful and adored,
kneels before the Bishop a wave of hysteria sweeps through
the convent. Only two remain distanced: Reverend Mother
and six-year-old Anna Murphy. Between them an unspoken
allegiance is formed that will sustain each through the years
ahead as *Mère Marie-Hélène* seeks to understand a childhood
trauma, to recover the power to love and combat her growing
spiritual aridity, and as Anna, clever, self-contained, develops
the strength to overcome loss and to resist the conventional
demands of her background. First published in 1941 this
complex and moving work offers both a luminous evocation of
convent life and a remarkable exploration of the nature of
human love and spirituality.

Kate O'Brien (1897–1974), one of Ireland's best-loved writers,
was born in Limerick. She is the author of nine novels, in
addition to plays, travel books and biography.

A PARTICULAR PLACE
Mary Hocking

In this, her most memorable and triumphant novel to date, Mary Hocking is confirmed as the successor to Elizabeth Taylor and Barbara Pym.

The parishioners of a small West Country market town are uncertain what to make of their new Anglican vicar with his candlelit processions. And, though Michael Hoath embraces challenge, his enthusiasm is sapped by their dogged traditionalism. Moreover, Valentine's imperial temperament is more suited to the amateur dramatics she excels at than the role of vicar's wife. Their separate claims to insecurity are, for the most part, concealed and so both are surprised when Michael falls in love with a member of his congregation, a married woman, neither young nor beautiful. In tracing the effects of this unlikely attraction, Mary Hocking offers humour, sympathy and an overwhelming sense of the poignancy of human expectations.

'Mary Hocking's wry straightness makes posher novels about marital unfaithfulness seem arch, pretentious and overdone by comparison' – *Observer*

'Mary Hocking is an undisguised blessing'
– *Christopher Wordsworth, Guardian*